The Terrible Wall
of Resistance . . .

"You didn't panic when I put my arm around you when we were coming home tonight, Kitt, and you're not only not panicking right now, you're being downright provocative."

"You know I wasn't deliberately——"

"That's the point. You were following your instincts. You wanted to touch me, so you did. I could see it in your face; you were leaning back with your eyes closed and a hint of a smile, enjoying the feel of me under your hands. Not only were you not trying to arouse me, it didn't even enter your head that you might be doing so."

"How do you know——"

"It's exactly the way I feel about you, love. I want to touch you." He stroked one hand slowly up her arm under the wide sleeve of her caftan. "I want to feel your skin under my hands and the shape of your body pressing against mine. I want to excite you and feel the heat rising in you and know that it's all there for me." His voice had become a hoarse whisper, his eyes again darkened to indigo.

Her breathing had shortened and her heartbeat quickened as he talked love to her. . . . Mesmerized by the dark heat of his eyes, she nevertheless felt a cold, hard knot of incipient fear in her center. . . .

ROMANCE LOVERS DELIGHT

Purchase any book for $2.95
plus $1.50 shipping & handling for each book.

___ **ROYAL SUITE** by Marsha Alexander. Fabulous success threatens the passion of new love.

___ **MOMENTS TO SHARE** by Diana Morgan. Her ambition might destroy the only man she ever loved.

___ **ROMAN CANDLES** by Sofi O'Bryan. In the splendor of the Eternal City she found a daring and dangerous lover.

___ **TRADE SECRETS** by Diana Morgan. Passion and power steam the windows amidst the world of publishing.

___ **AFTERGLOW** by Jordana Daniels. She had but one choice to make — glamorous romance or success.

___ **A TASTE OF WINE** by Vanessa Pryor. In lush vineyards, she took her first intoxicating sip of love.

___ **ON WINGS OF SONG** by Martha Brewster. In the glory days of opera, their voices mingled in passionate melody.

___ **A PROMISE IN THE WIND** by Perdita Shepherd. A peasant beauty captured by a ruling enemy, desired by a noble love.

___ **WHISPERS OF DESTINY** by Jenifer Dalton. While love bloomed in her heart, the seeds of war grew in her homeland.

___ **SUNRISE TEMPTATION** by Lynn Le Mon. Her defiant heart battled between the power of wealth and the pursuit of passion.

___ **WATERS OF EDEN** by Katherine Kent. She tasted the fruits of passion that grew wild in a lover's paradise.

___ **ARABESQUE** by Rae Butler. Two defiant hearts, one impossible love dared to challenge the might of a nation.

AGAIN THE MAGIC

Lee Damon

Paradise
Press, Inc.

Plantation, Florida

This novel is a work of fiction. Names, characters, places and incidents are either the product of the author's imagination or are used fictitiously, and any resemblance to actual persons, living or dead, events or locales is entirely coincidental.

EXCLUSIVE DISTRIBUTION BY
PARADISE PRESS, INC.

ISBN #1-57657-239-0

Printed in the U.S.A.

AGAIN THE MAGIC

Chapter 1

It was an unusually balmy day for the second Sunday in April, especially for the south coast of Maine, with clear, almost Wedgwood-blue sky, bright sun, a comfortable ocean breeze and the bracing scent of salt air. The busy tourist season was still two months away, and the small town of Kennebunkport was peacefully lazing through the quiet spring afternoon. At least, most of it was. On one stretch of Ocean Avenue, not far from Dock Square, the tranquility was somewhat disrupted by the sounds of laughter and a cacophony of voices, ranging from a deep male roar to a girl's high-pitched squeal.

"Quiet down, everyone, and pay attention. We're going to have a toast—to Kittredge Arlen Tate, new owner and moving spirit of the River Port Bookshop!"

To a male chorus of "Hear, hear!" and "Right on!" and a feminine cry of "Whoopee!," Ez Tate lifted his can of beer, barely visible in his big fist, in salute to the tall, handsome woman who was half-sitting, half-leaning against the wide railing around the second-floor deck. She laughed and bowed from the waist, first to the huge man who was grinning back at her and then to the two young men and the blonde girl lolling on an antique church bench.

"I thank you, one and . . ." Kitt's voice trailed off as a ululating "Aaroorooroo" interrupted her.

Three heads turned as one, and the young people on the bench stared in wide-eyed astonishment at the copper and white dog perched on the cushioned seat of a captain's chair. Familiar with such reactions, Kitt and Ez exchanged amused glances and chuckled. The dog cocked his head at them, pointed ears pricked forward deepening the wrinkles across his forehead, and then lifted his nose toward the sky and yodeled.

At the young people's incredulous expressions, Ez bellowed with laughter, sending half a dozen seagulls shrieking into the air. Kitt, still chuckling, moved over to the dog and rubbed him behind the ears with strong fingers.

"He's an African Basenji," she explained, raising her voice to be heard above Ez and the seagulls. "Their larynxes are shaped almost like a human being's, and they can't bark. But they do 'talk,' yodel, chortle, howl like banshees and, with great effort, sometimes manage a 'woof.'"

With amusement threading his deep voice, Ez added, "And he sits in chairs because he thinks he's people, except for the times when he thinks he's a cat!" Ez stepped over to stand beside Kitt, resting a brawny arm across her shoulders and teasing, "Actually, I think he's her familiar. You wouldn't believe what a witch she can be sometimes!"

Kitt laughed up at him, shaking a finger under his nose. "You be nice, Ez Tate, or I'll turn you into a toad and give you to Hero to play with!"

Charley, the brawny young man at the far end of the bench, suddenly leaned forward, his eyes shifting intently between Kitt and Ez. "Hey, you're twins! Peter, Midge, look at them! Now that they're standing together, it's plain as a pike."

Seen side by side in the bright light of the afternoon sun, it was quite obvious that Kitt and Ez Tate were twins. They had the same deep chestnut, thickly waved hair. His brushed the collar of his denim shirt, while hers tumbled to just below her shoulders. The sun brought out gold highlights in their dark hair and gilded their matching long, thick lashes. They both had wide, high cheekbones, straight noses and firm chins, the features larger and heavier-boned on Ez. His chin had a cleft; Kitt's was dimpled. Kitt's mouth was a bit wider, the lower lip fuller and softer, than his. Their most startling feature was their eyes—long, smoky blue-gray ovals, deep set and tilting up at the outer corners under well-defined brows. Those exotic eyes had caused much speculation over the years, and eager searching of the charts by the family's genealogy buffs. So far, nobody had found a clue as to how these descendants of a solid Scots-English line had ended up with eyes from southern Russia!

When Kitt and Ez were apart, their twinship was not as apparent. Ez's face was usually relaxed in an expression of easy good humor and interest in people and the world around him. He looked younger than his almost thirty years, whereas

Kitt not only looked her age, but showed signs of having struggled through some of those years. There were faint lines of strain between her brows and at the corners of her eyes and mouth. In repose, her face often had a pensive look, with shadows of remembered pain in the smoky eyes. However, over the past months her expression had gradually lightened as the sense of fun and zest for life of her earlier years had slowly returned and strengthened.

"You're right," Ez said, "and being a twin develops the old ESP. Mine is loudly screaming that everybody's hungry after all this work, so let's get cleaned up and find someplace to eat. Since you're natives, I'll depend on you to lead me to a large steak!"

Motioning to Charley and Peter to bring the bench, Ez tipped Hero off the chair and carried it inside.

"You guys can wash up at the kitchen sink. Midge and I will share the bathroom," Kitt said. "And lead us, please, to a *huge* steak. That," she continued as she whacked Ez across his midriff with the flat of her hand, "takes a lot of filling."

For such a big man, Ez moved remarkably fast. He grabbed Kitt's wrist with one hand, swung her around and then let her go as his other hand, with beautiful coordination, connected smartly with the seat of her tight-fitting jeans. Kitt yelped and spun around to stalk him as Ez backed, grinning, toward the kitchen.

"Now, now, there's no time for horsing around, Sis. And I'm so weak from hunger, you just might get the best of me. That would be a terrible blow to my ego."

Ez felt the edge of the low breakfast bar against the back of his thighs and sat down, quickly swinging his long legs over the counter to stand up in the kitchen. Still chuckling, he turned on the hot water faucet over the sink and started scrubbing his hands. Peter and Charley crossed the living room to join him, going around the breakfast bar rather than over it.

Midge and Kitt headed down the short hall toward the bathroom, Kitt yelling over her shoulder, "I concede. In physical confrontations with you, you big ape, it's a no-contest every time! Right, Midge?"

She glanced down at the much shorter girl, thinking with amusement of her first sight of Midge.

Kitt and Ez had arrived in Kennebunkport early that Sunday morning, driving their loaded vehicles into the graveled parking area in front of the bookshop. While Kitt unlocked and looked around both the first-floor shop and the upstairs living quarters, Ez loped back up Ocean Avenue toward Dock Square to find a source of coffee and food-to-go.

A bear of a man at six feet three, broad in the shoulders and chest, solid but lean through waist and hips, with long, strongly muscled legs, Ez looked like—and had been—a star half-back on his college football team. His easy, long-striding lope took him out of sight around the corner before Kitt had time to open the wide blue door to the bookshop.

Half an hour later, she was just returning to the car after settling Hero in the shop, when she heard laughing male voices almost drowning out female cries of "Put me down!"; "Dammit, I can walk by myself!"; "When I get loose, you big bully, you'll be sorry!"

Kitt stared, in mixed exasperation and amusement, at the group appearing around the corner from the square. Flanked by two laughing men, some ten years younger and a few inches and pounds smaller than himself, Ez strode briskly along the road, apparently unaffected by the violent squirming and kicking of the yelling girl draped under his right arm.

Roaring with laughter, Ez crossed the parking lot and swung the girl upright, setting her gently on her feet in front of Kitt. He quickly clapped his big hand over the top of her curly blonde head and held her off at arm's length as she indignantly tried to kick his shins. It was rather like a toy poodle attacking a mastiff. The girl was a diminutive pixie with big brown eyes in a pert face, her small but shapely figure dressed in jeans and a heavy turtleneck sweater.

"Here, now, stop before you dent a toe." Ez chuckled. "My shins are a lot harder than your sneakers. Just calm down and meet my sister, Kitt. Kitt, this pepperpot is Midge. She's the answer to your need for part-time and summer help."

Midge stood stock still, head tilted back, gazing up in wonder at Kitt. It was a long way up. Midge was all of five feet tall, while Kitt's normal height of five feet nine was increased at the moment to nearly five eleven by the heels of her leather boots. The two young men beside Ez were eyeing with interest Kitt's seemingly endless legs and slim hips, emphasized by her snug jeans, and obviously wishing they could get a better view of the long, supple waist and rather small but firm and nicely rounded breasts just hinted at under the loose fisherman's knit sweater.

Ez introduced Charley and Peter, explaining that he had met them and Midge at the restaurant in the square. "They kindly volunteered to help unload the pickup and trailer and carry the furniture upstairs. Midge mentioned looking for a job, so I hired her for you. She was a little reluctant to take my word, so I brought her along to meet you."

Kitt gave them a rueful grin, saying, "I can just imagine how much 'volunteering' you guys did! Ez is a past master at dragooning people into things they had no intention of doing."

She turned to the bemused Midge with a sympathetic smile, "I apologize for the caveman tactics." She leaned down, her voice dropping to a loud whisper easily overheard by the unrepentant Ez as she confided, "He's still got a strong streak of juvenile high spirits and tends to revert to ten years old on weekends. Would you believe he's a college professor in, of all things, medieval history, during the rest of the week?"

She straightened up and stood, hands on hips, gazing down thoughtfully at the younger girl. Midge, who had regained her composure, shot a look of total disbelief at Ez, and then returned Kitt's regard with one of interested speculation.

"If you really are looking for help, I'd like to apply. I'm just finishing my last year at the University of Southern Maine up in Gorham." She looked inquiringly at Kitt and asked, "Do you know of it?"

"Sorry, no," Kitt answered. "What have you majored in?"

"English. I'd really love to work in a bookshop, and I do need a job from now until at least the end of the summer. Gorham's a few miles outside Portland, about forty minutes' drive from here, and I commute, so I could work part time until classes finish in the middle of May and then work full time through the summer."

"Good enough," Kitt said decisively. "We'll settle the details later. Now, if you three lunks will get the heavy stuff unloaded, Midge and I will cope with the rest." Trailed by the younger girl, Kitt headed for her Camaro, asking over her shoulder, "Do you have another name? I assume 'Midge' is short for 'Midget,' for obvious reasons."

"Right. It was inevitable, I guess. I was always the smallest kid in class. My real name is Catherine, but no one calls me that except my grandmother. In fact, I'll bet everyone has forgotten it by now." Her brown eyes sparkled merrily as she added, "I usually do, myself."

Some ten hours later, Kitt and Ez collapsed gratefully into a pair of captain's chairs set out on the deck. They swung long legs up to rest their heels on the railing. Ez stifled an oath as Hero landed in his lap and then, catlike, stretched his thirty pounds in total relaxation the length of Ez's thighs.

"Really, Kitt, this beast is somewhat oversized for a lapdog." He gestured toward the river, some thirty feet beyond the back fence. "Now that's rather romantic— moonlight sparkling on the dark water, a balmy spring evening, and we've even got a bottle of wine. Maybe I should have coaxed the pixie into staying a while."

"I'll bet you wouldn't complain if *she* jumped into your lap." Kitt laughed. "Although if she hears you call her a pixie, she's more apt to break that bottle of wine over your head. Speaking of wine, how about opening it? Weren't we going to drink a toast to my new life?" Kitt held out the glasses for Ez to fill and then handed one to him.

They touched glasses as Ez said, "To you, the River Port Bookshop and a happy new life."

They sat quietly for a few minutes, sipping wine and watching the Kennebunk River moving swiftly by on its last mile to the sea. The bright moonlight flashed off metal fittings on the many boats tied up to docks on both sides of the river. It was a deep, tidal river, rising and falling as the ocean tides turned every eight hours. In the days of sailing ships, Kennebunkport had been a major shipbuilding center on the New England coast, sending tall ships out to sail the far oceans of the world.

"Kitt? You *are* going to be all right, aren't you? This isn't going to be too much for you to take on?"

"No, it's not. Oh, I couldn't have made it even two years ago by myself. But thanks to you, I've had time to get myself back together and, thanks to Grandma Arlen and her legacy, I've got my chance to be truly independent and do something

I've long wanted to do. If one can't own a library, the next best thing is a bookshop—and you know how I've always loved books and discussing them with people. Mrs. Stewart's been really great about teaching me the business end of it over these three years, so I'm not too worried about that part."

"I do believe you've really got your confidence back, and I couldn't be happier—not that I haven't enjoyed our being together these past few years, despite the fact that you were going through such a bad patch. At least you've been with me, and not thousands of miles away with strangers. And these last few months have been great." He smiled and lifted his glass in her direction. "It's certainly nice to have the old Kitt back again."

"Not the old Kitt—a new Kitt. Older, smarter, stronger and a lot more cautious. Never, ever, will I let anyone get me into that state again. I'm not sure if I could survive a second time, even with your help."

Ez turned his head away, hiding his face, suddenly harsh with frustration and pain as he recalled the time five years before when he'd heard about the horror his much-loved twin had endured in the two years of her marriage and the months after its breakup. He'd been half a world away, and it was all over before he knew what was happening. It was too late then to rescue Kitt, too late to vent his rage on Leon, too late for anything except to wrap his shattered sister in all the love he had and help her piece together what was left of a once joyous, trusting, outgoing girl.

In silent communion, Kitt reached over and gripped his arm, feeling the tense muscles. "Ez? Don't think about it anymore." Her voice lightened and she gave him a teasing look. "Have you considered where this leaves you, now that I'm out of your hair? You can now concentrate on developing a meaningful relationship with some lucky, deserving girl."

"Hmmmm. I've been giving that some thought today, in between hauling furniture upstairs, moving it around six times and tacking up umpteen yards of fencing. You may be seeing more of me than you expected." His voice was bland, but his eyes filled with merriment as he continued, "After all, it only takes a couple of hours or so to drive up here, and I'm not all that busy on weekends. This would be a nice, relaxing place to correct term papers."

Kitt chortled. "Transparent as glass. Fancy Midge, do you? Watch it, Brother. I have a strong feeling you may have met your match."

"One can only hope." Ez nudged Hero off his legs and stood up, stretching. "I hate to move, but I've got to get going. Got an early lecture in the morning." He carried the chairs inside while Kitt collected the glasses and wine bottle.

"Do I take it that I'll be seeing you next weekend? Or is that a silly question?"

Ez grinned and tugged gently on a lock of her hair. "Silly question. In fact, I get through early Friday, so you'll probably see me before suppertime. Ah . . . it might be nice to invite Midge to have supper with us, don't you think?"

"Delightful, I'm sure. Of course, I can always talk to Hero," Kitt teased. "You wouldn't consider bribing me to go to the movies, would you?"

"Funny, funny." Ez leaned to kiss her cheek. "I'll probably settle for sending you to bed early." He dodged her swinging hand and ran, laughing, down the stairs.

Later, Kitt strolled along Ocean Avenue with Hero pacing beside her. She was tired but relaxed and content, thinking about all they had accomplished that day, her first new friends, the quick rapport she had felt with Midge despite their age difference. She smiled to herself at a mental picture of big Ez holding off an infuriated Midge. It should be fun to see how that develops, she thought. She's certainly going to be a lively addition to the shop, and she likes books as much as I do.

It was very quiet. Kennebunkport was an old summer resort town which boomed in the season with summer residents and thousands of tourists. Off-season, it had the aura of a peaceful fishing village, although in recent years enough activity had developed on the weekends to make it worthwhile for resident owners to keep their shops open all year.

This end of Ocean Avenue was lined on both sides by one- and two-story frame buildings. There were old houses that were still maintained as individual residences; others had been converted into small shops or, as in Kitt's case, into a combination of shop and residence. Several of the buildings had started life many years ago as fishing shacks and small boathouses, and had evolved into restaurants, shops or imaginative living quarters. A very few of the buildings were new, but even they had been designed to blend in with the nineteenth-century aura of the village.

As she walked along the side of the road, Kitt noted a lighted window here and there indicating permanent residences, but also noticed that the majority of buildings were obviously still shut up for the winter. Only a few of the yards showed signs of tending, and not many of the shops had their signboards up.

She could hear her footsteps echoing back from the empty buildings at the end of the road where Ocean Avenue turned sharply to the right and then almost immediately made a sharp left turn into Dock Square. Hero's nails clicked against the pavement in counterpoint to the murmur of the river. Gravel crunched as they crossed the parking area to the stairs angling up the side of the building to the rear deck. Hero leaped up the steps, nimble-footed as a cat, and sat by the sliding glass doors waiting for Kitt.

She stepped onto the deck and strolled across to stand at the railing, facing the river and absorbing the peace and solitude along with lungfuls of salt air. Her body was utterly relaxed, her mind drifting among cloudy visions of the future—a misty picture of the shop filled with customers, an impression of lazing on a white beach, a fleeting glimpse of Hero romping in the backyard.

She turned to go in, feeling a welling of excitement at the thought that tomorrow would be the beginning of her carefully planned new life. But Kitt hadn't even the slightest premonition that before the week was over, her new life was going to be turned inside out.

Chapter 2

Shortly after seven o'clock on Friday morning, Kitt swung her dark blue Camaro into the parking area in front of the shop, pulling over to the far left near the outside stairs. She and Hero had been for an early morning run on Beach Road, and both were now more than ready for breakfast.

Kitt got out of the car, motioning Hero to follow. She walked over to the edge of the lot bordering the road and turned to study the building with a satisfied smile. It had been a very busy week so far. Between unpacking household and personal belongings and reorganizing the bookshop, she had had little time for quiet contemplation. It's beginning to shape up, thought Kitt, and will look even better when I get some flowers in along the front.

The building was old. Originally a private house, it had been remodeled several times in the course of 125 years. The last work had been done some six years previously by the Baxters, the couple from whom Kitt had bought the property and the business. They had obviously hired an architect to redesign the building, and he had used equal measures of imagination and practicality in doing so. The austere look of the typically plain, four-square coastal village house had been softened by the addition of large small-paned bow windows—two on the first floor, flanking the wide door, and two more on the second floor directly above them. The building was sided with gray weathered shingles; the shop door and exterior trim were painted a soft slate-blue.

Hands tucked in the pockets of her fleece-lined denim jacket, Kitt moved a few steps closer and examined the displays in the big shop windows.

I like it, she decided. Blessings on Midge for knowing about that collection of ship models. It was certainly nice of Mr. Everett to lend them. Should be an eyecatcher for the boat-people coming up over the next few weekends to get ready for the summer.

Her eyes traveled up to the second-floor windows. Like those below, they were six feet high and eight feet wide, taking up most of the front wallspace in the two bedrooms. Kitt stepped back a few paces to see how much was visible within the rooms. Well, that's not too bad, she thought. The plants fill up enough space to make it difficult to see details in the daytime, and the inside shutters work great at night. I'm glad I decided against drapes.

She started walking toward the stairs. "Hey, Hero, come on out of there! I just got those gardens spaded up, and I promise you there are no bones in them. Come on, now, I've got a lot to do today. Midge will be in at noon, and your favorite lap is landing in late this afternoon for the weekend. Surprise, surprise, can't imagine what the attraction is, can you?"

Kitt put in a fast-moving two hours after breakfast making up a bed for Ez in the spare room, giving the apartment a quick once-over with duster and vacuum, watering her jungle of plants and whipping up a couple of her twin's favorite pies. Just before ten, she was flipping on the lights and unlocking the front door of the shop.

Weekday mornings were still slow, so Kitt decided to tackle the deep cabinets under the work counter along the side wall behind the checkout desk. She had a strong feeling that there might be forgotten treasures in the far corners and, besides, with the summer rush coming up, she would definitely need that space. Midge had offered to clean out the cabinets, but Kitt felt that Midge's limited time would be better utilized in helping select summer stock for the shop.

Hero jumped up onto the folding director's chair kept behind the desk for his use and watched with apparent interest as Kitt started pulling things out of the cabinets. He was in a "talkative" mood that morning, and carried on a running "conversation" with Kitt as she commented on the degree of usefulness, fascination or worthlessness of her discoveries. Hero had an expressive voice. It rose and fell in tone, and combined a variety of sounds in different lengths with pauses in between, so that they sounded much like sentences. Occasionally, he even ended a combination on a rising note, much as a person would when asking a question.

Kitt was kneeling in front of the last cabinet, head and shoulders inside as she reached into the far corner, her voice muffled as she continued talking to Hero. She didn't hear the opening and closing of the door, and the firm footsteps coming across to the desk were softened by the carpeting.

Hero's remark of "Muruuroow arraoo" broke off abruptly. He came to his feet and watched, alert and tense, as the tall man leaned forward to place his hands flat on the desk. One corner of an expressive mouth twitched up in a half-smile, while deep sapphire-blue eyes gleamed appreciatively as they roved over the most visible part of Kitt—her slim but firmly rounded rump.

He watched silently as she wriggled backward on her knees to get room to pull her shoulders and head out of the cabinet. She sat back on her calves, straightening her body and lifting both hands to push her hair away from her face.

Still unaware of her silent admirer, Kitt waved a hand in a broad gesture, muttering, "Tell me, dog, what am I going to do with all this stuff? Hmmmm?" Hero growled softly. Kitt snapped her head around to look at him, and then half-turned to follow the direction of his stare.

She rose gracefully to her feet in one smooth motion and took a step forward, saying, "Sorry, I didn't hear you. . . ." Her voice died in her throat; she stopped breathing, stopped moving altogether except for the slow widening of her eyes as she stared incredulously at the man leaning on the desk.

Ten seconds dragged by. His face now mirrored the expression on hers. Total silence. Then Kitt drew in a shallow breath, followed by a deeper one, and stepped forward, reaching out slowly to place the tip of one finger on his chin.

"O'Mara?" Softly questioning at first, Kitt's voice grew stronger as her face lit up with a delighted grin. "Oh, Lord, O'Mara! I don't believe it! Whatever are you doing *here*?"

He was laughing now and straightened up to his full height of six feet four, holding out both hands, palms up, to Kitt. He closed his hands tightly around hers and leaned back a bit to examine her admiringly from the toes of her soft suede ankle boots to the top of her tousled hair.

"The original Kittredge Tate, all grown up, and very nicely, too." The laughter trailed off and, suddenly intent, the deep blue eyes lingered on her face. It was only a matter of seconds, but in that time a long-suppressed empathy flared into new life, and he saw much more than she realized. "I'd

say that sometime over the years you'd done some living."
The deep voice was thoughtful and slightly questioning.

"Well, it's been, what, twelve years? Must be. I was
eighteen that last summer, and I'll be thirty next month." Her
hands tightened on his for a moment before she withdrew
them from his clasp and slid them into the pockets of her cord
jeans. "Of course I have, O'Mara. Who could go twelve years
without . . . living?"

There was a note of despair in her voice on the last word.
Her mouth tensed and the stress lines between her brows
deepened as she closed her eyes for a moment. There had
always been something about this man that made it impossible for her to hide things from him. She took a long, slow
breath, visibly making herself relax, opened her eyes and
smiled at him.

"You haven't told me what you're doing here."

"I live here—at least, I live a couple of miles up the coast.
And how did you end up in Kennebunkport?"

"Oh, hard work and lots of luck. I've been saving for a long
time for something like this, and then my grandmother died
and left me enough to buy this place. It's just what I've always
wanted."

"Always? I seem to remember something about your
wanting to study physical education." The blue eyes teased as
he added, "In fact, you were the most complete tomboy I
ever knew. Can't think of a time when you didn't have a
scrape, bruise or bandage somewhere. You just wouldn't
admit there was anything that twin brother of yours could do
that you couldn't do as well."

Kitt chuckled, remembering, and mused, "True. But I
grew out of that . . . after a while . . . and other things
happened, and I was living a long way from Ez for a few
years." The strained look returned for a moment, until she
controlled it. He could see the effort she made to smile as she
continued brightly, "Ez and I have been sharing an apartment for almost five years—until last weekend, in fact, when I
moved in here."

He studied her face, his eyes knowing and alert, narrowing
as he tried to sort out the nuances in her voice and words.
Twelve years before, he had felt a strong rapport with the
younger Kitt, not as much as she had with her twin, but

enough so that they had often sensed each other's moods and thoughts. And one night, almost the last time he had seen her, he had recognized and answered a need she hadn't even been aware of.

It was bad. Whatever happened in those "few years" was a disaster. And it must have been a man. Where the hell was Ez? He loves her. How could he have let any man do . . . whatever it took to put that look in her eyes?

Kitt had come around to the front of the desk and sat back against the edge, arms folded across her midriff and long legs stretched out, while she looked over the tall, rangy figure. During the few moments he studied her, she assessed the changes that twelve years had wrought.

Physically, he was much the same. Even at twenty-two, he had been on his own for several years and had developed confidence and self-reliance. He had been easy-moving, well coordinated, with long, sinewy muscles in his arms and legs. *He hasn't changed much,* thought Kitt. *Maybe it's the heavy sweater, but he seems to have gained a few pounds. I hope so—he was always too thin. I used to tease him about counting his ribs.*

Her smoky eyes were almost analytical as they moved up the long, lean body, registered the strong neck and finally came to rest on his face. Not exactly a handsome face, but compelling and not easily forgotten. She remembered it as being harsher, obviously showing the tensions and pressures of a young man who had been working since he was seventeen to support himself and pay for college. She and Ez had discovered early on that O'Mara had a quick, clever wit and sense of the ridiculous that often lightened his usually serious expression. She thought now that his face was more relaxed, the laugh lines bracketing the wide mouth more pronounced. All in all, he looked . . . experienced, as if he had seen it all and done most of it, and now knew with certainty who and what he was and no longer needed to prove anything to anybody. As a young man of twenty-two, he had been an excitingly romantic figure; now, at thirty-four, he projected an image of total male maturity that was devastating.

Kitt was feeling slightly breathless as she shifted her gaze away from O'Mara's face. He still had a swath of black, not quite straight hair falling across his forehead. It was longer now, but still thick and looking as if he'd been in a high wind. She had been avoiding his eyes. Those brilliant, pure blue eyes—intelligent, inquisitive, sometimes mocking, often glinting with laughter as he had teased the young Kitt—those eyes had always seen too much, been too knowing.

She couldn't avoid them any longer, and she tensed defensively as she met his probing assessment of her face. Heavy black brows lowered in a slight frown as he noticed her reaction. Before he could speak, she turned away, coming to her feet and moving back behind the desk as if to put a barrier between them.

A quick, nervous spate of words burst forth. "Ez will be here tonight. He's staying for the weekend. I know he'll be so tickled to see you again. We've often wondered what had ever happened to you." She leaned over to rub Hero behind the ears. He was again sitting in his favorite position—on his rump, with his hind legs sticking straight out in front of him—watching the two tall humans with a puzzled frown. "Don't you like my dog? Come and make friends with him. I seem to remember your liking dogs. His name's Hero and—"

"Kitt," he broke in sharply. "Knock it off. What's the matter with you? I don't remember you as being at all jumpy." He walked behind the desk and rested one arm loosely across her shoulders, reaching down to let Hero sniff at his other hand. He felt Kitt tense again but ignored it. "Of course I like dogs. He's a Basenji, isn't he? They're crazy, but a lot of fun. Friend of mine in California breeds them."

He shifted his arm to rest his hand against her cheek, turned her head toward him and slowly rubbed his thumb over the tight muscle in front of her ear.

He looked in her eyes and saw a trace of fear. "Friend of mine right here, a very old and dear friend, is also acting a bit crazy."

She stiffened and tried to pull away from him. He let her go only long enough to cup her face in his palms, sliding his fingers into her heavy hair. "Kitt? What's wrong with you? I don't recall ever hurting you, so why are you so scared of me?" He tilted her head back slightly so that he could see her eyes, which suddenly glistened with tears as her thick lashes came down and her teeth bit into her lower lip.

"Please," she whispered. "It's not you, O'Mara. It's

just . . . I don't. . . ." Her hands were spread over his ribs, pushing him away. "Please, please, let go. I can't stand being touched. I can't. . . ."

Letting his hands drop away from her, he took a step back. He watched closely as she turned away for a minute. When she turned back to face him, her eyes were still rather bright but apologetic, and she managed an uncertain smile.

"I'm sorry, O'Mara. It really isn't you—it's something that happened when. . . . Oh, I just can't talk about it now. Maybe sometime I will." She pushed her hands into her pockets and hunched her shoulders. "The only one I can talk to is Ez."

She met his eyes and couldn't look away. The rapport that they once had was—incredibly—still there. She knew he was seeing more than she could tell him. Without knowing a single detail, he was sending her a message of hope. Warmth, caring, encouragement flowed from him to her. It took only seconds for the silent plea of *Oh, God, I need you,* to be answered as silently by *I'm here now.*

Slowly, Kitt held out her hands. He took them in a tight grip and smiled at her reassuringly. "Enough, now. I told you, I live here. There'll be all the time you need to talk to me whenever you're ready." His tone became more matter-of-fact. "Did you say Ez was coming tonight? When can we get together? I can't wait to see him. Is he still a bear?"

"Of course he's still a bear." Kitt laughed. "Did you suppose he'd shrink in twelve years? He should be here around five, so why don't you come to supper? Do you know Midge Bancroft?"

He nodded and Kitt continued, "She works for me and she'll be eating with us. Ez . . . well, I'll let you see for yourself. Get Ez to tell you how they met. And ask him about his interviewing technique. He actually hired her for me!" Kitt grinned reminiscently, shaking her head. "He's not to be trusted out without a keeper."

"Doesn't sound as though he's changed much," O'Mara said. "Supper would be great. I'll bring some wine. Do you want red or white?"

"Whatever you like with steak. And plan to stay for the evening, if you can. We've got a lot of catching up to do. I still don't know what you're doing living in Kennebunkport.

Thought you were going to work in Washington. Wasn't your degree in political science?"

"Good memory. And I did work in Washington, among other places. Look, it's a long story and I'll tell you all about it tonight. Save me repeating it for Ez."

He looked a little hesitant and half turned away from her. "Ahhh, would you mind if I brought somebody with me?"

Startled, and suddenly fearful, she said, "No, of course not. You're welcome to bring anyone you'd like. You always did have interesting friends, and . . ."

He burst into laughter, interrupting her. "Oh, Kitt, don't worry. It's a he. And *he's* nine years old."

Wide-eyed, she stared at him. "Nine?"

"Nine. And, yes, he's my son and no, I'm not married. At least, not now."

"Oh! That's great! I mean, it's great that you've got a son." Kitt was more than slightly rattled. Somehow, it hadn't occurred to her that he might have married. "What happened to your wife? No! I'm sorry. It's not . . . I mean, I shouldn't have asked that. It's . . . oh, damn . . . what's he like? What's his name? Who takes care of him? Oh, if he's nine, I guess—"

"Whoa! Kitt, take a deep breath and calm down. God, I don't believe this is the girl I knew. Now, one thing at a time. His name is, heaven help him, Augustus Edgar—but he only answers to Gus. He and Ezekiel will probably have a splendid time consoling each other. And, no, it wasn't my idea. I wasn't there when he was born, and his mother wasn't particularly interested, so she let her father name him. The birth certificate was filed before I found out, but it can always be changed when he's older if that's what he wants."

"What do you mean, his mother wasn't interested?" Kitt interrupted.

O'Mara ran a hand through his hair, pushing it back from his forehead, and stared out the window. "She didn't want a baby. She was mad as hell when she found out she was pregnant. We were divorced when Gus was six months old, and I've had him ever since. I'll tell you about it later, when we've got more time. Right now," he paused and checked his watch, "I've got to get going. It's almost noon, and I was supposed to be picking up milk and bread, among other things, for Mrs. Andretti. She's my housekeeper. Lower that eyebrow, Kitt. She's fifty-seven and very grandmotherly. I work at home most of the time, but once in a while I have to go off for a few weeks and she looks after Gus. She's been with us from the beginning."

He caught her hand and started walking with her to the door. Kitt stopped abruptly and exclaimed, "Wait! You never said what you came in for in the first place. And you still haven't told me what you're doing here."

He grinned ruefully. "It went right out of my mind. Wonder why. I came in to see if some books I ordered had arrived."

"Afraid not. I've been through all the special orders, and there's nothing for O'Mara."

"It wouldn't be under O'Mara." He tried to look serious, but couldn't keep the laughter out of his eyes. He watched her speculatively as he asked, "Do you have anything for Talbot?"

"Yes, as a matter of fact. There are three, no, four—" Her voice stopped and her mouth stayed half-open while she stared at him in utter disbelief. She finally found her voice and said wonderingly, "Talbot. And your first name is Michael. I always forget that. We always just called you O'Mara. Michael Talbot. *You're* Michael Talbot?"

"Oh, Kitt," he choked, doubled over with laughter. "If you could see your face!"

"Well, what did you expect? How would I have ever guessed that you'd be Michael Talbot? You never have your picture on the book jackets. Lordy, make sure Ez is sitting down when you tell him. If he falls over, he'll dent my floor. And I will leave it to you to tell him. I wouldn't think of spoiling your fun."

Eyes full of mischief, she said in a polite voice, "I must tell you, Mr. Talbot, that I've read all your books and so has my brother. We've found them most enjoyable and definitely a cut above what one usually finds in that genre. We've even seen two of the movies that—"

"Kitt, if you don't stop . . ." He took a step toward her, then paused, lifting an inquiring eyebrow. "Have you really read them? Or are you putting me on?"

"I've read them. We both have. And liked them. You do realize, don't you, that you've got a lot of explaining to do."

She glanced out the window. "Someone's coming in. Listen, we close at five, and Ez should be here about then. Can you get back here around five? I can't wait to meet Gus. Will he like Hero? I usually take him for a walk after I close up. Maybe Gus would like to do it today."

He moved to catch the door before it could close, nodding hello to the woman coming in. "Gus will love him, and he'll be delighted to take him for a walk. Now wait, today's Friday . . . Gus has baseball practice this afternoon, and I'll be picking him up at five. We can be here by quarter past. Do you think you can manage not to tell Ez? If we could surprise him, the look on his face when we walk in would be a nine-day wonder."

"It won't be easy, but I'll manage." Kitt couldn't contain a deep chuckle. "He'll go into shock."

She had stepped close to him to give the woman room to get by. He looked down into the face he had never quite forgotten. The sapphire eyes seemed to darken to almost indigo, and he said softly, "Dear Kitt, I'm so glad I found you again." And before she realized his intent, he leaned forward the few inches necessary and brushed his mouth along her cheekbone in a quick, gentle kiss. He straightened up, smiling at her, and with a "See you later" went out, closing the door behind him.

Slowly raising her hand, Kitt rested her fingertips on the place his lips had touched. She stared blankly at the closed door, unmoving, not thinking, hearing still the deep voice, soft, almost husky, saying "Dear Kitt."

"Excuse me. Miss? Excuse me? Are you the new owner?"

The woman's voice finally penetrated Kitt's daze, and she turned to take care of her second customer of the day, forcing all thoughts of deep blue eyes and warm, gentle lips to the back of her mind.

Chapter 3

Kitt managed to pull herself together enough to chat with reasonable intelligence with Mrs. Elbridge. Fortunately, considering Kitt's state of mind, Mrs. Elbridge was in something of a hurry and had only come in to pick up a special order. She left after a few minutes, and Kitt scooped Hero out of his chair, dropping into it herself and settling him onto her lap.

"Well, dog, and what do you think of that? O'Mara. Right out of the blue, and after all these years." She absently rubbed him behind the ears with the tips of her fingers, her eyes unfocused as she stared across the shop. "And it's still there. Something special . . . I don't quite know . . . it can't be possible. . . ." Her voice trailed off as she became lost in remembrance of the strong rapport she'd felt with him in that long locking of eyes. *I need you. I'm here.* It had been so intense, that feeling, as if they had spoken. She remembered, in wisps of recall, times in those long-ago summer days when they had shared a silent communication. Not as strong or deep as that of a few minutes ago, but in those days she hadn't yet experienced anything like the emotional disasters of these past years—and, perhaps, he hadn't either.

She stroked her hand over Hero's side, rubbing along his ribs with her fingertips, and he moaned with pleasure. "I think you're going to make a new friend this afternoon. Bet you'll like that, won't you, my Hero? Wonder what kind of a deal that was. She must have been an odd woman to take off and abandon her baby after only six months. To say nothing of O'Mara." She continued petting the dog, thinking dreamily of deep blue eyes and remembering, suddenly, the feel of those long, sinewy arms wrapped around her, holding her close to his strong, lean body. So long ago and—

The opening door jolted her back to the present, and she blinked to bring her eyes into focus as Midge bounced in.

"Hi! Wow! You don't know how glad I am that it's Friday.

Only three more weeks and I'm done, done, done! If I last that long. I have a feeling that Russian lit. final is going to be a beast." Midge boosted herself up onto the desk and sat with her small feet swinging two feet off the floor. "You look comfortable. So do you, Hero. Is this break-time?" She glanced at the littered floor in front of the cabinets. "Looks like you've been spring cleaning." Looking back at Kitt, she noted the bemused expression in the smoky eyes and had a strong feeling that the older woman wasn't quite seeing her. "Kitt? Are you all right? Hey!" She leaned over and snapped her fingers in front of Kitt's face.

"Hmmmm?" With considerable effort, Kitt brought her wandering mind back to the immediate moment. "Oh! Midge. Russian lit. Ahh, why don't you ask Ez about it? I'm sure he'd be enchanted to help you."

"Enchanted?" Midge grinned, and her eyebrows lifted out of sight under the blonde curls tumbled across her forehead. "That's not a word I'd think of in relation to your bear of a brother. Besides, he spends all week coping with students. I'm sure he'd rather get away from all that on weekends. Now, what's got you so starry-eyed? Don't tell me one of our local Lotharios has ventured in here. I didn't think any of them could read and, even if they could, I wouldn't have thought they'd appeal to you. Or have you run across an old boyfriend, perhaps?"

Kitt looked startled for a moment and then laughed, unconvincingly, as a light flush of betraying color tinged her cheeks. "I don't have any old . . . that is, he's not exactly . . ." She took a steadying breath, suddenly feeling much younger than Midge. *I am not going to let that man rattle me like this. It's ridiculous!* She stood up, dropped Hero into his chair and reached for a stack of publishers' catalogs and order forms.

"It was nothing, really. Look, let's go over these while things are quiet and see if we can figure out what the summer folk will want to read this year. You must have spent enough time in here in the summers to have a good idea what kinds of books the Baxters stocked."

Midge slid off the desk as Kitt started to sort out the catalogs and order forms. She leaned sideways on one elbow on the desk and looked up into Kitt's face inquiringly. "Did I step in it? If so, sorry. But you did have a very strange look when I came in, and you seemed to be miles away." She straightened up and reached for a stack of brochures. "How do you want these sorted?"

"Let's start by separating hardcovers and paperbacks. I think most of those big envelopes are from paperback publishers. The Baxters just piled them up for the last few weeks without opening them." Kitt wrinkled her nose in mock disgust. "They said they thought I'd like to pick my own stock. Which is true, but it would have helped to have some basic orders already in. I may have to take a trip down to the distributor's in Portsmouth to get what we want on time. Oh, well, at least we can look over this stuff and make a list." She worked rapidly through the pile of material at her end of the desk, separating it into two stacks. A few minutes later, she paused with a catalog in her hand. "Guess we'd better make a third pile, Midge. Ez would be interested in anything from the university presses. Or anything pertaining to history."

"Yo. Ah, when do you expect him? Is he still going to be here for supper?" Midge managed a fair imitation of casual inquiry, but Kitt caught the gleam of intense interest in the brown eyes as Midge slanted a look up at her.

Managing to control her impulse to smile, Kitt said lightly, "Nothing's changed since yesterday and the day before and the day before that. He'll still be here around five-ish." Unable to hold back a grin any longer, she added, "Maybe I should have made a sign, so you wouldn't forget."

"Funny, funny," Midge grumbled. Then she laughed. "Okay, so I'm interested. It's not often I meet a bear. Especially one who totes me around like a doll and has a sense of humor and is intelligent." She paused long enough to take a deep breath before continuing dreamily, "And besides all that, he's so handsome and . . . well, you may not realize it, Kitt, since he's your brother, but Ez is not exactly an everyday experience."

"Believe me, I realize it only too well." Kitt chuckled. She glanced down at Midge speculatively, wondering how she'd react to O'Mara's rather overwhelming charisma. Then it dawned on her that Midge probably knew him as Michael Talbot and saw him in a completely different light than she and Ez did.

Unable to resist the temptation, and curious about Midge's reaction, Kitt casually tossed out, "Oh, by the way, Michael Talbot and his son are joining us for supper."

She watched, first with interest and then with laughter, as Midge's brown eyes opened so wide in blank astonishment that they seemed about to pop out of her face. Midge sputtered and stammered and finally gave up trying to say anything for a minute. Eventually, she managed a squeaky "Michael Talbot! You actually *know* Michael Talbot! How? When? Where? Talk to me, Kitt. Don't just stand there laughing. It's not funny. He's famous, and all—absolutely all—the women under fifty are hot for him, and some older ones, too, and you just calmly say, 'Oh, by the way, Michael Talbot and his son are joining us for supper,' as if it's no big deal. Kitt! Stop laughing and tell me!"

"Heavens, Midge, you make him sound like . . . like some kind of superstud movie star or pop singer dripping with women. He's really very nice, you know, and down to earth. There's nothing to get so excited about."

"Oh, Kitt, he's a dream. How can you be so blasé? And those wicked eyes!"

"Not you, too," Kitt groaned. "I can still hear all those beach bunnies squealing 'Oooooo, what gorgeous eyes!' It was enough to make you sick."

"Beach? What beach? When have you been to the beach with him? Kitt, don't keep me in suspense like this!"

"Okay. Once through. Ez and I knew Michael Talbot years ago when we used to spend summers on Cape Cod. He worked a summer job at a resort hotel near our cottage, and we became friends. Except his name wasn't Talbot then; it was O'Mara. Well, it still is, I guess. I don't know where the Talbot came from, but his first name was always Michael. Sounds funny to think of him as Michael. We always just called him O'Mara."

"Never mind what he's called. Stick to the story. How long did you know him, and why haven't you said anything? Didn't you know he lived here?"

"No. We lost track of each other years ago. I never quite understood why. Ez and I knew him for three summers. We last saw him when we were eighteen and getting ready to start college. He was twenty-two and had just graduated with a degree in political science. It was the last summer he was working on the Cape. After Labor Day, he was starting a job in Washington, but we planned to keep in touch."

"What happened? How come you never saw him again?"

"I don't know. We wrote a few times, but the letters got further apart. You know how it is in college—all sorts of things going on and never enough time to fit them all in. After a while, when we didn't hear from him for a long time, Ez and I figured he'd gotten tied up in his job and . . . maybe other interests."

"What 'other interests'?" Midge narrowed her eyes, and Kitt could almost hear her deceptively sharp mind clicking rapidly through the possibilities. "Was there something between you two? Did you think he'd found somebody else?"

"No, it wasn't that exactly. Well, maybe. . . . Oh, I don't know how to explain it. The three of us were great friends right from the start, but that last summer O'Mara and I seemed to spend a lot of time alone and—"

"And?"

"And we liked each other." Kitt's fingers played idly with a pencil as she gazed thoughtfully out the window, her mind searching back to that last summer. "Maybe more than liked. I simply don't know, now. It was so long ago, and I—"

"You what?"

"Oh, I guess you could say I didn't know diddly damn about boys or men or . . . whatever. You have to understand, Midge, that that last summer was the first time I really *looked* at males. Until then, I'd been the world's greatest tomboy. Always chasing around after Ez and his friends, playing football, baseball, all kinds of sports, and keeping everything very buddy-buddy, one-of-the-boys. It was Ez's fault, too. We'd always been close and, since I was tall and athletic and could keep up, he always took me along."

"Didn't you date? Look at you—you're gorgeous! I should have thought you'd have guys in heaps at your feet."

"Nonsense. I'm not at all gorgeous. And I certainly wasn't anything like it then. Believe it or not, I was almost eighteen before I even started looking like a girl. Talk about arrested development! I was taller than most of the boys I knew and flat as a flounder in all directions. Then, in a few months, all of a sudden I finally got some curves. Not a lot, maybe, but enough to keep the top of my bikini in place."

"So, when you got a shape, what happened with Michael O'Mara?"

"I'm not sure. We understood each other in a very strange way. I mean, really strange. We didn't even talk a lot of the time. We just *felt* what the other one was thinking or feeling. I can't explain it. We used to walk on the beach a lot, early in the morning before he had to go to work, and hold hands. . . . I know that doesn't sound like much, but holding hands with O'Mara was like being kissed by someone else. No, it was better, because I never felt all that much from kissing someone else."

"Did he kiss you?" cried Midge, wide-eyed again. "Is that what you mean? Oh, drat, I don't suppose I should have asked that, should I?"

"It's okay. It's . . . just . . . .It was a long time ago, Midge, and we've both been living different lives. You can't just pick up something from where you left off after twelve years. At least . . . I didn't think you could . . . but it was so odd. . . ." Kitt's voice trailed off in a whisper as she closed her eyes, remembering that silent exchange.

"Kitt!" Midge shook her arm until she opened her eyes. "What was so odd? What happened this morning? That's when you saw him again, wasn't it?"

"Yes. He came in looking for some books he'd ordered, and—" She flung her hands out and laughed. "It was incredible! We were both so stunned, I don't think we said a word for the first two minutes. Oh! He forgot his books. Remind me to give them to him tonight."

"Never mind his books! What happened that was so odd?" pleaded Midge, her eyes gleaming with excitement.

"Nothing really earthshaking. It was just that for a few moments we sort of . . . talked without words. It's hard to explain. We were looking at each other, and he knew what I was thinking . . . well, I wasn't exactly thinking it . . . I was kind of saying something to him in my mind, and he knew and . . . answered me . . . I mean, I could . . . pick up somehow what he was saying in his head. Oh, damn, it sounds so crazy when I try to put it into words. It was like the communication we used to have, but much stronger. And it threw me. It really did. So many years, and . . . bang! *that* was still there. It didn't even take ten minutes from when I looked up and saw him standing there."

Kitt wrapped her arms around herself and looked at Midge with more than a bit of bewilderment in her eyes. "It's scary. The effect that man has on me. I don't want to get involved with anyone. And I just *know* he's not going to listen to a word I say. Oh, damn, when he finds out. . . ."

Midge waited, but Kitt turned away, picked up a catalog at random and started flipping through it. Finally, Midge said calmly, "It sounds to me as if you two have an unusually strong telepathic link. I'm not sure if I'd like that. It would be a hell of a disadvantage if my favorite man could read my mind. How could you ever win an argument? Or get away with anything?"

It broke the tension in Kitt, and she laughed at Midge's disgruntled expression. "Oh, but consider—if he could read your mind, then you could read his, and he'd be just as hard put to 'get away with anything' as you would!"

"Does it work that way with you and O'Mara?"

"I'm not quite sure," Kitt answered thoughtfully. "It seemed to be mutual this morning, but . . . I guess we'll have to wait and see how it really works. Uh-oh, here comes business. Look, why don't you take care of them while I get this mess cleaned up off the floor? We'll get back to figuring out orders after they go."

However, it turned out to be a busy afternoon, with a steady influx of customers until just after three o'clock. Kitt and Midge barely had time to snatch fifteen minutes in turn to run upstairs and gulp a tuna sandwich. When she had a spare moment to think about it, Kitt decided she was just as glad to be too busy to dwell on O'Mara's reentry into her life and what it might mean. She needed time to assimilate this new factor in what she had envisioned as a peaceful, rewarding, undemanding existence.

Kitt stood for a few minutes at the sliding glass doors which led out onto a small patio and then two steps down to the backyard. She'd just let Hero out, and she watched him racing around the yard and jumping over the obstacle course Ez had set up for him. In the background, she could hear the hum of talk from the shop. It was strangely soothing. Although she had told Midge that nothing earthshaking had happened, she knew that O'Mara had shaken *her,* and she wondered what the evening would bring. Hearing Midge call, she firmly pushed O'Mara to the back of her mind and went to help a customer choose a cookbook.

Finally, they hit a lull. Only one customer remained, and she seemed perfectly happy to browse by herself through the natural science section. Kitt dropped into Hero's chair while Midge scrambled up onto the high stool by the work counter.

Pushing her hair back with both hands, Kitt groaned a heartfelt, "Plagues and pestilence! Where did they all come from? There must have been thirty people in here."

"Plagues and pestilence?" Midge giggled. "Wherever did you get that expression?"

"Ez. Where else? He talks like that all the time. Well, sometimes, anyway. At least eighty percent of his reading matter is pre-seventeenth century. Sometimes I think he was born out of his time. Can't you just see him charging around on a big white horse rescuing maidens in distress and tossing them across his saddlebow?"

"What . . . what's a saddlebow?" gasped Midge. "It sounds awfully uncomfortable."

"Beats me. But in all the books I've read, the gallant knight is always parking maidens on it, and none of them seem to object."

"Speaking of which, knights and maidens and stuff," Midge grinned, "a thought occurred to me after the third person asked me today where we kept our romances. We don't have any. At least, not the books they were looking for."

"We don't?" Kitt frowned, mentally reviewing the various sections in the shop. "Hmmm. You're right, we don't, except for some historicals by some of the better-known authors. I remember seeing several of Roberta Gellis's books, and that series by Dorothy Dunnett. Holt, Eden, Whitney, a few others."

"And there's some Danielle Steel and Helen Van Slyke, but not much else for contemporary stuff," Midge added. "Maybe a few more. I haven't really checked that closely."

"Neither have I, yet. There's been so much to do this week that I've really only taken a quick look at what's in each section. I just assumed that romances were in with the paperback fiction." Kitt stood up and started around the desk toward the far wall. "Let's go see exactly what we have got."

The Baxters had designed the shop to look very spacious and open and yet provide room for a large stock with plenty of space for people to move about. On her first visit to the shop, Kitt had been impressed with the efficiency and convenience of its layout. Standing to one side of the door, out of the way of traffic, she had examined the arrangement of the shop with a critical eye. On the left, in the space in front of the bay window, was an island with an assortment of new hardcover fiction; new hardcover nonfiction was arrayed on wall-hung racks beyond the island. The rest of the wallspace on that side, as far as the working area, contained a comprehensive collection of material about Maine, the coastal area, the local area and New England in general. A round table and comfortable chairs were set out in front of this section.

Beyond the working area and desk was a large children's section—two low sets of bookcases built out from the wall at right angles, about twelve feet apart, with low tables and chairs placed in the open area. The space between the children's section and the back wall was enclosed to form a receiving/storage room.

To the right of the door, by the other bay window, was a small island which, together with the first section of wall shelves, contained books, pamphlets and other material relating to the current window displays. The remaining length of the shop on the right side was divided into sections by a series of five-foot-high by twelve-foot-long bookshelves set at right angles to the wall and spaced ten feet apart. It was a practical arrangement which provided a geat deal of shelf space while retaining a feeling of openness. The stretch of wallspace above the bookshelves was decorated with samples of posters and art prints which were for sale. Kitt had found the basic arrangement of the shop very much to her taste and had, as yet, made few changes.

Moving slowly along the shelves of the paperback fiction section, Kitt and Midge scanned titles and authors, pulling out a "slotted in" book now and then to check the cover art for one of the distinctive "romance" styles.

"You're right," Kitt said finally. "There's not much here except for the well-known authors. Wonder why. After all, the sexy historicals and the monthly lines are among the biggest-selling paperbacks these days. In the shop where I used to work, we couldn't keep the stuff in stock." She turned to Midge inquiringly. "Do you have any idea why the Baxters weren't stocking more romances?"

"I think they tended to be very conventional in their personal taste. If you notice, there's hardly any light fiction in the hardcovers, although I think they stocked a bit more in the summers."

"Well, I guess there is a tendency to let your own taste influence what you buy, but you have to overcome that. I couldn't expect to make a go of this if I bought only what I liked to read. I'd have thought that customers would have been asking for light reading, especially the summer people." Kitt swung slowly around in a half-circle, hands on hips, scanning the shelves again. "I don't even see any Gallen books. Or Harlequins or Silhouettes or Candlelights. Hmmmm. And the only Regencies are a few by Georgette Heyer. She's very good, of course, but there are some other excellent authors in that genre now."

Midge leaned against the end of one set of shelves, watching the graceful swing of Kitt's slender form with ruefully envious eyes. She sighed regretfully and brought her mind back to the problem at hand. "I think most of the year-round customers just accepted the fact that they'd have to pick up romances elsewhere. A lot of women go to the big bookstore opposite the Maine Mall in Portland. It's not that far up the Turnpike, and 'most everyone shops there at least a couple times a month. There's also a store in Kennebunk that carries a lot of current paperbacks. The summer people probably take what they can find. It wouldn't be worth special-ordering things for such a short time."

"I think we'll just see if we can change all that," Kitt said determinedly. "Why should I encourage local people to buy their books in Portland? Especially the lines that come out every month. That's a lot of books. Twelve Harlequins, eight Candlelights, six Silhouettes, four Gallens, three Second Chances. There are several others, but those are the best sellers, and if people buy one line, they'll usually buy the others."

Kitt's eyes were sparkling with enthusiasm and her hair was flying in all directions as she strode lithely across to the pile of publishers' material still on the desk. "Let's see if we can find

the forms for May and June for Pocket Books, Dell, Jove—
oh, just pull out anything on paperbacks from May on."

"Will there be time to send in orders? May's less than two
weeks away."

"No, not for May and maybe not for June. I'm still getting
my lines of credit established with the publishers and distribu-
tors. But I can take a list and a check down to the distributor's
warehouse in Portsmouth and pick up what I need once or
twice a month." Kitt flipped quickly through the still-
unsorted material, pulling out everything pertaining to paperback publishers. "We'd better check off everything on the
order forms that we think will sell. Then, we can compare
them to the orders that the Baxters put in. I rather think they
just ordered the top of the list. We should look over the other
special category shelves, or did you take note of what we've
got for science fiction, mysteries and adult westerns?"

"I didn't look that closely," answered Midge, ripping open
large mailing envelopes and sorting out the contents. "I think
there's a good selection of mysteries and science fiction. That
was the kind of thing the Baxters considered worthwhile light
reading."

"It sells well, that's for sure. So do the new western series,
and I don't think I saw any of them." Kitt glanced up as she
heard the door open. "Let's shift this stuff over to the work
counter. Now that we've got to spread it out, it's taking up
too much room here."

Working quickly, Kitt and Midge shifted everything over to
the long work counter. From the corner of her eye, Midge
saw that the two women who had come in were strolling
slowly toward the desk. "Why don't you help them, Kitt,
while I finish the routine sorting?" She climbed up onto the
high stool so she could reach the countertop more comfortably. "This part is a waste of your time."

"Okay by me," Kitt said. She stepped behind the desk as
the women reached it. "Good afternoon. May I help you find
something in particular?" Kitt's warm smile brought answering smiles from the two women.

"Good afternoon," said the older woman. "Do you have
May Sarton's books? We understand she lives in this area."

"Yes, she does." Kitt moved around the desk and started
across the shop. "We have a complete selection of her

work . . . right here. There's a special section for work by local authors."

"Oh, what a good idea!" the younger woman enthused. She looked up at Kitt with interest. "We're new here. We've just bought a summer home at Goose Rocks, and I'd like to find out something about the history of the area."

"I'm new here, too." Kitt laughed. "I've only owned the shop for a week." She waved a hand toward the opposite wall. "We have a very comprehensive selection of books and maps on the area. Why don't you browse through them? Take your time. If you have any questions, Midge could probably help you better than I. She's a native."

"Thank you. I'm sure I can find just what I want from all this."

Kitt walked back toward the desk, glancing at the clock as she went. "Oh, Lordy, it's after four and—"

"Ez!" squeaked Midge.

"What?"

"Ez just drove in. Oh, and I'm a mess!"

Kitt laughed as Midge ran her fingers through her tangled curls and then smoothed down the gold velour, vee-neck shirt which she wore outside her jeans. Remembering, Kitt leaned forward and spoke softly in Midge's ear. "Don't forget. Not a word about O'Mara. We want it to be a surprise."

"Who's O'Mara?" asked Midge with wide-eyed innocence.

"Good girl. Oh, birdlime, now what's he up to?" muttered Kitt, starting around the desk.

Ez stood just inside the door, arms thrown wide, head back. "Magnificent," he intoned in a deep, echoing voice. "It is the most magnificent bookshop I have ever seen. Ladies," he continued, bowing to the two customers and blowing kisses to them, "you are obviously women of rare taste and discernment. If I can be of any assistance whatsoever, you have but to call on me. A delight. Yes, it would be a pure delight to aid you in your search for knowledge and enlightenment."

For a moment, the two women looked at Ez in boggle-eyed amazement, but the gleam in his exotic eyes and his infectious grin soon reduced them to giggles. Kitt stood halfway down the shop, fists on her slim hips, and watched Ez's performance with a critical eye and an indulgent smile. When the mood struck him, he could be perfectly outrageous, but somehow his sheer size, good looks, abundant charm and untrammeled sense of humor always managed to carry him through his more public performances unarrested, unscathed and unrebuked. Kitt had, on more than one occasion, seen him turn an old prunes-and-pickles harridan into a cooing dove who patted his cheek and called him her "dear boy."

Now that Ez had charmed her customers into quivering jelly, Kitt waited with considerable interest to see what he would do next. A quick look to the side verified that Midge was also waiting with bated breath for the next act. Shifting her gaze back to her twin, Kitt noted that he had managed with typical luck to find a woolen shirt in the exact shade of blue-gray to match his eyes. Those eyes were now glinting with pure devilry as he slowly stalked toward her with arms outstretched.

"A goddess!" It was a muted bellow. The light fixtures trembled perceptibly. "An admirable Amazon! A voluptuous Valkyrie! A magnificent specimen of womanhood who will not crumble and collapse after a little hug." On the last words, Ez flung both arms around Kitt in a bear hug and effortlessly swung her off her feet and spun her around in a circle.

Kitt had long ago learned to move quickly, and she had lifted her arms out of the way as Ez grabbed her and firmly grasped two handfuls of his thick hair. She shook his head back and forth vigorously, kicked him on the shin and yelled in his ear, "Put me down, you idiot, you're cracking my ribs!"

Ez set her on her feet and pulled her hands out of his hair. Turning to his fascinated audience, he mourned, "Can you imagine? My own dear sister, who hasn't seen me for a week; and now," he sobbed, actually managing a tear in his eye, "she won't even let me express my brotherly affection."

He turned a pitiful look on Kitt which should have reduced her to abject apologies but, instead, inspired her to loud applause and a cry of "Bravo!" Midge was laughing so hard she had to hold onto the counter to keep from falling off the stool. Ez flicked a quick glance at her and then turned back to his audience. Shrugging and sighing, he said philosophically, "What can one expect from these oversized, independent women? It takes at least an hour just to wrestle them into their proper place. Now, me, I prefer the little ones." In an eye-blurring series of moves, Ez was across the desk and plucking Midge from her stool, swinging her high over his head with his huge hands wrapped securely around her small waist. "With the little ones," he chortled triumphantly, "you can put them where you want them and keep them there with one hand, leaving the other one free for all sorts of interesting activity."

He slowly lowered the breathless girl until they were practically nose-to-nose. He grinned into her flushed face and asked impatiently, "Well, aren't you going to kiss me hello?"

Midge was almost as quick-witted as the twins—no small feat since she'd had years less practice—and it took only seconds for her to toss out all thoughts of regaining her dignity, which would have been a difficult task anyway with her feet dangling almost a foot and a half from the floor.

Relying on Ez's extraordinary strength to hold her steady, Midge clasped her hands together under her chin, opened her big eyes as wide as possible in a look of reproachful surprise and breathed, "Oh, how can you ask it? Why, we're barely acquainted, and it's just . . . well, my mother . . . oh, it just isn't *done* in our family . . . I mean, I was brought up proper, I was. You," her face and voice expressed pure indignation, "you, sir, are a . . . a *masher!*"

Utterly ignoring the muffled laughter from Kitt and the two women, Ez threw back his head and roared at the ceiling, "Do you hear that!? I've braved the Friday afternoon traffic over miles of superhighways, crossed high bridges, inched my way through the pitfalls of Ogunquit and Wells, dared the intricacies of interchanges, overcome the obstacles in Dock Square and finally, FINALLY, I've reached my goal and I have my personal pixie in my grasp and SHE WON'T KISS ME!" This time, the light fixtures swayed back and forth. Ez brought his head down and peered intently into Midge's stunned eyes, whispering resonantly, "Why won't you kiss me, little wench?"

Totally carried away with the dramatics of it all, Midge flung her arms around his neck, leaned forward and kissed him on the mouth. She intended it to be short and friendly. Ez had other ideas. With typical speed and efficiency, he

rapidly shifted his arms, winding one of them tightly around
Midge's small frame to hold her in place and bringing his free
hand up to cradle the back of her head. When Midge tried to
end the kiss, she found herself unable to move. After half a
minute of Ez's idea of gentle persuasion, she didn't want to
move.

Kitt and her customers looked at each other with raised
eyebrows and indulgent grins. The two women, with occasional glances at the oblivious couple, moved back to the
bookshelves to continue their browsing.

Kitt's attention was caught by the sound of tires on gravel,
and she looked at the clock. It was only four-thirty, too early
for O'Mara. Realizing that more customers would be walking
through the door in a few moments, she moved behind the
desk and tapped Ez on the shoulder. This had no immediate
result since he and Midge were both completely involved in
what was obviously a deep and passionate kiss. Kitt tried
again, and finally heard a faint "Hmmmm?"

"Ez," she hissed, "if you must carry on with this victor-
and-his-spoils routine, will you please move it out back?
There are some customers coming in, and this is beginning to
look like 'Living Statues.' You know—the one called 'The
Kiss'? And while you're out there, will you bring in Hero?
Ez? If you don't go away, I'm going to pinch you in a very
uncomfortable place!"

"Hmmmm." Opening one eye but still kissing Midge, Ez
strolled toward the back door.

Chapter 4

After almost thirty years' experience with Ez's single-
mindedness, Kitt did not expect to see Midge back in the shop
before closing. As the clock hands inched up to five o'clock,
she crossed her fingers that Midge could continue to keep Ez
occupied and unaware of the hour until O'Mara and Gus had
time to arrive and arrange their confrontation with maximum
effect. Kitt saw the last customer out just after five, but she

left on the lights and opened the door partway so O'Mara would know where she was.

With her eyes scanning the backyard through the sliding glass doors, Kitt walked quietly toward the rear of the shop. As she neared the doors and her view widened, she realized that the yard was empty. Just as she paused, wondering where Midge, Ez and Hero could have gone, she heard Ez's deep laugh from the side of the patio. She inched slowly to her right, leaning forward until she could see Ez's feet on the bottom edge of a lounger. Taking another step forward, she had a full view of Ez, half-turned away from her, stretched out comfortably in the lounger with Midge nestled in his lap and Hero sprawled along his legs.

Catching Midge's eye while Ez's attention was concentrated on nuzzling her neck, Kitt made a "staying" motion with both hands and mouthed, "Keep him there." Midge untangled one hand from Ez's hair, gave an "okay" sign and happily set her mind on making him forget about time.

Kitt returned to the desk and quickly closed out the register, counting the cash and bagging it to take upstairs and put in the safe. She had just finished when she heard a car pull into the lot. Glancing at the back door to make sure Ez was still out of sight, she moved swiftly to the front of the shop just as O'Mara came through the door.

For a moment, all she could see was the big, again-familiar man standing there, holding out his hands to her and smiling into her eyes. She clasped his hands and found herself caught up in the intensity of his very blue, very warm gaze. Neither of them seemed able to speak, but before they had time to become completely lost in each other, a slight movement and a muted "Wow!" from beside O'Mara distracted Kitt.

She pulled her eyes away from O'Mara's and looked to her right for the source of that "Wow!" She blinked and found herself looking *down* into O'Mara's eyes! *Impossible! I've just fallen into the rabbit hole. He's shrunk! No two people could have eyes that color.*

Kitt swayed with shock and felt O'Mara's hands tighten on hers. Dazed, she looked back and forth between the tall man and the tall, thin boy standing beside him, both of them wearing identical grins as they chuckled at her stunned expression. *It's a time warp,* thought Kitt, *and I've got the adult O'Mara and the child O'Mara here at the same time.*

"Kitt, I'd like you to meet Gus," said O'Mara, still chuckling. "Gus, this is Kitt. Now do you believe me?"

Kitt stared at the boy, totally bemused by those sapphire O'Mara eyes looking so incredible in the young face and somehow *knowing* her just as his father's did. O'Mara let go of her hands as Gus stretched out his right hand to her.

"Hi. I'm very pleased to meet you, Kitt." He held her hand tightly and tilted his head, quirking an inquiring eyebrow in a gesture she'd seen O'Mara make dozens of times. "Are you all right? Dad said you'd be surprised, but—" He looked up at his father in concern.

"I . . . ah . . . yes, I'm okay." With a strong effort, Kitt pulled herself together and smiled at Gus. "I'm really perfectly fine. I was just . . . Your father, your very sneaky, sly father, who has a warped sense of humor, did not tell me that you looked just like him. Exactly like him. It's uncanny, but I'm sure I'll get used to it."

She gave O'Mara a ferocious scowl, then looked back at Gus with a delighted grin. "You and I are going to be the best of friends. I can tell. Now, what was this your father wanted you to believe?"

"He said you were someone very special and that I'd love you on sight." He looked at her with a familiar intentness and then stepped closer, tugging at her hand. "I think he's right. If you'll bend down a little, I can kiss you."

Laughing, Kitt leaned over and Gus kissed her on the cheek. He stepped back with a look of relief on his face, saying, "There. Enough mushy stuff. Dad says big girls like to be kissed, but I don't see what's so great about it."

"Oh, you will. No doubt about it." Kitt chuckled. "You are very definitely a trainee O'Mara."

"What's that mean?"

She leaned over and whispered in his ear, "I'll explain it sometime when you father's not listening." She slanted a teasing look up at O'Mara and found him watching them with what she considered an intolerably smug expression. She gave him an I'll-get-you-for-this look.

"It's a deal," said Gus, recalling her attention. He looked around the shop and then up at Kitt. "Dad said you had a super dog. Can I see him? And he said your brother was going to be here and that he's a crazy bear." He looked around again, his eyes sparkling with excitement. "Is he here?"

"They're both out back with Midge. She's keeping them distracted so you and your dad can surprise Ez. Tell you what—let's go down here by the desk. Gus, you stand over there out of sight for a few minutes, and you, Mr. Sly Know-It-All," she growled at O'Mara, "can sit on the edge of the desk. No, the other way, facing the front door. Great. Oh, wait. Here, take this. Pretend you're reading. Okay, now, hold your places. You're on."

Stifling her laughter, Kitt skipped to the back and slid open the door. "Ez," she called, "come on in a minute. There's someone here that I'm sure you'd like to meet."

Pushing Hero off his legs but still holding Midge in one arm, Ez rose smoothly to his feet and started for the door. "Who is it?"

"Ez, for heaven's sake," exclaimed Kitt, shaking her head at him in exasperation, "put that girl down. You can't just carry her around like some kind of a pet."

He stopped in front of Kitt and looked questioningly into Midge's flushed face. "Would you really rather walk?" he asked, with genuine interest, almost as if the idea were somehow abnormal. At her choked "Yes!" he set her carefully on her feet and looked puzzledly down into her sparkling brown eyes, now on a level with his chest.

"I don't know why you want to be way down there. It's much easier to talk up here. I'm going to get a crick in my neck." He looked rather put out at the thought of such inconvenience, and Midge and Kitt exchanged amused looks. After a moment, Ez turned his attention back to his sister. "Who is it that I should meet?"

"One of your favorite authors. He came into the shop this morning, and I invited him back to meet you." With difficulty, she managed to keep a straight face. "It's Michael Talbot. He lives just outside town." She stood back to let Ez and Midge through the door, Hero wriggling in between their feet.

"Hey, great!" exclaimed Ez, dropping an arm across Midge's shoulders to hold her beside him as they all started toward the front of the shop. "That's one writer I'd really enjoy talking with."

"Oh, you will, you will," muttered Kitt, trying not to give anything away. She brought them all to a halt a few feet away from the tall figure sitting on the edge of the desk. "Mr. Talbot, I'd like to introduce my brother, Ez Tate."

As O'Mara stood up and turned around, Ez moved forward and then froze in shock, one foot in the air and his right hand half-raised, as he first recognized and then accepted the reality of O'Mara standing in front of him.

"Saint George and all his bloody dragons," came out as an amazed whisper, followed immediately by a joyful bellow of "O'MARA!" which completely drowned out the laughter of Midge, Kitt and Gus. The laughter turned to cries of alarm, overridden by Kitt's yell of "You great idiot, put him down!" as Ez, enthusiastically uninhibited in showing his affection, grabbed O'Mara in a bear hug and lifted the taller man completely off his feet.

Gus watched them, open-mouthed and goggle-eyed, barely able to believe what he was seeing. O'Mara hardly had enough breath left to laugh, and after a few seconds his hands flicked in quick motion. With a grunted "Hey!" Ez let go of him and stepped back, roaring with laughter, then started throwing quick, jabbing punches which O'Mara easily blocked. Within seconds, the two big men were cat-footing around each other trading punches and karate chops and laughing uproariously.

Kitt, Midge and Gus, with a sure instinct for self-preservation, took refuge on the long checkout desk while Hero scrambled under his chair out of harm's way. Tucking their feet under their legs on the desk, the fascinated boy and the two women settled down to watch the show.

"What happens if one of them connects?" Midge asked interestedly.

"Well," Kitt said judiciously, "if O'Mara hits Ez in the head, nothing. Ez has a head like a rock. Same is true of his chest and stomach. O'Mara might slow him down a bit if one of those karate chops lands on a kidney or if he kicks him in the shin. Ez doesn't like that; it's how I slow him down."

Gus looked wonderingly from Kitt to Midge and back to Kitt. "Aren't you going to stop them? You act like you aren't even worried. Your brother's awful big. And strong. He picked Dad right up. What if he hits him?"

Kitt put her arm around the boy's shoulders and smiled

down at him. "No way would I get into the middle of that. They'd floor me and never even know it. Don't worry, Gus. They used to do this all the time, and neither of them ever got hurt. Besides, watch your dad. He moves faster than a blink. I doubt if Ez could touch him even if he were really trying."

Gus watched them for a moment and then looked up at Kitt. "You're sure?"

"Promise. They're only playing."

Kitt eyed the two men carefully, comparing them as they were now with the way she remembered them the last time they had roughhoused together. Both of them had filled out with solid muscle as they matured. However, Ez was broader and heavier through the shoulders and chest, while O'Mara had a rangy, sinewy build. Both were slim-hipped and long-legged, although Ez looked heavier in the thighs because of his exceptionally well-developed "halfback" muscles. O'Mara was an inch taller and had a slightly longer reach, but Ez could give him close to twenty pounds.

A small frown appeared between Kitt's eyes as she watched O'Mara intently. There was something new about the way he moved, an unusual quickness in his reactions, an instinct to move in the least expected direction. It almost looked as though he had practiced and trained to react *un*naturally. He's holding back, Kitt thought. If this were for real, he'd have had Ez down in the first minute.

Kitt looked over Gus's head toward Midge. "What do you think, Midge? Enough is enough? We've been left out of this reunion too long."

"How are you going to break it up?"

"Easy." Kitt threw back her head and let out a piercing rebel yell. Ez and O'Mara immediately stepped back from each other and flipped up their hands in a "draw" sign.

"You called?" O'Mara laughed as he started to walk toward Kitt.

"I just thought that since Ez wasn't getting anywhere with you, he might like to try his luck with a smaller O'Mara." Kitt stood up, pulling Gus off the desk to stand in front of her, facing Ez. "What do you think, muscleman? Would you have any better luck with this one?" She grinned understandingly at Ez's incredulous expression as his eyes darted between Gus and O'Mara.

She saw the delighted smile spreading over his face and just had time to mutter "Brace yourself" in Gus's ear before Ez swooped on him and swung him high in the air over his head.

"Ah ha!" he roared. "At last! An O'Mara I can handle with one hand." He flipped the laughing boy around and brought him down to sit on his shoulders. Turning to speak to O'Mara, he caught the words back and narrowed his eyes in speculation when he saw the look on O'Mara's face as he watched Kitt.

"Tell you what, old buddy. The little one over there," said Ez, chuckling and nodding toward Midge, "is all mine, but I'll divvy up the other two with you. I'll share Kitt if you'll share this twig, here."

"Ez! You—" Kitt felt the telltale color flaming in her cheeks and hissed at her twin when he laughed and winked at O'Mara. "You two!" she sputtered, shaking her fist at them. "Twelve years, and nothing, but nothing, has changed! Get you two together and you're totally impossible."

Kitt was just beginning to consider methods of retribution when Gus brought everyone's attention back to practical matters.

"Hey, Kitt, now that I've met the crazy bear, where's your dog?"

"Who's a crazy bear?" growled Ez, reaching up to take Gus's hands and then flipping him up and over in a somersault and setting him gently on his feet.

Gus laughed up at him. "You are! My dad said you were, and you really are." He turned around as Kitt called his name and then dropped to his knees and held out his hands toward Hero, who was hovering at Kitt's feet. "Oh, wow, he's neat."

"Hero, meet Gus. New friend."

Hero trotted forward, briefly sniffed Gus's hand, took two more steps and stood on his hind legs, resting his front paws on the boy's shoulders, and licked his nose. Gus giggled and threw his arms around the dog, reaching instinctively to rub him behind the ears with one hand.

"Oh, Kitt, he's super. Is his name really Hero? Sometimes dogs have long, fancy names, but you call them by nicknames."

"You're right, and 'Hero' is sort of a nickname. His real name is Hieroglyphic."

"Hiero—who? What kind of a name is that?"

"Hieroglyphic. It's old Egyptian picture-writing. Basenjis

were once the royal dogs of Egypt, so I gave him an Egyptian name. However, the crazy bear shortened it to 'Hero' because he said he felt like a fool yelling 'Here, Hieroglyphic' all over the park."

Gus twisted around and tilted his head back to look up at Ez with a grin. "I wish I'd seen that. It must have been funny."

Kitt stood transfixed, staring down at the handsome boy, and from a deep, long-buried dream a thought rose and burned across her mind. *He could have been mine. Oh, God, if only . . . he'd be mine now.* Her throat closed with a painful, choking emotion, and she could feel tears of regret and loss searing her eyes.

She had no idea how revealing her expression was or that O'Mara was watching her intently, his face mirroring a look of relieved satisfaction. A soft "Hmmm?" from Ez brought O'Mara's head around, and the two men exchanged a rapid series of silent questions and answers as their eyes locked for long moments. At last, Ez nodded and his mouth widened in a slow smile of approval and relief.

O'Mara's answering smile flashed whitely in the deep tan of his face as he murmured, "Some feelings never change, my boy. They just grow stronger and deeper."

Turning his attention back to Kitt, he read the imminence of tears and moved to her side, enclosing her hand in a strong, warm clasp. "Hey, there. I thought these two," motioning at the enraptured boy and dog at their feet, "were going for a walk. And we really ought to crack a bottle of wine to celebrate this extraordinary reunion."

Kitt, blinking back tears, looked up at him, somehow soothed by his nearness, and, meeting his eyes, sensed his awareness and understanding of what she was feeling. Drawing strength from his closeness and the warm clasp of his hand, she collected her frazzled emotions and turned a smiling face to Gus.

"Why don't you take Hero for his walk and get acquainted? If you'd like to, that is."

"That would be great!" exclaimed Gus, jumping excitedly to his feet. "Does he have a leash? Where should I take him?"

"We usually walk down the road toward the ocean. I don't think going the other way into Dock Square would be a good idea, or up on Maine Street. Too much traffic and too many other dogs." She bent over to rub one finger between Hero's eyes, and he arched his neck with pleasure. "I hardly ever use a leash. He's very good about staying close. If he goes exploring, just call him and say 'Heel.' Don't worry, you'll do just fine."

She started walking toward the front door with Gus, while Hero danced around them. "I'm going to lock up down here, so when you come back, come up the outside stairs. Okay? Oh, and Hero likes to run. Maybe you can both work off some energy." She laughed.

"We'll be back in a while," said Gus over his shoulder as he and Hero shot out the door and starting running across the parking lot. "Come on, Hero, race you!" floated back with the echo of thudding feet.

Kitt, smiling to herself, closed and locked the door. Turning around, she found herself blocked by an expanse of navy-blue wool stretched across a wide, solid chest. Before she could move back, a long, tanned finger tilted her chin up an inch, and warm lips brushed across hers in a feather-light kiss.

The gleam in those very blue eyes and the deep purr in his voice held Kitt immobilized. "Somehow I knew you two would take to each other. Ez isn't the only one I'm going to share him with, you know. And it's going to be a lot more than just weekends."

"O'Mara?" It was a just audible whisper.

Too soon. It's all happening much too fast. I'm not ready for this. She was afraid to believe what she was seeing in his eyes, and her own began to show traces of the panic rising in her. She felt the gentle touch of his fingers slowly stroking her cheek and watched his thick black lashes come down to hide his expression. It only lasted for a second or two, and when he opened his eyes again, they were glinting with laughter.

"Come on, my girl. We're supposed to be having a celebration, not a postmortem. You and I will have our time later." He caught her hand and drew her along with him. "I'm beginning to see what you meant about Ez and Midge," he said softly. "A bear and a kitten. Unreal."

"Just wait until you see a full, one-act production." Kitt chuckled, her amused gaze resting on the other couple where they sat on the desk, side by side, quietly talking.

Ez looked around at the sound of voices, his easy grin dispelling the last of the tension. "Hey, you two, I thought we were going to party. Where's the wine and song?" He winked at O'Mara and whispered resonantly, "No sense in asking for any more women. They'd never let us get away with it, and I'll tell you, the little one's got some nasty moves. I think Kitt's been giving her pointers."

"No such thing," Midge declared pertly. "I don't need pointers, thank you. When you're my size, you learn how to defend yourself against overgrown lummoxes. And just you remember, Ez Tate, the bigger they are, the louder the thud when they hit the ground!"

The men roared, O'Mara clearly delighted with the small, feisty girl, while Ez eyed her fondly, as if she were a favorite pet who had done something exceptionally clever.

"Chauvinists," said Kitt as she and Midge exchanged commiserating looks.

"If your miserable brother doesn't wipe that disgustingly patronizing look off his face, I'm going to do him a mischief," Midge stated loudly.

Ez growled and lunged at her, sweeping her up in his arms and, in one smooth motion, swung around to toss her, squealing, through the air to O'Mara, who caught her easily and threw her back to Ez. He plucked her out of the air and cradled her high against his chest, laughing down into her indignant face. Before he could throw her to O'Mara again, she grabbed fistfuls of his hair and yelled, "NO!"

Fists on hips and feet slightly apart in a challenging stance, Kitt scowled at the playful men. "Big boobies. Maybe you'd like to try that with someone closer to your own size," she threatened.

Laughing and holding his hands up in surrender, O'Mara scanned her slim but athletic five-foot, nine-inch figure. "No way, love. Pick you up and carry you around, yes. Toss you through the air and catch you, no. We'd both be flat for a week with wrenched backs."

"Cowards," Kitt muttered.

"I'll wrestle with you later," said O'Mara, grinning, "if you really want to play. Right now, though," he continued, turning to Ez, "I want to talk to you for a few minutes, if you can detach yourself."

"Sure. I can use a breather." Ez dropped Midge to her feet

but had to stay bent over since she still had a tight grip on his hair. Chuckling, he wrapped one hand halfway around her waist and held the other out to the side in a straight line with her small bottom. "Let go," he growled warningly.

Unafraid, Midge smiled sweetly into his face, which was just a few inches from hers, and purred, "You do and I'll bite your nose." She tugged his head down as she went up on tiptoe and kissed his nose, then let go of his hair and, with a quick twist of her agile body, she was free and racing for the back stairs, yelling over her shoulder, "Besides, I'd rather make love than war."

Ez straightened up with a baffled look on his face, which only made Kitt and O'Mara laugh harder.

O'Mara caught Kitt's eye and said, "If you'll go along and find the glasses, we'll finish locking up and fetch the wine. We'll only be a few minutes."

She looked at him questioningly but accepted his reassuring nod and followed Midge.

Chapter 5

Standing in the middle of the living room a few minutes later, Kitt ran her fingers distractedly through her hair and looked at Midge with an unconscious plea in her lovely eyes.

"Midge, do you mind? I . . . I've got to clean up and change. I spent most of the morning grubbing in those cabinets and . . . I need to be alone for a little bit. This is all . . . it's. . . ." She shook her head impatiently, sending her hair flying, unable to find the right words.

"No problem, Kitt. Go along and take your time. I know where the wineglasses are, and why don't I set the table? One less thing to do when the guys get back. And shall I take the steaks out now to get the chill off?"

"Yes, fine, if you're sure you don't mind. I don't mean to stick you with all the jobs. I'll do the salad when I come back, but perhaps you could scrub some baking potatoes. They can go in when Ez starts the charcoal. He should do that as soon as he comes up."

Kitt headed down the hall toward her bedroom, calling back, "Don't forget the size of those appetites when you're counting potatoes! And Gus is a growing boy."

"Just figure what a normal person would want and multiply by four," muttered Midge, pulling over the stepstool so she could reach the wall cabinets.

Kitt closed the bedroom door and slumped back against it with her eyes closed and her arms hanging loosely at her sides. She felt as if she had just run five miles on a mud flat. "Oh, damn, damn, damn," she whispered. "One O'Mara is more than I can handle. What the hell am I going to do with two of them? And, oh, that second one. A love. An absolute love."

She pushed away from the door and walked slowly toward the low, oversized bed. Kicking off her ankle boots, she dropped across the bed on her stomach, arms flung wide, and closed her eyes. It didn't help. Pictures of O'Mara flitted across her closed lids. O'Mara looking relaxed and impossibly young as he laughed with Ez. The strong, lean body twisting and bending to dodge Ez's punches. The beige cords stretching tightly over the flexing muscles in his long legs as he balanced to catch Midge. Blue—the gleaming, darkening, shifting, flashing, incredible blue of the eyes that kept telling her things she wasn't ready to know.

"No," she moaned. "I can't."

She forced her mind to concentrate on what she could put into the salad, mentally reviewing the contents of the refrigerator, while she rolled off the bed onto her feet and started undressing. Slipping into a white, floor-length, terrycloth caftan trimmed with navy-blue piping, she headed for the bathroom and a long shower.

Taking the few steps between her bedroom and the bathroom, she noticed the quiet and realized that the men hadn't come up yet. The only sound was the clink of silverware as Midge set the table.

Standing under the cascade of warm, soothing water a few minutes later, Kitt gradually became aware of just how tense she had been when she felt her cramped muscles slowly unknot and relax. She breathed in deeply, enjoying the heather scent of her soap, and tried to stop imagining the feel of strong, sensitive hands smoothing lather over her skin. It was one thing to tell herself that even if he were sharing the shower, she wouldn't be able to let him touch her like that; it was another thing to turn off her imagination and control her wishful thinking. The miracle was that she'd even want to think about a man touching her body again. Obviously, the reentry of O'Mara into her life was not going to be conducive to a peaceful existence. She *knew,* absolutely, that he was not going to believe that she wasn't affected by him, nor was he going to accept any nonsense like "I don't want to get involved with anyone."

She bent over, flipping her hair forward to get it thoroughly wet, and reached for the bottle of shampoo. The sting of soap in her left eye finally succeeded in diverting her thoughts from O'Mara for a while. Moving back from the stream of water, she squeezed the excess water from her hair and stretched a long arm through the shower curtains, groping for a towel to wrap around her head. She rinsed the last of the shampoo suds from her arms and reached for the taps.

As soon as she turned off the shower, she could hear the deep rumble of male voices, the frequent roar of Ez's laughter and the lighter sound of Midge's delightful giggle. Strange, she thought, Ez doesn't particularly like giggly women, but he sure gets a gleam in his eye when he listens to Midge. *That* giggle doesn't seem to turn him off a bit. In fact . . . The thought trailed off as she finished drying her legs, tossed the towel onto the hamper and reached for a comb.

"Damn this hair," she muttered, trying to untangle the wet snarls. "I've a good mind to thin out a pound of it and get a butch!"

The scowl faded and a smile lit her face at the sound of another bellow of laughter. Poor Midge, if he can rattle the window in here with the door closed, she must be practically knocked off her feet. Lord, the look on Ez's face when O'Mara turned around and he realized who it was. And, then, when he saw Gus! Wish I'd thought to take down the camera.

She plugged in the powerful blow-dryer and, brush in one hand, began the fifteen-minute chore of getting her thick hair dry. Faintly, she heard a higher male laugh and realized that

Gus and Hero must have returned. She smiled, remembering the instant rapport between boy and dog. Webs, she thought, beautiful silvery webs, and he's weaving them all around me. Twelve years of nothing, and then in a few hours he's fuzzing my mind with teasing little kisses, feather touches, sexy looks and his sneaky ESP, to say nothing of knocking me silly with understanding and compassion. And if that wasn't enough, he's got to bring in an utterly irresistible mini-O'Mara on me!

She put the hair-dryer away and donned her caftan, wincing as a loud thud shook the floor and wondering who was demonstrating what. The blast of sound hit her as she stepped out into the hall. Good grief, she thought, it sounds like a convention out there. How can two men make so much noise? She shut her bedroom door, muting the racket somewhat, and started getting dressed.

Clad in flowered bikini briefs and a matching lightweight bra, she sat on the bed to smooth on patterned knee-high nylons. She was barely aware of what she was putting on; her mind was back to worrying about what O'Mara's presence was going to mean in her plans. Right from the beginning, when she was fifteen, he'd understood her better than she understood herself. He'd always been able to bring her around to his way of thinking. Never pushing or being domineering, just looking at her with those damned *knowing* eyes and that *amused* little smile. He didn't even have to say it out loud, it was there in his expression: "Come along, Kitt, you know you want to do it my way." And she did. Even that last summer when she had finally started to gain confidence in being a young woman, she still followed where he led, letting him set the pace and rarely arguing with him.

Not that we never disagreed, she thought with a laugh. Oh, did we have some lovely discussions. At least, we called them discussions. But, somehow, when it came to a real argument, I never seemed to win. Hmmm, that's not an encouraging thought if I really want to keep him from taking over my life. Which I don't. I'd love to have him and Gus in my life, but . . . no, it's impossible. It's just too late.

She knotted the gold cord around her waist and stood back to look in the long pier glass. Dark green wide-wale cord jeans fit snugly on her long legs. The shape of her body was blurred by the pale green, hip-length cotton smock. With its high neck and long, full sleeves, it effectively hid any sign of bare skin. The addition of the belt kept the peasant-style top from being completely shapeless.

Turning sideways, she tugged, tucked and pulled at the top until it bloused enough to hide all sign of her breasts. She wasn't thinking about anyone in particular at that moment. It was an almost automatic procedure that she went through whenever she dressed. She was just turning to go to the closet for her shoes when there was a tentative knock on the door and Gus's voice called, "Kitt?"

"Come on in. I'm dressed."

He pushed open the door and took a couple of steps into the room. "Ez wants to know if you've fallen asleep. I don't know how you could with all the noise he and Dad are making. Boy, this is a weird room. Don't you have any windows?"

"Of course. Just open those louvered doors," Kitt said.

"Hey, wow, what a window! How many plants have you got? It looks like a jungle. What's that thing with the huge red flowers?"

"A giant amaryllis. Isn't it beautiful? I've got three more, and you can have one if you want. They're easy to care for, and they blossom a couple of times a year at least. I'll write down the instructions for you before you go tonight."

"Gee, great! You're sure it's okay?"

"Sure. Do you like plants?" Kitt was somewhat bemused by the turn of the conversation. She'd never known a young boy who was interested in growing plants.

"Yeah, I do, but I don't know much about taking care of them. Dad isn't into plants, and Andy only keeps geraniums."

Kitt was on one knee in the closet, looking for her clogs, and her voice was muffled as she asked, "Who's Andy?"

"She's our housekeeper, but she's really like a grandmother to me. She's been with us since I was a baby." He wandered over to the closet. It was double-width, with folding doors that matched those across the window. Only one section of the doors was open, and Kitt was leaning to poke through the boxes piled on the floor of the closed side. "What are you looking for? Want me to open this door?" Gus offered. "You could see better."

"Oh, men, you're so practical," Kitt grumbled. "I'm trying

to find my clogs—you know what they are, don't you? Okay, Mr. Efficiency," she laughed, "open that door and give me a hand. The ones I want are green leather and have open toes."

Gus dropped to his hands and knees and started opening boxes. "These aren't all shoes, Kitt. Why do you keep spices in your closet? Andy keeps hers in the kitchen."

"Ho, is this where they've been? I've hunted for them all week. You can put them outside, little wise guy, I keep mine in the kitchen, too." She glanced around at a scrabbling sound and exclaimed, "Hero! Out! We don't need your help."

"What on earth are you two doing? Digging for treasure?" Ez's deep voice startled them, and they both jumped. "Come on, Kitt, you and Gus can play later. The rest of us are hungry. The charcoal is just right for the steaks, but Midge doesn't know what you want to put in the salad."

"Coming. Just a minute. We're trying to find my shoes. Oh, those are the ones, Gus! Now just push all this stuff in—not the spices—and close the doors. Hero, will you get out of there? Go on, Ez, we're right behind you."

They were still sitting at the table two hours later. It had not been an elaborate, multi-course meal, but the steady talk and laughter had drawn it out. So far, most of the talking had been done by O'Mara, as he answered the dozens of questions thrown at him by Kitt and Ez. He had refused earlier to tell Ez anything about the past twelve years of his life, saying that it was all so boring he only wanted to go through it once and would wait for Kitt to join them. So he and Ez had spent an uproarious hour before dinner reminiscing about their summers on the Cape, with Midge and Gus a fascinated audience.

Once they were all seated at the table, though, the questions had come thick and fast.

"Okay, come clean, O'Mara. What happened to you?" Ez asked. "We wrote a few letters back and forth, but then, after a while, we never heard from you again. Kitt wrote asking if you were all right, and it was returned marked 'addressee unknown.' Where did you disappear to?"

"All I can tell you, even now, is that a few months after I started that job in Washington, I had a very good offer to go to work for a government agency. I can't tell you the name.

Most of the work was overseas, and one of the reasons I got the job was that I didn't have any family. No ties. No distractions."

"Sounds like you were some kind of a spy. Was that it?" Kitt asked.

"Something like that. They didn't like us to send or receive mail while we were training, and then I went on an assignment to. . . . Well, it doesn't matter. But it was almost a year before I got back."

"Was it dangerous?" asked Kitt, her eyes widening in sudden concern. "Oh, I suppose that's a dumb question. It must have been."

"Sometimes. I've got a couple of scars here and there, but nothing serious. I was lucky—I always managed to get out of the tight spots relatively whole."

Ez laughed and said, "I'll bet luck didn't have much to do with it. You always were tough as rawhide, and moved faster than anyone expected from a man your size."

"It helped. On the other hand, I made a rather large target."

"Ugh! Sounds awful when you put it that way," Kitt exclaimed. "What happened when you got back?"

"A couple of weeks in the hospital, and then a few weeks of leave. I met Laura, Gus's mother, then. I was staying at a rest house the agency owned down on Cape Hatteras, and she was visiting nearby. When my leave was over, I went back overseas on another assignment."

"Did you get married then?" As she asked the question, Kitt glanced at Gus, wondering if this talk about the mother he'd never known was bothering him. He was unconcernedly working his way through his second helping of salad.

O'Mara leaned back, sipping his wine. "No, not until I returned a few months later. My boss wasn't too happy with me, but he cooled off when I promised to take one more assignment out of the country. After that, I could transfer to an onshore job and stay put for a while."

Gus chimed in, "Dad was in . . . Oh, I'm not supposed to say . . . He was away when I was born. That's how come I've got this yuck name. If he'd been there, I'd have a lot better one."

"You know it." His father grinned.

Kitt smiled at the boy sitting across the corner of the table from her. "Oh, I don't know. I kind of like 'Gus.' It fits you. Besides, it could have been worse, Algernon or Bartholomew or Fotheringale," she slanted a sly look at Ez and added, "or Ezekiel."

Ez laughed and threw a cherry tomato at her. "You should talk. 'Kittredge' isn't exactly a typical girl's name." He turned back to O'Mara. "When did you start writing? What made you think of it?"

"It just sort of happened. The agency work was getting to me, and I had Gus to take care of. I wanted to spend more time with him as he got older, and writing was something I could do at home. Guess he was around three when I started the first book. Since I'd been up to my ears in political intrigue for five years, it seemed a natural choice for a plot."

"Political intrigue may have been a natural," Kitt said, "but your plots are anything but. Why didn't we ever realize what a devious mind you have? Positively Machiavellian."

"You weren't supposed to know," O'Mara said chidingly. "What's the point of being devious if everyone knows you are? It loses its effectiveness." He locked eyes with Kitt, staring at her intently, and said softly, "Be warned."

She looked puzzled and asked, "About what?"

"My devious mind." He laughed at her bewilderment and changed the subject quickly. "To finish this off—so we can get to what you two have been up to—after the second book did so well and the movie sale did even better, I decided to get back to New England. I always intended to live here eventually, and the time was right. I had enough money to afford the kind of privacy and the kind of place I wanted. It took a few months, but I finally found the house at Crest Rock, and we moved here a couple of years ago."

Kitt's dining arrangements consisted of an eight-foot antique harvest table with an equally long church bench on each side and a captain's chair at either end. She was sitting at one end, with Midge and Ez on the bench to her left and Gus and O'Mara sharing the one on the right.

Tiny Midge looked about ten years old beside Ez's bulk, and she almost sounded it as she cried, "Oh, but what about all those super places you go to and the movies you made? I read all about those. You were right there when they were filming, and what about that actress—" She broke off with a guilty look at Kitt.

Ez shouted with laughter. O'Mara smiled at her rather paternally. Gus looked from one to the other, puzzled, and Kitt blushed. She could have kicked herself.

"Put your foot in it that time, Thumbelina," Ez gasped.

"I'll tell you stories of my wild and wicked adventures another day," O'Mara said, "but right now I want to find out what the terrible twins have been up to."

Kitt grinned, her eyes gleaming with anticipation. "Has Ez told you yet what he does?"

O'Mara shook his head, watching her expectantly.

"Wait for this," Kitt cautioned gleefully. "Would you believe a professor of medieval history?"

There was a moment of stunned silence while O'Mara stared at Ez in blank shock. Then his mouth curved in a slow, wide smile and he said wonderingly, "Only you would carry a joke that far. You look like you should be wrestling bears or leaping tall buildings, so naturally you've become a college professor. I'll bet you're having a terrific time romping through life, chortling over the stunned reactions when you tell people what you do. Ezekiel, you fraud, you should have been *in* medieval history!" A dreamy expression came over his face as he gazed at the ceiling and said, "I can see you now, clanking around in full armor, trying to find a horse big enough to hold you and a hundred pounds of tin, while the fair young maidens—"

He broke off as everyone erupted in gales of laughter. When it quieted somewhat, O'Mara grinned at Ez and said, "You can fill me in on the details later. I'm having too much fun right now making up my own story." He turned toward Kitt, and with an odd note in his voice asked, "What about you, Kitt? What have you been doing with yourself all these years?"

Her facial muscles tightened, and she glanced at Ez with a hint of desperation in her smoky eyes before turning back to O'Mara to say hesitantly, "I . . . uh . . . I got my degree in phys. ed. and taught for a while and . . . Ez and I have been sharing an apartment for about five years. I was with a computer company for a while, and then I worked in a bookstore the last three years. When Grandma Arlen died and left me enough money to buy a shop of my own, I found this place and . . . Well, here I am."

She met O'Mara's sardonically amused gaze and quickly looked away. *Damn, he always sees too much!*

O'Mara shot a questioning look at Ez, who shook his head slightly. His eyes returned to Kitt, and he said, in a neutral tone, "That's certainly a succinct summary."

Pushing back her chair, Kitt jumped to her feet and started stacking dishes. "Oh, I haven't really done anything very interesting. Listen, why don't you all get comfortable while I clean up this mess? Ez, there's more wine. Gus, if you're getting bored with all this talk of old times, you can take the portable TV into my room. Is there anything you like to watch on Friday evenings?" She could hear herself babbling, but couldn't seem to stop. "Thanks, Midge, but it will go faster if I pile everything on the breakfast bar and you go around into the kitchen and work from the other side. Or I'll do it while you—"

She came to an abrupt halt when large hands closed gently over her upper arms and O'Mara's voice murmured in her ear, "Relax, Kitt. I'm not going to push you."

She knew he was standing close behind her, but only his hands touched her. They were resting on her arms more than actually holding her, and she realized that she could easily move away. He would let her go. But she stood still, hearing his slow, even breathing and feeling the warmth of his hands through her sleeves. Gradually, her muscles relaxed; she took a long, deep breath, let it out slowly, and turned her head to look into the compassionate eyes only a few inches away. And it was happening again. She could feel understanding and reassurance wrapping around her, and she said, just above a whisper, "I'm all right."

His voice was husky as he answered, "For now. We'll take care of the long term later. When you're ready."

She felt his hands slide down her arms in a light caress before dropping away as he turned and followed Ez across the living room.

The rest of the evening flew past, carried on clouds of nostalgia and gusts of laughter. Ez needed little encouragement to draw on his fund of stories about the pitfalls of dealing with female college students. O'Mara delighted

Midge with hair-raising stories of filming on location. Curled up at the end of the sofa, Kitt said little beyond adding a pithy comment now and then to Ez's outrageous tales.

"Shades of Charlemagne! It's time for all wee mites to be in bed," exclaimed Ez, glancing at his watch and then lunging to his feet. Two strides took him to the sofa where Midge was perched cross-legged. Wrapping his huge hands around her waist, he plucked her up and held her in midair, feet dangling over a foot from the floor. She grabbed at his arms, her fingers digging into his bulging muscles to secure a hold, and jack-knifed her jeans-clad legs up to rest her knees on his chest.

Grinning impudently into his face, she asked, "Now what are you going to do?"

"See you home, of course," he announced, giving her a mockingly lecherous look as he carried her toward the coat closet. He had to set her down while they put on their jackets, but then quickly swung her up in his arms and walked toward the sliding door to the deck.

"Will you stop wiggling, wench? This is for your own protection. I heard there's a gigantic lobster roaming the area, and he'd make an hors d'oeuvre out of a bit of a thing like you." Ez failed miserably in trying to keep a straight face, and Midge was laughing up at him, arms wound around his neck, as they disappeared into the darkness. Midge's faint "Goodnight, everyone" was definitely an afterthought.

Kitt and O'Mara had been amused observers of the performance and now looked at each other, laughing.

"Can you figure out who's making the running?" O'Mara asked.

"Oh, I think they both are—right at each other!"

"I wouldn't miss this for worlds. You're right, Ez's courting methods aren't to be believed!"

The laughter slowly faded from O'Mara's face. He leaned his chin on his hand, elbow resting on the arm of the large Victorian grandfather chair. He watched Kitt trying to avoid his eyes.

There was a waiting stillness. Tiny points of light flickered on Kitt's lashes as her eyes shifted about the room, inevitably coming to rest on O'Mara. She tried to concentrate on examining his navy-blue wool shirt and beige cord jeans, but it only increased her awareness of the powerful body and long, muscular legs under his clothes. The top buttons of his shirt were undone, and she could see a smudge of soft blackness in the open vee. She had a sudden vision of a younger O'Mara standing on the beach in swim trunks, his arms, legs and chest furred with soft, curling black hair, the thick mat on his chest narrowing down over his taut stomach to the edge of his trunks.

She felt every muscle in her body knot at the vividness of the memory. The stillness in the room thickened with tension, and her eyes darted up to meet his. *He's doing it again. He's reading my mind.*

Warily, she watched him rise to his feet and walk toward her, his hands held out to her. She hesitated, her mouth going dry with the beginning of fear. *I can't.* His eyes on hers were compelling, and she slowly lifted her hands to take his. As they touched, a frisson of dread shimmered along her nerve ends, and she was shivering as he pulled her to her feet in front of him. *O'Mara. This is O'Mara.* It was a litany running in an endless circle in her mind, and she clung to it as if it were a lifeline.

She'd kicked off her clogs some time earlier, and now stood in her stocking feet, still only a few inches shorter than he. He could feel the tremors shaking her, and increased the pressure of his hands. Every muscle in her body tensed, this time in determination rather than sexual awareness, as she forced herself to resist the nearly overwhelming need to yank her hands away and run.

"Shhhh. Quietly, Kitt. Just stand still." It was the same low, purring tone he might use to soothe Gus from a nightmare. At first, Kitt could barely hear it through the pounding of blood in her ears. Then, gradually, the words penetrated. "I told you, I'm not going to rush you. I know something is very wrong, but we've got all the time we need to sort it out. Now that I've found you again, there's no reason to hurry things. We can take it at your pace, and I'm not going to ask questions that you're not ready to answer."

She felt the easing of tension as her muscles unknotted, and she opened her eyes, raising them to the clear, calm reassurance of his gaze. "O'Mara." It was a statement.

"Nobody else," he said, smiling slightly. "Now, I've got to

get Gus home to bed, and I think you've had enough for one day. I've promised him a fishing trip tomorrow, and we'll probably be late returning, so I won't see you. Is the shop open on Sunday?" She nodded mutely, and he asked, "What time?"

"Noon." Her voice was hoarse.

"Good. Set your alarm early. I'll be by to pick you up at five-thirty, and we'll go to watch the sunrise and have breakfast. No, don't argue," he commanded as her mouth opened. "I'll bet you haven't watched a sunrise over the ocean in years."

"No. Not since the last time with you." Her face had a remembering look. She still stood before him, her hands lightly clasped in his.

"Stand easy, Kitt," he whispered as he bent his head and softly touched his lips to hers, straightening up again before she had time to do more than blink. He let go of her left hand and turned to walk down the hall toward her bedroom, drawing her after him by his hold on her other hand.

"Let's see what Gus is doing. Hope he's asleep. We've got to get off early in the morning."

He pushed open the door, and Kitt moved up beside him to look into the room. The TV was showing an old western, but the volume was turned down. Gus was sprawled on his side on Kitt's bed, his arm across Hero who was curled up tight against his stomach. Both were sound asleep.

Kitt and O'Mara exchanged indulgent smiles. "Seems a shame to separate them. However. . . ." He walked quietly to the bed and leaned over, speaking softly to the dog, and put his hand on Gus's shoulder.

"Gus. Time to go. Do you want to walk or shall I carry you?"

The boy sat up, mumbled, "Walk," and slid off the bed. His father's hands on his shoulders steadied him as he staggered, still three-quarters asleep, toward the living room. Kitt followed, carrying a potted amaryllis bulb. She collected their jackets and handed O'Mara his, turning to help Gus. Hero leaned against the boy's legs, and Gus slitted his eyes open to look down at him.

"Bye, Hero," he muttered. "See you soon. Nice supper, Kitt. See you, too." He yawned and stood swaying while his eyes closed again. "Walk," he protested sleepily as O'Mara picked him up.

"Not down those stairs." He settled Gus against his shoulder, holding him securely in one arm, and reached for the pot that Kitt was shifting from hand to hand as she put on her jacket.

"I'll carry it down. Hero's got to go out anyway."

In the parking lot, O'Mara opened the door of his Jeep Renegade and set Gus down in the passenger seat, tucking his plant in beside him. Hero scrambled into the back, turned around twice, and collapsed in a comfortable ball, his nose tucked under his hind legs.

"Come out of there, you nut." Kitt laughed, opening the driver's door and snapping her fingers. Slowly, and with obvious reluctance, Hero uncoiled, stretched and finally jumped out of the jeep. O'Mara slid into his seat and closed the door. Rolling down the window, he grinned teasingly at Kitt and said, "Don't forget. Sunday at five-thirty."

"You're mad, you know," she groaned, and then laughed. Hands in pockets, she stood watching as he swung out of the lot and turned down Ocean Avenue.

Chapter 6

Kitt walked a short distance down the road with Hero, moving in a semi-daze, barely aware of her surroundings. Her mind was a twirling kaleidoscope of flashing scenes from the evening, from the years of her marriage, from those long-ago summers. The colors were vivid, reflecting the emotions flickering through and around the jumble of pictures: blazing, blistering reds, oranges and acid yellow of anger, hate and violence; cool blues and greens and warm lemon of peaceful, endless summer; grays, browns and soft beige of numbness and despair; and, strongest of all, the spring green of new life and the deep, flaming blue pulling her inexorably into that life.

It was too much. Her head was aching with confusion and, with every ounce of willpower she possessed, Kitt blanked it all out. She turned and walked back toward home, head down, eyes on her feet, counting her steps. Her concentration on nothing was so total that she didn't hear Ez's car or see him waiting for her.

"Yeoo—" She choked off the yelp of surprise and grabbed Ez's arms to regain her balance. His hands reached out to steady her as she bounced off his chest.

"You really are in a fog, pet, when you can't see something this big," Ez said, a faint question in his voice.

"Sorry. Guess I was rather out of it." Kitt started up the stairs and said over her shoulder, "I think I had a bit too much wine. How about some coffee?"

"Sounds good. You sure it's just wine that's got you walking into barn doors?"

"What else?" asked Kitt, sliding open the door. She dropped her jacket onto the back of the sofa and headed for the kitchen. She tried desperately to keep a nonchalant expression on her face, knowing it was a futile effort; the mental link between her and Ez was incredibly strong, even stronger than that between her and O'Mara.

Throwing his jacket over hers, Ez moved lazily to the low breakfast bar and sat down, leaning forward on his crossed arms and watching Kitt intently. "It could be O'Mara. Didn't you find it just a little bit intriguing that we still had that old rapport going, even after all these years? And don't try to tell me you don't know what I'm talking about. Ten minutes after you walked into that room tonight, you two were so aware of each other that even Midge picked it up. In fact, I could see smoke rising a couple of times when we were in the shop."

"Ez, it isn't . . . I don't. . . ." Kitt's hands were shaking, and she set down the jar of coffee with a clatter. Hands pressing flat on the counter, she dropped her head, squeezing her eyes shut.

"Oh, damn, damn. I don't need this!" Her voice was ragged with the effort to suppress tears. "Everything was going so well. I finally had it all together—peace and work I liked in a place I liked. And *he* walks in and. . . ."

"And?"

Kitt pushed away from the counter, swinging around to

face Ez and holding out her hands in appeal. "It just doesn't make any sense. Ez, you can't wipe out twelve years, can you? It was all there, just as though we'd only been apart for weeks. All the feeling we used to have for each other . . . and . . . and something more. I don't know . . . I can't explain what it is. But, Ez, I'm not ready to handle it. I couldn't. . . ."

He got up and swung his legs over the low counter. "Look, go sit down before you fall over. I'll fix the coffee."

"Now," Ez said a few minutes later, handing Kitt her coffee and dropping into an easy chair. "Take a few swallows of that and calm down. Nobody's going to force you into anything, least of all O'Mara."

"I know. That's what he said—that we've got plenty of time and he wasn't going to push me."

"Did he say that after we left?" Ez asked. "What happened? You were certainly off somewhere in limbo when you walked into me."

"Nothing much happened. He held my hands and . . ." Her voice dropped to a whisper that Ez had to lean forward to hear, "He kissed me."

"Kissed you!" Ez yelped. "And you call that 'nothing much'? Dammit, Kitt, you haven't even been able to let a man touch your arm, never mind hold hands or kiss you, for five years. And now you say it was 'nothing much'?"

Kitt was sitting on the sofa, her knees pulled up and her arms wrapped around them, and now she rested her chin on one knee and smiled faintly at Ez.

"Well . . . I suppose if you look at it from that viewpoint, it was something of a breakthrough. Understand, though, it was all I could do not to pull away from him and run like hell. And the kiss was so quick, I didn't have time to react. He did it deliberately—I know he did. It's scary how much that man knows without anybody telling him anything." She paused and cocked an eyebrow at Ez. "Unless you said something to him?"

"No. I wouldn't. Not without talking to you first." He paused to give her a searching look and then continued, "He did ask me what had happened to you. Said you were obviously an overwound watch."

"Terrific. What did you tell him?"

"Just that you'd been through a bad patch some time ago and were still getting it together." Ez possessed a deep understanding and compassion that few people other than Kitt ever saw. His face reflected that perception now as he asked softly, "Do you want me to tell him what happened?"

"Hmmm . . . no . . . I don't think so. I don't know. Ez, I don't really know what to do or to think about it. It's all so out-of-the-blue—I never expected anything like this to happen."

"For what it's worth, I think any explaining should come from you. Oh, maybe not right now. It's got to be when you're ready to talk to him about it. But, Kitt, that's going to be the real breakthrough—when you can care about a man again, care enough and trust him enough to tell him about Leon and all that happened and ask him to help you."

"O'Mara. That's the man you think I can ask?"

"From what I remember of the way it was with you two that last summer, and from what I sensed tonight, I'd say he's probably the only one you'd ever be able to ask. You were both falling in love back then, and if you'd had a little more time, I think you both would have changed your plans and spent these years together."

"I've thought of that sometimes over the years," Kitt said pensively. "But, old saying, it was the wrong time and the wrong place."

"And now it's a different time and a different place, and it looks to me as though you're both picking it all up from where you left off." Ez smiled when Kitt shook her head in denial. "Oh, yes, Sis. What I could feel zinging back and forth between you two tonight wasn't anything like the *beginning* of love; it was a continuation of what you'd had."

"He said he'd found me again."

Ez stood up and stretched and then reached for Kitt's hands to pull her up. "Oh, he has, he has. But, then, you've found him again, too, and that may be the start of a full, complete cure. C'mon, you're out on your feet. It's been an emotional day for you, and right now you need sleep more than anything else."

Much to her surprise, Kitt did sleep, almost from the moment her head touched the pillow. It was a sound, healing sleep, and she awoke a little after seven feeling considerably calmer than she had when she'd watched O'Mara drive away the night before.

She stood and stretched, suddenly feeling energy surging through her body, and pushed open the shutters to see a beautiful, bright April morning waiting for her. Scooping Hero off the foot of the queen-sized bed, she bounded out the door and into Ez's room. He was still sound asleep, sprawled on his stomach diagonally across another big bed. She dropped the dog beside him and ordered, "Hero, wake Ez."

A banshee howl filled the room and echoed from the walls. Ez went straight up in the air and came to rest on his knees in the middle of the bed. Wearing only pajama bottoms, he looked formidable with the broad bare expanse of chest and shoulders rippling with muscles as he lunged across the bed, growling and reaching for Kitt. Still laughing, she leaped back and whirled out of the room.

"Hurry up and get dressed. It's a great morning and we've got time to take Hero for a run before breakfast," she called back.

It was a busy Saturday, and Kitt moved through the day filled with a sense of vital well-being. She rode with it, not trying to analyze the feeling of expectancy that kept bubbling through her. When Midge came in, they exchanged conspiratorial grins and needed no words to understand each other's mood. As it turned out, there was little time for talking anyway. It was a lovely, warm April Saturday, and the town was full of day-trippers and weekenders, at least half of whom seemed to find their way to the bookshop.

Ez strolled in a few minutes after five and lifted an inquiring eyebrow at the dozen or so customers still milling about the shop.

He leaned over the cash register where Midge was making change and said, in a whisper loud enough to rattle the windows, "I thought you were closing at five."

Kitt's laugh rang out from across the shop, and she called to the embarrassed Midge, "Ignore him, Midge. He's been out in the fresh air all day and is probably starving. Why don't you two run along? I know you've got reservations for dinner." She had gradually edged through the customers to the desk, and now, with her back to them, she scowled ferociously at Ez. Still in a carrying voice, she said, "I'm in no hurry to close up. It'll be another half hour or so before I'm through sorting out the art books."

Ez grinned unrepentantly. "Just trying to be helpful. Sure you don't mind if Midge leaves? We've got just time enough to change and make it to Ogunquit."

"Don't you want to change your mind and come with us, Kitt?" Midge asked. "You're going to be alone all evening— you did say O'Mara wasn't going to come by tonight, didn't you?"

"So he said, but we've got a dawn date tomorrow, and I'll be going to bed early. I'm fine. And you two don't really need a chaperone, do you?" Kitt teased.

"Hardly," Ez drawled. "Now that would really cramp my style." With one large hand encompassing her shoulder, he turned Midge around and propelled her ahead of him toward the door. "I'll run you home and then come back to change."

Kitt's evening was quiet. She'd let the late customers take their time, and it was almost six before she locked up and went upstairs to fix a light supper. After a short walk with Hero, she stretched out on the sofa to watch a spy movie on TV. She was so involved in the intricate plot that she didn't hear the phone until it rang for the second time.

Her hello was a bit breathless.

"Is that gasping expectancy, or did you run from somewhere?" Even softened, O'Mara's deep voice vibrated over the phone line.

"Hate to disappoint you, but it's neither." Kitt chuckled. "You startled me, and when I jumped for the phone, I fell over a hassock. Are you just getting in? How was the fishing? Did Gus catch anything?"

"Yes. Great. Yes. And I also caught a few, nice of you to ask. Have I lost you to my son even before I had a chance to get a firm grip?"

"Possible, possible. He's a charmer. Can't imagine where he gets it, unless it's from the same source as those very blue and sexy eyes."

"Are you flirting with me, Miss Tate?"

"Ummm, maybe."

"Feel safe at the other end of a phone line, do you?" His voice dropped to a suggestive murmur. "Try it in the morning when you're an arm's reach away."

"O'Mara. . . ."

"Is that a tinge of panic? No need. It'll all come in its own good time. What are you doing?"

"Watching a spy movie, except I've just missed the ending. Ez took Midge out to dinner and whatever. I decided they could manage without a third party. I'm going to bed in a few minutes, since you're hauling me out at that ungodly hour in the morning."

"I'd love to suggest a more convenient arrangement, but . . . maybe next time." O'Mara's soft chuckle set up vibrations in the pit of her stomach. "Are you blushing, my Kitt?"

Drat the man! Her face was flushed, and she groped for words.

Amusement threaded his voice as he asked, "Speechless, love? We'll have to discuss this odd habit you're developing of blushing and stammering when you talk with me. You didn't used to do it."

"I'm not . . . you . . . you're impossible, O'Mara. And I'm going to bed. See you in the morning."

"Good night, love. Dream nice dreams—preferably about me." And with that provocative comment, the connection clicked off, leaving Kitt, with a bemused expression on her face, staring at the buzzing receiver.

Moving in something of a fog, she turned off the TV, wrote a note asking Ez to take Hero out and got ready for bed. She set the alarm and, after turning out her light, opened the shutters to let the moonlight fill the room. Tall and slim in her tailored pajamas, she stood by the window for a few minutes enjoying the silver night before sliding into bed. She stretched out full length on her back, ankles crossed and hands clasped behind her head. She closed her eyes but could still see a faint glow of the bright moonlight through her lids.

Dream of me. The deep purr echoed in her mind. She could picture his face, the lazy smile, the warm blue glow of his eyes only inches from her own. Her breath caught as the hazy picture became actual memory, and she let it all flow back, realizing just what scene her mind had brought up from her subconscious. It was the last part of their last evening together so many years ago.

They'd gone with Ez and his date to the end-of-summer dance at the hotel. It had been an evening of magic and moonlight, the kind of evening that every girl dreams of having at least once in her life and that she remembers nostalgically for years afterward.

It was a formal dance, and her gown was a whorling blue-green swath of supple jersey, with a halter top that left her shoulders and back bare. She delighted in the silky, sensual feel of the long skirt swirling about her legs as she and O'Mara moved in perfect harmony around and around the ballroom in an endless waltz. Her high heels made it easy for him to rest his cheek against hers, and she could feel the warmth of his breath on her bare shoulder. Warmth, the slow golden warmth of honey spreading over her nerve ends, glowing into heat where he touched her—her bare back where his hand slowly stroked the smooth skin; her thighs as they brushed against his in the movement of the dance; the side of her breast pressed against his hand clasping hers between them. They didn't talk. They lost themselves in their senses, aware only of each other in a world that turned and glided in rhythm with faintly heard music.

She was so lost in a dream that she never knew the moment when he slowly whirled her through the open French doors and down the wide veranda overlooking the beach. Gradually, she realized that the distant music was only a thread of melody over the sound of the sea, and that he had both arms around her holding her close to the lean, hard length of his body. She blinked her eyes open, momentarily dazzled by the silver blaze of moonlight, and turned her head to meet his dark, intense gaze. Caught in the gleaming indigo net, she was vaguely aware that at some point she had wound her arms around his neck and that they were no longer dancing but standing still against the veranda railing.

His mouth touched hers, gently at first, and then as her arms tightened and her eyes closed, he deepened the kiss, the pressure of his mouth opening hers for his exploring tongue. There was no thought; it was all sensation and response. She could feel his muscles tensing and swelling as his hands pressed firmly down over her hips, the strong fingers curving and gripping as he pulled her tightly against the warm hardness of his body. The growing urgency of his tongue sent a white glow of heat surging up from deep within her to jolt the breath from her lungs. Her hands clenched desperately in his hair as she felt weakness spreading down her legs and heard a roaring in her ears.

Slowly, awareness returned. She was still in his arms, but held more gently now, and his hands were soothingly stroking her back. Her face was against the curve of his neck, his head resting on hers. She felt his lips brushing her ear as he whispered, "Shhh, my Kitt. It's all right, now. I didn't mean to let things get so out of hand."

Her voice was a mere breath, and he felt her words more than he heard them as she asked, "What happened to me?"

"You blacked out for a few seconds." There was a thread of laughter in his voice when he added, "I always knew there was a strong potential for passion between us, but I never imagined it would knock you out if we let go a bit. Next time I kiss you like that, I'll make sure we're lying down."

"Are you going to kiss me like that again?" Anticipation strengthened her voice, and she lifted her head to look at him.

"Do you want me to?" he teased.

"Yes!" She laughed joyously. "What I'd really like to know is why you didn't do it before. You've kissed me a dozen times this summer, but never like that." Her voice was gently scolding, but the smoky eyes were glowing with desire.

His arms closed around her, one hand sliding into her hair, and he held her tightly for a long minute, his head lowered to press his warm mouth against her neck. The brush of the balmy night breeze felt cool on her overheated skin when he stepped back, holding her away from him with his hands on her shoulders.

"You weren't ready before. I'm not at all sure you are now." For a moment, his face was somber, and then his expression lightened as he smiled and said, "Come on, let's walk home along the beach."

Kitt abruptly opened her eyes and sat up, pulling her knees up to wrap her arms around them. The room was bright with moonglow. She turned her head to stare out the window, not really seeing the lacy silhouettes of her plants. It's all as clear as if it happened yesterday, she mused. How can I possibly remember so much detail after so long? She smiled to herself as she recalled the oh-so-interested looks that the women had given him as she and O'Mara had strolled into the ballroom.

Lord, he'd been handsome that night—I couldn't blame them for staring, although some of them were old enough to be my mother! Only someone as tall, broad-shouldered and totally male could have gotten away with the lace and ruffles of that lemon-yellow shirt. But it had looked great with the deep blue dinner jacket. We must have been moon-mad that night, walking two miles home along the beach and leaving his car sitting in the hotel lot! Good thing Ez had known how to hotwire it so he could get his date home.

Falling back on the bed, she rolled over onto her stomach and wrapped her arms around the pillow. She closed her eyes, and the fuzzy picture that had been trying to coalesce sharpened and became dimensional.

The hotel, the people, the music were far behind, out of sight and hearing. They walked on the hard-packed sand near the water, the wide, empty beach stretching out ahead of them to darkness. The nearly full moon hovering over the ocean cast a rippling silver path that seemed to move with them. The sea was calm, the half-tide waves small. Their shushing and the crunch of O'Mara's shoes on the sand were the only sounds. Caught up in the magic of a once-in-a-lifetime night, they walked as if in a dream, linked by their tightly clasped hands, occasionally turning from the silvered sea to look at each other.

Kitt was barefoot, her shoes and his tie tucked in the pockets of the jacket slung over his shoulder. He'd undone the top buttons of the ruffled shirt and rolled the sleeves up to his elbows, and the dense fur on his arms looked frosted in the shimmering light. They didn't speak at all during the long walk. They didn't need to—they were absorbing each other through their senses. The warmth of his hand spread from hers through her entire body. Whenever she met the intent look in his eyes, she could feel a fevered yearning welling up from the core of her being.

His face was all sharp planes in the cool light, the skin taut over the prominent bones and tightened muscles. His dark hair was ruffled by the same soft breeze that pressed her long skirt against her legs, emphasizing their long, slim length. Every few minutes, a frisson tingled over her skin as all the fine hairs rose on her arms and legs and across the base of her spine. Because of the low back and deep vee of the halter top of her dress, she wasn't wearing a bra, and due to the warm evening, she hadn't worn stockings. Now, she was sensuously aware of the silky brushing of the soft material against her body, naked under the dress except for nylon bikini briefs.

She looked at O'Mara, wondering if he knew how little she was wearing, and realized that he must after the way his hands had moved over her. In that silent communication they shared, she knew that he was aware of what she was feeling. Keeping his eyes on hers, he slowed his steps, and then, gently pulling her after him, moved at an angle across the deeper sand toward the dunes rising behind the beach. She gazed around dreamily, and one part of her mind registered that they were just short of the last bend in the beach before coming into sight of her cottage. She stopped when O'Mara paused at one of the paths leading up into the dunes.

She lifted her face, thinking he was going to kiss her, and the dark blaze of his eyes burned into her, stopping her breath and rocking her on her feet. She wavered, trying to catch her balance, her lips parted to draw air into her empty lungs, and her eyes widened with instinctive awareness as her senses responded to a flaring sexual need that her mind did not yet understand. He tightened his grip on her hand to support her while she regained her equilibrium, and bent his head to brush a light kiss across her mouth. When he lifted his head, his face had relaxed into a smile.

"I want to kiss you goodnight," he said huskily, "but not on your porch and not in the middle of the beach."

"Yes," she whispered.

"Will you come up here for a few minutes? I know a sheltered place where we can still see the ocean."

"Yes."

They climbed the path, slipping a bit in the soft sand, and at the top he led her to the right until they reached a small hollow between two dunes. The side toward the beach was worn away, and when they sat down, they could see that the glistening path of moonlight was still beckoning them across the water. They sat quietly, side by side, not quite touching. After a few minutes, catching movement out of the corner of her eye, she turned her head and watched in dazed curiosity as he emptied sand from his shoes, then stuffed his socks into them. Picking up his jacket, he pulled her shoes out of the pockets and tossed them over beside his. He twisted around toward her and reached back to spread the jacket on the sand behind her.

She waited, barely breathing, watching the play of muscles under his shirt as he moved. Her eyes lingered on the darkness of the thick furring of hair on his forearms and in the opening of his shirt. On the beach, she'd often teased him about how furry he was and had run her palm over the dense mat of soft curls on his chest. Now, she wondered what they would feel like against her bare skin, and suddenly raised her eyes to meet his and knew he was reading her mind. His mouth quirked in a half-smile, and he leaned toward her, braced on one arm, his other hand sliding slowly around her waist and across her bare back, pulling her into his kiss.

Her mind turned off; her head was full of swirling mist; there was nothing left of the familiar world but sensation. The smell of salt and the faint residue of his aftershave lotion. The hardness of his arm under her head, the pressure of his fingers gripping her shoulder, the softness of his jacket against her back. His mouth was tender on hers, the warm, moist tip of his tongue brushing back and forth on the sensitive inner flesh of her lower lip. She wanted him closer and tightened her arm around his back, burying the fingers of her other hand in the soft thickness of his hair.

His lips firmed and moved demandingly on hers to open her mouth wider for the passionate thrusting of his tongue. She fought for breath as the weight of his torso pressed her against the sand, but pulled him closer still with all her strength. Then his hand was tugging on her arm, pulling it down from his shoulder, and he lifted away from her until his chest was barely touching her. His mouth slowly eased its pressure, and he whispered against her lips, "Unbutton my shirt, love. I want to feel your hands on me and your skin against mine."

Her hand trembled as she slid it between them, and her fingers fumbled with the buttons. "Don't be scared, my Kitt, I just want to love you a little," he whispered, tracing the line of her jaw with his mouth. "I'm not going to do anything you're not ready for." She felt his hand moving at her nape and then the pads of his fingers trailing lightly across her collarbone and down between her breasts. The soft material of her halter tickled her taut nipples as he slid it down to her waist.

When his large, warm hand closed gently over her breast, she moaned his name and restlessly turned her head back and forth, pressing it hard against the sand as she instinctively arched her back, offering her breast to his descending mouth. Her hands stroked the hard ridges of muscles and ribs and then gripped convulsively as his gently tugging lips drew waves of spiraling heat from deep within her body. Twisting and turning, trying to press her full length against him, she was lost in the driving needs of instinctive sexual reaction, responding reflexively to the passionate arousal of his hands and mouth. From a dim distance, she could hear a moaning litany of "Please, please, O'Mara, please," and then his mouth was on hers, opening it wide with bruising force, and his full weight came down on top of her.

Kitt snapped to awareness at the sound of footsteps coming down the hall and Ez's low voice talking to Hero. Drawing a deep, painful breath, she realized that all her muscles were knotted with tension and that she had been holding her breath in the excitement of achingly vivid memories. Forcing herself to breathe slowly and steadily, she consciously relaxed her tight muscles. There was a soft click of Ez's door closing, followed by muted sounds as he moved around getting ready for bed. She heard Hero pushing open her door and then felt a slight jar as he jumped onto the bed and thumped down by her leg.

Closing her eyes, she concentrated on blackness, refusing to let any more memories surface, and in a few minutes Nature took over and dropped her into a deep sleep. It wasn't until the predawn hour, when her internal clock was starting to bring her out of sound sleep, that the dreams began. At first, they were the nice dreams that O'Mara had wished her—scenes from the long-ago summers and, finally, as she tossed restlessly and kicked off the covers, the continuation of her earlier memories of that last night. She twisted in the lighter sleep and one arm lifted and reached out as she pictured O'Mara suddenly rolling away from her and sitting up, head down on his arms resting against his upraised knees, his back heaving with deep, rasping breaths as he fought for control. She lay stunned for a moment and then pushed up on one elbow, oblivious to her half-naked state, and reached to

put her hand on his back. He spun around, fist raised and
swinging at her face, and she screamed as she realized it was
Leon's face, contorted with rage, that was behind the moving
arm. She rolled frantically to avoid the blow and came awake
as she landed in a sprawl on the floor.

Pushing herself to her knees, shaken with deep, dry sobs,
she didn't hear Ez's call or the thud of his running feet. Her
numbed mind was just beginning to register her surroundings
as he dropped to his knees beside her and his big hands closed
gently on her shoulders.

"Kitt, are you all right? What was it, another dream? You
screamed. It's been a long time since you've done that."

"I'm . . . I'm okay," she gulped, trying to get control.
"Let me stand up. I'll be all right in a minute."

He stood, pulling her up, and reached for the robe draped
over the foot of the bed. "Here, put this on; you don't need a
cold along with everything else."

"You're a fine one to talk." She laughed shakily. "I'll bet
you don't even know where the top to those PJs is. You're
coming out in goose bumps."

"Never mind me. Are you sure you're okay?"

"Now that I'm awake, I'm fine." She pushed her tangled
hair back. "Look, why don't you go back to bed. I was going
to get up in another half-hour anyhow. O'Mara's picking me
up at five-thirty. Now that I'm more or less awake, I'll have a
cup of coffee and then get dressed."

"Oh, well, I'm awake now, too, at least temporarily. I'll
have coffee with you and then sleep a few more hours." He
pushed her toward the door. "You go get the coffee ready
while I put on a sweater. It really is freezing in here. I'll turn
on the heater in the bathroom," he called after her. "It
should be warm by the time you finish your coffee."

Chapter 7

An hour later, in the gray light of dawn, the scrunch of tires on gravel sent Kitt dashing for the door, Hero bounding at her heels. They reached the foot of the stairs in time to see O'Mara extricating himself from an elegant, cream-colored sports car, whose classic lines were in sharp contrast to his very casual attire.

Kitt stopped a few feet from him, and they both started laughing as they eyed each other's worn running shoes, faded jeans and black and gray alpaca sweaters—his sweater was gray with a black design, worn over a black cotton-knit turtleneck, while hers was gray on black over a white turtleneck.

"Great minds?" Kitt asked.

"ESP. We've always had it. This just proves it's still working." He grinned, walking around to open her door and tilt the seat forward. "Into the back, Hero. Come on, let's go or we'll miss sunrise."

She tucked herself into the low bucket seat, glancing around the luxurious interior of black leather and walnut while he walked around and slid behind the wheel. Eyeing the complexities of the instrument panel, she asked, "Whatever is this piece of extravagance called? And what happened to the jeep?"

Tossing her a quick grin as he pulled out of the lot, he scolded, "Woman, speak with respect. This is a Mercedes 450SL. The hardtop comes off in another week or so, and it's a convertible for the summer." He gave her a sly look from the corner of his eye and added, "You'll love it."

Ignoring the provocation, she shook her head and sighed mournfully, "It's a shame how success changes people. I remember when you were a man of simple tastes, who appreciated sunrises and watching sandpipers scurry along the beach, and were perfectly happy with your charming old Chevy."

O'Mara tried to say something, choked on his laughter and finally managed to gasp, "You've got a wicked tongue, to say nothing of a faulty memory. That charming Chevy was falling apart. You should know—you helped push it often enough. And I still like sunrises. I'm taking you to one, aren't I?" Serious now, he glanced at her and said consideringly, "As for my tastes, they couldn't have been all that simple. I chose you, didn't I, and there was never anything simple about you, my girl. Innocent, yes, but never simple."

Her head jerked around, and she stared at him disbelievingly. "What . . . what do you mean you 'chose' me? We were friends . . . the three of us were friends . . . and whatever happened between you and me just sort of happened."

"Kitt, Kitt, you make an elegant ostrich. But if you feel more comfortable believing that's the way it was, go on believing it. For a while. But we've already lost too many years. I'm not going to let you slip through my fingers again."

"O'Mara. . . ." Kitt took a deep breath. She was half-turned in the seat, watching his face, trying to decipher his expression. "I don't understand . . . All right, there was something between us, maybe . . . love, or the beginning of it . . . I was never sure. You were the first man who'd ever touched me or really kissed me. Afterward, in those first months at college, I used to think about us a lot and try to figure out whether what I felt was just a crush or . . . the real thing. If I could have seen you again, or even if you had called me . . . but there were just those few chatty letters about your new job and not a word about us, and then nothing."

He was frowning, his lips pressed together in a thin line, by the time she finished speaking. She couldn't see his eyes to read his expression, but she did notice that his knuckles whitened as his tanned hands clenched over the steering wheel. Not sure that this was the right time to discuss the past, she was still impelled by the memory of those sleepless nights and the hurt she had felt when he had apparently dropped her without a word of explanation. And it *had* hurt. Oh, how it had hurt.

She shifted her gaze down to where her hands were tightly gripping each other in her lap, and waited with trepidation for him to break the fraught silence. Perhaps she had angered him by implying that he had been unkind or thoughtless. It had all been so long ago that it would be stupid to pick a fight now over an adolescent disappointment. No, dammit, more than just a disappointment.

She flicked a quick look at him. He was concentrating on the road, but a muscle was twitching in his cheek, and his mouth was still tight. She shifted around and stared unseeingly out the window. After her vivid recollections of the night before, the details of the ending to that last summer were fresh in her mind. Thinking about it now, with the hindsight of experience, she knew she couldn't have been wrong—he had been as emotionally involved and as aroused as she had been. He had taken them to the edge, and she had been willing . . . no, more than willing . . . eager, flamingly eager, to fall over that edge with him.

Resting her elbow on the top of the door, she pressed her fist against her mouth and closed her eyes, feeling again his weight on her, the soft brushing of fur against her bare breasts, her heated response to his coaxing tongue and, most of all, the hot, aching need that had thrust her hips against his hardness. She had been so lost in her first experience of passion and in her feelings for O'Mara that she'd been unaware of practical details. She never remembered who'd pushed his shirt off or why her legs were suddenly bare and no longer constrained by her skirt. It was his voice, almost unrecognizable, groaning hoarsely in her ear, "Kitt, my Kitt, we can't," that had brought her to a hazy realization that they were almost naked in each other's arms.

She must have made a sound, and O'Mara's questioning "Kitt?" brought her abruptly back to the present. Cautiously, she turned her head to meet his gaze, not sure how much her face was revealing. Quite a lot, apparently. She bit her lip and looked away from the amused understanding in his eyes. *Damn him, I don't even have private thoughts anymore.* She forced herself to look back at him, only to find that he was again concentrating on the road, but now, his expression was no longer angry or bitter. And since he already knew where her mind had been, and they had more or less already started the discussion. . . .

"What happened?" It came out as a husky whisper.

He glanced at her quickly and then turned back to face front. She was puzzled at what seemed to be an expression almost of self-disgust.

"Oh, the nobility of man," he finally said sardonically. "I

was trying, Lord help us, to be fair to you. At least, that's how I started out. You were so damn young in so many ways, and I'd been fighting my own battles for what seemed like forever—I was determined to 'make it.' I'm not sure if I even knew exactly what that meant to me then. Getting to the point where I didn't have to worry about next month's rent and feeling that I was doing something productive, I guess. But one thing I was sure of, I couldn't afford a wife, and there was no other way I could have taken you to Washington with me. Besides, I didn't think it was fair to you to tie you down with that kind of commitment, then."

She gasped, and his attention was momentarily diverted from the road as he scanned her startled expression. "Oh, yes," he said softly, looking back at the road. "I thought about it. Quite seriously. But . . . it wasn't that I didn't want you with me, Kitt . . . I did . . . but you were just beginning college, and you hadn't had a chance to date anyone but Ez's friends or me. I wanted you to have your college years and a chance to meet other men and make sure that what you felt for me was strong enough and important enough to last a lifetime."

"How were you going to find out if you never saw me or kept in touch?"

"That's the biggest mistake I ever made," he said bleakly. "Do you remember when I wrote you that I wanted to come up to Massachusetts that first Christmas to see you, but I couldn't get time off? I planned to take a few days when you were home for spring break. But then, just after the first of the year, I was approached by . . . a government agency, and offered a different kind of job. They were interested in my abilities and educational background, they said, but most of all they were interested in the fact that I had no family ties or close friends who would become concerned if I disappeared for periods of time."

"O'Mara, were you a—"

"Don't ask," he cut her off. "I still can't talk about it in any specific detail. Let's just leave it that it was a very high-risk occupation, and the money was fantastic. It was also supposed to be for a limited time—no more than four years of active work out of the country. After that, I could stay on in a position near Washington, or they would help me get into something else. At the time, it seemed too good to turn down."

"You're mad. From what you said the other evening, it was dangerous," Kitt wailed.

"Don't get upset *now*." He chuckled. "Oh, I know it wasn't at all sensible, but then, neither was I in those days. It seemed like a heaven-sent opportunity. By the time I was through with the basic commitment, you'd be graduating and we'd have enough money to start a life together without having to budget too tightly." He hit the steering wheel with his fist and groaned, "Talk about blind, one-track minds! Don't think I haven't kicked myself purple more than once over the years."

"You never considered that you might meet someone else?" she asked wistfully, thinking of all they might have had, if only. . . .

"No!" The explosive exclamation scattered her thoughts and brought her attention back to what he was saying. "And, since this seems to be a moment of truth, I'll tell you that Laura wasn't really 'someone else.' She was fun, a good-time girl, someone to laugh and relax with while I was recovering from some . . . injuries. It wasn't serious for either of us— just a casual couple of weeks in the sun. When I left, I had no plans to see her again."

Kitt leaned back in her seat, gazing out the window and becoming aware, for the first time, of the road they were traveling.

"This is Route One," she said, puzzled. "Where are we going?"

"Ogunquit Beach. It's a beautiful beach for walking. Have you been there yet?"

"No, not yet," she said absently. She turned to look at him, her expression becoming more alert and a bit quizzical. "If it wasn't serious, how come you ended up married to her?"

He glanced over at her with a rueful tilt to his mouth. "You might call it an accident." His eyes returned to the road as he continued, "I was back in Washington a few months later on another leave, and a friend invited me to a party. Laura was there, and we sort of picked up where we'd left off. I was only going to be around for a few weeks, and she didn't care for long-term relationships."

He glanced at Kitt again and smiled slightly at the disbelieving look on her face. "I told you, she was a good-time gal. Fun and games and no involvements. She wanted bright lights, parties, lots of laughs . . . and someone to pick up the checks."

"So how did she—and you—end up married and expecting a baby? If she was that much of a playgirl, I should have thought she'd know how to take care of herself."

"One would think so. But evidently she had a bit too much to drink one weekend and forgot to take her pills. She didn't realize it until way too late. At least, I considered it too late. She came raging to me to pay for an abortion, and I refused. It took me some time to convince her that I had a right to an opinion, and even longer to talk her into marrying me. She only agreed because I promised that she'd be free to go after the baby was born."

. Kitt stared at him blankly and then started to laugh. "O'Mara," she gasped, "only you would make that kind of a deal. It's usually the man who wants out and only marries to give a baby a name—and a lot of them don't even do that. Whatever did you plan on doing with a baby and no mother?"

"Just what I did—find a motherly woman as housekeeper and nurse." He took a deep breath and let it out in a gusty sigh. "I know it sounds crazy, but you have to understand— that was *my* baby, and I had no other family. Maybe it had something to do with being orphaned so young, or maybe it's just that we all need at least one person who belongs to us and to whom we belong. You should know what I mean—no matter what happens, you've got Ez and vice versa."

"You're right, and I do understand how you felt. Furthermore, since meeting Gus, I have to say that it was all worth it. He's super."

"You two seem to have a mutual admiration society going. He spent half of yesterday making plans for the summer, and at least eighty-two percent of them included you and Hero." He tossed a quick grin at her as he slowed in the center of Ogunquit Village to make the left turn to the beach parking lot.

"Love me, love my dog," she said, laughing.

"I adore your dog. He's a total eccentric." His lips twitched in an effort to restrain a grin, and he quickly flipped his elbow up to block the punch she aimed at his arm. "Control yourself for a few minutes. If you've got that much energy, I'll let you chase me down the beach. It'll help work up your appetite for breakfast."

He swung the car into the parking lot and stopped at the edge facing the sea. The predawn light was pearling the sky above a dead-calm ocean. Seagulls wheeled and dipped, their raucous cries breaking the expectant hush of the new day.

She sat quietly, letting her gaze drift over the wide expanse of gray water broken here and there by the jutting of black ledges. Off to her right, the sea lapped against huge, tumbled rocks around the base of a headland. Amused, she briefly noted the mixture of architectural styles of the many buildings topping the low cliff. She turned to look past O'Mara at a large, three-story motel which faced the road and parking lot on one side and the wide beach on another.

Stubbornly, determined for once not to let him have it all his own way, she refused to meet his eyes, which she could positively *feel* traveling over her face. In a way, he had explained several things that had troubled her for a long time. Now, despite her understanding of his motivations and the unkind workings of fate that had kept them apart, she still felt somehow cheated. Cheated of the life they could have been sharing all these years, cheated of the joy of knowing that Gus—and perhaps other children—could have been hers, cheated of the ecstasy of learning about love and passion and caring from the man who should have been her teacher. And, inevitably, she resented what seemed like arrogance on his part in deciding the course of their lives without even discussing it with her. Perhaps, if her experience with Leon had left her with just one remotely happy memory . . .

"Kitt, don't, please." There was a note of pain in his low voice, and it finally drew her eyes to him, wondering at his harsh, self-accusatory expression. She could not know how clearly her thoughts had been mirrored in her face.

He reached out to press his hand against her cheek. "It *was* all my fault. I can't believe I could have been so damn stupid. Especially now that I've finally found you again and realize—"

"Don't look like that!" she interrupted urgently, reaching for his free hand and holding it tightly with both of hers. "All right. It was dumb and damn stupid and . . . oh, hell, yes, I'm mad. You had no right to decide such a thing for me. But that was then and this is now, and . . . well, one minute I think it's the same with us, but then I know that we've . . . I've got a major problem, and I don't think it *can* be the same."

He started to speak, and she shook her head violently, a look of despair clouding her eyes. "Oh, why, why, couldn't you have tried to contact me again before it was too late?"

"I did, Kitt. But by the time I got everything sorted out, and Gus settled and me out of my commitments, you and Ez had graduated and I couldn't find you. I tried to contact your parents, and that was the first I knew that they had died." He tightened his fingers around her hand. "I'm sorry about that. I liked them, although I knew they didn't think I was half good enough for their daughter. No family, no money, no established future."

"That wouldn't have mattered to me, you know. Besides, how do you know that they felt that way? They never said anything to me . . . or to Ez. He'd have told me."

"There are some things that don't have to be said." One corner of his mouth tilted. "I know it wouldn't have mattered to you, but I guess, in a way, it did influence some of my thinking. Kitt? I did try, but I didn't know how to reach anyone else in your family."

"It's okay. Well, maybe not entirely, but it's a bit late now to get all upset about it. What's done is done. Oh," she groaned, "how I hate platitudes."

His expression suddenly lightened, and he finally managed a full smile. "I have a strong feeling that you're going to make me pay for my mistakes, and I'm not at all sure it's going to be anything I'll enjoy. You, my love, when you put your mind to it, can be every bit as outrageous as Ez on his best day."

It was useless. Try as she might, she simply could not stay angry with him, and at last she started laughing. "You're right, and I'm going to give it a lot of thought. And you'll get no warning, O'Mara."

"Nasty witch," he growled, still smiling. He glanced around at the sky and exclaimed, "Damn! All this soul-searching will have to wait. We've only got a few minutes left. Let's get down the beach a ways before the sun rises."

They got out of the car, followed by Hero, who immediately charged at a large beige seagull strutting across the pavement. The gull flapped into the air with insulting ease, and Hero quickly turned to race after Kitt and O'Mara as they headed for the steps to the beach.

"Oh, it's beautiful!" Kitt exclaimed as she gazed up the endless sweep of beach and dunes to her left.

"I knew you'd like it," O'Mara said with a laugh. He sobered and looked into her eyes for a timeless minute before saying softly, "It reminds me of another beach we walked one night."

Before she could think of a reply, he caught her hand and, pulling her after him, began running along the hard-packed sand in an easy, ground-eating lope. Within a few strides, she picked up the rhythm, and their long legs moved in unison as she ran easily beside him. Hero raced ahead of them, dashing in and out of the shallow wash from the small waves escaping from the unruffled sea.

After a few minutes, when they were well down the deserted beach, O'Mara veered left into the soft, dry sand and suddenly stopped, giving a hard yank to Kitt's hand. Taken by surprise, she was pulled off-balance and felt his strong hands on her arms, turning her and pulling her down. When she could regain her breath, she found herself sitting in the sand with her back against O'Mara's chest, his arms looped loosely around her and his long legs stretched out, knees slightly bent, on either side of hers.

She leaned forward, shifting her hips in the sand to get away from the pressure of his hard thighs, her hands grasping his wrists to pull his arms from around her.

"Sit still, wiggle-worm." His voice was a deep murmur in her right ear, and she could feel his warm breath on her cheek. His arms exerted just enough pressure to hold her still against his chest. "Watch the sky. It's starting to color up. And for heaven's sake, relax." There was a thread of laughter in his voice as he added, "It's a bit chilly on this beach when you're sitting still, and I need you to keep me warm."

Her eyes on the slowly changing shades of rose and yellow in the eastern sky, Kitt gradually relaxed. With each slow breath she took, her muscles uncramped one by one until she was resting easily back against O'Mara's hard chest with her hands loosely clasped around her upraised knees. He lifted one hand to brush her hair away from his face, tucking the silky strands behind her right ear. His hand stroked her throat, and the long fingers wrapped around the far side of her neck while he rubbed his thumb along her jaw, exerting just enough pressure to turn her face so her cheek rested against his.

She felt his warmth winding around and through her, and she was totally aware of being enclosed by the heat and strength of him. A feeling of surprise welled in her consciousness to become overlaid by a growing wonder. *I'm not afraid. Not of his nearness or his arms around me or his strength. I should be in knots, waiting for the bruising fingers and painful bites. But I'm not.* She closed her eyes and pressed her cheek tightly against his.

"Look, Kitt," he whispered against the corner of her mouth.

She opened her eyes to a sweeping pastel wash of pinks, yellows and pale oranges filling the sky and reflecting in the mirror sheen of the ocean until it was impossible to tell where one began and the other ended. A matching glow seemed to fill her soul with a great sense of peace.

Unmoving, hardly breathing, they watched a thin curve of brilliant red-orange widen to a crescent as the rising sun defined the horizon. The colors in sky and sea deepened and brightened before slowly fading as the blazing ball rose above the ocean and flamed a path of shimmering red almost to their feet.

Kitt took a deep, shuddering breath and realized that her face was wet with tears. Before she could lift her hand, O'Mara shifted her around until her head was resting on his shoulder. Pulling a handkerchief from his hip pocket, he gently wiped away the traces of tears. Their eyes locked, his tender and very blue, hers questioning with the beginning of belief. She watched the blue darken as he bent his head to rest his warm mouth against hers. The gilt-tipped lashes feathered down, and she waited, half-afraid of what he might do next and half-eager to find out if the long-ago magic could be recaptured.

Chapter 8

O'Mara lifted his head a hairsbreadth and whispered, "My Kitt." Then he was turning her into his body, his arms closing around her. His mouth was firm and sweet on hers, asking for response as the tip of his tongue teased her lips to part for him.

She couldn't help it. It was an instinct bred of years of fear and pain. She knew that this was O'Mara, that his arms were tight but not crushing her, that his kiss was loving, not punishing. Her conscious mind knew it all, but the deep-rooted, subconscious instinct for self-protection burst out of her control.

Suddenly, from one breath to another, she was a struggling, twisting, kicking, punching armful of fury. She was a strong, athletic woman, now in a state of nearly total panic, and O'Mara knew he couldn't subdue her without hurting her.

Saying her name over and over in a crooning voice, he let her go, quickly shifting his arms to protect his face from her flying fists, but making no other attempt to restrain her. Hero scrambled up from where he had been sprawled beside them and started snarling at O'Mara, his growls partially drowning out Kitt's breathless cries of "No, no, no."

O'Mara sat still and relaxed, but his voice was commanding when he said, "Quiet, Hero. Sit." He didn't change tone when he turned to Kitt. "That's enough, Kitt. I'm not touching you now, so you can just calm down and get control of yourself."

She was crouched on her knees, hips resting back on her ankles, her hands spread flat on the sand with her head hanging down between her outstretched arms as she panted for breath. The panic slowly subsided, and her breathing became even. And now, how do I explain that, she wondered. Why, oh, why did this have to happen with *him?* She felt half-dazed from the aftermath of the blind, mindless fear, and from the shock of having reacted so violently to O'Mara's gently loving kiss.

It was very quiet. Kitt didn't move for several minutes, and then she opened her eyes and slowly sat back, tossing her hair out of her face. She brushed her hands over her thighs to remove the sand, and then tugged her sweater back into neatness. She could feel O'Mara's eyes on her, and the waiting stillness was so thick she felt she could almost grasp it in her hand. Unnerved by both her violent reaction and the necessity of making some explanation, she kept her eyes down while she tried to get her chaotic thoughts in order.

Finally, unable to dither any longer, she hesitantly raised her eyes to meet his. He was sitting much as he had been, long legs stretched out, his heels braced in the sand on either side of her knees. He was leaning forward with his forearms resting on his knees, sifting handfuls of sand through his fingers. The bright blue eyes were intent on her face, examining, questioning and—her breath drew in sharply as she realized it—still warm and reassuring.

"I . . . I'm sorry," she whispered, her eyes wide and troubled. "Did I hurt you?"

His mouth twitched with a repressed smile as he answered, "No. At least, not permanently. I'll probably have a few bruises for a couple of days. You swing a mean punch, love."

"I didn't . . . It wasn't. . . ." She struggled for words, trying to find some way of explaining away her furious rejection of his tenderness.

She chewed her lower lip, turned her head from side to side and looked blankly up and down the beach. Her restless hands twitched at her sweater, fussed with her hair and, finally, came to rest on her thighs, fingers curling and digging into the muscles until she winced with pain. Frantically, she considered and rejected one explanation after another. She knew he'd never believe most of them—they weren't even explanations; they were weak excuses that didn't have the slightest ring of truth. Truth. Could she tell him the truth? If he felt pity for her, she couldn't bear it. Not from him. But he wasn't going to believe anything else. He knew her too well not to know that it had taken something unbearably horrible to make her react to him like that.

She looked at him and saw the patient receptivity in his face. And she knew, beyond all doubt, that she was going to have to tell him. A heartbeat later, she also knew that he was the only man who would ever be able to help her overcome her fears. He could teach her again, as he had years before, to delight in his touch, to respond with her own warm passion to his hands and mouth, and to know the aching joy of needing him as much as he needed her. All she had to do was to trust him, right now, and to believe in the love she could see in his eyes.

O'Mara had been watching her change of expressions, sensing her confusion and following her groping progress toward decision. He knew her as well as he knew himself. He always had. It was an inexplicable, instinctive awareness that had existed between them from the beginning. He could always sense what she was feeling and, often, what she was thinking. That awareness was one of the reasons he hadn't coaxed her into marriage twelve years before. At eighteen, she wasn't too young to love him, but she was too young and unknowledgeable about life to make the kind of total commitment to him that he needed from her. He had gambled with time, then, and lost. Now, he wasn't about to gamble again, nor was he going to lose her a second time.

He knew the minute she reached her decision to trust him. He could see the easing of tension in her face and body and, looking deep into the smoky blue-gray of her anguished eyes, he could feel her vulnerability and almost hear her plea of *Help me*.

He held his hands out to her, palms up, and said very softly, "I love you. I always have. I know you're hurting badly, even if I don't know why, and I know I can help you if you'll trust me and tell me what it is. Can you take my hands now?"

Keeping her eyes on his, Kitt slowly loosened the tight grip of her fingers and rubbed her hands over her thighs, then lifted them and reached to slide them into his waiting clasp.

He tugged gently on her hands. "Come a little closer, just enough to be comfortable. I won't touch you except to hold your hands. Okay?"

"Okay." Her voice was just above a whisper, but her hands tightened on his. She raised up enough to move her legs and knee-walked a couple of feet forward between his legs before settling back down. Closer, but still not touching except for their tightly clasped hands now resting on her knees, they watched each other expectantly. They knew they were on the verge of something that could eventually reestablish the intended pattern of their lives that had been interrupted so many years before.

"Can you tell me now?" he asked.

"I think so. At least, I'll try. But, oh, damn," she choked, with tears filling her eyes, "you are going to be so upset with me. I was so stupid, and you never did suffer fools, gladly or otherwise." She blinked back the tears and looked at him despairingly. "I'm such an awful mess now, and I've probably ruined any chance for us to . . . to . . ."

"You're just a minor mess," he teased, trying to ease her grief. "And nothing is ruined for us. It's just beginning. Listen to me, love," he said firmly, leaning toward her and tightening his clasp on her hands. "I'm not going to be upset with you. It's perfectly obvious that . . . Look, will it help if I tell you what I've figured out for myself?"

At her relieved nod, he continued, "You've obviously been badly hurt both physically and emotionally, and it had to have been done by a man. I think that most of the emotional damage has been healed, probably with Ez's help. You said the other night that you'd been with him for the past five years. From the way you respond to me, emotionally and mentally, I don't think there's any problem there anymore, is there?" He raised a questioning eyebrow.

"No," Kitt said. "Not now. But it took a long time to put me back together, and I couldn't have done it without Ez. You'd never believe the shape I was in when he finally got there."

He started to say something, then paused and visibly changed the thought. He studied her face closely, and then his eyes lifted to linger on the red and gold lights glittering in her hair from the strengthening sun. After a few moments, he smiled encouragingly and said in a firm voice, "I'll believe you must have been a shambles. You didn't get those strain lines in your face or that look I've seen in your eyes from simple, everyday problems."

She shook her head but didn't say anything. Keeping her eyes locked on his, she waited for him to continue.

"If it's no longer an emotional trauma that we've got to deal with, it must be physical." She nodded, and he swore under his breath, his jaw tensing and his eyes becoming dark with rage. "Dammit, Kitt, are you going to tell me that some . . . did you let . . . no, wait, I know you too well. It had to be someone who got by Ez, and that means you thought he was okay."

She couldn't stand his anguish, couldn't bear to let him grope for the answers. Pulling her hands free, she leaned forward and reached to hold his face between her palms. "Oh, please, please, don't look like that! O'Mara, it's been over for a long time, and I've gotten almost all of it into perspective. I understand how it happened and why and—"

She stopped abruptly and sat back, lifting her hands to push her hair back and then clasping them around her neck. Stretching and arching her head back to relieve the tense muscles, she closed her eyes and didn't move for several minutes. She could *feel* the simmering anger running through him, his need to strike out against whoever had hurt her, and she knew that she was going to have to take her own personal giant step. Somehow, she was going to have to explain the past and, simultaneously, dilute his anger and then give him hope for their future. Because they were going to have a future together. She didn't know how they were going to overcome her terror of physical violence, but she had boundless faith in O'Mara's ability to get what he wanted—and he unquestionably wanted her. Now all she had to do was to explain the problem and dump it into his lap. Well, there's no time like the present, she thought, and it worked a while ago, so maybe it will again.

She suddenly relaxed, opening her eyes and dropping her hands to her thighs. Noting his tenseness and the arms folded tightly across his chest, she managed a wavering smile and asked, "Will you help me?"

His "Of course" was more growled than spoken, but some of the anger faded to be replaced by curiosity.

"Would you . . . please . . ." Her voice cracked, and she almost lost her courage, but finished in a rush, "Will you please hold out your arms to me?"

She held her breath, watching his expression change rapidly from curiosity through disbelief and questioning to hope. Within seconds, he had started to smile, and he unfolded his arms and held them out to her.

"Come here, love," he said softly, knowing what the request had cost her. "We'll take it at your speed. Just tell me what you want me to do, or not to do."

Letting her breath out in a shaky laugh, Kitt scrambled forward, turning and wriggling backward until she was sitting as she had been when they watched the sunrise. Stretching her arms out under his, she threaded her fingers through his and folded their arms loosely around herself.

"Do you think you can hold me just like this? No matter what I tell you?" she asked. "Some of it's going to make you awfully mad, but please try not to tighten your arms around me. If I feel I can't get free, I panic."

"Don't worry about it. Now that you've warned me what to expect, I won't hug you no matter how much I might want to. Okay? Can you relax back against me now? Let me have my right hand for a minute so I can tuck your hair back away from my mouth . . . that's better . . . I love it, but I don't want to eat it for breakfast." He turned his head just enough to touch her cheek gently with his mouth. "Can you tell me now?"

"Yes. At least, I'll try. Not all the ugly details, but enough so you'll understand." She swallowed hard and then, staring unseeingly across the water, began talking in a flat, impersonal voice.

"His name was Leon Darcy, and he was a pro football player—a linebacker. I met him in California a few months after I graduated from college. I was a phys. ed. instructor in a little town just up the coast from Los Angeles. Ez was in England doing graduate work on a fellowship, and he never met Leon until the day before we were married."

"Oh, God," O'Mara whispered, and she felt a tremor go through his body.

"I know," she cried in an anguished voice, turning her head toward him. His eyes were closed and his mouth was tight with pain. She rubbed her forehead against his cheek and whispered, "I'm sorry, I'm sorry. It wasn't that I'd forgotten you or what was between us, but it had been years since I'd heard from you, and I didn't think I'd ever see you again."

"Did you love him?"

"No, but by the time I knew that it was too late. At first, I thought I did. Oh, damn, I told you I was stupid, so stupid." She turned back to stare at the ocean, pressing her cheek against his. "A couple of Ez's college teammates were playing pro ball out there, and they used to take me out once in a while. That's how I met Leon. He was big—even bigger than Ez—and as tall as you. Dark wavy hair and blue eyes. Not as blue as yours and he didn't really look anything like you, but his coloring was similar and he was kind of quiet. Oh, hell, it had been a long time since I'd seen you, and in some ways he reminded me of you, and I was a bit lost without Ez—it was the first time we'd ever really been apart—and I convinced myself I was in love with him.

"He helped matters along, too. He was affectionate, admiring, understanding—at least, he put on a super act. I found out long afterward that he had made the big play for me because he thought that other men envied him. He had an ego you wouldn't believe, and a mass of seething insecurities that he kept so well hidden nobody, but nobody, even suspected what a psychotic he was.

"Anyway, he romanced me to a faretheewell, and I fell for it all. I don't even remember exactly how we happened to decide to get married, but it was very fast. I did insist on calling Ez and waiting long enough for him to fly over for a few days, but it all happened in a couple of weeks—before I had time to think twice."

"Didn't Ez see any of this?" O'Mara asked. "He's always been very sharp about people."

"He didn't take to Leon, but there wasn't much time for him to figure out why. He arrived the day before the wedding, and I was floating around starry-eyed and not listening to anything anyone was saying to me. I was so happy when Ez got there, I guess he didn't want to bring me down on the basis of a vague uneasiness. He's suffered agonies of remorse since then for not following his hunch."

"So, what . . ." O'Mara's voice was a croak, and he cleared his throat before asking, "What happened?"

"It's so hard for me to say it all out loud. While it was happening, I didn't understand why—that came later. He. . . ," She paused for several moments, trying to find the right words. "Do you remember that night we came so close to making love? I never went beyond a few kisses with anyone else—I never wanted to. Even with Leon, while we were going together, it never went beyond kissing. He seemed to hold back, and I wasn't sure enough of myself to encourage

him. Oh, damn, to be honest, I wasn't excited enough I guess.
It wasn't anything like it was with you, but I decided—in all
my stupidity—that what we'd had was a fluke, a one-time
phenomenon. I figured that it wasn't usually like that, and
that Leon and I would manage just fine."

"Dumb." O'Mara kissed her ear and blew into it gently. "I
wish to hell I hadn't stopped that night."

"So do I. You'll never know how many times I've wished
it." Her voice started to break and her lips were quivering as
she choked out, "You should have been the first. Oh, God,
how I wish you had been. You wouldn't have hurt
me . . . and you'd have . . . made sure I liked it . . . and
. . . and you'd have loved me."

Her eyes were squeezed shut, trying to hold in the tears,
and it was a moment before she felt the tight grip of his hands
on hers and the flexing of muscles in his arms as he struggled
not to clamp them around her. He bent his head to press his
face against her neck, and she could barely hear his muffled
words.

"Kitt . . . my lovely Kitt . . . how could anyone hurt you?
What did that—" He choked off a gutter term that she barely
understood.

She pulled her knees up further and wrapped her arms, and
his, tighter around her body. The silent tears ran down her
face, and her voice was barely audible as the disjointed
phrases tumbled out.

"He raped me . . . horrible . . . tore my nightgown off
and . . . he just . . . attacked me . . . I tried to fight him
off . . . hit me . . . always like that. Except he didn't try
to . . . very often . . . sometimes it was weeks and weeks
. . . kept hoping he'd forget . . . he always said he was sorry
days afterward . . . didn't know what to do . . . Ez so far
away . . . afraid if I called . . . Ez would kill him . . . I
didn't think anyone would believe me . . . so normal and
charming all the time to everyone . . . except when he . . .
begged him not to but he . . . so strong and I couldn't stop
him . . . couldn't hide the bruises . . . he was so mad when I
had to go . . . doctor saw . . . hit me with his fist . . .
couldn't get away from him . . . knew my ribs were cracked
. . . it hurt so . . . the doctor asked so many questions . . .
didn't believe I fell . . . teethmarks . . . I couldn't hide them
when he taped my ribs . . . told me . . . counseling clinic and

I ran and ran and . . . and they helped me get away . . . and then. . . ."

She was panting for breath; her head was tilted to lean her cheek against the thick cushion of his hair. At first, she thought the wetness on her neck was from her tears. Then she felt the uneven motion of his chest against her back and heard the rasping of his breath.

She felt his agony and knew that it was feeding from her to him and back. They were sharing their pain as they had shared elation and joy and passion. And slowly it eased. Something hard and hurting deep inside of her seemed to dissolve and dissipate like smoke. At the same time, she felt the tension draining from O'Mara's body.

They sat very still, eyes closed, totally concentrated on each other. It was as if there were a channel connecting them, so real that she wanted to lift her hand to touch it. Love, caring, understanding—it all flowed from him and filled her being, spreading in a slow, glowing warmth along all her nerves, muscles and veins, seeping deep into the marrow of her bones. It filled her like an ever-rising tide, and as it overflowed she channeled it back to him, subtly changing its texture with the female aura of her own love and tenderness.

For those timeless minutes, they were in another dimension of existence. They had gone beyond physical need and awareness into a unique communion of mind, emotion and soul—the mutual surrender to each other of their individual identities, a total melding of self with self, and then a return to individuality. But now something of each one had become part of the other, and neither of them would ever really be alone again.

It was a rare and stunning experience, an act of total giving and receiving that few people achieve. Kitt and O'Mara were in a semiconscious state, unaware of where they were or why, utterly overwhelmed by the strength and wonder of the commitment they had just made to each other. It was long minutes before the sound of children yelling and laughing penetrated their dazed minds and brought them back to earth.

O'Mara lifted his head, and Kitt half-turned to look at him, seeing the wonder that she felt reflected in his face. They moved toward each other at the same moment. It was an undemanding kiss, very gentle, their lips soft yet clinging to each other's in a tender, loving affirmation of the incredible experience they had just shared.

Drawing back a few inches, Kitt smiled into his eyes and said softly, "In the immortal words of somebody or other, 'Oh, wow.'"

" 'Out of this world' might be more appropriate," he said, laughing. In a quick change, he became very serious and cradled her face in his hands. "That was the most beautiful experience I've ever had. It could only have happened with you, my Kitt." His voice grew husky as he went on, "Someday soon, we're going to share our bodies and passion and ecstasy, and it's going to be absolutely incredible for both of us. But nothing, not even making love with you, could be as unbelievably beautiful as what we just shared."

She tried to speak, but the words were locked in her throat by such a strong welling of emotion that it brought tears to her eyes. O'Mara smiled and rocked her head gently between his hands. "Idiot. Don't cry anymore. Come on, it's breakfast time. Let's get some food into you—and me—all this intense emotion is making me hungry."

"Men! Is there anything that doesn't make you hungry!?" Her laugh was a bit ragged, but at least it was a laugh.

Standing up, they brushed the sand off their jeans and turned to walk back along the beach toward the parking lot. There were more early morning strollers and joggers now, some with dogs, and Hero stayed close beside Kitt. Very naturally and without saying a word, Kitt reached over and slid her hand into O'Mara's. He looked at her with a glint of satisfaction in his eyes, said, "Breakthrough!" and started laughing. Her joyous laughter pealed out to join with his, and it was suddenly the most glorious day that either of them had known in twelve years.

Chapter 9

Over breakfast, they discussed O'Mara's books, and he told her about the new one he was researching. By unspoken agreement, they avoided any mention of what had happened between them on the beach. It was too soon to put it into words, to try to analyze and dissect a nearly inexplicable experience. Kitt felt bewildered; in fact, totally disoriented. It was as if she had been picked up off of solid ground, shaken hard, spun around and then set down on shifting sand. She knew that her carefully planned life had just been blasted apart, but she still wasn't sure what O'Mara had in mind as a replacement.

Looking at him across the table, watching his changing expressions as he talked about his work, she had a feeling of inevitability. It was as certain as her next breath that he loved her and that she loved him. It had taken less than three days for them to wipe out twelve years. Actually, it had taken less than three minutes from the time she had turned around Friday morning and seen him standing there watching her. But, she thought, let's face it—the twelve years weren't really erased, no matter how much she wished them to be. They had happened, Leon had happened, and now she could not have a natural relationship with the man she loved.

Something of what she was thinking must have shown on her face. O'Mara broke off in the middle of a sentence and peered at her intently. He reached across the table and loosened one of her hands from its tight hold on her coffee cup. He held her fingers in a loose clasp, rubbing his thumb lightly over the delicate bones in the back of her hand.

"You're tightening up again, love." His voice was a soothing murmur. "Will you stop worrying about it? Oh, yes, I know what you're doing—going round and round fretting about this trauma of yours. I wish you'd concentrate on trusting me. Will it help if I tell you that I've got an idea of how we can overcome your little problem?"

"Little problem!" she cried, and then a flush tinged her cheeks pink as she realized that everyone nearby had heard her. She glanced around self-consciously and found several people gazing interestedly at them.

O'Mara's eyes gleamed with suppressed laughter as he teased, "You always did get overexcited about minor setbacks. Why, I remember once when—"

"Stop it, you beast," Kitt muttered. "It's not funny. How can you talk about 'little problems' and 'minor setbacks' when I can't even let you hold me without going to pieces—never mind being able to . . . do anything else?" She looked at him pleadingly. "Have you really figured a way to . . . what . . . cure me . . . make me a whole woman again?"

"I'm not positive, mind you," he said, now very serious. "But, yes, I do have an idea." He shook his head when she started to speak. "No, I don't want to tell you yet. Let me think about it a bit longer, and then I want to discuss it with a friend of mine."

"No!" Distress was plain in her voice and her face. "Please . . . I don't want—"

She broke off as the waitress appeared beside the table, offering them more coffee from the steaming pot in her hand. Tightening his fingers around Kitt's to prevent her instinctive withdrawal, he said a quiet "Yes, please" to the waitress, and then waited for her to move away before speaking calmly to Kitt.

"It's all right, love. My friend is a psychotherapist, and he's an expert in the battered wife syndrome. In fact, Kenton Thorp has developed several of the therapy programs which are widely used in helping women in situations similar to yours."

He looked at her searchingly. "You do realize, don't you, that you're by no means the first woman who's been brutalized by her husband? There are thousands of wives in the same ugly predicament."

"I know," said Kitt, her smoky eyes showing traces of remembered pain. "The doctor who treated me sent me to a clinic that specialized in helping women who had been—" She stopped abruptly, her hand gripping his convulsively. Meeting his steady gaze and drawing strength from the encouragement she read there, she continued, "Once I understood that

I wasn't alone in having a . . . brutal husband, and that there were legal steps I could take. . . . Oh, Lord, you don't know what a relief it was just to find people who not only believed me, but who could help me, too."

O'Mara's mouth thinned to a grim line, and his eyes sparked with anger. "What about Ez's friends?" he growled. "Surely they'd have helped you."

"They'd have beaten him bloody," Kitt said bleakly, "and then they'd have called Ez—and he'd have killed him. I mean it literally, O'Mara, and you know it. Ez would have killed him with his bare hands. You've never seen him in a rage. I have. Once. And I hope I never do again. You know Ez—easygoing and loves the world—a big, happy bear. It's almost impossible to get him mad, but when it happens, he goes utterly berserk."

"I believe it. When did you ever see him in a rage?"

"Years ago. We were home on vacation from college and went into Boston one evening to see a new movie. Afterward, we were walking back beside the Common to the parking garage when we heard a girl scream. You know how dark parts of the Common are with trees and shrubbery, and how many weird characters roam around in there at night. Well, we couldn't see anything much except some movement, but the scream choked off and then we heard men's voices and a girl crying. Ez went charging toward the sounds, and I chased after him as usual, yelling at some people on the street to call the cops." She shook her head with a rueful grin at O'Mara's exasperated expression. "Don't say it. I know I should have stayed out of it, but it was an automatic reflex."

He grinned back at her. "I'm not surprised. You always did run at Ez's heels, no matter where he went." He reached across the table to tap her on the nose with a long tan finger, and laughed into her bemused eyes. "And mine, come to that."

Tilting her head, Kitt inquired in a mock-sweet voice, "Is that where you want me—at your heels?"

"Witch! You know it isn't. You'll stay beside me—all the time." He paused, and a wicked gleam sparked in the sapphire eyes while his voice dropped to a sensuous murmur as he added, "Except in bed . . . where you will definitely not spend all your time *beside* me."

He shook with silent laughter as Kitt's face flushed dark pink and her eyes widened in a delightful mixture of questioning apprehension and expectant wonder. She caught her lower lip between even white teeth and tried to think of something non-stupid to say. *Good grief, I'm thirty years old, and I'm blushing like a schoolgirl and groping for words as if I'd never heard of sex.*

"My Kitt," O'Mara chuckled, "you are going to be such a delight to teach, and I'm going to enjoy every minute of it." He leaned forward, raising her hand to his mouth, and gently ran his lips and the tip of his tongue across her knuckles. Holding her eyes with the blue flame of his, he said softly, insinuatingly, "You will, too."

Kitt was mesmerized by the blazing sensuality of the promise in his eyes and of his tongue tracing patterns over her fingers. The noise and light of the restaurant faded off somewhere into the background. All of her senses were filled with O'Mara's overwhelming male presence. Dazedly, she let a thought drift to the surface of her mind. *God, how can he make me feel like this just by holding my hand and looking at me? Whoever would believe that his tongue tickling my knuckles could be so sexy? I wish he were—*

She was jolted to awareness by his teeth nipping the end of her thumb. In what seemed like a cacophony of babbling voices and clattering dishes, their surroundings intruded and broke the heated, erotic spell.

"You . . . you great tomcat," Kitt exclaimed in exasperation. "Look at you. If you had whiskers, you'd be twitching them. And stop laughing at me!" she hissed. "You did that on purpose!"

"Of course I did, love," he said soothingly, trying to subdue his mirth. Sitting back in his chair, he released her hand and, with a very satisfied expression, watched her flustered movements as she fiddled with her coffee cup. "Since I can't court you yet, in the usual way, it's necessary to devise alternate methods." One thick black eyebrow lifted inquiringly and the blue eyes widened in mock innocence. "I thought I was rather creative. No?"

"No . . . yes! . . . oh, you . . . you just wait."

"I am waiting," he answered, grinning, "but this is hardly the place for you to retaliate." He pushed back his chair and stood up, holding out his hand to her. "Let's go, love. You can finish telling me about Ez and the muggers on the way back."

There was little traffic on Route One at that hour, and they were pulling into Kitt's parking lot less than thirty minutes later. Hero leaped up the stairs ahead of them and, by the time they were halfway up, they could hear him "talking" to Ez. Stepping onto the deck, they found Ez and Midge seated at a card table, obviously having just finished breakfast.

"Did we return too soon?" asked Kitt, all innocence. "You did say you were going back to bed, brother, although you didn't specify when. Now, let's see, it's just after nine, and you had to get Midge over here, cook breakfast, eat it and, yes, it does look like you've had most of that pot of coffee, so you couldn't have had time—"

She dodged behind O'Mara as Midge and Ez reached for the last two muffins with a purposeful gleam in their eyes.

"Wait a minute!" yelped O'Mara, pulling Kitt around and holding her in front of him. "I wouldn't think of commenting on your domestic arrangements, Ez. If you can find someone to cook your breakfast and entertain you at this hour on a Sunday morning, I'm all admiration. Besides, it would be a crime to waste those muffins. They do look good."

Giggling, Midge put the muffins on a plate and pushed it, together with the butter dish, toward O'Mara. "Here. Pull up a chair and help yourself. Uh, I'll make another pot of coffee; this one seems to be empty."

As Kitt and O'Mara moved toward the table, Ez caught his sister's eye and gave her an intently questioning look while asking, "Did you . . . enjoy the sunrise? Where did you go?"

"Ogunquit Beach, and it was beautiful." She slipped her hand into O'Mara's and smiled happily at Ez. "We also had a long talk, and it's going to be all right eventually. Isn't it?" she asked O'Mara, turning to him for reassurance.

"Oh, yes, love. No question." He didn't have time to say more before Ez sprang to his feet and grabbed his hand in what to a weaker man would have been a bone-crushing grip.

With a rather dreamy look on her face, Kitt stood and watched the two big men grinning exultantly and pounding each other on the shoulder.

"What in the world—Ouch! Watch where you're tromping!" Midge dodged around the men to reach Kitt's side. "What's gotten into them? Did somebody win the lottery?"

Kitt beamed down at her and explained, "Sort of. O'Mara and I . . . well, I guess it's mostly what I . . . we've finally . . . or I've finally—"

"Thanks," Midge said with a long-suffering look. "I'm really tickled to have such a thorough explanation. Can't tell you how pleased I am that you and O'Mara, or is it just you, or maybe it's O'Mara and Ez, or perhaps we should consider—"

Laughing, Kitt dropped into a chair, shifted it sideways and crossed one long leg over the other. "Sorry, Midge. It's just that it's a bit difficult to explain. You see, there was something I needed to tell O'Mara, but it was a very hard thing to talk about, and I thought it would take a long time before I could do it, but it didn't and I told him this morning."

"Terrific. I think I know almost as much now as I did after your first explanation. No," she admonished, holding up a staying hand, "don't spoil it by telling me anything that makes sense."

"All right, I won't." Kitt laughed, reaching over to pat Midge on the cheek. "I'll let Ez explain it all to you. It will give you another excuse to sit on his lap," she teased gently. "Isn't that where all little ones perch when they listen to a story?"

"I'll see if the coffee's ready," gasped Midge, blushing furiously and running for the door.

"What's gotten into the pixie?" asked Ez, settling back into his chair.

"She's getting the coffee," Kitt said blandly as she rose and started stacking the used dishes. "I'll just get all this out of our way. Well, perhaps not quite all. Ez, how about giving me a hand?" She gave him a compelling look that brought him to his feet, and he followed her inside, passing Midge on her way out with the fresh coffee.

"What is it?" asked Ez as he helped Kitt rinse and stack the dishes.

"I've told him the basics. No real details. I . . . I can't . . . just cold facts . . . it's too . . . oh, when I talk to him about it, I get upset and that upsets him and so does what I'm saying, and then I get even more upset because he's—"

Ez placed his hand across her mouth, cutting off the breathless jumble of words. "Calmly, calmly now. Just take a deep breath and quietly tell me what you want me to do." He moved his hand until only one finger was across her lips. "Just the basics, huh? Did you tell him how it all ended?" She shook her head. "Do you want me to tell him?" She nodded, her eyes wide and pleading. "Okay, but not today. Next weekend, I'll bring up all the documentation and let him read it for himself. Anything else?"

She pulled his hand down and held it in hers. "Could you . . . would you fill him in on the details? Once I know he knows, then I think I can discuss it with him. The hardest part is telling him for the first time . . . I mean, for *me* to have to tell him and know that it's . . . hurting . . . and making him so angry . . . not with me, but because it happened to me and . . . well, I think it would be easier on him if you told him first, and then we . . . he and I . . . could talk about it. Don't you think so?" She clutched his hand and looked at him appealingly.

"Oh, Kitt," he sighed, putting his arms around her and holding her gently. They stood quietly in the middle of the kitchen, her forehead resting on his shoulder, and communed in their own special way.

After a few minutes, he held her away from him and looked reassuringly into her troubled eyes. "I think you're probably right. It would be easier on him if I filled in the blanks. The important thing was for you to be the one to tell him that you were married and what kind of a marriage it was—at least, to tell him enough so that he realizes why you pull away from him."

"I did. I just couldn't—"

"It's okay. I'll talk to him about the rest." He turned her toward the living room and the door to the deck, his arm around her shoulders bringing her along with him out into the sunshine.

As soon as she saw them coming through the door, Midge poured their coffee. She and O'Mara were sitting opposite each other at the table, and he reached out to draw Kitt to a seat at his right while Ez dropped into the remaining chair. Hero ran frustratedly around the table until Ez leaned over and lifted Midge out of her chair and into his lap. With a whoop of satisfaction, Hero jumped into the empty seat and settled into his "people" position, looking around at the laughing humans with a puzzled frown.

"I told you your dog was a total eccentric." O'Mara

chuckled, leaning toward Kitt and pushing her disheveled hair back from her face. "Everything okay?" he asked very softly.

"Just fine." The smiling face she turned to him suddenly seemed years younger, the strain lines erased and the pallor chased away by the delicate flush of healthy color across her cheekbones.

He glanced from her to Ez and back again with a questioning look. "Something?"

Seeing that Ez and Midge were engrossed in their own conversation, Kitt leaned closer to O'Mara and said quietly, "Later on, if it's okay with you, Ez will fill you in on some details you should know. I think . . . well, we both think it will be easier on you . . . and me, too . . . if he tells you and answers any questions and. . . ." Her voice trailed off and she looked at him with a mixture of uncertainty and appeal.

"Okay. You're probably right. While you gals are upping the reading tastes of the local populace this afternoon, Ez and I will go out to my place and have a talk. Okay if we take Hero along to amuse Gus, or vice versa?"

"Sure. Ah . . . will you be coming back later?"

"What's your next dumb question?" His expression was only mildly interested, and Kitt grinned at him unrepentantly.

"Hey, you guys," Midge interrupted, "Ez says he doesn't have to go back until morning. His first class isn't until eleven. So, why don't we all do something interesting tonight?"

O'Mara and Ez locked eyes, grinned, and chorused, "All of us together? Just how interesting do you want it to be?" They broke up in laughter at Midge's outraged expression, highlighted by the tide of fiery red that spread over her neck and face.

"Never mind them," Kitt consoled. "We've got all afternoon to think up something really nasty to pay them out."

"F'sooth," said Ez, chuckling, "now what do you think a couple of bits of baggage like you two can do to us?"

"Idiot!" O'Mara groaned. "I'm not sure yet about the little one, but you should know better than to toss a challenge like that at the big one. Got a wicked, evil turn of mind, has my Kitt."

"Warty toads, the both of you!" Kitt laughed. "You just wait and see what's going to happen to you."

The morning was rapidly warming up under a bright spring

sun, and the four of them lazed on the deck for another hour, enjoying the tangy air and watching the boats on the river. By unspoken agreement, they kept it all very lighthearted—laughing, teasing, talking about tastes and hobbies, and making tentative plans for the next weekend. Finally, Kitt glanced at her watch and broke up the party.

"Ugh! Eleven, already. I've got to change and get downstairs. What do you think, Midge, can the two of us do a fast inventory of the paperback fiction in half an hour? I'd really like to get an accurate idea of what we need before we spend time going through catalogs and order forms."

"Don't know why not." Midge wrinkled her small nose in disgust. "There isn't what I'd call an overabundance of it. Can't imagine why the Baxters let the stock get so low."

"Well, if you two are going to start talking shop, we're off." Ez set Midge on her feet and then stood up to stretch. Wrapping one big hand around her neck, he walked her over to the stairs and stood on the second step down, turning to face her at eye-level. With a teasing smile, he declared, "It's all up to you, pixie." His hands closed over her shoulders as she leaned forward to fold her arms around his neck and kiss him.

Kitt and O'Mara watched them for a minute, and then turned to each other with quirked eyebrows.

"He should patent that technique," O'Mara said thoughtfully.

"If we were smart," Kitt mused, "we'd be getting this whole courting routine on film, complete with sound. We'd make a fortune."

"Hmmm," murmured O'Mara, standing and bringing Kitt to her feet facing him. "At the moment, I'm more concerned with my own courting problems." His eyes gleamed as he watched the flush deepen on her cheekbones, and he took her hands in a loose clasp, gently tugging until she stepped close to him. He smiled slightly, watching her trying to evade his eyes, but he finally captured and held her gaze. "Kiss me?" he asked in a whisper.

She hesitated, her eyes searching his for any hint of demand, but all she could see was warm anticipation, undemanding, leaving it up to her. Finally, she leaned forward, tilting her face up, and he bent his head so she could touch his mouth with hers. It was a tentative kiss, very light, and she seemed poised to back off at any second. He could feel the tension coursing through her, and he held totally still, letting her decide where she wanted to take them. When she tipped her head slightly to shape her mouth more closely to his, it took all his control to remain relaxed and keep his hands loosely entwined with hers. It only lasted for a few seconds before she drew back and looked up at him in a mild daze.

"I did it," she said wonderingly. "I really did it."

His mouth widened in a slow smile that had more than a hint of satisfaction in it. "Little acorns," he murmured.

Suddenly, her tension was gone, and she laughed joyously. "I'm not at all sure I want to be a mighty oak tree. Couldn't I be a willow or a lilac?"

"More like a monkey puzzle tree." He chuckled, starting toward the stairs with her beside him. "You're every bit as mad as old crazy bear there."

"I'm working on it," she said blandly. "It's all suddenly coming back to me. Wonder why?" She slanted a teasing look at him and felt joy bubbling through her at the promise in his eyes.

"Sassy, too." He laughed, kissing her fleetingly on the cheek. "We'll see you later. Oh, by the way, we're all eating out tonight. No, I'm not telling you where." He paused behind Midge, enclosed her small waist in his long hands and plucked her out of Ez's arms, swinging her around and setting her down beside Kitt. "Enough, Ezekiel. You can continue this dalliance at a more propitious time. Besides, much more of such carrying on and you'll both be tumbling down the stairs." Laughing and pushing Ez ahead of him, he called back, "Stay out of mischief, you two. We'll be back around five."

A moment later, a piercing whistle sounded from the parking lot, and Hero leaped from his chair, dodged between Kitt and Midge and scrambled down the stairs.

"Why do I keep thinking that's my dog?" Kitt asked of the blue sky.

"Well, you know, man's best friend. I never heard anyone mention woman's best friend." Midge chuckled as they gathered up the coffee cups and headed inside.

Chapter 10

Kitt and Midge did manage to compile a checklist of the deficiencies in the paperback fiction section, but they had little time during the afternoon to work on the order which Kitt would need to take to the distributor's warehouse. It had turned into a golden spring afternoon, and half of the population of eastern Massachusetts seemed to have decided to "take a ride to Maine" for the day.

"Don't they have bookshops in Massachusetts?" groaned Midge in mid-afternoon.

"Of course they do, but it's more fun to drive two hours to romantic Maine to pick up a book on exotic plants than it is to walk four blocks along dirty city streets," explained Kitt with a straight face.

"*Romantic* Maine?" Midge squeaked disbelievingly. "Have you ever spent a winter here? Try jogging around at twenty below with a sixty-mile-an-hour gale whistling in off the ocean and snow up to your bippy, and then tell me about romance. You're nuts, truly nuts," she declaimed positively.

"Why would you be jogging around in weather like that?" asked Kitt with great interest, turning her head to hide the glint of laughter in her eyes. "I thought all you Maine-iacs hibernated in the winter." She turned back to Midge, her eyes widened in alarm. "You mean I've got to go *outdoors* in a mess like that? Oh, dear, I thought now that everyone had inside plumbing—"

Kitt began to chuckle as she watched a puzzled Midge slowly catch on to the joke. It was the last break they had for the rest of the afternoon. After the last customer left at ten past five, Kitt collapsed across the cash register with a "Whew" of relief, while Midge dropped bonelessly to the floor in the middle of the main aisle, spread-eagled on her back and looking as if she were about to melt into thé carpet.

"Lordy," Kitt moaned, "if it's like this on a Sunday in April, what's it going to be like in the summer? I swear, at one point there must have been fifty people in here climbing over each other."

"Um," Midge mumbled. "Try to concentrate on the money you've made. And don't even look at the kids' area."

"I'm trying not to look at any of it. Do you know any psych. majors? They could certainly find all the base material here for a study on why people don't put things back where they found them. Just look at that reading table. It's covered a foot deep with stuff from all over the shop."

"Far as I'm concerned, it can stay that way until morning," Midge said emphatically. "And before you get the idea that I'm dumping all the cleanup on you, remember that I don't have any classes tomorrow. I can be here any time after eight, and with both of us fresh and fully functional, we can put this place back together by ten with no trouble."

"Ah, the optimism of youth," declaimed a deep voice from the back door, and Ez and O'Mara strolled lazily down the aisle.

"This place looks like a nor'easter struck it," O'Mara said, chuckling, as he sat down on the desk and reached over to push Kitt's tousled hair back from her face. She wrinkled her nose at him when he added, "At least a Force-Seven gale from the looks of you two."

There was a slight thud as Ez dropped, cross-legged, to the floor above Midge's head. With assumed clinical detachment, he leaned forward to peer, upside-down, into her face. "Gadsooks! It blinks! Its nose twitches! That rather interestingly shaped chest is moving up and down! I do believe it's alive, O'Mara. Perhaps a little mouth-to-mouth resuscitation will revive it completely." Cradling her head in both hands, he started to bend down further, only to be halted by Kitt and O'Mara's laughter. He looked up at them crossly and chided, "Please. No levity. This is a serious scientific experiment."

"Looks more like a gorilla examining his dinner," said O'Mara, still laughing.

"Or a vampire bear selecting his favorite vein," chimed in Kitt.

"I'll overlook the gorilla crack, but really, Kitt, a vampire bear?"

"Whoever saw a bat that size?" she demanded convincingly.

With a quick twist and a flip, Midge was on her feet. "I," she stated firmly, "don't care if it's a gorilla, a bear or a bat—I'm not going to be anybody's dinner." With a gleam in her brown eyes, she bent over and rested her elbows on Ez's shoulders, purring into his amused face, "That resuscitation sounds interesting, though."

The words were hardly out of her mouth before she found herself pulled down into his arms and thoroughly kissed.

Shaking their heads and grinning, Kitt and O'Mara quietly disappeared up the stairs.

"Where's Hero?" Kitt asked a minute later, realizing that her dog hadn't come in with the men.

"We left him with Gus for the evening. Gus was feeling a bit abandoned when we told him that the four of us were going out to dinner, but he perked up when Ez said that Hero could stay with him." He caught her hand, pulling her around to face his inquiring look. "I also bribed him with a promise that you'd come to dinner Tuesday night. You will, won't you?"

"I'd like that." She smiled at him, and then, suddenly realizing that something had seemed different about him downstairs, stepped back to run her eyes quickly from his neck to his feet and back again. "My, my," she said wonderingly, taking in the full effect of the slim navy slacks and the muted navy and hunter-green plaid jacket that had obviously been tailored to the wide shoulders and taut waist and hips. The dark green silk tie was held in place against the pale blue shirt with a small gold lion's head tietack.

"I'm not at all sure I can live up to all this elegance," she teased, running a finger over one of the brass buttons on his jacket and then flattening her hand to stroke her palm over the soft wool. She was suddenly speechless as she realized what she was doing and froze, raising startled eyes to meet his amused gaze.

"Don't stop now, love. I'm waiting with bated breath to see where you're going with this."

"Oh!" seemed to be all Kitt could manage, but she didn't draw back when he brought his free hand up to hold hers against his chest. She felt suspended in time, held immobile by the compelling look in his eyes, the air around them glowing golden in the light from the lowering sun shining through the window wall. Bemused, she pressed her palm against his chest, feeling the steady beat of his heart. Turning her other hand slightly, she slowly moved her thumb over the inside of his wrist until she found his pulse. Everything seemed to fade to insignificance except the two of them standing so still in their golden cocoon while his life force flowed through her body from hand to hand, his heartbeat vibrating against her palm and his blood surging rhythmically under her thumb, influencing her own rhythms until they blended with his. Simultaneously, they closed their eyes and concentrated their special sense of each other on opening the channel between them again.

For long seconds, Kitt was mindless, only able to feel every cell in her body shimmering with a strangely soothing heat, to feel the beat of her life mingling with his, to feel the balm of love flowing over the contours and into the crevices of her consciousness, and to sense the same shimmering, beating, flowing feelings in him.

Blinded by the sun blazing into their eyes as they reached the top of the stairs, Ez and Midge were several steps into the living room before they saw the two standing so still and lost in each other. Ez's abruptly cut off "What are—" was enough to snap them back to the present. Blinking as if they were just awakening, which in a sense they were, Kitt and O'Mara slowly turned their heads to look at the other two.

"Oh, hi," Kitt murmured vaguely.

"Is it time to go?" O'Mara asked with equal vagueness.

Ez shook his head pityingly, heaving a deep sigh of resignation. "You see what I mean, now," he said to Midge. "They're gone, poor devils, lost to us forever. And here I am, left alone, fated to wend my solitary way through life unless, of course, I can find a sympathetic soul to keep me company. Uh, a female soul, you understand."

Midge stepped back to stand, hands on hips, looking up at him. Wide-eyed, she gasped, "Incredible! I never knew they could pile it so high!"

It was enough to bring Kitt and O'Mara back to reality with shouts of laughter. Ez picked Midge up and tossed her over his shoulder. As he passed O'Mara on his way to the door, he flipped a thumb at Kitt and said, "If you could manage to concentrate her attention on getting dressed, we just might be ready to go in time to make our reservation. I'll drop this one off and be back to change myself; we can pick her up on our way."

Midge's muttered, "God, how I hate to be organized!" trailed off into unintelligible scolding as Ez closed the door behind them and ran down the stairs.

Kitt turned her head just enough to slant a hesitant look at O'Mara, and found him watching her with an enigmatic smile.

"Ah . . . I'd better get dressed, I guess. Are we . . . it looks . . . you look . . . I mean, what should I wear?" *This is ridiculous. I can't even get a sentence out in one piece. Why do I let him keep doing this to me?*

"I know what I'd like you to wear, but I doubt if you'd do it," he said suggestively, managing a creditable leer. He laughed at her quick scowl and pushed her ahead of him toward the hall. "Come on, silly, show me what you're hiding in your closet, and I'll pick out something appropriate."

"Now, wait just a minute, O'Mara," she demanded, bracing her feet and grabbing the back of the sofa. "I can choose my own clothes. Just tell me what kind of place we're going to."

He took the last step, which brought him against her back, moving his hand around to her waist and holding her lightly against him. While he worked at prying her hand off the sofa, he bent his head and murmured in her ear, "Don't be stubborn, love. If I leave it to you, you'll come out draped neck to toe in some kind of tent. Look at this shirt you're wearing. There's room enough in there for two of you. Come on, now," he coaxed, "let me pick out something I'll enjoy looking at. Trust me. You'll still be covered up—more or less."

She hissed at him and stamped a foot, narrowly missing his toe. "It's the less I don't like. Please, O'Mara—"

"No, don't grab the sofa again. Here, hold my hand. It will help me resist the temptation to put my other arm around you." She could hear laughter threading through the soft purr and felt a warm, melting sensation in her belly, which suddenly intensified as he slowly traced the rim of her ear with his tongue.

"Trust me," he whispered again. "I promise you won't be uncomfortable. And no one's going to bother you. Who's going to argue with both Ez and me?"

"Oh, you wretch," she sighed, leaning back against him and turning her head so his lips brushed her cheek. "You can look through my closet, but—"

The rest was lost as he tipped her face up and kissed her. Before she had time to pull away, it was over, and he was tugging her along with him down the hall.

Still reluctant, she paced after him, her brows drawn together in a frown as she tried to decide whether to laugh or swear. Kitt had developed very definite ideas about how she wanted to appear in public. Although she was perfectly willing to admit that her choice of clothes was inspired by a defensive need for concealment, she refused to face the fact that she subconsciously chose fabrics, colors and designs that enhanced her natural handsomeness and long, lithe form. When she looked in her mirror, she saw only a tall figure whose shape was blurred under loose sweaters and shirts or the straight lines of shift-style dresses and caftans. Ez could have told her that when she was moving with her long, graceful stride and elegant carriage, her slenderly curved body was far from hidden from the discerning eye.

Kitt was still muttering under her breath as O'Mara pushed open her closet doors. She returned his amused look with a scowl, and he tch-tched at her as he began flipping through the hangers. With her temper beginning to simmer at a slow boil, she paced around the room thinking up devastating comments about domineering males and pushy people who leap in uninvited and try to reorganize other people's lives. Loving and sharing were all very well, but choosing her clothes was something else. She'd been dressing herself for a good many years without any help and—

"Ahhh, now this I like." His admiring comment interrupted her mental diatribe and brought her head around to see what had pleased him so much. Head tilted consideringly, he was examining a long caftan which he was holding out at arm's length, its hanger hooked over one finger.

Grudgingly, Kitt had to admit, if only to herself, that it was one of her favorite gowns. Made of heavy natural silk in a rich ivory shade, with gold leaves embroidered around the neck, sleeves and hem, it was designed to be loose enough for comfort but narrow enough to skim the wearer's figure when she walked. Needless to say, Kitt had never seen herself walking in it; in her mirror, it hung straight from shoulder to ankle, and one of the reasons she liked it so much was that—she thought—it didn't show her shape at all. She also liked the neckline, cut in a shallow vee both front and back, which enabled her to slip the gown over her head without fussing with zips and hooks.

"Kitt?" He kept his voice low and undemanding, accurately reading the signs of incipient rebellion in her flashing eyes and the stubborn set of her mouth. Watching her out of the corner of his eye and gauging her reactions, he lifted one of the wide sleeves and held it out, admiring the graceful, almost medieval line.

"It would be just perfect for the Tidal Inlet," he murmured. "I'll bet it's really elegant on you, too."

"Is that where we're going—the Tidal Inlet? It's rather fancy, isn't it?"

His mouth twitched, but he managed not to smile and kept his voice bland as he answered, "Not exactly. It's . . . ah, how shall I put it? . . . quietly restrained. Yes. I thought it would be good experience for our courting couple. After all, there will be many occasions when they will have to subdue their natural high spirits and—"

"Oh, damn you, all right," interrupted Kitt, torn between laughter and exasperation. "But don't think I'm going to let you take over *everything* in my life."

"But I have no intention of it," he said, straight-faced. "Don't worry, love, I really couldn't cope with running a bookshop. When would I ever find time to write? Besides, it makes a nice little hobby for you and keeps you out of mischief while I'm busy. Not that I wouldn't like having you around all day, you understand, but—"

"You patronizing, overbearing . . . oh! . . . 'nice little hobby,' my foot!" Sputtering and shaking a fist under his nose, Kitt followed him as he backed slowly away from her. "O'Mara, if you think for one minute that I'm going to put up with . . . stop laughing, you wretch . . . it's not funny. I won't be—"

He stopped with his back against the wall and, still laughing, pushed her fist aside, cradled her head in his hands and kissed her, effectively distracting her attention. After an initial "Mmf" of surprise, Kitt placed her hands flat against his chest, ready to push herself away. However, she somehow found herself caught up in the comforting feeling of his wide mouth tentatively molding itself to the shape of hers.

Confused, with fragments of thoughts tumbling through her mind, she hovered on the brink of movement, unable to decide which way to go. *No panic. Yet. Oh, that feels nice. Why so lightly? He's leaving it up to me. I should stop this. Now. I can feel his hands shaking. If he grabs— But he won't. Hmmm. That's better. And if I tilt my head, it's even better. Strange. There are some things you never forget. Like kissing O'Mara. No! Don't!*

She stiffened and pulled back as his hands closed over her shoulders, and he immediately dropped them to his sides. Leaning back against the wall, he folded his arms across his chest and watched her with a calm expression. Only a slight tension at the corners of his mouth betrayed the effort he was making to maintain that look.

After the one step back, she hesitated and then relaxed, reaching out to touch his hand and giving him a tentative smile.

"At least this time I didn't belt you," she said huskily.

"You did very well, love. You even kissed back." He kept his voice encouraging and warm, giving no indication of the battle he was waging with himself to keep from pulling her down onto the wide bed, just a tempting four feet away from them. He wondered whether she had been aware of what she was doing just before she pulled away from him. Even knowing what her reaction would be, he hadn't been able to stop his instinctive grip on her shoulders when he felt the warm, moist stroke of her tongue across his lips. He'd taught her to do that long ago, and he sensed that once she'd reacted to the feel of his mouth on hers, the old, well-learned response had been automatic. He watched the play of expressions across her face and wasn't surprised when she changed the subject.

"Did Ez . . . talk to you . . . about . . . about. . . ." She struggled to say the words, but couldn't get them out.

"About Leon and what you went through? Yes, he did. In fact, we spent a large part of the afternoon discussing it."

He had himself under very tight control now, and she couldn't read anything in his face or his eyes but compassion. However, she could sense a seething fury tamped down under an iron will, and for a moment she felt a blazing flash of the old bitterness and hate sear through her. Unknowingly, she grimaced, as if in pain.

"Kitt? You all right?" He straightened away from the wall and smoothed her hair back. "We thought you wanted him to tell me." There was a faint question in his voice.

"I did. It's . . ." She turned and paced restlessly across the room. "I'm glad he told you. Really I am. I wanted him to because I couldn't think how—" She looked at him pleadingly from the far side of the room.

"I know. It was hard enough for Ez to tell me. It would have been even harder for you. But now that I know, try and see if you can bring yourself to talk with me about it. Not now. When you're ready. Okay?"

"Okay." It was just above a whisper, and he read her lips more than he heard her.

Deliberately changing the mood, he started purposefully toward the door, saying briskly, "Enough of this dithering about, my girl. If you want to get the shower before Ez, you'd best get a move on."

Her laugh was a bit shaky, but it was there. "You know it. It's not just that he wallows around in there forever, but he uses all the hot water. Must be a reaction to all those years of scrambling for quick, half-cold showers in locker rooms."

Halfway out the door, he turned back and said softly, "Don't be long. I've spent too much time without you as it is." He closed the door behind him and went whistling down the hall.

Kitt felt lightheaded. It was partly relief that O'Mara finally knew what a mess her marriage had been and just what had made her react to him as she had. Part of it was due to a growing hope and belief that he would figure out how to bring her back to normal. Most of all, she was caught up in the joyful acceptance of love. She was still drifting dreamily around her room, slowly undressing, when she heard the crunch of tires as Ez pulled into the lot. With a muttered "Damn, damn," she yanked off the rest of her clothes, grabbed her robe and raced for the bathroom.

There was no more time, then, for wishful thinking, tentative plans or faint doubts. Spurred on by Ez's intermittent bellows of "Move your butt, Sis," accompanied by periodic thumps on the door, she practically leaped in and out of the shower, brushed her teeth, whipped on her robe, yanked open the door and dodged just barely in time to miss being punched in the nose by Ez's big fist.

"Hey!"

"Sorry, Sis," an unrepentant Ez said, grinning, "but how the hell was I supposed to know you were about to open the door?" He whacked her bottom as she went past and called to her closing door, "Don't lollygag around in there. We've got to pick up the pixie in half an hour."

As it was, Kitt was ready fifteen minutes before Ez made his appearance, and she and O'Mara shaded their eyes and groaned at the sight of his brawny torso draped in lime-green cashmere over a navy-blue silk shirt.

"God, Kitt, can't you do anything with his color sense?" moaned O'Mara. "I'd never have believed it could have gotten worse, but . . ."

"Oh, I don't know. That's not too bad. The white tie and pale gray pants kind of tone it down a bit," Kitt gurgled. "What I'm worried about is what Midge will be wearing. There's not much that goes with lime."

"Especially that amount of lime. There must be yards of it. Midge could use it for a blanket."

"Very funny, you two," Ez growled. "You just don't recognize class when you see it. I think this is a very striking color."

"Strikes me blind, it does," O'Mara commented dryly. "Time's fleeting. Let's move it, or Midge will be wondering if that giant lobster got you."

Fortunately, Midge had decided on a russet velvet outfit of flared pants and trim vest teamed with a full-sleeved chiffon blouse in a swirly pattern of pale lemon and peach. Kitt and O'Mara, sharing the middle seat in Ez's station wagon, found the ten-minute drive to the restaurant strangely peaceful, since Midge spent the entire time staring at Ez's lime-green and navy splendor in open-mouthed disbelief.

As Ez swung into the parking lot, Midge turned to look back at Kitt and O'Mara and managed, "Ahhh . . ."

"Exactly," Kitt agreed.

"Know just how you feel, Midge," O'Mara sympathized. "Hang on another few minutes, and we'll get you some brandy. It won't tone down the color, but after a glass of that you won't be able to see it anymore."

Ez maintained a façade of aloof detachment, ignoring all jibes and the double-takes of the people in the lounge when the four of them entered to find seats while they waited for their table. An impartial observer would have noted that Kitt and O'Mara drew as many looks of admiration as Ez drew of astonishment.

Within a few minutes, they were settled at a small table, Kitt and O'Mara on a banquette against the wall, while Midge and Ez occupied leather-upholstered swivel chairs across from them. Kitt leaned back, sipping her white wine, and let her gaze drift about the room. Her attention sharpened within a few moments as she noted how many people, mostly women, were smiling and nodding at O'Mara. She slanted a look at him as he half-lifted a lazy hand in acknowledgment of a group of people in the far corner.

"Friends?"

"More like acquaintances. Well, four of them, anyway. I don't know the others." He gave her a teasing smile. "Better start getting used to it, love, but keep it firmly in your doubting little mind that you're the woman I take home."

Her eyes flashed, but before she could speak, she felt a touch on her arm and turned to find Midge on her feet.

"I'm going to . . . ah . . . finish doing my hair. I was so rushed, I only had time to run a comb through it." There was a lilt of question in her voice and a definite appeal in her eyes that brought an immediate response from Kitt.

"Good idea," she said, smoothly rising to her feet. "I can feel some of these pins slipping. Maybe you can get them in more securely for me." She brushed a hand lightly over the loose chignon at her neck and divided a bland glance between O'Mara and Ez, who had risen to their feet. "Excuse us for a few minutes while Midge anchors my hair."

A smile twitched at the corners of O'Mara's mouth and he said softly, "Wouldn't bother me if you lost all your pins." The warning glint in her eyes brought the smile out fully, but all he said was, "I'll order another glass of wine for you. Very good for the nerves, white wine."

Ez gave her a questioning look as she followed Midge past him, but all Kitt could do was shrug slightly and murmur, "I don't know."

She trailed Midge through the crowded room, accommodating her normally lithe stride to Midge's shorter legs.

Although she answered several greetings with a smile and a "Hi, there" or "Nice to see you," Midge didn't pause, but kept moving steadily toward the foyer. Kitt, with her attention fixed on the small, stiff shoulders in front of her, didn't notice the disappointment on several male faces when Midge ignored the opportunity of introducing them to the intriguing newcomer. In fact, she would have been dismayed had she realized how much interest her graceful progress was attracting from all over the room. She would have been even more dismayed if she could have heard the exchange between O'Mara and Ez.

"Something?" O'Mara asked quietly, his eyes fixed on Kitt's back as she moved away.

Ez took a swallow of his drink, swinging his chair around so he could watch the mismatched pair making their way toward the entrance. "I don't know. She's been uncommonly quiet ever since we picked her up. I really didn't think this jacket was all that shocking." A faint smile touched his mouth. "Look at those two. Half the men in here are falling out of their chairs. The long and the short of it. Between them, they've got something for everyone."

At the rare note of uncertainty in Ez's voice, O'Mara tore his eyes away from the enticing movement of Kitt's hips and looked at Ez with a mixture of surprise and comprehension. A slow smile widened his mouth as he drawled, "Well, well, the old bear's finally found his honey pot." He chuckled and then laughed out loud at the incredible sight of Ez blushing.

"Maybe," Ez said broodingly, noting with a jaundiced eye how many men Midge was acknowledging. "Hell, does she know every man in here?"

"I wouldn't think so," O'Mara teased, "but do try to keep in mind the fact that she's lived around here all her life. She's bound to know a lot of people."

"And most of them men," growled Ez, looking around the lounge. His attention was arrested suddenly, and he quickly scanned the room again and then cast a sly grin at O'Mara. "On the other hand, I'd say most of that chop-licking interest is going a bit over Midge's head."

"Won't do them a damn bit of good," O'Mara stated positively, a combative gleam in his darkening eyes. "Everything that one has is all mine and always has been." He met Ez's level look and said firmly, "All right. You don't have to say it. I made a stupid move once and lost sight of it. Never again."

"Don't rush her," warned Ez. "It's going to take some time. And you've got to realize that she's not exactly the same girl you used to know. Besides the problem we've already talked about, she's become very independent, with a strong mind of her own."

"I don't object to that," O'Mara said magnanimously, "just as long as she houses it under my roof and rests it in my bed." He and Ez exchanged a long look of total masculine understanding. "Don't worry, Ez," he said reassuringly, "I'll be careful with her. I'm not about to blow it now."

"Oh, I'm not worried," Ez replied blithely, "If I had even a tiny doubt, do you think you'd get within a mile of her, old friend or not? Oh, no. I failed her once, but you can bet your life I never will again."

"No. Neither of us ever will again." O'Mara's expression was momentarily bleak, before he visibly brought his mind back to the present and signaled to the waitress for another round.

Dropping her evening bag onto the counter, Kitt sat down on a low-backed chair and looked in the mirror at Midge, who was standing uneasily behind her. "Okay, peanut, what's the matter? So far, you've hardly said two words. I know Ez's color sense is excruciating, but it's not—"

"It isn't that," muttered Midge with a wan smile. "Do you want me to re-pin your hair?"

"No, it's fine, and don't change the subject," Kitt said gently as she glanced at her reflection. For a change, she was wearing her heavy hair pulled loosely back into a low knot on her neck, her face framed by the deep waves of chestnut silk. "Now, quickly, before someone comes in, tell me what's wrong."

"Me. I'm wrong. Oh, Kitt, didn't you see how all those women were looking at him?" She bit her lip and looked forlornly at herself over Kitt's shoulder. "Look at me. I hardly come up to his chest, and I look like a fluffy-headed doll. It's a joke. And they were all dressed to the nines and tall and sophisticated . . . and . . . older. I mean, not *old*, but nearer his age."

"Midge—"

"Oh, I know we have fun and kid around a lot, but he is

nine years older and I think he thinks I'm a . . . a playmate or—"

"Hold it. Just calm down a minute." Kitt swung around and looked up at the distressed girl. "You're getting slightly incoherent, and it's all over nothing. You're right. Ez is nine years older than you, and so am I for that matter, so listen to me for a few minutes."

She glanced around at the sound of the door opening and then lowered her voice so that the three women at the other side of the room couldn't hear her. "Believe me, Midge, if Ez wanted to be with one of those tall, sophisticated, probably empty-headed fashion plates, then that's just where he'd be. Nobody, but nobody, ever makes Ez do something he doesn't want to do. If he asked you to come with him tonight, it was because he wanted to be with you. Furthermore, if he really thought you were nothing more than a fluffy-headed doll, he wouldn't waste more than ten minutes on you. Ez doesn't go for dumb bunnies."

"But—"

"No buts." Kitt put a hand over one of Midge's tightly clenched fists and squeezed. "I know Ez carries you around like a doll," she said, grinning, "but have you considered that he uses it as an excuse to touch you? Seems to me that he's managed to find one reason or another for keeping at least one arm around you a good ninety percent of the time you're together. I didn't get the impression that you minded all that much," she teased, "since you don't exactly scream with fright when he's tossing you around. In fact. . . ."

"In fact, I rather like it. So, okay," said Midge, managing to look both contrite and sheepish, "this is all a tempest in a thimble. I guess I just . . . well, it was kind of weird walking into that lounge with the three of you. You're all so tall and . . . for a few minutes, I felt . . . almost like I wasn't there. I . . . it's hard to explain . . . you've never been five feet nothing and. . . ." She trailed off into embarrassed silence and nibbled on a thumbnail.

Standing up and towering over Midge even more than usual since her high-heeled sandals brought her close to the six-foot mark, Kitt laughed down at the petite girl and turned her toward the door with a friendly hand on her shoulder.

"Silly cluck. We all know you're there, and Ez knows it most of all. Be a good pixie and stop worrying about minor details. Take heart from the fact that if all Ez wanted was female company, he wouldn't have to come way up here every weekend to find it. He's got them falling at his feet all over campus. No, believe me, it's the company of one particular female that's bringing him up here."

"Really? Do you *really* think so?" asked Midge, tipping her head back to look up at Kitt as they crossed the foyer.

"Oh, yes, indeed. Just hang in there and let things take their natural course and—" She broke off as her gaze went over Midge's head and zeroed in on their table. "Now, what in the name of all the Knights Templar do those two think they're up to? Looks like a scene from *The Sultan's Selection.*"

"What are you—" Midge had stopped when Kitt halted in the entrance to the lounge and, standing on tiptoe, had craned to see what had caught the older woman's attention. Now, her eyes widening in consternation, she could only manage a feeble "Oh" at the sight of Ez and O'Mara surrounded by at least half a dozen obviously fascinated females.

Kitt had caught O'Mara's eye and lifted a sardonically inquiring eyebrow, receiving a wink and a smug grin in return.

"Tomcat!" she growled, snapping Midge's head around and up and widening her gaze in alarm at the steely glint in Kitt's exotic eyes.

"Kitt!" she hissed. "Don't get carried away in here. What are you going to do?"

"Pour a bucket of sauce over a couple of randy ganders."

"Kitt!" gasped Midge, choking back laughter.

"Will you stop saying 'Kitt' and get helpful?" There was a gleam in the smoky eyes that was every bit as wicked as any O'Mara had ever had. She started moving slowly into the room, muttering under her breath to Midge, "Half the men in here are watching us. Do you know any of them? Smile and introduce me and then start bubbling. Two minutes should do it."

"What are you talking about? Ouch! All right, don't pinch." Glancing around, Midge let her eyes rest on a good-looking, sandy-haired young man and smiled mischievously at him. "Hi, Ted. How are you? Haven't seen you around for weeks. Have you met Kitt Tate yet? She's just

bought the bookshop, and I'm working for her. Kitt, this is
Ted Robertson. His sister and I were in school together. Oh,
Stevie. When did you get back from California? Have you
met Kitt Tate?"

In less than a minute, they were surrounded by eager men
ranging in age from twenty to early thirties, laughing and
joking with Midge with the ease of long acquaintance, and
making their interest in her stunning friend more than
obvious. With the unobtrusiveness of experience, Kitt had
backed against a table and casually swung one of the swivel
chairs around in front of her. Now, as she bantered with the
laughing group, she idly spun the chair back and forth,
effectively keeping everyone an arm's length away.

Although a frustrated Midge couldn't see past the surrounding men, Kitt had no trouble flicking quick glances over
their shoulders at the table where O'Mara and Ez were
sitting. After a few moments, she leaned toward Midge and
whispered, "Brace yourself. Ez has the strangest look on his
face, O'Mara is practically blowing smoke rings out his ears,
and they're both headed this way."

She straightened and turned a laughing face to a big,
ruggedly handsome man who was offering her a drink and
watched, with no little satisfaction, as a delighted sparkle lit
his eyes. Suddenly, unexpectedly, elation bubbled through
her as she realized just how long it had been since she'd
fearlessly exchanged quips and laughing, teasing looks with a
group of men.

Still smiling happily, she turned and met O'Mara's smol-
dering gaze as he stepped beside her and draped a casual arm
across her shoulders. She glanced past him to see Ez drop his
huge hands onto Midge's shoulders, almost buckling her at
the knees, and she split a wickedly sparkling look between the
two big men as she drawled, "Well, well, if it isn't the busy
ganders."

Mouths half-open with the beginning of no-doubt pithy
comments, Ez and O'Mara exchanged startled looks which
were rapidly supplanted by dawning comprehension and,
finally, roars of laughter. The bewildered group of admirers
looked inquiringly at Kitt and Midge who, with satisfied grins,
were giving each other thumbs-up signs.

O'Mara, with practiced ease, flashed a knowing smile
around the group and said, "Sorry, fellows, but these two

seem to have lost their way to our table. Have you all met Ez Tate, Kitt's twin?" Quickly but politely, he introduced Ez who, with equal aplomb, exchanged handshakes while easing his and Midge's way through the group and toward their table, followed by O'Mara pulling a laughing Kitt along with him.

"Stupid goose," growled O'Mara, pushing Kitt down on the banquette. "Wait till I get you home." The muscles spasmed along his jaw as he held back a smile. "Feeling your oats, are you?"

Taking him, and herself, completely by surprise, Kitt impulsively leaned toward him and kissed his cheek. A slow smile spread from his mouth to his eyes as he took in her stupefied expression. "Shock yourself?" he asked huskily.

"Did I really do that?" she whispered.

"Mmmmm. We're certainly progressing in leaps and bounds today. I can't help but wonder how you're going to say goodnight."

"I'll think of something," she said dreamily, leaning back and letting her eyes drift to Ez and Midge. She blinked and sat forward, her mouth open to protest at the sight of Ez holding a fuming Midge firmly seated on one hard thigh. "Ez!"

"Don't you start, Kitt. I know damn well that was all your idea, but this one isn't getting out of my hands again. I'm not spending the evening retrieving her from that wolfpack." He glared at Midge, who glared right back.

Kitt watched her twin incredulously and said, dazedly, to anyone who cared to listen, "I don't believe this. He's jealous! My sweet-tempered, love-'em-and-leave-'em brother is jealous of a little bitty pixie he could stuff into his pocket. I may just faint from the shock."

"Do you get the impression of a bear guarding his personal honey tree?" O'Mara asked, chuckling in her ear.

"Yeah," agreed Kitt. "But he'd better watch it. The queen bee looks like she's about to bite his nose."

"Well, she can't now. Fred's just signaled that our table's ready. Let's see if we can get Godzilla to let her go long enough to eat."

Chapter 11

"Hmmm. I do like home comforts. Now, tell me, you devious witch, who were you trying to send up, Ez or me?" O'Mara kept his eyes closed, but a knowing smile hovered on his lips. He was stretched out the full length of the long sofa, his bare feet propped on one arm and his head resting in Kitt's lap while she leaned back against the other arm. His jacket and tie were draped over a chair, and the discarded shoes and socks were placed neatly underneath.

"Both," Kitt said succinctly. Shifting slightly so she could rest her head against the sofa back, she let her eyes play over the long, rangy body which somehow still exuded an aura of vitality even when it was totally relaxed. With the detached sense of someone watching a silent movie, she saw her hand slide across his shoulder and rest on his chest for a few moments, rising and falling with his slow, even breaths, before the fingers moved and unbuttoned the next three buttons of his shirt. Then the dark, soft curls were winding around the fingers as they idly stroked through the thick mat. A quick, arrested motion brought her eyes down to the long, tanned hands clasped loosely across his stomach, but they were quiet now, barely moving with the rhythm of his breathing.

It was peaceful in the dimly lit room, with just the hint of sound from the river penetrating the double-glazing of the window wall. With a continuing detachment, Kitt let her eyes wander the length of his legs as he recrossed his ankles and, with a completely objective appreciation of a well-developed physique, watched the flexing of his sinewy thigh muscles. The fine wool fabric of his slacks was pulled taut by the angled position of his legs, and her curious eyes drifted across his hips and flat abdomen and lingered unthinkingly on the soft mound of his groin. Her mind was concentrated on the warm, solid weight of his head on her thigh and the tickling of his hair on her palm as she lightly brushed her hand back and forth across his chest.

"Do you have any idea what you're doing to me?" The husky voice jarred her into full awareness, and her eyes widened in alarm as she became conscious of several disturbing factors all at once—a slow stirring at his groin which was tautening his slacks even more, the whitening of his knuckles as his hands gripped tightly together, the gaping shirt which, unknowingly, she had almost completely unbuttoned, the deepening rise and fall of his chest under her stilled hand, the shape of his head under her other hand which had somehow become buried in his thick hair, and the possessive eyes, darkened to indigo with arousal, catching and holding her gaze.

"I . . . I wasn't thinking . . . I just . . . oh, my," she ended on a moan, closing her eyes.

"Don't shut me out, love. Look at me." The deep voice was coaxing, still with a touch of huskiness, and she opened her eyes. He brought one hand up to gently circle her wrist and guide her palm down over the vee of fur across his stomach. "I didn't mean for you to stop. Do you realize that the fact that you wanted to touch me and did it so naturally is another giant step on our path?"

"I guess it is, isn't it?" Her wondering look was replaced with a slow smile of delight, and she deliberately smoothed her hand up over his ribs, enjoying the warm tightness of his skin stretched over bone and muscle.

With a rather breathless laugh, he caught her wandering hand and held it with both of his. "Slow down, love, or you'll be off the path and into the rocks."

"O'Mara!"

"Sorry," he choked. "No pun intended. But if you'd been a properly brought up young lady instead of trailing around with all those blunt-speaking athletes, you'd never have interpreted it that way."

The again-sapphire eyes laughed up at her, and the thickening tension in the room was suddenly dissipated.

"Kitt? Were you and Midge really miffed about those women coming over to talk to us?"

"Ummm. I don't know if that's quite the word. Mildly annoyed? Provoked? Yeah. Provoked comes closer. Really, O'Mara, we'd only been gone five minutes!"

"Ten." It was a teasing incitement.

"Whatever. It still didn't seem long enough for you two to become so damn bored you had to collect a harem."

"Jealous?" he drawled, giving her an assessing look.

"No!" She bent over him, narrow-eyed, trying to read his bland expression. "Are you trying to pick a fight?"

"Not at all. There's no point in picking a fight with you until you're in shape to make it worthwhile."

"Now what are you talking about?" she wailed in exasperation. .

"Making up after our fights. That's going to be the best part, although," he murmured consideringly, "there could be some other interesting moments."

"But I don't—Oh!" She felt her face warm with telltale color as she finally caught onto his teasing. "O'Mara, I'm beginning to think you have a one-track mind."

"Not really," he chuckled, bringing her hand to his mouth and kissing her palm. She felt the jolt of heat up her arm as his tongue flicked over the sensitive center. "But I will admit that, for right now, I'm concentrating on how to get you over this little problem you have about letting me touch you. Once we've got that out of the way, we can go on to other things."

"There you go again with your 'little problem,' which you know—"

"What I know is that you've kissed me more than once today and managed to stand still while I kissed you. Not really a proper kiss, perhaps, but we're getting there. You didn't panic when I put my arm around you when we were coming home tonight, and you're not only not panicking right now, you're being downright provocative."

"You know I wasn't deliberately—"

"Hush. I know you weren't thinking about what you were doing. But don't you see? That's the point. You were following your instincts. You wanted to touch me, so you did. I could see it in your face; you were leaning back with your eyes closed and a hint of a smile, enjoying the feel of me under your hands. Not only were you not trying to arouse me, it didn't even enter your head that you might be doing so."

"How do you know—"

"It's exactly the way I feel about you, love. I want to touch you." He stroked one hand slowly up her arm under the wide sleeve of her caftan. "I want to feel your skin under my hands and the shape of your body pressing against mine. I want to excite you and feel the heat rising in you and know that it's all there for me." His voice had become a hoarse whisper, his eyes again darkened to indigo.

Her breathing had shortened and her heartbeat quickened as he talked love to her. She could feel her nipples hardening, and her breasts seemed to swell in the constriction of the light bra she was wearing. Mesmerized by the dark heat of his eyes, she nevertheless felt a cold, hard knot of incipient fear in her center.

Something must have shown in her face, because he suddenly lunged to his feet and stood at the end of the sofa with his back toward her, his dark head bent and his feet slightly apart as if he were having trouble balancing. His shirt moved, stretching across the muscled back, and she knew he was rebuttoning it.

She sat forward on the edge of the sofa with her eyes fixed on his back. Half of her wanted him to come back down beside her and take her in his arms. Maybe more than half. Most of her. But there was still that one small part that recoiled and screamed "No!" at the thought of hard arms closing around her and the heavy weight of a male body pressing her down and trapping her, a victim of whatever dark demons took possession of him in the flame of passion. She bent forward with an inarticulate moan and buried her face in her hands.

"Don't, love. I'm sorry. I shouldn't have . . . I didn't intend to scare you. Kitt? Are you crying?"

His voice was strained and low, close to her ear. She could feel his warm breath on her temple, and his hands seemed to be almost trembling as they gently smoothed back her hair. There were little tugs at her nape, and she realized that he was pulling the pins from her chignon. Keeping her head down, she spread her fingers just enough to see that he was kneeling in front of her.

"Kitt?" He was finger-combing her thick hair out of the twisted knot and spreading it over her shoulders.

"I'm all right," she whispered, brushing her fingers across her eyes and then straightening up partway but still leaning forward with her elbows on her knees. She lifted her head and discovered the worried blue eyes only inches away. Lifting her hands to his face, she trailed her fingers lightly across his hard cheekbones and down to the corners of his mouth. With intent concentration, she watched her finger graze back and forth across his lower lip until he finally caught the end of it between his lips. She felt his tongue licking around the fingertip and raised her eyes to meet his.

Drawing back a bit, he brought his hands down to capture hers and then leaned forward again until his mouth was a bare inch away from her suddenly dry lips. Nervously, she ran her tongue over them, watching his head tilt slightly and come closer.

"Do that again," he whispered. "Now." And his mouth was shaping itself to hers. Her breath caught painfully in her throat as she hesitated, and then with a sigh she parted her lips against his and slowly traced the inner curve of his bottom lip with the tip of her tongue. There was a sense of familiarity in the flood of pleasure washing through her, and she had a flashing memory of sitting in the front seat of his car, his arms around her, excitement coursing through her as he taught her how to kiss him.

Strange. I never kissed Leon like this. Never even wanted to. Oh! His tongue touched hers, teasing, coaxing, until he caught the tip gently between his teeth. At the first hint of her withdrawal, he moved his head back just enough so he could look at her. The smoky eyes were clouded with the beginning of passion, and her mouth was soft, half-parted, asking for more.

Still holding her hands, he leaned forward to brush his mouth slowly across hers and then brought them both up to their feet.

"You have some decaffeinated coffee, don't you?"

"Hmmm?"

"Come along, love. We could both do with a cup of coffee, but neither one of us needs any more stimulation. You've had enough for now, and I've had . . ." His voice caught in his throat and he cleared it before finishing, "almost more than I can take."

Kitt was only half-hearing his words. Still in a state of emotional confusion, not quite sure exactly what had happened between them, she fixed unfocused eyes on his mouth and watched the words forming without understanding what they were.

"Kitt!"

"Hmmm?"

"Coffee."

"Oh."

"Oh what?" he asked patiently, trying not to laugh.

"Would you like some coffee?" she asked dreamily.

"That would be very nice. Thank you." His shoulders shook as he watched her weave an erratic course toward the kitchen.

"Welcome." She drifted across the kitchen, not bothering to put on a light, and started filling the kettle.

"Oh, love," he moaned, "at least see if you can get the kettle onto the same burner that you turn on. I'll dole out the coffee." He entered the kitchen, flipping on the light over the sink, and reached for the mugs. "At the rate you're going, we'd probably end up with dog-food mush."

"Hmmm? Did you want something to eat?"

"No, love." He leaned back against the counter, smiling indulgently, and watched her wander over to open the refrigerator. "What are you looking for, Kitt?"

"Dog food?" She frowned, puzzled. "Why do you want dog food?"

"I don't. Ah . . . do you keep it in the refrigerator?"

"I don't think so. Maybe I'm looking for something else?"

"Oh, Kitt!" he gasped, "I can't stand it!" He reached past her shoulder and plucked a jar of potent whole-seed mustard out of the door-shelf, thumbed off the cap and waved the open jar under her nose.

Two breaths later, she jerked her head back, blinked, gasped and doubled over in a hard sneeze. Straightening up, she gave him an irate glare, opened her mouth, and sneezed again.

"Damn. What do you think you're doing? And why mustard? I thought we were having coffee."

"We are. I had to do something to bring you out of your fog. Settle down now, I want to talk with you. No, not in there. We'll sit at the counter. At the moment, the combination of you and a sofa is more than I can handle."

"Okay," she sighed. "If you insist." She swung around on the stool to face him. "So what are we going to talk about? Your harem?"

"No, you witch, and it had nothing to do with harems. I knew four of them, and the others were simply friends of theirs. You going to listen?"

"Yes." She gave him a wry smile and shrugged. "But you're not really going to be telling me something I don't already know. You're well known around here as Michael Talbot, a celebrity, a famous author. That alone would draw a lot of women. Add the fact that you're tall, dark and handsome and have those *wicked* blue eyes, and really, O'Mara, one wonders why you're not perpetually leading a parade of panting popsies!"

His head went back and he shouted with laughter. Moments later, gasping for breath, wicked eyes glittering, he managed to moan, "Oh, you wretched woman. What an appalling picture. It's never in the world as bad as that! 'A parade of panting popsies'!? I think maybe we should get you your own typewriter and turn you loose. You just might end up making more money than I do and collecting your own coterie of crooning Casanovas!"

Kitt broke up in a fit of giggles, finally gurgling, "Never!"

"You're right. I wouldn't put up with it for a minute. However," he continued, sighing gustily, "there's not much I can do about the attention I sometimes receive in public. For several reasons, I am well known in the area, and not just because I'm Michael Talbot. There's also Gus, and I've become involved in sports and school activities with him, which means I've met half the parents in town. Then there's the fact that I've been a bachelor ever since I've moved here, and get invited to a lot of parties, to say nothing of the handful of genuine friends I've made. So, incidents like that in the lounge are bound to occur sometimes when we're out."

"O'Mara," she said in exasperation, "do you really believe that I'm going to get all warped out of shape because a bunch of poor, misguided, overeager women drape themselves all over you? Oh, stop laughing. And I'm not jealous. It was just . . . well, I guess it was a kind of envy because . . . because I couldn't be that relaxed and uninhibited with you, and I want to be."

"And that little performance you and Midge put on? What was that all about, then?"

"Ahhh, well, it was partly pique," she explained, intently

examining her fingernails, "and partly to prove something to Midge. She was having . . . temporary insecurity problems, and I decided to demonstrate her . . . high appeal as bear bait."

"Bless us one and all," O'Mara groaned. "You twit, you just about sent Ez around the bend."

"Hmmm," Kitt murmured noncommittally, an enigmatic look making her eyes seem even more slanted than usual.

"Yeah. Well, all right, I was none too pleased myself. You have no idea, my love, of your effect on the male population. You could have sealed every envelope in town with the tongues hanging out in that room. If you've reached the point where you want to try out your wiles," he said, his voice dropping to a seductive purr, "I'm always available and don't mind at all being used as a guinea pig."

Eyes glinting with mischief, she fluttered her lashes at him and purred just as seductively, "Thank you. I'll put your application right in the front of my file."

"Sassy. Very sassy. Watch it, wench," he warned, "I'm keeping score."

"And thinking up interesting forms of retribution?"

"All in good time." He stood and stretched, his eyes going to the kitchen clock. "Good Lord, no wonder you're looking so smudgy-eyed. It's almost two. Where the hell is Ez? For that matter, I'm not exactly wide awake myself. Do you realize we've been up since five this morning?"

"Yes, indeed, and I'm about ready for bed. You don't have to wait for Ez. All the doors are locked, and he's got his own key. I'm alone here all week, you know."

"Not quite. You've usually got Hero. By the way, I'll bring him back in the morning."

"Okay. Look, you really don't have to wait. Who knows when he's coming back? You won't get any sleep."

"Sure I will. Just give me a pillow and a blanket. That couch is plenty long enough."

"Don't be ridiculous! You can't—"

"Unless you'd like to share?"

Meeting his level look, she reached out to take his hands in a convulsive grip, and there was pain in her eyes when she said, "You know I *want* to, but—"

"I know. But be patient, love. After today, I don't think

it's going to take all that long to knock down those hurdles. Aha, the building shaketh as in an earth tremor. Ez has arrived."

"You still here, O'Mara? Or are you staying over?"

Jacket dangling from a finger, tie gone, shirt half-undone, and looking extremely pleased with himself, Ez strolled through the door.

"Oh, my, yes, indeed," said O'Mara with a knowing smile. "If I ever saw a bear who'd been sampling the honey . . . and I wouldn't dream of asking what she did to your hair. But, ah . . . why braids? No!" He held up a hand. "Please don't tell us. We can spend a quiet evening this week making up our own story."

"I have no intention of explaining anything," Ez said loftily, eyeing Kitt as she walked a slow circle around him, examining his head from all angles.

"What I want to know," stated Kitt with obvious interest, "is how long it took her to do all those tiny braids. You look like Bo Derek after she met Jack the Clipper."

"Are you lecturing like that tomorrow?" O'Mara asked with the air of a reporter conducting an interview. "Do you think it will increase or decrease attendance? Is this intended to start a new fad, or is it perhaps a live demonstration of a fifteenth-century coiffure?"

"No, no, O'Mara," Kitt exclaimed, "you've got it all wrong. It's a new style for athletes. Now that the coaches can't insist on short hair anymore, this is just perfect for keeping it neat and out of their eyes, and then in the evening, just comb it all out and—eureka!—waves and curls and nobody can accuse them of a sissy thing like setting their hair. Am I right, Brother?"

"You're both weird," Ez said calmly. "Just because I decided on a change of hairstyle, there's no need for you two to start poking fun. If you're too hidebound and conventional to appreciate a truly creative approach to the expression of one's individuality through the medium of innovative hair arrangement—"

Whoops of laughter drowned out the rest of his exposition, and he watched Kitt and O'Mara with a slightly raised eyebrow and a placid expression until they finally collapsed on the sofa and got themselves under control.

"Oh, Ez," O'Mara moaned, "if only I had a tape of that. You'll never be able to do it again without missing something."

"Nonsense. Of course I can. Remember, I did my post-grad work in England. University denizens over there talk like that all the time. For that matter, haven't you ever listened to Bill Buckley?"

"He's right, O'Mara," said Kitt. "Give him a couple of stiff drinks, and he can go on like that for hours. It's appalling. He's been known to clear out a faculty meeting in fifteen minutes."

"I can well understand why." O'Mara had put on his socks and shoes and now shrugged into his jacket. "However, I'm leaving for quite a different reason—namely, I'm falling asleep. Goodnight or morning or whatever, Ez," he said to the broad back moving down the hall. "Come on, love, walk me to the door and be sure you lock it behind me."

They stopped beside the door and stood close together, not quite touching except for their clasped hands. Kitt met his eyes and read encouragement, inquiry, warmth and just a hint of tightly controlled desire. As his head bent, she swayed forward until she was leaning lightly against him, and lifted her mouth to meet his. Eyes closed, she savored the warm pressure, loving but undemanding, and the hardness of his chest against her breasts. All too soon, to her mind, he was stepping back, his hands coming up to her shoulders to steady her until she found her balance.

A shadow of disappointment flickered in her eyes, and her voice held a note of reproach as she protested, "I wasn't afraid."

He brushed a finger across her lips and smiled. "I know, love. That's why I stopped. I want you to go to bed with a good memory. Don't forget to lock this behind me. I'll see you in the morning."

Kitt locked the door and stood for a few moments listening to his descending footsteps, which were remarkably light for such a big man. Humming *The Second Time Around*, she floated across the living room, turning off lights, and did a waltz turn down the hall.

"Hey, Sis, come here and give me a hand, will you? I can't get these damn things undone." Ez's exasperated rumble came from the partly open bathroom door, and she pushed it all the way back to find him leaning over the counter, peering into the mirror as he tried to untangle his hair.

Leaning against the doorjamb, she couldn't help giggling at his look of total frustration. "Why don't you leave it? I think it's kind of interesting. Different, definitely. Ahhh . . . why did she do it, or shouldn't I ask?"

He gave her a sidelong, sheepish look in the mirror. "She was kind of miffed with me." Pausing, he straightened up and regarded his image ruefully. "I didn't realize just what it looked like until I got in here. We were in the car when she did it." Finally, he chuckled. "Dippy broad. God, that looks ridiculous! Kitt? Come on," he coaxed, "help me get them out."

"Oh, all right," she said with a long-suffering sigh. "What are sisters for, except to stay up till dawn unbraiding their brothers' hair?" She hooked the stool from under the counter with her foot. "Sit down so I can reach this mare's nest. Oh, damn, she tied them all off with strands of hair. I'm going to have to clip the knots out."

"Like hell! You're not going to go snipping chunks out of my hair!"

"Don't be vain. It's only little bits of ends." She pulled open a drawer and rummaged in her manicure kit for small scissors. "It won't even show. If it bothers you, you can get a trim tomorrow. You need one anyhow—your hair is curling over your collar. Won't hurt a bit to get an inch taken off."

"Half an inch. Oh, toads' nails, look at the kinks. I'm going to have to wash it to get all those out."

"It'll take more than that. Hold still, before I chop a chunk out of your ear. Once I've got all these undone, if you'll just lean over the sink, I'll give you a shampoo and a creme rinse. That should get rid of most of the kinks, and, if I blow-dry it with a brush, I can get the rest of them out. You'll be as good as new in half an hour."

"With raggedy edges," Ez grumbled. "That woman is demented, and she has an evil temper."

"You still haven't explained how she could have done this without you knowing. Or did you? It must have taken some time."

He met her eyes in the mirror, flushing and looking rather sheepish. "Oh, well, I was distracted and . . . ah . . . well, if you must know, we were parked down by the beach, talking and watching the surf and . . . I was sort of resting my head back against her . . . er . . . shoulder, and she was playing with my hair . . . I . . . we kind of lost track of the time, and we talked and—"

"Watched the surf. Sure you did. What you're trying to tell me is that the conversation was so interesting that Midge could braid up all your hair, and you do have quite a bit of it, into tiny braids without you even knowing it. Right? That must have been some talk—this had to have taken well over an hour."

Ez merely grunted, his gaze fixed morosely on the mirror as he watched Kitt snipping away at the ends of the braids.

"Cheer up," she urged, glancing at his unhappy expression. "I'm really being very careful."

"I know." It came out on a gusty sigh. "You and O'Mara seemed very *simpatico* when I came in. Everything progressing?"

"Umm-hmmm. Fine, so far. He's wearing his kid gloves and being very cautious. I'm doing better than I ever thought I could." For a few minutes, she concentrated on the last of the braids, then met Ez's concerned gaze in the mirror. "How did he react when you told him about . . . Leon?"

"With rage. Total, nearly uncontrollable rage. He came up with some terms that I'd never heard, went on for ten or fifteen minutes without repeating himself once, and then switched to several other languages for another quarter hour. Near as I could keep count, he knows every curse there is in at least twelve languages. We were walking around the cliff path on the top of Crest Rock, out in front of the house, when I told him. Right off, he flung the can of beer he was holding out to sea. Then, while he was roaring curses at the ocean, he started heaving rocks over the edge. I figured it was as good a way as any to work it all off, so I found a comfortable boulder and let him go at it. It was an education. The man knows more basic Anglo-Saxon than I do."

"Guess it's just as well that you were the one to tell him. Did he . . . what did he say when he cooled down?"

"Blamed himself. Also told me I was a damned mealy-mouthed fool for not stopping you. After he got that out of his system, we settled down and talked about you and how you'd reacted and what it had taken these last five years to get you back together. We . . . ah . . . talked a bit about a couple of ideas he has for getting you through the rest of it. Did he say anything to you?"

Kitt was adjusting the water temperature, and now she pushed his head down and reached for the shampoo. "Get your hair good and wet. That's fine. Now close your eyes. He didn't say much. Just that you'd talked about it, and now he knew, he . . . it would be good for me to tell him myself . . . when I'm ready. Stick your head under the faucet again. I know he's right, and I guess I'll probably do it pretty soon. It's something we *have* to go through. Okay now, keep your eyes closed while I work this rinse into your hair. Ugh, next time you get a haircut, have him thin some of this out. How do you get a comb through all this? There. Stay still for a few minutes."

Pulling a clean washcloth out of a drawer, she pushed it into his hand. "Here. Use this if it starts running into your eyes. Did you and the pixie sort out *your* difficulties? Or has this little stunt put you back on Start?"

"No, not really. This is just a manifestation of her warped sense of humor, and *that* is probably a result of being smaller than almost everyone else. I'm not chewing nails, you know. It was rather funny, and I can understand why she did it. As far as making up, we . . . ah . . . did that. Not that there was any great problem, except a bit of poorly timed one-upmanship. How long do I have to stay like this?"

"That's it. Just let me rinse it out. Okay. Here. Get the excess water out while I find a brush. Are you coming up next weekend?"

"Of course. If you think I'm leaving her to the weekend wolfpack, think again."

"One could almost believe you were jealous, if one didn't know that you've never been jealous in your life. On the other hand," Kitt continued blandly, "there's a first time for everything. Yes?"

"Mmmm. Maybe. If so, I'll have to do something about it. Jealousy is a destructive emotion, and I'll be damned if I'll let myself get that bent out of shape. It'll be something to ponder this week during my long, lonely evenings."

"Don't try for sympathy from me. One short whistle and you'll have all the company you can handle."

"True, but I rather think I'd find it a bit boring after the pixie."

"Falling off the edge?"

"Maybe. Time will tell."

Kitt paused with the hair-dryer in her hand, her thumb on the ON switch, and studied him for a moment. With a slowly widening smile, she asked, "How much time?"

"Not much," he murmured with an answering smile, and Kitt turned on the dryer.

Chapter 12

An April Monday on the Maine coast tended to be very quiet and peaceful. The weekenders were gone, it wasn't the season for midweek day-trippers, and the permanent residents were going about their normal Monday pursuits and recovering from the previous two days of hectic activity.

Yawning and blinking to keep her eyes open, Kitt leaned against the counter and waited for the water to boil. After her extraordinarily long Sunday, she'd only gotten a little over five hours of sleep, and now, coming up on eight-thirty, she was longingly considering the idea of keeping the shop closed for the day. Mondays were very slow anyway, and, at the moment, she had absolutely no enthusiasm for anything beyond falling back into bed for another three or four hours.

The sound of trudging footsteps on the outside stairs, followed by a feeble knock on the door, brought her away from the counter and across the living room to grope for the cord to open the long drapes. She squinted, eyes watering, into the bright glare of the morning sun as she flipped the lock and pushed back the door for a less-than-lively Midge.

"If you say 'good morning,' I'll pound you into the deck," Kitt growled.

"Wouldn't think of it. Got any coffee?" A sleepy Midge tottered across to the counter and dropped onto a stool, propping her chin up with both hands, elbows on the counter.

"Mmmm. Instant in a minute. I haven't the energy to make fresh." Kitt stifled a yawn and reached for another mug. "Ought to make you do this, Miss Clever Fingers. You must have gotten at least an hour's more sleep than I did."

"Don't yawn. It's catching. Why'd I get more sleep?"

"Because, you evil elf, you didn't have to stay up until after three undoing a hundred and fifty-two tiny braids and then shampooing and blow-drying out the kinks."

For the first time that morning, Midge's eyes were wide open as she stared at Kitt in total dismay. "Oh, God, I never thought about . . . It never dawned on me that . . . Oh, Kitt, I'm sorry. It was a joke. Well, sort of a retribution, but I intended Ez to have to get them out. It never occurred to me that you'd have to do it. Oh, damn!"

" 'S okay. I'll think of a suitable revenge once I'm awake." Kitt dredged up half a chuckle. "He really did look incredible."

"Ah, yes, well, maybe I'd better disappear for a while. He *is* still here, isn't he? I saw his car out front."

"Coward. You stay right there. He's still asleep." She glanced at the clock. "He should be getting up if he wants to make it back in time for his lecture. Perhaps," said Kitt with a deliberately malicious smirk, "I should let you wake him up. It just might even the score."

"Have a heart, Kitt," Midge wailed. "He's not going to be any too pleased with me this morning."

"Take it like a trouper. Here, you'd better go bearing coffee. By the time he gets it down, he'll have considered the consequences of strangling you."

Midge, looking rather apprehensive, clutched the mug in both hands and moved reluctantly down the hall. Incomprehensible mutterings drifted back until they were cut off by the closing of Ez's door. Smiling to herself at the thought of his reaction to being awakened by Midge, Kitt wandered into the living room and stretched out on the sofa. She turned on her side, pushing a small pillow under her head and wriggling around until she had her bare feet tucked up under her long terrycloth caftan. Yawning widely, she closed her eyes, telling herself it was just for a few minutes.

When O'Mara pushed open the door some ten minutes later, he found her sound asleep, quite undisturbed by the muffled squeals and inarticulate rumblings coming from the direction of Ez's room. Hero trotted over to the sofa and nuzzled his damp nose into Kitt's neck. Without opening her eyes, she drowsily mumbled, "Good boy. Go see Ez."

Before she had a chance to fall all the way back into sleep, she felt a moist tickling around her ear and warm breath blowing gently into it. A large hand was lightly kneading her shoulder, and a teasing voice was urging, "Wake up, Griselda. How are you going to find your handsome prince if you don't kiss the available toads?"

She turned her head slightly and opened one eye to find O'Mara's mouth an inch away from her own. "Mmmm. The toads in this neighborhood are certainly improving." She slipped one hand around his neck and pulled his mouth down to hers, kissing him with soft lips and slowly stroking tongue-tip in that way that was rapidly becoming habit again. Drawing back a bit, she opened both eyes wide and looked at him wonderingly. "Good heavens," she breathed. "It works!"

"Of course." He grinned smugly at her and settled himself more comfortably on the floor beside the sofa. With the hand on her shoulder, he pushed her back and nestled his head into the curve of her neck, his other hand coming up to stroke her cheek and play with her ear. At the gentle tugging of her fingers in his hair, he sighed and relaxed against her, closing his eyes.

"What's going on down the hall?" he murmured.

"I sent Midge to wake up Ez."

"Oh, my."

"Mmmm. But she deserved it, and I told her so. It took me forever to undo her handiwork. Doesn't sound as if he's too upset. She's giggling. Did you get any sleep?"

"Enough. I don't need much. I can manage for quite a while on four or five hours a night. On the other hand, I wouldn't mind another couple hours right now with you."

"I can't imagine that you're very comfortable there on the floor."

"You'd be surprised. By the way, what have you got on under that?" he asked, tugging on her caftan.

"Ahhh, nothing."

"Wretched woman," he groaned. "You had to tell me."

"You asked."

"Why don't we go curl up together on your bed and—"

"Hey, you two," bellowed Ez, leaning over the back of the sofa, "enough of this lollygagging around. I'm starving. What's for breakfast?"

"If we ignore it, maybe it will go away," Kitt whispered. At that moment, she could have wished her adored twin six feet under a rising tide. She wanted to savor the peace and the feeling of rightness of O'Mara's head resting on her shoulder, his warm breath against her throat, and the soothing movements of his hands.

"No such luck," O'Mara growled. "I can hear its stomach rumbling from here."

Sounds of cabinet doors opening and closing and the muted thump of the refrigerator door were quickly followed by Midge's clear voice complaining, "There's nothing to eat! We must have cleaned you out yesterday morning, Kitt."

"Oh, hell," O'Mara groaned. He lifted his head, turned Kitt's face toward him and, totally ignoring the interested presence of Midge and Ez, kissed her slowly and thoroughly, shifting so that all his weight was on his elbow and she knew she was free to move away if she wanted to.

She didn't. After an initial tensing, she relaxed and slid her hands around his neck. A slow, heated languor spread through her, and she was pleasantly jolted by his teasing tongue opening her mouth and leisurely exploring its smooth contours. She could feel his blood pounding under her hands as they stroked the warm skin stretched taut over the strong muscles and tendons of his neck.

And then it was over, and she opened drowsy eyes to be caught in the indigo blaze of his. A breathy "O'Mara" was all she could manage.

Regaining control of his immediate inclinations, he forced a nearly normal smile and said huskily, "If I thought it would work, I'd give them ten bucks and send them out for breakfast. However—"

He rose smoothly to his feet, then bent over the sofa and, with little apparent effort, lifted Kitt into his arms and started carrying her toward the hall. Her protesting "O'Mara!" was drowned out by his deep-voiced complaint of "Some peoples' brothers have absolutely no understanding of a recently transformed toad's need for peace and privacy in which to enjoy his new princely privileges."

"Ha!" Ez exploded. "And you talk about my convoluted language!"

"O'Mara! Wait!" called Midge to his disappearing back. "Aren't we going to have breakfast?"

Her only answer was the slam of Kitt's bedroom door as O'Mara kicked it closed behind him. Grinning down at a laughing Kitt, he leaned back against the door, still cradling her in his arms.

"Idiot. Put me down before you do something awful to your back. I'm not exactly a featherweight."

"Never mind that. The big question is 'are you afraid?' You don't seem to be, if the way you're clinging to my shoulders is any clue."

"No, not at all," she said in slowly dawning amazement.

With a satisfied expression, he gradually let her legs down until she was standing. Shifting his hands to rest lightly over her hips, he brought her a step forward to rest the full length of her softly curving body against his. Her arms were still around his neck, and she tightened them now to bring his mouth down to hers.

Nothing had changed in the last five minutes. The same heat washed through her body, and she could feel the increased beat of his heart against her breasts. With a pang of remorse, she sensed the strain he was enduring to keep from crushing her against him. Her mind was rapidly becoming fuzzy as his seeking tongue accelerated her arousal, but she was still aware of the tremor in his hands as he fought to keep their touch light while they skimmed slowly over her hips and up the long, supple contours of her waist and ribs to come to rest against the outer curves of her breasts. Mindlessly, instinctively, she thrust her hips and pelvis against him, and it was not until she felt the hard ridge of his arousal pressing against her belly that the first chill of fear uncoiled deep inside and sent its muscle-tensing message to her brain.

By then, they were so closely linked in their private rapport that he sensed her burgeoning fear almost as soon as she did, and he unhurriedly but firmly ended the kiss and moved her a step back, breaking the contact of their bodies. He held her steady with his hands still high on her ribs, his palms against the sides of her breasts. Desire glazed their eyes as they looked at each other with matching triumphant smiles.

"Okay?"

"Yes. It didn't have time to get a hold."

"I'm getting so I can sense it sooner and stop before you begin to panic."

"It's getting longer each time before the fear comes."

"Is it gone now?"

"Yes."

"Then take hold of my wrists so you know you're in control, and stand still."

With his eyes fixed intently on hers, watching and judging her reactions, he slowly and very gently moved his hands forward, curving them to fit the soft swell of her breasts. Her hold closed tightly around his wrists, but she didn't push him away. With waves of pleasure sweeping through her, she heard herself moan his name as her back arched to press her swelling breasts into his hands.

Then, suddenly, the warm, enveloping pressure was gone, and she was spun around, his hands gripping her shoulders, his forehead resting against the crown of her head.

"God, love, any more of this and I'll have you on that bed, ready or not." His deep voice was an agonized groan, and she could feel his breath gusting hard and fast against the back of her neck. "Get into some clothes, lots of clothes, and we'll all go out for breakfast."

"Okay. Lots of clothes." With great effort, she gathered her wandering wits and regulated her breathing. "Ah, it would be easier if you'd let go of me." She moved several steps away as his hands dropped, and half turned to give him a teasing look. "It would also be quicker if you waited out there with the odd couple."

"You're absolutely right." He ran his fingers through his thick hair, pushing back the swath from his forehead but ignoring it when it promptly slid forward again. He stopped halfway out the door, looking back at her with a wicked gleam. "Be prepared. When we get you over this minor obstacle, we're going off by ourselves somewhere and we aren't going to get out of bed for at least a week."

"Only a week?" Kitt asked demurely, but with a gleam that was nearly as wicked as his.

"You mean you can go longer than that without food?" Chuckling, he closed the door on her startled expression and strolled down the hall singing *Roll Me Over in the Clover.*

It was a relaxed, laughing group seated around the table in the small Dock Square restaurant a short while later. At nine on a weekday morning, there were only a few other customers, and O'Mara and Midge exchanged greetings with most of them, as well as with the waitress and the young counter-girl. Although she was intelligent and remarkably quick-witted, Midge was still young enough and unsophisticated enough to derive considerable satisfaction from the admiring and interested looks directed at her companions. Casting an encompassing glance around the room, she realized that they were drawing the same half-envious, half-fascinated attention that had been centered on them the evening before at the Tidal Inlet.

"Midge? Something wrong?" Ez's rumble came from above her right ear, and she tilted her head back to look up at him.

"Not really. It's just . . ." She groped for words, trying to explain her sudden uncertainty in a tactful way. "I noticed it last night and now again here—wherever we all go together, everyone seems to stare and . . . well, look at those two girls over there. I went to high school with them, and they're looking at me as if I'd grown two heads."

Ez directed his gaze over her head to the girls, whispering together across a table against the wall, their eyes fixed in obvious envy on the group by the window. Pure mischief lighted his blue-gray eyes as he turned to O'Mara and Kitt and quirked an eyebrow. Midge watched curiously as the three exchanged silent messages, devilry dancing in their eyes, and then leaned back in their chairs and toasted each other with their coffee cups.

"I'm going to have to run as soon as we eat." Ez's hearty tones bounced off the walls of the small room. "We should make some plans for next weekend, so I'll know what clothes to bring with me."

"Will you be here in time for dinner Friday?" Kitt's clear alto easily carried to the openly listening ears of the other patrons. At Ez's nod, she continued, "Why don't we plan on going somewhere special, then? Midge and I are going to have a busy week, and we won't feel like cooking at the end of it." She turned to O'Mara with a blatantly seductive smile and smoky eyes that raised the pulse rate of the four men watching from the counter.

Midge's eyes were wide with delighted fascination as she realized what they were doing, and she fought to hold back a giggle as O'Mara's heartstoppingly sensual smile and deep purr of "Of course we'll take you out, love" brought a flush to Kitt's cheeks and audible moans from at least three of the enthralled women in their captive audience.

Moving his arm from the back of Kitt's chair to her shoulders, he pulled her closer and kissed the corner of her mouth. With obvious effort, he tore his eyes away from her and smiled warmly at Midge. "What do you think, Midge? The Standish Reef at Cape Elizabeth? If I call today, we should be able to get a window table."

"Oh, yes," Midge exclaimed happily, picking up her cue without losing a beat. "That view over the ledges when there's a good surf is incredible, and they've got a great group playing in the lounge." She looked up at Ez with an impish grin. "We can dance after dinner."

There was a moment of silence while her tall companions tried to envision tiny Midge dancing with Ez.

"It boggles the mind," O'Mara groaned.

"Stilts, maybe?" Kitt offered.

"Dancing is an overrated sport," Ez proclaimed. "We'll sit in a dark corner and neck." The comment set them all laughing and brought shocked gasps from several of their audience.

Midge dug an elbow into his ribs and hissed "Ez!" Enclosing the back of her head in one large hand, he leaned over and stage-whispered in her ear, "Don't worry, honey, we'll save the heavy stuff for when I take you home." Since Ez's idea of a whisper could easily be heard in the kitchen over the rattle of pans, it was little wonder that Midge's ex-schoolmates were staring in open-mouthed, goggle-eyed dismay and envy.

Making a quick decision in favor of savoir faire, Midge shrugged nonchalantly and caroled, "Promises, promises."

Before Ez could say anything even more outrageous, the waitress arrived with their breakfasts, and they all settled down to concentrate on hot muffins, cheese and fresh mushroom or sausage omelettes, O'Brien potatoes, ham steaks and thick slices of toasted homemade honey-wheat bread. They shared a pitcher of orange juice and jars of marmalade and blueberry preserves.

"Good cook," said Ez, buttering a muffin thick with blueberries.

"All the baked stuff is made here," Midge explained.

"This omelette is super," Kitt murmured. "So are the potatoes. Ez! Don't pig the ham. Let me try some. Ummm. Mustard."

O'Mara watched her enjoyment with a fond smile. "This is the best place for breakfast for miles around." He eyed Midge's plate and asked off-handedly, "Is that a sausage omelette? How is it?"

"Scrumptious. But I'll never finish it all." She looked up at him hesitantly. No matter what Ez and Kitt called him, she was very much aware that this incredibly sexy and famous man who seemed to want to share her breakfast was actually *the* Michael Talbot. A quick glance around showed her that no one had left the restaurant; they all seemed to be held enthralled by the four people at the window table. She looked back at O'Mara's questioning expression and offered, "Would you like some of it?"

"Thought you'd never ask." His warm smile flashed white against his early tan as he held his plate out to Midge.

"What about me?" Ez asked plaintively.

"If you eat any more, old son, you'll flatten every tire on your wagon," teased O'Mara. "Kitt, grab that last muffin before he gets it. We'll split it. Do you want some, Midge?"

"Uh-uh. I'm stuffed. We've got Friday night taken care of, but what about the rest of the weekend? There's a really good theater company doing *The Taming of the Shrew* at the Civic Center in Portland on Saturday evening. How about that?"

"Sounds good," said Ez, splitting a villainous look between Midge and Kitt. "We might pick up some useful ideas, don't you think, O'Mara?"

The bright blue eyes flashed an amused look at a scowling Kitt, then flicked to a bristling Midge before returning to Ez's anticipatory expression. "No comment. You can easily hold that one at arm's length where she can't do any damage, but this one is definitely a challenge to control without acquiring dents, bruises and a lump or two. Feisty, both of them, but a gentle hand on the reins—"

Kitt and Midge groaned in unison and muttered "Chauvinists!" in identically disgusted tones.

Still grinning, O'Mara turned around to locate the waitress

and signal for more coffee. Unobtrusively, he noted the interested observers and deliberately let his voice out as he turned back to the table and said, "That takes care of Friday and Saturday evenings, and Sunday we'll have a cookout at my place."

He might as well have dropped a bomb in the middle of the room. As friendly and unassuming as Michael Talbot was with the townsfolk, it was widely known that he guarded his privacy, and only close friends were invited to his home on Crest Rock. He met Midge's stunned gaze and winked at her.

"Oh, wow," she breathed. "Wait till my sister Angie hears this."

Shaking his head at her dazed expression, Ez said to O'Mara, "You really must explain this dumbstruck awe that you seem to inspire in the female population around here."

O'Mara laughed and slanted a look at Kitt. "I'd like to see the day I inspire awe in this one." Turning to Ez, he continued, "Next weekend, while the girls are working, we'll have an enlightening discussion of the advantages and disadvantages of fame and fortune."

"Sounds promising, but if I don't get a move on, I'm going to be late."

Midge, Kitt and O'Mara waved Ez off outside the restaurant and then walked the short distance to the shop. After they left the restaurant, Ez had capped their virtuoso performance by picking Midge up, in front of the wide window in full view of their audience, and kissing her long and thoroughly. Since she was still a bit unsteady on her feet, Kitt and O'Mara tucked her in between them and guided her steps in the right direction.

"Love this square," commented Kitt, looking around at the buildings. "Such a wild mix of styles, from eighteenth-century no-nonsense to Victorian kitsch to a twentieth-century brick block, and everything in between. I really must take time to go through some of those books on local history."

"*Not* any of *my* time," O'Mara stated firmly. "We've got too much catching up to do. However, you can make a start this evening because I've got a long-standing commitment to speak to a literary club in Portland, and these things usually drag on forever."

"Much as I like your company, I won't pine for you tonight. I'm going to bed early to catch up on my sleep."

"We could shift off today, and each get a nap," Midge piped up hopefully.

"Don't put temptation in my way," Kitt groaned. "You *know* what a mess we left the shop in last night. And we've got to get that order ready for me to take to Portsmouth. Oh, drat! I forgot to ask Ez if he could leave the wagon here next weekend and take my car back with him."

"What do you need the wagon for?" O'Mara asked.

"Next week is the first week of the month, and piles of new releases will be out. I've got to pick up a stock of them, together with backlist stock, from the distributor in Portsmouth. There's no way all that will fit in my Camaro."

They crunched across the parking lot and waited while Kitt unlocked the shop door. O'Mara trailed Kitt and Midge inside. Midge promptly busied herself in the back, leaving the couple alone. "Listen, love, there's no way I want you to be heaving around cartons of books, either. Can't you go this week? I could borrow a van or a trailer and go with you."

"I'd still have to go back next week. Over half of what we need, the current stuff, won't be in the warehouse until then. Can't you—Oh, I forgot. Your European trip. When do you leave?"

"Next Tuesday. A week from tomorrow. So don't make plans for any evenings this week. I want to spend as much time with you as I can before I leave. That's going to be a long couple of weeks."

"I thought you said you'd be gone two and a half weeks."

"Not if I can help it. It depends on how long it takes me to track down three of the people I want to see. They tend to move around a lot and keep low profiles."

"Until you explained the background of this new book last night, I never realized how involved research could be. I wish—" She broke off, biting her lip and looking at him longingly. Part of her wanted to tease him into putting off the trip; after twelve years apart, she didn't want to lose another day of being with him, talking with him, touching him and, most of all, continuing the progress they were obviously making in overcoming her fear of his touch. Sliding her hands under the edge of his sweater, she pressed her palms and wide-spread fingers over the warm, smooth skin at his waist, watching the quick flare of desire flash in his eyes. She sensed that if she asked, he'd change his plans, and she swayed toward him, her mouth lifting to touch his, the words "Don't go" on her lips.

She didn't say them. The pressure of his mouth stopped them, and then she forgot them as she seemed to forget everything when he kissed her. His hands resting lightly on her shoulders gently urged her closer, and she pressed her suddenly taut breasts against his chest, opening her mouth to his softly probing tongue and sliding her hands around to his back, feeling the tremors shivering through him in reaction to her touch.

Revelation hit her with the impact of a Force-Ten gale, sweeping every other thought out of her head. *I have as much power over him as he has over me. At the moment, maybe more.* Slowly, hesitantly, she moved her head back, gradually breaking the kiss, and looked at him, reading the need and passion in his face and eyes.

"Kitt? What is it?"

"I—" She dropped her head onto his shoulder. "Just wait a minute, please."

"All right, love. Take your time." Stroking soothing hands back and forth across her shoulders, he stood relaxed, taking some of her weight as she leaned lightly against him.

The thoughts jumbled through her mind, and she strove desperately to sort them out and make sense of this new knowledge. *Except this shouldn't come as such a surprise. It's been perfectly obvious that I excite him. I know how much control . . . well, not know, exactly . . . more like I've sensed that he's been clamping an iron hold over his passion and trying to keep his physical arousal under control. He's afraid of scaring me, but it's gotten away from him a couple of times. Last night and this morning. But he's been so careful that I just didn't realize how strong his reaction to me is. I could feel it, really feel it, just then. That same fire jolting through him that I feel when he touches me. Why didn't I know that? After that incredible oneness that we experienced on the beach, I should have known . . . but he's so much more . . . what? . . . self-confident, surer of himself as a man, stronger . . . than he used to be . . . but he was always sure of himself . . . and strong . . . now he really knows who and what he is. It fooled me. So strong, I never realized that I could send him up in flames just as fast as he does it to me. Can I?*

She didn't think about it any longer, just followed her instincts. Turning her head, she nibbled kisses up the side of his neck as she took half a step forward and brought the rest of her body, from thigh to belly, tight against his. He wasn't expecting it and had no time to control his reaction. Before she could draw in her breath, his hands were curving over her buttocks, pulling her hips into the surge of his groin.

"My God! What are you doing?" The deep groan in her ear vibrated through her, shocking her to awareness, and she jerked away from him to stand, hands clapped over her mouth, staring at him in wide-eyed dismay. *Oh, dear God. Did I really do that? I couldn't have!* She watched him fight for control, his head bent, hands clasped around his neck, a long, shuddering breath rasping through his chest.

After what seemed like an hour, but was only a minute or two, his head came up and his questioning eyes met her half-fearful ones. "Don't look so scared, love. I'm perfectly all right and not the least bit upset. Just curious." He tucked his fingers into the front pockets of his jeans and shifted his weight to stand hip-shot and relaxed. "You took me completely by surprise, or I would have had better control."

"It's not . . . I'm not scared. At least, not by anything you did. It's just . . . I don't believe I did that. I just realized that . . . oh, it sounds so . . . something . . . to say it straight out."

"Never mind what it sounds like. Tell me."

"It sounds dumb and stupid. I can't believe I was so wrapped up in myself that I didn't realize how you felt. But . . . it just came to me when you were kissing me that I could . . . what is it the kids say? Light your fire? . . . just as you do to me. Each time you've kissed me, you've been keeping so much control over yourself, right from the beginning, that it seemed to take you even longer than it did me to . . . well, I just hadn't understood that—" She stumbled to a stop and looked at him with troubled eyes.

"Silly wench." The tension started to leave her face as he smiled at her. "Lest there be any further doubts in your sometimes fuzzy head, let me assure you that you don't have to go to all those lengths to find out how much I want you or how quickly I react to you. If I hadn't been sitting down in the restaurant when you gave me that very sexy, how-soon-can-we-find-a-bed smile, I'd have embarrassed both of us. Haven't you had any idea of the agony I've been suffering trying to keep a lid on all my natural instincts and needs where you're concerned?"

"I . . . I sensed some of it, but I guess I've been so busy worrying about my own reactions and not being able to be—Oh, damn. I love you so much, and I should have *known* what was happening with you."

He closed the distance between them and took her hands, raising them to kiss one and then the other before sliding them around his neck. Holding her eyes with his, he lightly traced his fingers down her arms, over her ribs, and brought them to rest on her hips.

"Your eyes have dark smudges, and you're too tired to think straight. You've got the rest of the day to get through, and this is no time to start an in-depth analysis of our emotional states or anything else. Mmmm. I like that. Feels good. Since you like playing with my hair so much, isn't it lucky I've got all this fur all over me? As I recall, you always did have a thing about it."

"I used to wonder—"

"No!" He cut her off abruptly, but there was a glint of mischief in his eyes. "Don't tell me now. Save it for when you can show me what you used to wonder. At the moment, I couldn't cope with your erotic imaginings. Oh, love, are you blushing? There's nothing wrong with that—just as long as I'm the one you're dreaming about."

"O'Mara. . . ." Her voice was a husky, pleading whisper, and she pulled his head down so she could reach his mouth.

"No more now, love." His voice was muffled against her mouth, his words interspersed with quick, light kisses. "If we don't . . . stop this . . . your early customers . . . are going to . . . get the shock of their . . . lives when . . . they walk in that door."

"I don't care."

"Kitt!" Laughing, he pulled her arms down and held her away from him. "Behave yourself, Griselda, or I'll turn back into a toad. Damn, look at the time. I've got to get back to the house and make some phone calls. If I don't try the overseas ones before noon, I'll miss their afternoon office hours."

"Okay," she sighed. "If you've got to go, I suppose I can manage. But just barely. If you have to go to Portland this evening, when am I going to see you?"

He started walking toward the door with her, one arm draped loosely around her shoulders. "I'll probably be late getting back, so I won't see you until sometime tomorrow. I'll call you in the morning. No, wait. You take Hero for a run early on, don't you? What time? I'll try to go with you."

"Seven? Eight? What's comfortable for you?"

"Somewhere in there. Can you just wait until I get here?"

"Sure. With a pot of coffee?"

"Sounds good." He glanced back over the shop, a slight frown between his eyes. "Where's Midge? I should at least say goodbye."

"Probably curled up in a corner somewhere, asleep." Kitt chuckled. "I'll pass it along."

Opening the door with his free hand, he pulled her close with the arm around her shoulders and kissed her briefly.

"O'Mara. . . ." It was a protest, asking for more.

"Not now, you witch, or I'll never get out of here. Get some rest. I'll see you in the morning."

Chapter 13

Kitt stacked the last of the dishes in the drainer and tipped the sudsy water out of the small dishpan, rinsed it and leaned it upside-down against the side of the sink to dry. Yawning and stretching, she padded barefoot across the kitchen and into the living room. She wandered aimlessly over to the window-wall and stood, hands tucked into the back pockets of her navy cord jeans, watching the boats surging upriver to their docks and moorings.

She was tired. The day had seemed to drag on forever, and that, she thought, undoubtedly had a great deal to do with the fact that she wouldn't see O'Mara tonight. She and Midge had spent a couple of hours putting the shop back together, and then worked halfheartedly through the afternoon on the stock order. Fortunately, it had been a slow day for customers. Not that I welcome the lack of income, she mused, but neither of us was in top form for answering questions intelligently.

The movement of the water, glittering and flashing in the light from the lowering sun, was hypnotic, and she tore her eyes away from the river to scan the evening sky. Should be a great sunset, she decided. Those clouds feathering across the western sky are going to pick up lots of color, and there'll be a lovely reflection on the ones overhead and to the southeast. I should be comfortable enough on the deck with my heavy jacket . . . another cup of coffee . . . boots.

Trailed by Hero, she detoured through the kitchen to put the kettle on and then started hunting for her fleece-lined ankle boots, first in her bedroom and then back to the hall closet, finally locating them under the sofa.

"I wish you could tell one pair of footgear from another, Hero. It would save me enormous amounts of time if I could just send you to find these things. No. Let go, beast. This is not a game, and that's not your shoe. Yours is under my bed."

Still sitting on the floor by the sofa, she pulled the boots on over her bare feet, elbowing a playful Hero out of her way. She glanced out the window at the sky and, noting touches of color on the clouds, rose to her feet and hurriedly fixed a mug of instant decaffeinated coffee, grabbed her sheepskin-lined suede jacket from the closet and dragged a captain's chair out to the deck. By the time she was settled with her feet up on the railing and the warm mug cradled in her hands, the first fragile colors of the sunset were just beginning to tint the clouds.

With a warning "Mewf," Hero jumped into her lap and stretched out along her legs. Kitt automatically stroked one hand along his back, her eyes and attention fixed on the gradually changing colors in the sky. More clouds had appeared, and now there was a rising broken band of them spreading in an arc from east to south, glowing rose and pale pink from the reflection of the setting sun. Her head tipped back as she followed the drift of clouds across the dome of the sky, the pinks shading to lavender where the clouds were wispy against the blue background until, high in the western sky, the wash of pale lemon began. It brightened and intensified to deep yellow and glowing gold as her eyes scanned down the plumy clouds to where their lower edges blazed with a molten, white-gold fire.

Flickering light caught her attention, and she dropped her eyes to the river, now a swift, shimmering rush of blazing orange. It drew her gaze back to its origin in the west, and she watched the deepening flames of color spread upward, lightening to peach and rose-gold in the eastern and southern skies. Suddenly, the very air around her turned pale peach, and she looked from side to side to find that the immediate world was lit with an intense, pale gold glow. It created an otherworldly feeling, distorting the normal perception of color and distance, fuzzing sharp edges and changing the familiar shapes of trees and fences into something dimly seen in a dream.

Enchanted, Kitt gazed around at what seemed to be a fairy-tale land, hushed and waiting under a spell, its eerie silence unbroken even by the usual screaming of the gulls. After long minutes, the light started to fade through all the pastel shades of orange and yellow until it was gone and, with what almost seemed to be a jolt, the world returned to its proper dimensions and colors.

Drawing in a deep breath, Kitt lifted dazzled eyes to the sky and, still in a state of wonder, watched the sweeping, tumbling cloud formations shade and blend in ever-changing tones of yellow, orange, rose, red, scarlet, lavender, orchid, purple and brilliant silver-gold until, finally, the spectacle ended with an intense display of magenta flame filling the western horizon.

Kitt sighed, feeling peaceful, relaxed and content, as she watched the dark river that was barely discernible in the dying light of dusk. Somehow, the awesome display of Nature's power and magic had reduced all her problems to insignificance, while at the same time reinforcing her faith in the strength of the love and trust between O'Mara and herself. Everything had suddenly been refined and reduced to one simple fact: their coming together and their sharing of the rest of their lives were as natural, inevitable and magnificent as that sunset.

Huddled in her warm jacket, with Hero's body heat

keeping the cold from at least part of her legs, she lingered on the deck for another quarter-hour watching the clouds drifting across the starlit night sky. At last, the chilly dampness rising from the river drove her inside. Shrugging out of her jacket, she shivered in the cool room and pulled an Aran sweater on over her blue and white Oxford-cloth shirt. She'd forgotten about the coffee, and it had gone cold. Since she had to stay up until at least ten so she could take Hero out, she headed for the kitchen for another mug, flicking up the thermostat a couple of degrees as she passed it.

Her mood was a strange mingling of tranquil acceptance of the truth of O'Mara and herself and an exaltation welling through her as the vision of the sunset lingered in her mind. Flicking through the stereo cassettes, she pulled out *Northland Rhapsody* and slotted it into the player, settling at one end of the sofa to sip her coffee and listen to the evocative music of the mysterious North Country. She leaned her head back and closed her eyes, envisioning the endless green sweep of the deep woods broken only by roiling rivers and clear lakes reflecting the intense blue of a smogless sky. The character of the music changed, sending the chill of glaciers and mountain snowfields shivering up her spine before sliding into a haunting, desolate evocation of the barren, icy wastes of the Arctic. Kitt was lost in the intensity of the shifting moods of the music until she became aware of the tears on her cheeks as the final passage began—the impression of the eerie, sibilant, rising and fading, unearthly singing of the Northern Lights.

The music ended, but she sat unmoving, her mind filled with the mystery and wonder of the strange song of the heavens. She'd read about the phenomenon in a variety of books and articles on the Far North, and knew that there was considerable controversy over it. Many who had lived all their lives in that harsh country swore that the Lights had never made a sound, but others vowed with equal vehemence that they had heard them more than once and had even produced tape recordings.

Dreamily, she envisioned O'Mara and herself standing in a snowfield, watching the dancing Lights filling the sky and listening to the mystical music. Oh, you daft wench, she chided, the man has got you in a rare fine state. Next, you'll be dreaming of getting away from it all in a hideaway in the mid-Atlantic trench! What's a little problem like breathing under water? After all, love conquers all! Nut! You're a total nut, Kitt Tate.

Jumping up, she shook off her fanciful imaginings and strode briskly to the kitchen, forcing away tiredness for a while as she fixed another mug of coffee, inspected cabinets and refrigerator, and made a shopping list. Remembering O'Mara's promise to spend as much time as possible with her, she smiled to herself and went back over the list, adding here and increasing quantities there. She checked it over again, trying to recall his preferences in those distant summers, and found herself, instead, picturing Gus.

Boys were easy. She quickly added chocolate chips, brown sugar, nuts, oatmeal, a large jar of peanut butter, baking chocolate, preserves and more fruit. Flipping open cupboard doors, she rechecked her stock of flour, sugar and shortening. Enough for now, she decided. If I run out, I can always pick some up later in the week. Hope he's planning on Gus being with us some of these evenings. Can't wait to get to know him better. Oh, he's such a delight! And that budding sense of humor. He's going to be as quick-witted as his father.

She wandered back to the sofa and sat down, leaning forward with her elbows on her knees, her hands stroking Hero as he stood between her feet. "You like him, too, don't you? Did you have a good time the other night with Gus?"

At the sound of the boy's name, Hero cocked his head inquiringly and wagged his tightly curled tail. "Rrorrf?"

"Right. Gus. I think you've found a new best friend, haven't you? You won't even have time to miss Ez."

"Arrarow rarroo."

"O'Mara likes you, too. In fact, dog, you're going to end up with more attention than you'll know what to do with. That might almost apply to me, too. I've got a strong hunch that that man is going to insinuate himself into every nook and cranny of my life."

"Oouooar raoowr."

"I know. You're absolutely right. It's not such a bad thing, maybe. But I think, after a while, when we've gotten used to being together again and I've overcome this damn panic about sex, we're going to have to work something out. I'm not the kind of woman to live only through a man. I've got to have something for myself, something that's my own achievement." With her hands on either side of his head, fingers rubbing behind his ears, she tipped the dog's face up to hers. "Do you think he'll be able to understand that, my Hero?"

"Raar arro-woow."

"Hmmm. Maybe. He's a very together man, and he doesn't need to prove anything by submerging my identity in his. However, he does have a tendency to make all the decisions and, one way or another, get me to go along. There's just so much of this it's-for-your-own-good stuff that's valid. Some of it's okay, but not all the time about every little thing. Maybe, right now, it's just overreaction or overpossessiveness because we're together again so unexpectedly. I suppose that was as much of a shock to him as it was to me. And I certainly feel possessive about him. Strange, that. I'm not the possessive type. At least, I never thought I was, but I sure didn't like all those drooly women hanging on him in that lounge."

"Maarroo?"

"No, not yet. First things first. The most important project at the moment is to get rid of my damn trauma. And we do seem to be making some progress. Wonder if he had time today to call his friend about that. Although his own system seems to be working rather well."

She turned her wrist to check the time. "Close enough, Hero. Come on, out we go, but make it fast. No long rambles tonight. I've got to get some sleep."

With Hero's cooperation and a bare minimum of bedtime routine, Kitt was sound asleep within half an hour. It would have taken a lot more to awaken her than the faint clicks at the deck door three hours later or Hero's light bound off the foot of the bed or the hushing whisper and soft rustling beside the bed. She stirred but still didn't wake when the long body eased down beside her and stretched out full length along her left side, not quite touching her as she lay on her back with the bedclothes pushed down to her waist.

There was enough light coming in the big bay window from the streetlights and a half-moon to show the dark head propped on one hand as he watched the sleeping woman. Perhaps sensing something different, she sighed and turned her face toward him but continued sleeping. His gaze moved over her face in a loving examination, noting how much younger she looked with the relaxation of tension that always seemed to be hovering over her. In the dim light, her lashes were a smudge against the high cheekbones, and the wide mouth was soft, the lips slightly parted. The corners of his lips twitched in amusement as his eyes shifted down and he took in the plain, no-frills, silk pajama jacket. Slowly, taking care not to touch her, his steady fingers deftly slid the buttons from their holes until his progress was halted by the folded-back blanket. It was enough. With thumb and index finger, he pulled gently on the pale green silk until it slid far enough to the side to uncover her left breast.

His finger was feather-light as it started trailing a circling path around the soft, slightly flattened mound. His eyes were intently watching her lashes as his finger reached her tautening nipple and started teasing it. At the first flickering movement of awakening, he gently closed his hand over her breast and leaned to rest his mouth against hers, slowly stroking the tip of his tongue between her lips.

The first faint pings of warning never made it out of her subconscious. Probably because they weren't very strong. After all, nothing truly threatening had happened. No thuds, crashes or shatterings. No snarls, howls or yells. Just a vague, barely perceived feeling that something was . . . odd, out of the normal, unfamiliar. The tiny tickle of strangeness did no more than cause a sigh and a slight shifting of her head.

The dream drifted in like a zephyr, a brushing of soft wings across her breast, a breath of warm air on her face. Butterflies. A lovely iridescent blue and green one settled on her breast and tiptoed around, climbing to the peak where it hovered fluttering the fragile edge of its wing against the tight nipple. It tickled. And there was something else, a . . . something . . . a presence . . . nearby. What? Must wake up and move the butterfly. So beautiful. Wake up now. Now. Oh.

Kitt's eyes opened wide, straining to see, as consciousness crept into her mind. Somebody. Man. Mouth. Hand. Her body knew instinctively before her mind was aware, and her back arched to the warm hand, her mouth opened for the seeking tongue and one of her hands moved to bury itself in the soft, thick hair. Her eyes recognized the shape of his head, her nose knew his scent and her mouth welcomed the familiar tongue. Questions fluttered through her mind, but they didn't seem important at the moment. Only the heat and need rising in her were real. She struggled to free her left hand, trapped under the covers. She wanted to touch him, to hold him in both hands, to—

"Mmmmm. I must wake you up more often."

"O'Mara?"

"It better not be anyone else."

"Where did you—How did you get in? What time is it?"

"One-thirty, and I picked the lock."

"How?"

"Easily. I'll show you sometime."

"Ohhh-oh. That feels good. O'Mara?"

"Mmmm?"

"Why are we whispering?"

"So we won't wake Hero."

"Some watchdog. He usually wakes me if anyone sets foot on the place."

"He's a brilliant dog. Knows just who belongs here. He met me at the door and led me right to your bed. Turn on your side, love, facing me."

"But—"

"No problem. I can play with the other one."

"Are you laughing at me? Beast. It's just that it feels nice."

"Only nice?"

"Weellll . . . Very nice? Oh!"

"Oh, indeed. Told you it was no problem. That's one thing that's helpful about having a matched pair."

"You pick . . . the damnedest times . . . ohh . . . to . . . tease."

"Who's teasing?"

"O'Maraaa . . . oh, yes . . . don't stop."

"Easy, love. You're going to take out a handful of hair in a minute. Mmmm. Wait. Can't you take this thing off?"

"I—"

"It's all right. You don't have to if it makes you nervous."

"N-no. I'm not. . . . You won't hold me down, will you?"

"Uh-uh. We'll stay like this. You can move away whenever you want to. All right? Are you afraid?"

"Not like this. Touch me again?"

"Like this?"

"Oh, yes. Yes."

"Ken was right. Great minds."

"What?"

"I called Ken Thorp this afternoon, and we had a long talk about how to cope with your . . . our problem."

"What did he say? Ahhh, if you keep doing that, I'm not going to be able to concentrate on this discussion."

"Yes, you can. It's all part of the program. Why don't you let go of my hair for a minute . . . what is this thing you've got about hanging onto fistfuls of hair, love? . . . and unbutton my shirt."

"I like the feel of your hair, that's what. Are you sure about this?"

"Mmm-hmm. Ken says that I've started out right, getting you used to my touch, but that things will probably go faster if we distract your attention from what *my* hands are doing by talking about something else and, at the same time, keeping *your* hands busy with their own concerns."

"So I won't have time to worry about what you might do?"

"Something like that. Except that you shouldn't worry about it anyway. You *know* I'm not going to do anything you won't like or that will frighten you. It's a matter of . . . mmm . . . programming. Getting you so used to my touch, in a totally nonthreatening and natural way, that you'll actually miss it when I'm not with you."

"I miss it now. I mean, I did tonight."

"Not as much as you're going to."

"What else did he say? What about being able to hold me?"

"Not yet. In fact, he said that I shouldn't even try. He thinks we should . . . what are you doing?"

"I love the fur on your chest. It's so soft. Ez's is rough and so was—I've always liked your pelt. Remember?"

"Oh, indeed I do. All right. Help yourself. It goes right along with Ken's suggestion, in fact."

"What suggestion?"

"He thinks we should come at this from two directions. Both of them are going to call for a lot of trust on your part, absolute blind faith that I'm going to keep control no matter what either of us does. Do you understand, love? You've got to believe it without question or the slightest shadow of doubt."

"And then what?"

"Look at me. Can you do it? Have that kind of faith in me?"

"Of course. I'm here, aren't I? I'm lying on this bed with you, and you've got your hand on my breast and I'm touching you, and I'm not panicking."

"And that covers both directions. Ken said that we should work on getting you used to my hands, just as I explained a few minutes ago, and at the same time you should try to let yourself go and . . . well, take the lead. Touch me, put your arms around me, kiss me, whatever you want to do . . . or feel like doing . . . or want me to do. You'll set the pace, but I'll encourage you to go a little bit further each time. And always we'll stop when you say so, the second you start feeling uneasy or afraid."

"Do you think it will work?"

"Yes. It may take a while, but I'm sure it's the answer. Can you do it?"

"Oh, yes. I'm sure I can. And I'm certain it will work. It's got to."

"Don't push it, though. Just let it happen naturally."

"I am. What's that?"

"A scar. Nothing much. Just a scratch. Ahh, if you're going to explore my ribs, use a firmer touch, love. That tickles."

"O'Mara? This isn't going to be easy for you, is it? I mean—"

"I know exactly what you mean. No, it isn't going to be easy in some ways. I want you more than you can begin to imagine, and it's going to be hell to keep all that tamped down. On the other hand, I love to touch you and to feel your hands on me, and I'm cherishing the thought that all my extraordinary self-control is going to be well rewarded in the near future. You *are* going to make all this up to me, aren't you, my love?"

"Mmmm. I'm sure to think of something. There must be a book or two of helpful suggestions downstairs."

"Witch. Never mind your damn books. I'll teach you anything you want to know, and probably quite a few things you'd never think of by yourself."

"Promises, promises. Aaaiie. Ohh. Yes. Yes."

"Strange. Why do your breasts taste like lemons?"

"My soap. Sometimes it's heather. Do it some more. Please."

"Greedy . . . I remember . . . once I started this, before, you didn't want to . . . let me stop."

"I still don't. Why are you?"

"So you can kiss me. This is supposed to be a group participation effort."

"Two isn't a group. Mmm. *You* taste like lime."

"Aftershave. Three is a group. Open your mouth, love, and stop talking."

"Uummm."

"Now what?"

"Who's the third?"

"Hero. He's curled up against my legs. Stop laughing, wench."

"I love you. My personal toad-prince."

"You're getting giddy. I knew I shouldn't start kissing your breasts."

"Yes, you should. In fact, you should do it more often."

"I will. Now what are you doing? Oh, love, if you're going to start undressing me, we're going to have a problem."

"Just your shirt. I want . . . mmmm . . . that. Your fur is like silk . . . tiny feathers of silk . . . against my breasts."

"Is your fur like silk?"

"I don't have—Oh!"

"Never mind. One of these nights, I'll find out for myself. Mmmm. Was that a tease, or are you really going to kiss me?"

"Does that answer your question? Are you all right?"

"No. You're driving me slowly out of my mind doing that."

"Don't you like it?"

"Mmm. Love it. But you're still giving me a temperature, between rubbing your breasts across my chest and adventuring all over the place with your busy tongue—"

"It's just your neck . . . and your ear. . . ."

"And my mouth and my shoulder. What are you doing now?"

"The blanket's in the way."

"Leave it there. Kitt!"

"But I want—"

"I know what you want, love, but let's not put too much strain on my willpower. Just leave the blanket where it is, you under it and me on top of it. A nice safe arrangement."

"O'Mara? I think I could—"

"No, you can't. And you're not going to try. Not yet. Thank you for the thought, though, love."

"Oh, damn. None of this is fair to you at all. And what if it makes you sick?"

"Kitt! For godsake, where do you get these ideas? I'm all right. At least, I will be as long as you stay under that blanket."

"But—"

"I am not going to get sick from a little abstinence."

"A lot."

"Okay, a lot of abstinence. I'm still not going to get sick. Where do you get such weird ideas?"

"I probably read it somewhere."

"Stop reading about sex. If you want to know something, ask me. If I can't demonstrate it, at least I can explain it."

"Okay. Why can't I—"

"No. Not tonight. I already told you—Oh, you witch, are you ever going to pay for all this. Come on, now. Kiss me goodnight. I've got to get home, or I'll never make it back here by eight."

"Why go home? You can stay here."

"You're out of your tiny mind. If you think for one minute that I could sleep with you and not—"

"I'm not totally stupid, toad-prince. You can sleep in Ez's room. What time is it? You won't get any sleep at all by the time you go home and then come back. It's ridiculous."

"Mmmm. Maybe. It's almost three. Lord, have we really been here that long? You do have a way of making time fly, my Kitt."

"We're both mad. At this rate, I'll probably get rid of my kink because I'll be too tired to panic."

"That's not my main worry, you dingbat. If this is the method we've got to use, by the time I can make love with you, we'll have to spend that week in bed catching up on our sleep. And that's not at all what I have in mind."

"With your deviously inventive imagination, I have every

confidence that you'll come up with a solution. Are you sure you don't want to sleep here?"

"Positive. It's impossible. Ummm. Very nice. Now, right now, let me up."

"I'm not the least bit afraid yet. Not a twinge."

"You've got all the makings of a wanton, love. Not that I mind, as long as you confine your experiments to me, but . . . stop it, you tease . . . that's enough for now."

"My, but you move fast, O'Mara. A regular hoppy toad. Aren't you going to kiss me goodnight?"

"I just did, and that's all you're getting for at least the next five hours. Does Ez have any pajamas? And is there a lock on that door?"

"Why do you need—"

"I want to make sure you stay in your own bed."

"O'Mara! It's not funny. As if I'd—Well, maybe I would at that. All right, all right, I'll stay here. There are some pajama bottoms in the second drawer of his bureau. Don't ask me where the tops are. I think he throws them away."

"Goodnight, love. Ahhh, you'd better put that back on before you get cold. 'Night, Hero."

"Good morning, toad-prince. Don't worry, I'll wake you up by eight."

"Why do I sense a threat in that? If you dump cold water on me, I'll blister your butt."

"Would I do anything so obvious?"

"Much as I love you, there are moments when I don't trust your weird sense of humor an inch. In your own delightful way, you're every bit as crazy as Ez."

"Hold the thought. 'Night, O'Mara."

Chapter 14

Tousle-haired and sleepy-eyed, Kitt leaned in the doorway of Ez's room with Hero cradled in her arms and lovingly watched O'Mara sleep. Only half-awake, her instincts and inclination urged her to join him on the big bed. The strong, tanned expanse of bare back practically cried out to be stroked, and she wondered if the rest of him were naked, too, under the sheet tangled around his hips and legs. Maybe he hadn't bothered trying to find pajama pants, especially if he didn't usually wear them. Somehow, she rather thought he slept in the raw, and she leaned hard against the doorjamb as her knees weakened at the vision of the two of them spending endless nights naked in each other's arms.

God. The man is turning my mind to mush. She straightened up, mentally kicking herself, and decided firmly that what they both needed was a strong dose of fresh air and exercise. Slowly and silently, she moved to the foot of the bed and carefully set Hero down.

"Wake him."

She leaped back to the doorway as Hero's banshee howl echoed around the room.

"What the hell!?" By the time the second word was out, O'Mara was off the bed and crouched in the middle of the floor, blinking around for the source of the unearthly ululations. It took only seconds for him to add Hero to a laughing Kitt and come up with—

"Wake up call!" trilled Kitt, and then dissolved in giggles as she spun around and dove for the bathroom with O'Mara one jump behind her. She flipped the lock on the door just as his palm hit it, and she leaned back against it, laughing.

"Damn your eyes, woman. That's a hell of a way to wake a man out of a sound sleep. It's a wonder I didn't crack my spine."

"I knew you wouldn't," she called through the door. It sounded as if he were leaning on the other side of it, she thought. "I wake Ez up like that all the time, and you're in every bit as good shape as he is."

"I think I'd have preferred the cold water," he said in a disgusted voice.

"But I didn't want a blistered butt," she protested.

"You may get one anyhow," he growled. There was a pause, and she could hear him laughing softly. "Kitt? I'll forgive you. Open up. We'll take a shower, and you can scrub my back in atonement."

She turned her head so her mouth was next to the edge of the door. "Mmmm," she purred. "It truly is a fascinating offer, but I'm not going to take a shower right now. I'll wait until we get back from running."

"Coward. How will I get my back scrubbed?"

"I've got a nice extra-long-handled bath brush. Don't go away. I'll only be a few minutes."

"Wait! Kitt? I've only got the suit I wore last night. Did Ez leave any clothes here? Jeans or something?"

"Yeah. All kinds of stuff. I think there's a couple of warm-up suits in there, too. Help yourself."

Within half an hour, they were in the Mercedes on their way to Beach Avenue. Kitt glanced over at O'Mara, thinking how easily they had meshed their morning routine. While Kitt brushed her hair and her teeth and had a quick wash, O'Mara had called home to reassure Gus and Andy that he was all right and would be along later. He took over the bathroom, and she started the coffee before scrambling into a smoky blue warm-up suit, which somehow, for all its looseness, seemed to accentuate the slim length of her legs and the firm shape of her breasts.

As she left her room, she could hear him moving around in Ez's room and called, "Coffee's ready. Will toast and strawberry preserves hold you for now?"

"Fine. Be right there." His voice was muffled, and she wondered what he had found to wear.

She had the answer two minutes later when he strolled into the kitchen in a warm-up suit that exactly matched hers.

"Thank heavens for drawstrings. Ez is a couple inches bigger around than I am."

"Mmmmm," she murmured, her eyes fixed on the dark cloud of fur visible where he'd zipped the jacket only halfway up.

"Behave yourself, love," he chided, laughing.

"If I must," she sighed.

"Where is your mind, love?" At the soft question, Kitt blinked and realized that they were stopped beside the beach.

"It was . . . ah . . . um . . . on other things." She tried hard for an insouciant look, but ended up blushing and laughing.

Shaking his head, he gave her a very *male* smile, murmuring, "I *knew* I shouldn't have kissed your breasts."

"O'Mara!"

"Come on, you oversexed wench. Let's run."

It was a beautiful, brisk morning, and they loped easily along Beach Avenue, past Lords Point and out to the end of Great Hill Road before turning and heading back to the car. Kitt recognized several of the morning regulars and smiled a greeting. It was a few minutes before she realized just how much attention they were attracting, and raised a questioning eyebrow at O'Mara.

"I don't usually run along here. And definitely not with a tall, delectable toad-kisser." His grin was pure challenge. "Most particularly not in his-and-her outfits. Add one darling dog, and everyone in town is going to know what's going on by noon."

"I hope Ez's shoes pinch your big toes." She gave him a formidable scowl and stuck out her tongue.

"Hmm. Later, love." He laughed and grabbed her hand, holding it for the rest of the run.

Since Kitt still hadn't food-shopped, he insisted on taking her to breakfast again at the small restaurant in the square. They bantered and laughed their way through omelettes, freshly baked, still-warm cranberry-orange muffins, home fries and grapefruit juice. Over their second cups of coffee, they made tentative plans for the rest of the week.

"Tonight, you and Hero are invited to supper. Andy is agog with anticipation. As might be expected, Ez wrapped her around his little finger Sunday. She was practically panting over him and spent two hours making her special lasagne and a Black Forest cake when he 'just happened' to mention that they were two of his favorite treats."

"He has an appalling effect on older women," said Kitt, straight-faced.

"Women have been spoiling him rotten all his life. I don't

know how he does it. He gets this look on his face, utterly pathetic, that seems to say 'Inside this great, hulking body is a poor, starved little boy,' and they fall all over themselves to feed the poor, deprived mite. Yuck! Stop laughing. That's exactly what he does."

"I know, I know," Kitt gasped. "But I think you're just jealous. Ooo. Brute. Don't grab my knee like that. I take it back. You've got more than your share of females flinging themselves at your feet."

"Mmm. But they aren't offering home-baked goodies," he teased.

"Never you mind," she purred, a challenging gleam in her eyes. "I'll take care of the goodies, home-baked or otherwise."

"I'm counting on it." His smile promised delights that she thought it best not to dwell on at the moment.

At the sound of gasps and a muffled groan from her right, Kitt glanced around to discover four pairs of dazed female eyes fixed on O'Mara. She turned back to watch him curiously to see what he would do.

He directed the smile, now turned down a few notches, toward the young women at the next table, nodded, and murmured a polite "Good morning, girls."

"Oh, subtle. Very subtle," Kitt said, grinning.

Reaching across the table for her hand, he raised it to his mouth and slowly kissed each finger, a wicked glint sparking in the sapphire eyes as he played to his audience. "You give me confidence," he claimed audaciously. "Now that I've got you to protect me from importunate females, I can—"

"You can stop the blarney, O'Mara," she hissed. "You can also stop nibbling on my fingers. Have another muffin. Wicked toad. Behave. You're giving those girls spasms. Oh, damn you."

Resisting all her efforts to pull her hand away, he held it to his mouth while he wrote messages on her palm with his tongue. Stifling a nearly uncontrollable desire to giggle, she didn't even try to decipher his words—the outrageously sensual blaze of his eyes said it all.

"O'Mara!"

He released her hand with obvious reluctance and an unrepentant grin, winking conspiratorily at the fascinated girls.

"You're impossible," Kitt groaned.

"Hmm," he agreed. "Now, about the rest of the week. This is Tuesday. Tomorrow evening we'll leave open until we can talk with Gus, but Thursday evening he's in a school play. You will go with me, won't you?"

"Love to. What's the play and what part does he have?"

"It's something to do with a Little League team facing it's first experience with a girl teammate, and he plays the captain, who doesn't think much of female baseball players. I'm not going to tell you any more, or it will spoil the suspense."

"Sounds great! I love school plays. The kids get so involved if they've got the right coaching, and sometimes they turn in remarkably good performances besides having a lot of fun. And that takes us to Friday, when the Midge-and-Ez Show rolls again."

"Lord help us all," O'Mara intoned. "At least we've got two very public evenings planned, which should keep them under reasonable control part of the time."

"Don't count on it," she warned. "He gets worse as he gets older, and an audience only encourages him to wilder flights. Unfortunately, he's such a natural comedian that even his most outrageous performances make everyone laugh. Not too long ago, I saw him tie up traffic for fifteen minutes at a busy city intersection while a couple of hundred people, including three cops, fell all over the place in hysterics."

"What in the world was he doing?" asked O'Mara, folding his arms on the table and leaning forward in anticipation.

"You know the intersection of Boylston and Tremont Streets in Boston?"

"Oh, my God," he said in awed tones.

"Indeed. Well, we reached the middle of it in conjunction with one of Boston's feistier cabdrivers, and you know how belligerent they can be. Neither he nor Ez would back off, so they both ended up in the middle of the street debating the rights of man, cabdrivers and civilians."

"I can hear it now."

"I only wish you could have. Ez was at full parade-ground bellow, which was positively echoing off the Prudential Tower and the John Hancock Building—and you know how far away they are—while this five-and-a-half foot cabby was literally jumping up and down in rage trying to make himself heard. It was ludicrous. Ez is looming there, roaring at the skies, and this little cabby is trying to shake his fist under Ez's nose but can't reach him. People were lining up on the sidewalks, and finally the drivers of all the waiting cars got out and joined in the debate. After two or three minutes, when he'd gathered a nice crowd, Ez climbed up on the hood of the car, flung out his arms and roared, 'Let the people decide!' He then appointed a judge, twelve jurors and the prosecuting and defense attorneys from among the spectators."

"You're making all this up," O'Mara gasped. "I don't believe it."

"Could I make up something like this? Listen. I don't know how he does it, but he got them all to go along with it. I think by then they were so stunned by the noise and fascinated by his act that they just got carried away. He kept it going for at least ten minutes, coaching everyone in their parts and conducting both the prosecution and the defense. Just about the time that police sirens could be heard heading our way, he waved everyone back to their cars, directed the cabby to a parking space, found one himself, gathered up the cabby, the cops and a few bystanders, and took us all to Jake Wirth's for knockwurst and dark beer. What with one thing and another, we never did make it to the matinee performance of the play we were going to."

"Who needs the theater when you've got Ez?"

"Too true. Yipe! Look at the time. I've got twenty minutes to get changed and open up."

The rest of the day seemed to fly by. Somehow, Kitt kept feeling that she was losing an odd hour here and there. Late in the afternoon, she finally decided that the clock wasn't skipping but, rather, her mind kept drifting off into enticing scenarios of her and O'Mara in a variety of isolated places such as sand dunes at midnight, mountain cabins and a houseboat anchored in mid-ocean.

When Midge arrived at three, she took one look at Kitt's smudgy eyes and not-quite-with-it expression and pushed her toward the stairs. "Go take a nap or you'll fall asleep in the middle of supper. O'Mara's house is supposed to be fabulous, and you're not going to be able to keep your eyes open wide enough to see it. Go on, Kitt. I'll close up and make sure you're awake before I leave."

"Okay. I'm sold," mumbled Kitt as she half-stumbled up

the stairs and drifted down the hall. She was asleep seconds after pulling a quilt over herself.

The persistence of something tickling her cheek and nose and the sound of boyish chuckles finally impelled her to open one eye, and she found herself looking into Gus's laughing face. It took a few seconds of disorientation before full awareness returned and her mind started receiving a jumble of messages. Lying on stomach. Gus must be kneeling on the floor. That's Hero on my feet. Something's tipping the mattress. O'Mara sitting on the edge of the bed. Suppertime.

She opened the other eye and smiled at Gus. "Hi. If it isn't my favorite mini-O'Mara." Her voice was sleep-husky, and she cleared her throat. "What's everybody doing here? Thought I was coming to your house."

"We came to get you so you wouldn't have to drive home alone late tonight. Dad says I should start getting used to taking care of you." His grin was pure imp. "Uh, I think maybe I'd have better luck with Hero. I bet you can hold your own with anybody, especially if you've been taking lessons from the crazy bear."

"I'll bet I can hold my own with you, my lad," cried Kitt, suddenly throwing back the quilt and grabbing Gus, hauling him up on the bed and tickling him. Laughter and breathless protests intermingled as they wrestled back and forth across the wide bed, watched by an indulgent O'Mara. Hero, trying to join in the melee, almost got knocked to the floor before O'Mara caught him up and held him in his lap.

"Okay, you two, break it up." O'Mara set Hero on the floor before plucking a laughing Gus off of Kitt's stomach and dropping him beside the excited dog. "Gus, you take Hero for a quick run around the block while Kitt gets herself put together. Don't be long. We want to show her the house before it gets dark. Hustle, now."

"We're gone. Come on, Hero. Wait'll you see our captain's deck, Kitt."

O'Mara dropped back down onto the edge of the bed and leaned over Kitt, his hands braced on either side of her. "You look very enticing like that. Hair all mussed, buttons half-undone, and you'd better get that gleam out of your eye or we'll embarrass Gus when he gets back," he ended in a deepening voice.

"One kiss?" She deliberately fluttered her lashes at him, but spoiled it by giggling.

"Come and get it," he said softly.

In a quick, fluid move, she was kneeling beside him with her arms wound loosely around his neck. "Just one, now," he murmured provocatively as her mouth touched his.

When she felt his hands on her hips, she instinctively started to tense up, but then relaxed again as she realized that he was just going to let them rest there. In another moment, as his tongue touched hers, she forgot about where his hands were.

"Mmmmmfff . . . behave . . . I said just . . . witch . . . let go . . . this bed is . . . too tempting. . . ."

The hands on her hips tightened momentarily, and she found herself swinging through the air and landing on her feet in the middle of the room.

"Coward! I thought I was supposed to set the pace," she complained.

Laughing and fending her off, he dodged out the door, calling back, "Within reason, love, within reason. Hurry up and get ready. I really do want you to see the Rock for the first time in daylight."

Kitt hurried. Within twelve minutes, she had showered, whisked a brush through her hair and scrambled into navy cords and a plaid velour vee-neck pullover—which just happened to blend with the navy cords and plaid Pendleton shirts worn by Gus and O'Mara. She lifted a sardonic eyebrow at the identical smug grins on their faces as they realized what she had done.

"We're a matched set," Gus exclaimed happily. "Too bad you haven't got a plaid collar for Hero."

"Sorry, chum. It never occurred to me."

"Maybe I can get him one for his birthday. When is it?"

"Never mind the dog's birthday present," O'Mara groaned. "Will you two get a move on?"

Within a couple of minutes, he had Kitt settled in the front seat of the Renegade while Gus and Hero shared the back, and they were heading out Ocean Avenue paralleling first the river and then, at the river's mouth, swinging left to follow along the oceanside, past Walker Point, and then losing sight of the water for a while as the road bent inland. A little more than two miles from Kitt's, they turned right onto a narrow, winding road that brought them back to the coast, climbing along the sea-washed ledges. They passed four widely spaced, half-hidden and obviously expensive summer homes, rounded a curve, and slowed to a stop to give Kitt her first view of Crest Rock.

For long moments, she just stared, unable to think of any appropriate words. It was so much more than she had expected that she could do nothing but try to take it all in. The Rock was an enormous granite outcropping that jutted some thousand feet out into the ocean almost due south, and rose nearly two hundred feet above the water at low tide. From where she was sitting, she was at eye-level to a point about halfway up the Rock and could see both the waves crashing against the rocks and ledges at its base and part of the roof and upper portion of a house at the top. She blinked at the bright flashes of the lowering sun reflecting off of what seemed to be a wide expanse of glass. It was difficult to make out many details through the mass of greenery and weather-twisted pines edging the top of the Rock.

"Kitt?"

"Oh, wow."

"Isn't it a neat place to live, Kitt?" Gus leaned forward between the seats, trying to see her face. "Do you think you'll like it?"

"It's incredible. What happens in a storm? Don't you get blown off the top?"

"No way. Wait till you see how everything's anchored down or protected and all the great things they did when they built it so you can really see a big storm. Wait till you see—"

"Enough, Gus," O'Mara chided. "It's got to be a surprise, or she won't get the full effect."

"Oh, okay, Dad. But let's go quick."

"What's all that glass? Have you got a window-wall? It must be a marvelous view. That's facing—what?—due west? What a great place to watch a sunset!"

"Better than you'd ever guess." O'Mara chuckled. "Patience, love, and you'll see for yourself." He let up on the brake and swung back onto the road.

Another curve and the ocean was out of sight. Still climbing gradually, the road was now bordered by a high stone wall backed by trees, and Kitt realized that they were on the land side of the Rock. O'Mara swung the jeep through a wide, gateless entrance onto a two-lane paved driveway, which curved in a shallow, sweeping *S* as it steadily sloped up through a field studded with rock outcroppings and clumps of low-growing bushes.

"In another few weeks, this'll be very colorful. I've left it to grow in a natural, untamed way," said O'Mara, waving a hand at the expanse of wilderness. "Those rocks are covered in wild roses, and the field is brilliant with all kinds of wildflowers. That mass of high bushes over there runs all the way back to the road and is a mixture of four or five colors of lilacs that have just gone wild."

"What are these bushes?" asked Kitt, gesturing to an unidentifiable tangle of thin brown branches that edged a curve.

"I'm not up on plants and stuff. Some of them have flowers, and I know that's forsythia," he said, pointing to a blaze of yellow. "I think there's some honeysuckle in there somewhere and—"

Laughing, Kitt waved him down. "Never mind. I'll explore myself sometime. Besides, it will be easier to identify them when the leaves are out. Ohhhh."

They had rounded a high ledge and stopped in a courtyard. Kitt tried to look in all directions at once and managed to bump her head scrambling out of the jeep. Slowly turning in circles, she moved out into the middle of the wide, paved area, totally unable to decide what to examine first. O'Mara and Gus leaned against a fender and watched her rapt expression with satisfied smiles.

Finally, she stopped turning and walked to the far side of the courtyard, away from the house, and stood at the low brick wall looking down over a randomly terraced lawn. It took a moment for her to realize that the terraces followed the ledged contours of the underlying rock. There was an opening in the brick wall which led onto a wide flagstone walk that descended via shallow steps down two terraces to a magnificent natural swimming pool formed in a deep depression of the native rock. White sand filled in and smoothed out the roughness of the ledge around the pool, and then gave way to lawn and a sizable flagstone patio with a permanent barbecue. Kitt could picture it in the summer: white wrought-iron furniture with colorful, weatherproof cushions and umbrellas, steaks sizzling on the grill, people splashing in the pool and lounging comfortably around, while Gus and a horde of tanned, long-legged kids raced over the rolling lawns. Off to the right, partially screened by what looked like rhododendrons, she could see a tennis court and, below that, on another terrace, a horseshoe pitch.

Tucking her hands into her pockets, she took a deep breath, holding down her rising excitement, and slowly turned around to face the house. Perfect. Just perfect. If she could have sketched the ideal house, it would have looked like this. Long and low, pale gray shingles with a blue roof and white trim, a dark red door, wide, small-paned windows, a deep overhang to the eaves to shade and protect the second-floor windows, a wide, roofed porch across the front and a narrow strip of bark-mulch set with azaleas and boxwoods between the courtyard's brick edging wall and the porch. She couldn't even guess at how many rooms there might be, but it was a large house. Besides the main two-story section, there were two single-story wings on a slightly lower level angling out at either end of the irregularly shaped courtyard. At the left was a four-car garage, and on the right was what almost looked like a separate apartment with its own entrance. It boasted a huge floor-to-ceiling bay window, and Kitt could just make out the shapes of furniture and a wall of books.

"Kitt?"

"Hmmm?"

"Do you like it?"

The deep voice was just above her right ear, and she turned to look at him with dreamy eyes and a musing smile, strands of hair blowing across her face in the crisp breeze. "I love it. It's all . . . so perfect."

He curved a gentle arm around her shoulders and urged her foward. "Come in and see the rest of it and meet Andy. She's been peeking out the kitchen window, consumed with curiosity and impatience."

"I can't wait. Oh, where's Gus? And Hero?"

"Look." He half-turned and nodded toward the huge, contoured lawn. Gus and Hero were racing across the broad sweeps of grass, dodging around bushes and leaping over rocks.

"I know that's a lot of room, and then there's all that thick undergrowth around the outer edges, but what if a kid or an animal gets too close to the edge of the cliff?"

"Don't worry. It's not very visible because we've let vines and bushes grow up over it, but the whole perimeter of the Rock is securely fenced or walled. In fact, as you'll see when we go in, the house is quite near the front curve of the cliff, and for added safety I had five-foot fences installed from the back corners of each wing out to the perimeter fence. The only way through to the front from here is via two locked gates. Gus and his friends play on this side."

She scanned across the acre or so of lawn and murmured, "They've certainly got room enough for just about anything."

"And the wherewithal. Besides what you see there, there's a basketball hoop that fastens to the garage and a volleyball net that goes up down there in the summer. We use that large, flat area at the bottom for croquet, and there's a slide that fits by the pool. Believe me, they don't have any need to explore around front!"

"It all sounds wonderful, and I won't worry about Hero sprouting wings. Why do you call the other side the front? This looks like a front to me."

"You'll see," he answered mysteriously. "Hey, Gus, we're going in! Are you going to help show Kitt around?"

"Yes! Wait for us! Come on, Hero, run!"

Kitt looked around again, this time with a puzzled frown. "I can hear the surf, and I know we're surrounded on three sides by water, but I can't see any of it from here."

"Not on this side. I was struck by that right off the first time I looked at the place. It did seem strange, and I couldn't understand why the owner, who was also the man who designed and built the place, hadn't cleared some vistas. He explained that there's always a wind up here, which can vary from a gentle breeze to a roaring gale. If the trees and bushes were cut back to open up viewing areas, it would give the winds too much sweep at ground level, and we'd have trouble keeping the plantings intact, to say nothing of what it would do to the lawns and pool. As it is, this whole back area is quite protected, and we have very little damage even in the winter storms."

"I can understand the reasoning, but it seems a shame not to be able to see the ocean. It must be spectacular from up here."

Gus and O'Mara exchanged laughing glances, and Gus grabbed Kitt's hand, tugging her toward the door. "Come on, Kitt. We'll show you the ocean!"

With both O'Maras urging her onward, she had only a fleeting impression of the large, light hall—white-painted paneling, gold-framed mirrors and paintings, several doors, another hall off to the left and, incredibly, a wide, graceful staircase curving up from the center of the main hall.

"Oh, wait! Let me see!" She tried to stop, tipping her head back to look up at the lovely spiral.

O'Mara's hand on her back pushed her onward. "Later, love. First, the ocean."

Gus and Hero had run ahead and were now waiting by the open French doors at the end of the hall. Dazzled by bright sunlight, Kitt couldn't make out details until she and O'Mara had stepped from the dimmer hall into what, for a moment, seemed to be the outdoors.

Kitt stopped short as her eyes adjusted to the light and the full impact of what she was looking at hit her. She gasped in wonder and her head swung from side to side as she tried to take in the unbelievable panorama. She was barely aware of Gus and O'Mara taking her hands and leading her forward until she heard the deep, laughing voice in her ear.

"Well, what do you think? Is that enough ocean for you?"

"I'm speechless," she breathed finally, looking around and up and realizing just where she was. The bulk of the house was behind her, and she was standing in the front part of a large, triangular glass room with a polished wood ceiling. The base of the triangle was the house-wall, which contained three pairs of French doors and a wide, rock fireplace. Two walls of large glass panes, divided by sturdy white-painted wood strips, angled out from the house to meet at a point some fifty feet from the edge of the cliff. All of the underbrush had been cut back to give an unimpeded, one-hundred-and-eighty-degree view of rocky coast, island-dotted ocean on the left, open sea straight ahead and to the right, with a few ledges breaking the surface in-shore.

"It's like being on the very front of a ship," Kitt said wonderingly. "If you watch the movement of the water for a minute, you even feel as if you're moving up and down. It's fantastic. Look at that ocean—it just seems to go on forever.

And the sky! I've never seen so much sky. Oh, glory, we are going to watch the sunset from here, aren't we?" She turned to O'Mara, her face alight with eagerness.

"Nope. We've got an even better place for sunset-watching when the winds are within reason."

"Up on the captain's deck," exclaimed Gus.

"I thought this was—"

"Oh, no," said Gus, bouncing with excitement, "This is the bridge. The captain's deck is up on top."

O'Mara glanced at his watch and checked the western sky. "We've got maybe thirty minutes before that sky gets interesting. Just time for a quick look through the house while it's light. You can take your time later and browse around all you want."

"You mean there's something else that comes up to this room?" Kitt pulled her eyes away from the view with considerable effort and turned her attention to examining the bridge. She only had time to note the low, cushioned benches along the glass walls and the casual scattering of lounge chairs, comfortable-looking sofas and low tables in various sizes, everything fitting into a nautical color scheme of red, white and blue. Her eyes halted in their survey as she caught a movement from the French doors at the right, and she watched an attractive, middle-aged woman walk toward her.

O'Mara moved to meet her, putting an affectionate arm around her shoulders and bringing her directly to Kitt. He laughed down at the smiling, dark-eyed woman and teased, "I don't know how you've contained your curiosity this long. Why didn't you come out sooner? Here she is, Andy. This is my Kitt."

At the unmistakable note of love and pride in his voice, Kitt's gaze lifted to meet his, and for a long moment she was lost in the blaze of happiness she could see in his eyes. She knew, as clearly as if they were speaking, that he was thinking about sharing this home with her, planning the days and nights of their lives together. His voice was husky as he continued, "Kitt, this is our chief dragon and favorite mother-figure, Mrs. Andretti, more widely known as Andy. You might as well give up without a fight, right now, because she'll end up managing you for your own good, too."

"Michael! Behave yourself. You'll have the young lady

thinking I'm an old witch or something. I'm very pleased to meet you at last, Kitt. I haven't heard about anything but Kitt and Ez and Hero for days."

Kitt laughed and held out her hand. "Oh, poor you! That must have gotten terribly boring after a while. I hope I can redeem myself."

They smiled at each other over their clasped hands, and Kitt felt a relaxing of an inner tension which she hadn't even realized was there. Until it was gone, she hadn't known that she was worrying about Andy's reaction to her. After all, she had been the only mother Gus had ever known. Also, it had been obvious from the way O'Mara talked about her that he had great affection and respect for her, and Kitt had sensed that this was more than reciprocated by Andy. It wouldn't be at all surprising if she were wary of Kitt's sudden advent into the O'Maras' lives as a potential wife and stepmother. But as Kitt intently examined the older woman's expression and listened to her voice, she discovered only warmth and friendly interest.

As Gus and O'Mara nudged them across the bridge toward the left-hand doors, the two women chatted easily about Ez and Hero, exchanging laughing compliments on how well they had done in handling the males in their lives.

"Don't get overconfident, you two," O'Mara commented. "Remember, counting Hero, you're outnumbered four to three even if you bring in Midge for reinforcement."

"That doesn't make any difference," Andy said complacently. "Cleverness wins over brute force every time. Isn't that so, Kitt?"

"I should have known better than to get you two together," O'Mara groaned.

Led by Gus and Hero, it was a convivial group that quickly toured the house, pausing only to point out the highlights to Kitt. O'Mara was eager to reach the captain's deck in time to watch the sunset. Kitt took in the huge family/recreation room which they entered as they left the bridge, noting big, comfortable sofas and chairs, game tables, a pool table, a folded-up Ping-Pong table pushed back against one wall, an upright piano, a small soda fountain in one corner with a marble-top bar and swivel stools, paneled walls hung with animal and sporting prints, another rock fireplace which backed on the one on the bridge, and wide, many-paned windows looking out over the ocean on one side and onto the courtyard and lawns at the opposite side.

A bubbling Gus made sure that Kitt didn't miss any of the features of his paradise as they slowly crossed the big room toward the wing with the huge bay window.

"Easy, Gus," O'Mara chided. "You can bring her back later and show her everything in detail."

As they reached the far side of the room, Kitt paused at the top of four broad, shallow steps and looked back, trying to orient herself. "This looks like it takes up one whole end of the main house."

"It does. The former owner did a great deal of entertaining, and we sometimes end up with a houseful of guests in the summer," O'Mara explained. "I changed the type of furnishings and equipment, since Gus will be using it for some time to come with his friends. It's practically indestructible, which also makes it a great place for adult parties."

"To say nothing of a playroom for Ez!" exclaimed Kitt, laughing. "Now, what's down here?"

"This is my bailiwick," said O'Mara, leading her down the steps and sliding open double wooden doors to give access to a rectangular hall. He pushed open a door immediately in front of them. "Full bath." Giving Kitt time for no more than a glimpse of dark green, white and tan, he urged her toward the door at the left end of the hall. "This is where I work, and don't start getting the 'neatening bug,' because even Andy leaves this room alone."

Kitt walked slowly into the bright room, easily twice as long as it was wide, with one long wall almost entirely made of glass opening the room up to a stupendous view of ocean and rocky coast with the spires and roofs of Kennebunkport in the distance on the right. Tearing herself away from the riveting view, she turned to examine the rest of the room. The long wall opposite was almost filled with modern horizontal files and bookshelves. She walked through the room, noting the well-worn leather chairs, a couch, the big L-shaped oak desk and its upholstered swivel chair, an IBM typewriter on a large, movable table and, finally, at the far end, an archway that led into a small but fully equipped kitchen.

"Good heavens, O'Mara, you could hole up in here for

weeks. Are you one of those writers who hibernates when the creative urge hits?"

"Not really, although it's handy for snacks and coffee at odd hours. This wing was designed as an apartment for the original owner's aunt. Open that door on the other side of the kitchen. Go on. That was the living room, but I've made it into a library. What do you think?"

"It's beautiful," gasped Kitt, taking in the casual elegance of the room. Somehow, she knew that O'Mara had arranged this room, just as he had the others, and she was more than a little surprised at the many facets of his taste she was seeing in this fascinating house. Where the other rooms had been designed for a combination of comfortable living and hard use by active youngsters or a busy man, this room was obviously intended for quiet contemplation and study. The long inner wall was centered by a small fireplace of green-veined black marble with intricately carved wood panels rising above it to the ceiling. On both sides, the wall was lined with floor-to-ceiling bookcases except for the doors at either end. The outer end-wall contained a door to the outside and a wide window framing a pretty rock garden with a path winding through it between the door and the courtyard. The chairs and sofas, which were arranged in casual groupings by the fireplace and the big bay window, were of a traditional, faintly Victorian styling and were upholstered in jewel-toned Belgian cut-velvet, which somehow managed to blend rather than clash with the soft creams, blues and greens of an almost-room-sized antique Oriental rug.

O'Mara watched Kitt's bemused face as she looked around the lovely room and smiled to himself with considerable satisfaction. Taking her hand, he pulled her toward the door leading back to the main house, saying softly, "I think we've found you your own special place."

"Oh, yes. It's . . . is that a Pembroke table? And that looks like Hepplewhite."

"They are. We'll come back and you can look to your heart's content later. Right now, I want to get upstairs before that sunset gets away from us."

They were halfway up the curving staircase when the phone rang, and Andy, pausing in the hall to answer it, called up, "It's for you, Michael."

"Will you take a message and tell them I'll call back shortly, please?"

"Michael . . . it's a woman. . . . She says she's Mrs. O'Mara."

Chapter 15

Kitt swayed and groped for the banister as shock blasted through her with icy numbness. Dimly, she heard Gus's mutter of "What's *she* want?" and O'Mara's snarled expletive, and then O'Mara's hands were on her shoulders pushing her down to sit on a stair.

"Kitt! Don't look like that, love. It's only Laura doing her best to cause trouble. Look, you go on up with Gus while I get rid of her, and I'll explain later. Kitt?"

She blinked and shook her head as if she were coming out of sleep, then focused her gaze on his concerned expression. For a long minute, they looked at each other, and then, as she felt the reassurance emanating from him, she gradually relaxed. A pressure against her side and the feel of a thin arm sliding around her waist brought her head around, and she discovered Gus sitting beside her and patting her arm, his face mirroring his father's concern.

"It's okay, Kitt. We're not going to let her bother you. She's just trying to twist Dad's arm to get money." The young voice was very matter-of-fact, as if he were discussing the distasteful antics of a stranger. And, really, that's just what he's doing, thought Kitt as she put her arm around his shoulders and hugged him. He's never seen her, and he's so smart that he must know she doesn't give a damn. Oh, I'd like to shake her teeth loose! No, I'd like to send her somewhere far away where she can't ever upset him again. She'd be a rotten mother, obviously, and he's done far better without her.

"Kitt? Are you all right?"

"Yes." Her voice was strong and very positive. "I'm fine.

Go talk to her while Gus shows me his room. Go on, now, we're going to be too late for the sunset if you dawdle around here. Come on, Gus. Where's Hero?"

As she and Gus reached the top of the stairs, she could hear O'Mara's voice, full of barely controlled fury, echoing up the stairwell. She had the fleeting thought that she was just as happy not to be on the receiving end of *that* before she turned her attention to her surroundings. The upper hall was lit by a pair of sliding glass doors that opened out onto the captain's deck. At this moment, Gus only let her look out for a quick scan of the triangular area, floored with redwood decking and enclosed with a waist-high safety guard formed from panels of clear, inch-thick Lexan bolted to a strong metal framework.

"We'll go out in a couple of minutes when Dad gets here. Come this way, now, and see my room." Gus tugged on her hand eagerly, and she followed him along the hallway to the left and through the first door on the right. "Those are guest rooms and baths on the other side, but my room is here, then the baths, mine and Andy's, and then her room goes all the way to the end on this side. There. Isn't it great? It's double-sized and so's Andy's. And Dad's is even bigger. It's on the other side of the stairs."

"Wow! Oh, Gus, what a super room!" Kitt's surprised delight was genuine. The big room was a boy's dream, and the long expanse of windows running the full length of the outer wall and making the panorama of sea and sky seem like an extension of the room was the frosting on the cake. Kitt stood just inside the door, taking it all in as Gus darted around pointing out the major features: low, wide window seats that were also storage bins; rugged oak furniture with brass trim; inlaid vinyl tile floor in a geometric pattern of brown, orange and yellow softened with several thick, dark brown area rugs; a large section of built-in shelves including a swivel bracket for a small TV and fittings for a stereo rig, records, tapes, speakers and a recording setup; a workbench with model airplanes and cars displayed on the shelves above it; a large aquarium; and a large, fine-mesh cage sitting on its own table by the windows.

"Listen, Gus, since you've got an extra bed . . ." Kitt let her voice trail off suggestively and grinned at him.

"Oh, Kitt, you wouldn't fit in that bed." He chuckled. "It's for when I have a friend stay over. Besides, I think Dad has something else in mind for you." He broke up in laughter at the look of consternation on her face.

"Ahhh . . . I don't think you're supposed to understand that, are you?" she asked doubtfully.

"Well . . . we do talk about a lot of things that I don't think the other guys talk to their fathers about. Come see Fifi." He pulled her over to the cage, and she looked at him questioningly when she could see nothing but a collection of large, flattish rocks piled up rather haphazardly.

"Maybe it's a silly question, but why do you need this big cage to keep rocks in?"

"Watch." With a definite O'Mara gleam of devilry in his bright blue eyes, Gus started drumming his fingers on the top of the cage. After a few seconds, Kitt saw something moving between the rocks, then a quick blur of motion, and she was suddenly staring in frozen shock at a coiled rattlesnake, its head lifted and slightly weaving while its tongue darted in and out and its tail vibrated noisily. Instinctively, she grabbed Gus, pulling him back from the cage, and looked frantically around for Hero.

"Kitt! Kitt! It's okay. She's harmless." Between gusts of laughter he managed to get her attention, patting her arm in reassurance.

"Harmless? That's a rattlesnake!"

"Honest, Kitt, she's okay. She's been defanged. Ohhh, the look on your face." He went off into another peal of laughter.

"Gus! You didn't spring Fifi on her without any warning!" The deep voice was equally divided between chiding and laughter, and Kitt turned to find O'Mara striding across the room. "You handled that very well, love. Not even a scream. You should have heard Ez yell."

"And he jumped backward halfway across the room," said Gus, chortling.

The look Kitt split between them promised future retribution. "You, my darling toad, have been warping this otherwise delightful boy's sense of humor. *Fifi?*"

Gus slanted a look up at his father and then gazed at Kitt in wide-eyed innocence. "It's 'cause she shakes her tail. Dad named her."

She tried but couldn't hold it back. She rocked with laughter and finally collapsed on the window seat, holding onto her aching ribs while tears ran down her face.

"I don't believe it," she moaned. "Ez must have loved it. Fifi!"

O'Mara reached for her hands and pulled her to her feet. "Come on out on the captain's deck. That sky's about right." He led her over to a sliding glass door at the end of the windows and out onto the deck.

Gus took her other hand and urged her over to the point of the triangle. "Isn't this something, Kitt? It's just like being on the prow of a ship."

"Unreal," breathed Kitt, pushing her blowing hair out of her face and looking out and down at the heaving ocean. Feeling O'Mara's arm around her waist, she leaned back against his shoulder and looked up at the color-streaked sky.

"Are you warm enough? The wind's coming up a bit," he said softly in her ear. "We can go down and watch this from the bridge if you're cold."

"I'm not going to be cold. Between you and my mini-O'Mara here," she chuckled, wrapping her arms around Gus and holding him in front of her, "I'm going to be warm as can be."

Watching the changing hues of the sunset, they stood quietly talking.

"This is a great spot for sunbathing," Kitt said a bit wistfully.

"Hmmm. With or without strap-marks and white patches," O'Mara murmured in her ear with an accompanying kiss. "No one can see you up here when you're lying on the deck, except from our own second-floor windows."

"Tempting thought."

Gus twisted his head around to look up at her. "We've got chairs and stuff we put out here in the summer, and when it's not too windy, we have picnics up here."

She turned her head to meet O'Mara's heated gaze and caught her breath at the vividness of the vision that flashed into her mind, a vignette of the two of them lying naked in the sun and sharing a picnic of wine and cheese. O'Mara's slow, knowing smile told her that he was reading her mind again, or perhaps this time she was reading his, and she suddenly became aware of the tautness of her breasts and the clenching of her abdominal muscles as desire flared through her.

"Ouch! Kitt, you're squeezing me!" Gus's laughing protest

broke the spell, and she tore her gaze away from O'Mara's, bending to kiss the boy's cheek and apologize.

"In case you're interested, those doors on the left lead into our bedroom," O'Mara whispered in her ear. "At least, it will be *ours* before too much longer."

"And when do I get a tour of that?" Kitt asked softly.

"How about now? Ready to go in, Gus? Run along and get cleaned up for supper. We'll meet you downstairs in a few minutes."

"Okay. Come on, Hero. You can play with Fifi while I get washed."

"Oh, wait a min—"

"It's all right," O'Mara said, laughing. "She really is harmless and quite tame. She belonged to a stuntman on one of the film sets I worked on. He was having trouble traveling with her, so he gave her to Gus. Hero just likes to watch her. Gus taught him to tap the cage to get her moving around."

He pushed open the sliding door into his bedroom and, with an arm around her shoulders, urged Kitt through ahead of him. It was dim in the room with the fading light, and she took only a couple of hesitant steps forward before turning back to him. He smiled at her encouragingly as he flipped a light switch and filled the room with a soft glow from several floor and table lamps.

Her attention was fixed on that smile, and she felt again the sexual awareness that had been aroused in those brief moments on the deck. Unthinkingly, she leaned into him, bringing her hands up to rest along his hips and lifting her mouth to his. She felt the light stroke of his hands up her back and then his fingers threading into her hair to cup her head and tilt it so her mouth was where he wanted it. Everything else went right out of her mind as he gently teased her lips apart with his tongue and feathered the tip of it around the inside of her mouth until, frustrated, she caught it with her teeth.

"Umm. Witch! Don't bite unless you want more than you're ready to handle." The deep voice was warm and amused, and the large hand that made abrupt contact with her rump was more caressing than chastising. "Control yourself for a minute or two, and tell me what you think of our private quarters. You haven't even looked around yet."

"You distract me," she murmured, still reluctant to move away from him.

Chuckling, he shook his head at her in mock-despair and turned her around to face the big room. Her eyes widened as she assimilated the full impact of a room that might have been designed and decorated just for her. Moving slowly forward and then turning to take it all in, she tried to come to terms with the dawning realization that, unbelievable as it seemed, O'Mara had planned it all with her in mind.

"Do you like it?" The soft question drifted in the waiting stillness.

"How did . . . how did you know?"

"I've always known what pleases you."

Still soft, their voices were faintly husky with emotion. He watched her intently, seeing the wonder and awareness in her expression and the deepening pleasure in her eyes.

"But you didn't know I'd ever see it. It had been so long, so very long."

"I knew. I looked for you, and I knew that someday I'd find you again. And this would be waiting for you. Our own private place."

"It's beautiful. So beautiful. It's the most beautiful room I've ever seen. Or could ever imagine."

She kept discovering new things, or perhaps it was just that the initial shock was wearing off and she was really *seeing* it all. Hesitantly at first, and then with growing eagerness, she moved about the huge room. Some twenty feet wide and more than twice as long, it was divided into sleeping and lounging areas by a floor-to-ceiling brass screen which extended ten feet into the room from halfway down the long inner wall. The screen had the dulled-gold patina of age, and its primary motif was a magnificent rearing dragon. The room was held together as an entity by the wall-to-wall expanse of deep, plushy, dark blue carpeting and the unbroken stretch of floor-to-ceiling windows along the outside wall. At the same time, the areas of the room were subtly defined by carrying through the Oriental theme with beautiful antique rugs in muted tones of blues, minty green, old gold and soft rose on cream and ivory backgrounds.

One large rug indicated the lounge area at the end of the room nearest the deck. Between the door to the deck and the end wall was a small, natural rock fireplace, taking advantage of the chimney rising from the double fireplaces on the first floor. A long, curving, deep-cushioned sofa covered in smoky blue velvet and piled with cream, gold and rose velvet cushions was flanked by intricately carved antique mahogany end tables, while a long, low Persian brass table served as a coffee table. Kitt stroked her fingertips over a bronze lion crouched on one of the end tables as she admired the porcelain table lamps, several other animal sculptures in bronze, pewter and jade, and an intriguing throw tossed over one end of the sofa.

"O'Mara, tell me I'm wrong. That can't possibly be a fur . . . what? . . . blanket? Rug? What is it?"

"Would you believe mink? Oh, yes, indeed. Don't look so stupefied, love. And, no, I didn't buy it. It was a gift, which it would be just as well for you not to question too closely. Just enjoy the advantages."

"What advantages would those be, you sybaritic Romeo?" Kitt gave him a very knowing look accompanied by a quirked eyebrow and the closest thing to a smirk that she could manage.

"I've never claimed to have had a monkish existence." His grin was totally unrepentant. "However, just consider that you, my lovely Kitt, are going to reap all the rewards of my . . . um . . . research. For instance, just try and picture a stormy winter's night, the sound of the surf crashing against the Rock, the room lit only by flickering firelight, and you and me lying naked on that mink rug in front of the fire. . . ." The words trailed off, muffled against her mouth. After a moment, he lifted his head just far enough to add, "You'll love the feel of mink against your bare skin."

"O'Maraaa . . ." she moaned, desire flaming through her as the erotic picture he'd painted filled her mind. She pressed her full length against him, winding her arms around his shoulders and pressing her hot face into his neck. With effort, he kept his touch light as he stroked his hands up her sides and brought them to rest against her breasts.

"Why are you wearing that silly bra? You don't need it," he whispered.

"I—"

"Of course, I'd just as soon you took off the shirt, too, and—"

"Stop it, you beast. I've got to go down and face Andy and

Gus in a few minutes, and . . . and what's in those cabinets?"
Determinedly pushing away from him, she moved toward the
built-in cabinets along the end wall.

"Coward. All right, this time I'll let you get away with it.
Go ahead and open them. Stereo, tape deck, records, tapes,
speakers, color TV, odds and ends. You can examine it all
later. Come on over here and see the rest of our conveni-
ences."

He caught her hand and led her across to where a round
brass table and two brass side chairs, with seats and backs
padded in rose and cream velvet, were positioned on an oval
Oriental rug in front of the windows near the deck door. "For
breakfast, if we want to be alone, or midnight snacks. Before
you ask, look down at the other end . . . see, the alcove
beside the windows. That's one of those compact units that
contains a sink, a small refrigerator and a couple of electric
burners. Dishes and stuff are in the cabinets. Of course,
anything elaborate would have to be fixed downstairs in the
kitchen and carried up, but coffee and simple stuff can be kept
here."

Kitt looked at him disbelievingly. "You're quite mad,
aren't you? Do you have kitchens stashed all over the house?
Not that it isn't a super idea and the absolute height of
dissolute living, but—"

"Oh, no, it isn't. You haven't seen the, excuse the expression, bathroom, yet."

"What else would you call a bathroom?" asked Kitt in
bewilderment.

"This one defies description. I . . . ah . . . got a bit carried
away."

"Well? Where is it? Let me see it."

"Down here. You can check out our bed on your way by."
He gave her a sly, laughing glance as they moved around the
brass screen. "Well? How do you like it?"

"Good grief!" She stared in total amazement at an enormous bed, easily seven feet wide by eight feet long, with a
fantastic brass tree as a headboard, spreading graceful
branches the width of the bed and up to within two feet of the
ceiling. The stretch of wall behind the headboard, between
the brass screen and the corner, had been painted a smoky
blue to match the silk spread on the bed, and the patina of the.

beautiful tree gleamed mutedly against the soft background color. The bedside tables were large squares of pale green marble set on narrow, gracefully curving brass legs. Kitt was so mesmerized by the huge bed that she barely noticed details such as delicate brass lamps with cream silk shades, matching Oriental runners at each side of the bed, and cunningly designed, small, fitted brass cabinets on each table to take the place of the usual drawers and shelves.

"O'Mara, where . . . oh, where . . . did you find that bed? Ez would give his soul for a bed like that. We could sleep a family of six in that bed."

"Not on your life. That bed is for us—you and me—and nobody else. Ez can find his own bed. Hero can sleep with Gus, and the rest of the kids can have the rooms across the hall." He pulled her back against his chest with his hands on her shoulders and nuzzled his warm mouth into her neck, whispering, "Lots of room to exercise all kinds of imagination, sideways, endways and even upside-down." He felt the blush spreading up over her neck and into her face and growled suggestively against her ear, slowly running his tongue around the rim.

"I . . . oh . . . I'm not . . . even going to ask about upside-down." Laughing breathlessly, she turned and slid her arms around his waist, stretching up to feather kisses across his cheek to the corner of his mouth. "It's a magnificent bed, but aren't you afraid you'll lose me in it?"

"Never. I don't intend to let you get out of reach." His hands, lightly curved to her buttocks, encouraged her another half-step closer as she shaped her mouth to his and hesitantly urged his lips apart with her tongue, tentatively exploring the textures and contours of his warm mouth.

This can't be me doing this. What will he think? I know what he's thinking. He likes it and wants more. He did say I could do whatever I wanted to, and I want to know what his mouth feels like . . . tastes like . . . he does it to me . . . and I love it, so he must. Does his stomach melt away when he does this? Damn that shirt . . . I can't feel his skin . . . such a long, strong back . . . oh, no . . . no, it's fine . . . he's not really holding me . . . I wish I could let him . . . but I can feel that cold knot forming when he starts to close his hands on my bottom and pull me close . . . but he let me shift back . . . I

can move away . . . umm . . . OH! Is that what you're sup-
posed to do! Why didn't he tell me? . . . Beast. I can sense him
laughing in his mind . . . he knows I'd never have thought of
that by myself. Oh, yes, yes . . . give me your tongue, smarty,
and just see how quickly I learn . . . now . . . now . . .

"If you're that fast on the uptake with everything I teach
you, we'll have a very busy honeymoon, love." The husky
voice was muffled against her neck, and the slow stroking of
his hands up and down her sides was gentling rather than
arousing. Her head rested on his shoulder while she tried to
steady her breathing and convince her knees that they were
not made of custard.

"Oh, you great gormless toad, why didn't you ever show
me that before?" she groaned complainingly. "Look at all the
time you let me waste. Do you realize that—"

'"Love, love," he chided, a thread of laughter in his voice,
as he held her away from him. "One thing at a time. Get used
to this, and then we'll try the next step. Now, tell me, were
you scared? I thought you started to tense up once."

"Just a little. It did start, but as soon as I moved away and
you loosened your hands, it was all right."

"I thought—"

"Hey, Dad! Kitt! Andy says supper's on in ten minutes."
O'Mara and Kitt half-turned to peer through the brass screen
as Gus came bounding in from the hall.

"Okay. You're just in time to catch Kitt's first reaction to
my bathroom." O'Mara ruffled Gus's hair as they grinned at
each other conspiratorily. "What do you think she'll say?"

"I wouldn't even try to guess." Gus giggled. "Ez said
'Great pillars of Hercules!' and roared, so she'll probably
come out with 'Shades of Charlemagne' or something weird."

"You two are killing me with suspense. What on earth is in
this bathroom?"

"You gotta see it!" exclaimed Gus, grabbing her hand and
tugging her toward the hallway she'd noticed in the end wall
beyond the bed. O'Mara's guiding hand on her back kept her
moving when she tried to stop to admire a pair of beautiful
Chinese chests of black lacquer inlaid with flowers and birds
of silver, ivory and jade, which flanked the entrance to the
hall.

"Later, love. Now, along here on the right are all sorts of

built-in drawers and fitted shelves for anything you could think of, and on the left—wait a second, Gus—through this door—*voilà!* a dressing room with more drawers and racks and stuff. No, you can look at it all later. Onward."

"Ready for this, Kitt?" Gus turned to grin up at her, one hand on another brass screen which was hung as a gate across the end of the hall. He pushed it open and led her through into darkness. Before she had taken more than two steps, lights started coming on in one area of the big room after another.

Kitt's mouth opened in amazement and her eyes grew wider and wider as they darted around the big room, skipping from one fascination to another and then returning here and there to take in details. She was vaguely aware of O'Mara and Gus watching her reactions with gleeful grins lighting their faces, but for a couple of minutes she was too busy taking it all in to think of anything to say. It was initially a jumble of impressions: the deep blue carpeting continued from the bedroom and hall . . . more brass screens with Oriental motifs separating areas of the room . . . a sauna?! . . . a shower room that looked big enough for a family, with pale green tile and a full-size tiger stalking through long grass across the back wall . . . two toilets in Chinese red porcelain just visible behind a screen . . . no, one's a bidet . . . twin sinks in the same red porcelain set in a wide, marble-topped counter . . . corner room with all those windows on two sides . . . whatever is that tiered platform? . . . a whirlpool tub! . . . big enough for a party . . . and red, too, with a brass fence around the edge of the platform and railings on the steps . . . clever idea to carpet the tread and tile the risers . . . where did he find that tile? . . . looks just like meadow grass and wildflowers . . . love those windows rising from the edge of the platform to the ceiling . . . how extravagant to sit in that tub and look out over the ocean and no one can see in . . . a lounge area?! . . . floor-to-ceiling windows in the front corner and that smashing old wicker lounge and the matching low table . . . like the white with red and green cushions, but it needs a big floor plant . . . a fig tree, maybe . . . and those neat wicker benches in front of that long vanity table . . . that must be the front wall and what a marvelous view in daylight to look at while doing your

hair . . . a double length? . . . ah, that's a shaving mirror
. . . clever . . . his-and-her dressing tables . . . oh, look at
that wall above the sinks . . . what is it? . . . pillars and an
Oriental garden . . . he had to have had these tiles specially
designed . . . I don't believe any of this.

"Kitt? Say something!"

"Scheherazade's skivvies! O'Mara, what *Arabian Nights*
fantasy were you having when you dreamed this up?" She
started laughing delightedly and waltzed across the expanse
of blue carpet. "You could hold a party in here. How did you
ever tear Ez away from that hot tub? It's even big enough to
swim in."

"Not for Ez." O'Mara chuckled. "Gus might just manage a
couple of strokes, though. Do you like it? I'll admit I got a bit
carried away."

"A bit! You're totally balmy. Look at this shower. What
kind of group sports did you have in mind when you thought
this up? Never mind! I can tell by that gleam that you
shouldn't answer that in front of Gus."

"Oh, Kitt," Gus giggled. "I'm not dumb. I'll bet you and
Dad—"

"Thank you, Augustus, but I'll make my own plans for
what Kitt and I will do in that shower. Come along, you two,
before Andy sends out a search party for us."

Kitt was allowed only brief glimpses into the guest bedrooms on the opposite side of the central hall, receiving an
overall impression of attractive color schemes and the warmth
of antique furniture. O'Mara wouldn't let her linger to
examine the many interesting-looking paintings along the hall
or in the various rooms; she hadn't even had time to admire in
any detail the several large seascapes in his suite. To all her
cries of "Oh, wait a minute, let me see," he laughingly
answered, "Later, love. Supper's on."

At the far end of the hall, beyond Andy's suite, O'Mara
guided her through an archway and down an angled flight of
carpeted stairs. At the bottom, she had just time enough to
note a large laundry room and a lavatory before being guided
through another archway into a big, cheerful, country-style
kitchen.

"Well, it's about time," Andy said. "I was about to send
out my last messenger if I could tear him away from this
roast." She nodded, smiling, toward Hero, who was perched

on a stepstool, his eyes fixed on her every move as she deftly carved thick slices from a beef roast.

"What a super kitchen!" exclaimed Kitt, walking around the center-island work area with its twin sinks, marble-topped work surfaces and various-sized drawers and cupboards. Above the island, dish cabinets had been suspended from the ceiling with fluorescent lights built into their bases to provide even, bright light over the work area. More marble-topped cabinets lined the far, inner wall and continued at right angles along under the wide inner window overlooking the courtyard.

"This must have been designed to cater for a crowd," Kitt observed. "Six . . . no, eight countertop burners and a double-size grill, two ovens, another one . . . oh, that's a microwave, and . . . What's this, Andy?"

"A warming mat, the man called it. It's that pyroceram material. You just flip that switch at the side, and the whole piece heats up just enough so that you can drain vegetables and then put the covers back on the pans and set them on that. It keeps everything hot but won't burn it or cook it any more. I won't put good china on it, but it works fine with earthenware or the ovenproof dishes."

"Must be handy when you're cooking for a party."

"Don't know what I'd do without it. There, Michael, if you'll take this platter and Gus takes the potatoes . . . Kitt, would you—Kitt?"

Kitt backed out of a doorway in the corner and swung around inquiringly, starting quickly toward Andy when she saw her holding out a bowl of peas. "Oh, sorry. I was so surprised to see a pantry. Aren't they the handiest things? You never find one in new houses. Do you want me to carry anything else?"

"No, that's fine. I've got the rest of the hot dishes, and everything else is on the table. We're eating in the breakfast room, just through here. This is closer to the kitchen, and cozier for the four of us than the formal dining room."

With laughter and an easy exchange of conversation, they settled around a mellow pine trestle table in the comfortable, pine-paneled room which continued the warm, country theme of the kitchen. In answer to a question from Kitt, O'Mara explained that all the paneling and the cabinet and drawer fronts in the kitchen and breakfast room had been made from old pine barn boards. Through much of the meal

Andy, O'Mara and Gus answered Kitt's many questions about the house and grounds and described things she hadn't seen yet.

Kitt, attuned to the interplay of voices and expressions, quickly realized that these three people had a closeness and deep affection for one another that she was eager to share. For the first time since being reunited with O'Mara, she truly understood that their relationship was not going to be simply a continuation and deepening of their old emotional tie, but would have to expand to include his love for Gus and Andy and theirs for him. She knew by the time the leisurely dinner was over that there was nothing she wanted more than to become an integral part of this close family circle, to give and receive her share of the interest, understanding and love that was implicit in all their exchanges.

There was no question of the depth of her emotional involvement with O'Mara. Very simply, they were part of each other. And she wasn't really worried anymore about being able to reach a physical fulfillment of their love. Sooner or later, O'Mara would take her beyond the panic point. Even now, in the few days they had been together, she had managed to overcome an amazing amount of her deep-rooted distaste and fear of physical contact.

He turned from speaking to Andy and met Kitt's intense gaze. "Where's your mind, love? You're going to wear through the bottom of that cup if you stir any longer."

"I . . . ah . . . does that go out to the patio I saw from the bridge?" Flustered, she motioned toward the window wall with its sliding glass door.

"Yeah," Gus answered. "We eat out there a lot in the summer. Do you like the house, Kitt? Wouldn't you like to come and live here with us?"

She grinned at his eagerness and cast a teasing look at O'Mara before leaning toward the boy and widening her eyes, asking wonderingly, "Are you proposing to me, Augustus O'Mara? Well, overlooking the slight age difference, I just might be interested—except for two things."

"What?" choked Gus, stifling a giggle and trying to look serious.

"First, I don't know if I'd really feel easy sharing a room with Fifi. And, second, I'm not at all sure your father fancies me as his daughter-in-law. I rather think he has something else in mind."

"Oh, Kitt, you're as nutsy as Ez sometimes!" Gus broke up in laughter, joined by Andy, while O'Mara leaned back in his chair and met Kitt's laughing gaze with a blatantly seductive grin.

He waited until he saw the tint of pink in her cheeks before he said, blandly, "We'll discuss what I have in mind after Mr. Big Ears is in bed."

Kitt decided that she'd be in trouble no matter what she said at that point, and jumped up and started clearing the table. With everyone helping, it only took a few minutes to clean up, stack the dishwasher and store the leftovers. She and Andy chatted easily, establishing the groundwork for a deepening friendship, while O'Mara and Gus built a fire in the family room and then began a game of pool, which, Gus explained, was an evening ritual.

It was a relaxed, peaceful hour, a foretaste of the strong family relationship she would enjoy and become part of in this marvelous house. She already loved Gus, not just because he was O'Mara's son, but for himself—for the intelligent, funny, affectionate, laughing boy he was—and she felt that he was quickly coming to love her. She watched the two of them as they moved around the pool table, so much alike, O'Mara a living vision of what the boy would become. She was totally unaware of the revealing expression on her face as her eyes lingered on the tall, rangy figure leaning forward to make a shot, the muscles in his thighs and back straining against the fabric of his jeans and shirt. Smiling understandingly, Andy saw her eyes close and her mouth soften as she remembered the feel of those sinewy back muscles under her hands and the strength of his legs pressing against hers when she kissed him beside that incredible bed.

"They *both* need you, you know." Andy's soft-voiced comment brought Kitt's eyes open and her attention back to her companion.

"I need them, too, Andy. And you, if you'll take me on." Kitt's smile was warm and appealing, and would have melted a much harder heart than Andy's.

"Oh, I rather think I shall," she said airily. "Not only will you be just what they need, but I've rather taken a fancy to this darling dog." She patted Hero, sprawled out on the sofa beside her, and winked at Kitt, adding, "And then, there's that marvelous twin of yours. Now there's a man who truly appreciates good cooking."

"And lots of it," interjected Kitt, laughing.

"Ah, but that's the challenge, you see, Kitt. It takes skill to provide both quality and quantity, to say nothing of variety. Yes, indeed, it will be a delight to have him around." She tilted her head, brown eyes twinkling, and looked at Kitt consideringly. "Have you realized what a very interesting package deal you are?"

For a moment, Kitt's eyes widened in surprised inquiry, and then she started to laugh, quickly joined by Andy.

"What are you two finding so amusing?" called O'Mara from across the room.

"Andy has just pointed out what a great bargain I am," Kitt chuckled.

"There was never a doubt in my mind," answered O'Mara with a distinctly suggestive grin, "but we may be talking about different benefits. Okay, Gus, that's the game. Good shot on the seven ball. Now you'd better get off to bed."

"I know. School tomorrow." He ran across the room and scrambled across the sofa to throw his arms around Kitt's neck. "I'm glad you like our house, Kitt. You *are* going to come to live with us, aren't you? And Hero?"

Kitt leaned back slightly so she could look into his unusually serious face. The normally bright blue eyes were dark with an intense longing that held just a touch of uncertainty. She wrapped her arms around the wiry young body and hugged him, ducking her head to nibble quick, tickling kisses down his neck which made him giggle.

"I rather think we shall—just as soon as your father and I work out a few minor details." She sent a speaking glance toward O'Mara.

"Terrific!" crowed Gus, jumping up. "Wait till I tell the kids who's going to be my mother! When, Dad? Kitt, how long is it going to take? What details?"

Laughing, O'Mara stretched out a long arm and caught the excited boy, swinging him up over his head. "Calm down, you jumping bean. It won't be long, believe me. Off to bed, now."

"Oh, okay. Can Hero come up with me, Kitt?"

"Sure. I'll collect him when I go." She came gracefully to her feet as Andy stood up.

"I'll go along with Gus and see him into bed. There's a TV show I usually watch, so I'll say goodnight now, Kitt." Andy held out her hand, and Kitt took it in both of hers, bending over to kiss the older woman on the cheek.

"It was a lovely dinner, Andy, and I've so enjoyed getting acquainted with you at last."

Chapter 16

Five minutes later, after an exuberant Gus had kissed everyone goodnight at least twice and raced up the stairs with Hero, followed by Andy at a more sedate pace, Kitt and O'Mara settled onto one of the window seats near the front of the darkened bridge. They kicked their shoes off and sat sideways on the wide bench, Kitt wriggling back between O'Mara's thighs to rest her back against his chest. For a while, they were quiet, relaxing and enjoying the peace of the calm, starry night, watching the progress of a ship so far offshore that its running lights looked like moving stars.

"O'Mara?"

"Hmmm?"

"Are you going to tell me about that phone call, or just leave me wondering?"

"It was Laura. She likes to upset people, and when she heard a woman answer, she jumped to conclusions."

"Does she call often? Doesn't she know Andy's voice?"

He tilted her head back against his shoulder so he could see her face. "No and no, my worrywart. There's absolutely nothing for you to get disturbed about, so take that frown off your face. I doubt if Laura even knows I've got a housekeeper, never mind what her name is or what her voice sounds like. Laura knows nothing about how we live—except that I've got a fair amount of money these days. That's what she's after, love. Just money."

"Do you give her money often? I thought you said—"

"Oh, Kitt," he sighed. "Look, you are not going to have Laura on your neck, if that's what's worrying you. I gave her a lump sum payoff when she signed the divorce papers, and she also signed an agreement that she was accepting that amount in lieu of all future claims. I hadn't heard a word from her until about three months ago, when she called asking for help."

"What happened? Why did she need help all of a sudden?"

"I can only guess. I didn't believe half of what she said. From what I remember of her, I'd say she's finding it a bit difficult these days to attach the kind of men who have the money and inclination to buy her the good life. At least, her version of it. Too many parties, too many men, too many years. It's got to start showing sometime, and I think she's discovering that what you can tease out of men when you're young and gay is a far cry from what they're willing to give to an overage, overused party girl."

"That's rather brutal, isn't it? How do you know—"

"I know." He cut her off abruptly, his voice hardening. "Remember, I've kept in touch with her parents, and I take Gus down to visit them every few months. They love him, and he's made up a great deal for the disappointment and sorrow she's brought to them. She's a thoroughly selfish woman who's caused a lot of trouble and unhappiness. Don't feel sorry for her."

Kitt shifted a bit and half turned so that she could see his face in the dim light from the family room. "Are you . . . ?" She didn't know quite how to finish it, unsure of just what his feelings were for this woman who had given him a son and then wiped them both out of her life.

"Oh, hell. She's pathetic more than anything else, Kitt. That's all I feel for her. I told you before that there was never anything between us except a casual affair. And it was casual on both sides. If she feels anything for me now, it's resentment because, one, I made her have Gus and, two, I've made a lot of money while she's been going downhill. Before you ask, yes, I did give her some money when she called a few months ago. Well, I didn't exactly give it to her; I told her to send me the bills she was worrying about and I'd pay them, which I did. I also told her that it was a one-time arrangement and that she'd better get herself a normal job and start living on what she earned, because I wasn't going to pay any more of her bills."

"So why is she calling you for more money now?"

"Because Laura only hears what she wants to hear. I figured that once I helped her out, she'd be back for more. I told her 'no dice' and that it wouldn't do her a bit of good to keep bugging me."

"But not quite in those terms?"

"Ah, not quite. They were strong enough for even Laura to get the message."

"What about her parents?"

"They won't help her anymore, either. At first, her father gave her money when she came with a sad story of needing help to pay medical bills and who knows what. Then he found out that she was taking the money and using it for trips to Europe or Mexico or wherever else the Beautiful People congregated. The next time she came around, he told her to give him the bills and he'd pay them himself. He made the same discovery I did—the bills were for expensive clothes, jewelry, a luxury apartment, credit card charges at first-class hotels and restaurants, and on and on. He also told her the same thing I did: 'Get a job and live within your income, because I'm not paying for any more high life for you.' She kept right on living it up, and he refused to shell out again."

"If you knew about that, why did you pay?"

"Two reasons. One was psychological, just in case she got cute with attempted legal action to claim part-custody of Gus. Of course, she hasn't a chance, but she could cause considerable unpleasantness. Not that I mind so much for myself, but I don't want Gus involved in that kind of mess. In any event, I wanted to spike any guns she might try to bring up in claiming that I refused to help her when she needed it. Once around, keeping a list of exactly what the bills were that I paid, with a clear emphasis on the fact that none of them were what the normal person would call necessities, would be clear proof that I was willing to help her out. It would also explain why I didn't feel the need of extending further aid, since she was obviously making no attempt to live on a reasonable scale."

"It doesn't make sense, O'Mara. Why would she bother trying to get Gus when she knows she can't possibly succeed? And she doesn't really want him anyway, does she?"

"Of course not. It would only be a threat, a form of blackmail, to try to get me to pay her off. She wouldn't expect to get anywhere in court, but she could create a great deal of nasty publicity since I'm fairly well known. I've been careful over the years about my public image, mainly because of Gus, and there are some scandal sheets that would love to get a first-hand account from my ex-wife about how mean and miserable I am toward her and how I won't let her have any contact with her darling son."

"But—"

"I know. It's not true and I can prove it, but by the time I did so and a retraction was printed at the bottom of page forty-two in small type, who would pay any attention? All the public would remember would be the headlines."

"Okay. I can see your reasoning. So, what was the second thing?"

"I wanted to get a list of her creditors. That was why I told her to send the bills to me. Her father told me that when he wouldn't pay any more bills for her, she claimed that she would have no trouble having them sent to me."

"Would she?"

"Oh, she could have gotten away with it once. Of course, the first time I received a bill from anyone for her charges, I would have sent back a letter explaining the situation. Again, to simplify things and prevent unpleasantness, it was easier to get hold of her current bills, pay them, and include a letter of explanation specifying that I was not responsible for her future financial dealings and that the recipient would do well to investigate her credit standing."

"Hmmm. You can get rather nasty, too, can't you?"

"Only if pushed."

"I'm surprised that she'd hit you up again. If she knew you at all—"

"That's just it. She doesn't. Besides, she was ripping mad. Several of her favorite shops and a couple of credit card companies have cut her off after checking her rating and source of income. Naturally, she blames me."

"How did you leave it?"

"No more money. I absolutely won't guarantee her credit. She'd better get a job and scale down her lifestyle. Threats aren't going to get her anywhere. That's it."

"What do you think she'll do now?"

"Who knows? She's so damn erratic it's impossible to second-guess her half the time. I'll give my lawyer a call in the morning and fill him in so he'll be ready for any odd moves. I'm bored with the subject of Laura. Let's talk about how soon you're going to take up residence here."

His arms were looped loosely around her, barely touching her, and she felt no uneasiness in their gentle enclosure. In fact, she wasn't thinking about being restrained at that moment; her mind was still on Laura and how much of a threat she might be to Gus's peace of mind. O'Mara was more than capable of taking care of himself, but Gus was only nine, and Kitt had no clear idea as to just how much he understood of the situation. She was trying to formulate a leading question when O'Mara distracted her by trailing kisses from her ear down to her collarbone and slowly stroking one hand up the length of her leg.

"Oh, wait. O'Mara, stop changing the subject. I want . . . Will you stop that for a minute? I want to ask you something."

"Mmmm. I would much rather find out how we're progressing in our project."

"All right, but not this minute. Please. Toad. Come on, O'Mara, this is important. I need to know how Gus feels about Laura, or I won't know what to say or not to say to him. What are you doing?"

"Unfastening your bra. Why the hell do you bother with the silly thing? You don't need it. Ah, that's better. Lean back and relax. You can hold onto my other hand, and you can move away whenever you want to. Okay?"

"This is a hell of a way to carry on a serious conversation. How am I supposed to concentrate with you doing that? Are you going to tell me about Gus?"

"If I must. But you do pick your times, love. Is that making you nervous?"

"That's not exactly the word I'd use, you devious toad. You know perfectly well what that's making me. Tell me about Gus and how he feels about Laura. How much does he know?"

"When did you develop this one-track mind? Ow! Don't pinch. I'll tell you. He knows just about everything. He's much too bright to try to fool or fob off with half-truths. I didn't think it was fair, either, to let him fantasize about his mother coming back full of remorse and overdue love. We've talked about it quite a bit at one time or another, and I think he's very well adjusted to the situation. Several times, we've discussed the possibility of finding just the right woman to be a mother to him and a wife to me, and I told him about you and said that you'd be exactly what we needed if I could find you again."

"Ha! I had a feeling. He said something the other evening that made me suspect that he'd already heard quite a bit about me before last Friday. O'Mara?"

"Mmmm. Turn around. I can't kiss you from here."

"That was a short discussion. On the other hand, I'm rather losing my train of thought. Ahhh, that's nice."

"Just nice?" His voice was muffled against her neck. She arched her head back and turned toward him, pushing his head up until she could reach his mouth with hers.

"Very nice," she whispered against his mouth, pressing her bare breasts into his warm, waiting hands. His touch was firm but gentle; he let all the pressure come from her, leaving her free to move back whenever she wished.

Kitt had no thought of moving away. She loved the feel of his hands on her, his fingers gently stroking, his thumbs teasing her nipples to hardness. Eagerly, she opened her mouth for him and wound her arms around his shoulders, burying her fingers in his thick hair, reveling in its sensuous softness under her hands.

Eyes closed, all her senses concentrated on him and what he was making her feel, she stopped trying to think coherently or to analyze what was happening between them. She let her mind go its own way, filling with the awareness of her rising heat and his obvious arousal. It went on for a timeless span before he finally brought his hands up to frame her face and ease her a few inches away from him.

"Softly now, my Kitt," he murmured huskily. "Let go of my hair and relax."

"Not yet. Please."

"Shhh. Now is just the right time to calm down, before we push it to the point where you get scared. Come on, love, sit up and give me your hands."

"But I want—"

"I know what you want, but you're not ready yet. You

know you're not, love. And I don't want you to react to me with fear, so we should stop before it gets to that stage."

Pushing her hair back, she sat up, swinging her feet to the floor and leaving a couple of feet of space between them. As her breathing returned to normal and her heartbeat slowed, she slanted a rueful look at him. "It's your own fault, you know. You touch me like that and I forget all about being afraid of . . . the rest of it." She sighed and stood up, turning away from him to fumble for the fastening to her bra. "But I know you're right about rushing things. It's just that. . . ."

He swung to his feet as her voice trailed off and she stood, tense, staring out at the dark, moving mystery of the night ocean. Coming up behind her, he started massaging the tight muscles in her neck and shoulders, finally feeling her relax under his hands and, at last, lean back against him, reaching up to take his hands and bring his arms around her. She turned her head against his shoulder and smiled at him, saying softly, "It's okay."

"We've got almost a week before I leave for Europe. Let's just take it day by day and one step at a time. No pressure. No trying to force things. All right, love?"

"All right."

Although she agreed with him at that moment, she didn't really believe that they would be able to keep from trying to consummate their deep love for each other much longer. Her knowledge of his desire and need for her went far beyond sensing; she could actually *feel* the strength of his passion driving through him whenever he held her, or even when she was merely close enough to touch him. As for her own feelings, she was torn between frustration and anger and exasperation. She was filled with an overwhelming longing to *be* with him, completely, totally; to find out at last the ending of what they had started so many years before; and, at the same instant, to begin fulfilling the promise of their new life together now. Still, despite her blazing, aching need of him, which grew stronger every time they were together, there remained that tiny, cold, twisted lump of fear lodged deep in her vitals, just waiting to burgeon into panic when her subconscious screamed, "Trapped! Can't move! Can't get away! There's going to be pain!"

She tried again and again, far into the night hours after

O'Mara had brought her home, to convince herself that she would not panic. This was O'Mara, and he loved her far beyond anything she could put into words; he would cut off his hand before he would cause her the slightest pain; he had the patience and experience to bring her to the ultimate pleasure without ever causing her the least discomfort; he would teach her everything and make sure she gloried in the learning.

She sat up in the middle of her empty bed, huddled in a tight ball with her arms wrapped around her knees, rocking back and forth. Somehow, it had to go away. She had to force it out of her system. There must be a way to get rid of the fear, especially since she was eons away from being afraid of him. She loved him. She had emptinesses that only he could fill—physical, mental, emotional spaces. She knew she wouldn't be complete until she was with him, living with him, sharing all the experiences of life with him. And the frustration of not being able to get rid of that damn nub of panic was making her mad enough to spit!

The list of both their individual and mutual frustrations that week was a long one. Kitt tried everything she could think of to tease, tempt and inveigle O'Mara into at least trying to make love to her. To her surprise, he remained adamant in his conviction that they should not try to force the issue. Much to his surprise, and her delight, she discovered hitherto unsuspected talents for playing the seductress. With a heady combination of fascination, bemusement and appreciation, he watched her kick her inhibitions into the river and concentrate her unfettered imagination on the problem of wrapping him around her little finger.

For the first time in years, she looked at clothes as more than a means of covering as much bare skin as possible. In fact, it had been so long since she had given a thought to dressing to please a man that she was hesitant to trust her own judgment in choosing among the many new styles. A quick conference with Midge, and she had acquired a new part-time clerk for a couple of hours in the afternoon, leaving Midge free to go with her on a three-afternoon shopping spree.

Enchanted, Midge watched a new Kitt emerge—a vibrant, laughing woman who looked years younger, her eyes sparkling with mischief as she suddenly became aware of her own attractiveness and appeal and plotted, with Midge's enthusiastic assistance, to knock O'Mara back on his heels. There wasn't a doubt in her mind that he knew perfectly well what she was doing, but he encouraged her transformation by voicing his admiration and approval of her new image.

It was O'Mara, standing back and thoroughly examining Kitt's outfit for dinner at the Standish Reef, who finally pinned a label on her new look when he murmured, "Hmmm. Subtly enticing. I like it. You'll be lucky if you get out of there without some green-eyed female stabbing you with her butter knife."

"Or some overheated male attacking her," chimed in Midge, casting an envious glance at Kitt's elegant length draped in finely pleated, pale gold chiffon evening trousers and a sleeveless, cowl-necked overblouse of the same material belted with a gold cord. When she was standing still, the costume was merely elegant, but as soon as she moved, the thin, drifting fabric molded to her every curve.

The glinting look Kitt cast in O'Mara's direction made it clear just which overheated male she'd like to have "attack" her. Laughing, he caught her hands to pull her close and whispered, "You look very sexy, love, but I'm still only going to let things go just so far."

Much to Kitt's chagrin, he stuck to his position, and it wasn't until their last evening together before he left for Europe that he relented and, even then, it was because she took him by surprise and he reacted before he had time to think.

Monday afternoon was slow, and Midge chased Kitt upstairs at four o'clock to get ready for the evening. O'Mara and Gus were due to pick her up at five to take her out to dinner and then back to the Rock for the rest of the evening. Her first view of the O'Maras standing nonchalantly in the middle of the shop stopped her in her tracks, and she had the fleeting thought that Midge's bedazzled expression must surely be mirrored on her own face. They were truly splendid, casually posed in the ultimate in father-son ensembles, watching her with matching mischievously gleaming eyes.

Regaining her aplomb, she walked around them in a circle, valiantly ignoring the telltale shaking of O'Mara's shoulders as she absorbed the details of deep sapphire velvet jackets, two or three shades darker than their eyes, white silk-knit turtleneck pullovers, pale gray slacks and intricate gold chains. She bent over Gus to examine the gold device on his chain and discovered it to be an inch-high, finely detailed Tyrannosaurus rex.

Still leaning over, she raised her eyes to Gus's, kissed him on the nose and pronounced, "You are truly splendiferous!"

Straightening up and turning to O'Mara, she managed to slide her eyes quickly past his waiting gaze and concentrate on the glitter of gold on his chest. As she realized what it was, she suppressed a gasp of laughter but couldn't control the mirth that filled her eyes. Gleaming against the white silk was a magnificently warty toad, sporting a distinct leer and winking at her with a glowing sapphire eye.

Breathlessly, she managed, "Wherever did you find—" before she finally met his laughing eyes with her own.

It set the tone for much of the evening. Absorbing the love and admiration emanating from O'Mara and Gus, Kitt was relaxed and happy; the faint misgivings she'd felt about the bareness of her dress, still a new experience, disappeared under O'Mara's appreciative comments and his apparent inability to keep from touching her every few minutes. Since all of her interest was centered on the look in *his* eyes, she was totally unaware of the attention she attracted as she followed the maître d' across the restaurant dining room. More than a few male eyes lit with pleasure at the sight of her long, slim legs enhanced by the swirling knee-length skirt of her turquoise jersey dress, and the firm curves of her breasts subtly emphasized by the soft gathers of the dress's bodice, cut high in front but baring her back almost to her waist.

O'Mara, however, had not missed the assessing looks. Once they were seated, he clasped Kitt's hand to gain her attention and murmured teasingly, "I love your new wardrobe. Make no mistake about that. But I'm definitely going to start carrying a voluminous cape around with me for occasions such as this."

Her startled eyes met his, and then followed his drifting gaze around the room. As she realized how many men were eyeing her, she bit her lip in consternation and a flush stained her cheeks. Turning back to O'Mara, she opened her mouth to speak but was forestalled by Gus asking, "Why do you want to wrap Kitt in a cape? I think she looks great!"

Laughing, teasing, bubbling with plans and discussions, the

three of them ignored the rest of the patrons and concentrated on deepening their rapidly developing sense of being a family.

Daylight saving time had come in over the weekend, and it was still light when they left the restaurant and strolled across the parking lot toward the Mercedes. Kitt was turned away from O'Mara and talking with Gus, so she didn't notice his distraction until they reached the car. When he didn't step forward to unlock the door, she turned and saw him standing several feet back, his attention fixed on something on the far side of the lot.

"O'Mara? What's wrong?"

With a last look over his shoulder, he joined them. "Nothing. Just . . . I thought I saw . . . someone I knew."

The Monday evening traffic was light on Route One, and they made good time back to Kennebunkport. Half-turned in her seat so that she could include Gus in the conversation, Kitt gradually became aware of the inordinate number of times O'Mara checked the rearview mirror and that he was often only half-hearing what they were saying to him.

"Is something wrong, O'Mara?" she asked softly when Gus's attention was diverted by the boats as they crossed the river. "You've been watching that mirror all the way back."

"I'm not sure. Probably it's coincidence, but there's been a red Toyota following us since we left the restaurant, and I noticed a similar car a couple of times earlier today." He shrugged, adding, "It's probably just an early tourist who happens to be going to the same places we are."

"Seems logical. After all, lots of cars are seen around for a few days and then disappear. I've been getting quite a few tourists in the shop these past couple of weeks."

They stopped briefly at the shop to pick up Hero, and then went on to the Rock. Gus stayed up an extra half-hour, taking advantage of it's being his father's last night at home for at least two weeks, and Kitt and Andy kibbitzed a wild Ping-Pong contest between father and son. After hot chocolate and mint cookies, Gus and Andy retreated upstairs, leaving Kitt and O'Mara to wander out to the bridge.

There was a spring storm building up at sea, and they watched as the large waves smashed over the offshore reefs, sending silver fans of spray twenty feet into the air. Clouds raced across the moon-bright sky, driven by strong upper-air winds, and they could hear the crash of the sea against the base of the Rock and the rising sound of the wind sweeping around the house. Standing at the point of the bridge, Kitt felt almost as if she were out in the midst of the turmoil and shivered.

"Let's go in and sit by the fire for a while before I take you home." His voice was soft in her ear, and she could feel his breath on her cheek and his warm hands stroking up and down her arms.

Something changed, stopped and then started again, shifted its balance—she didn't know exactly what happened, but from one breath to another she blazed with heat and a driving need of him. Perhaps it was the combination of the warm, strong security of his presence at her back and the wildness of the elements around them—whatever the cause, she was suddenly taken over by her own elemental instincts, and she turned into his arms, pressing her body and legs against his, wrapping her arms tightly around his waist, reaching for and finding his mouth with hers, already open and seeking.

She took him completely by surprise, and he reacted instinctively, unthinkingly doing what he had dreamed of for days. He met her mouth with an unleashed hunger, his arms closing around her, drawing her even tighter to his instantly aroused body. One hand pressed firmly down the length of her spine, the long fingers spreading and curving to fit the shape of her buttocks and pulling her pelvis tight against the hard ridge of his manhood.

They swayed on their feet, almost off-balance, muscles straining as they tried to get closer to each other, breaths panting, her low moan smothered under the force of his urgent, thrusting tongue. He was so lost in the passionate delirium of holding her, possessing her, that it was almost too late when his dazed senses picked up the panic signals. Within seconds, his extraordinarily strong willpower had tamped down his soaring passion, relaxed his straining body and brought his mind back to reason. Her hands were on his hips, pushing him away, her body was stiffening and a keening sound was starting in her throat as she twisted her head away from his, when he finally loosened his arms and brought his hands up to rest lightly on her shoulders.

"No, no, love. It's all right," he whispered. "Don't pull

away from me. Relax. See, I've let go. You're free. You can move wherever you want to, but I'd like it best if you came back against me. I won't hold you again. I promise. You took me by surprise, then. Just come back to me. One step, that's all. I'll keep my hands right where they are, and you can move away if you want."

Soft and soothing, repeating key words and phrases, his voice drew her back from the edge of panic. Shaking back her hair, she looked at him and saw love and took a step forward, sliding her arms around him again and leaning her head on his shoulder.

"I didn't think it would happen," she murmured. "It felt so good to be in your arms and I wanted you so much, I really thought it had gone away. Oh, why—"

"It's all right, my Kitt. We're getting closer." His deep chuckle vibrated against her cheek where it rested on his shoulder. "If I can't yet hold you in my arms, at least I'm in yours—and that's the next best thing."

Chapter 17

O'Mara left on Tuesday morning, and in the ensuing days Kitt discovered that Time had a fey, fickle will of its own. A morning would disappear without a trace or a memory, an afternoon dragged into a week, an evening fluctuated between hours that were seconds long and minutes that were endless. She threw herself enthusiastically into the task of expanding the scope of the shop, working energetically for half a morning, only to be brought back from a lovely daydream of life with O'Mara when Midge arrived to nudge her into reality.

By the middle of the first weekend, she caught onto the conspiracy. It had somehow escaped her notice until then that she had rarely been left alone since Tuesday morning. Midge was around in the afternoons, working, and Gus had popped in after school on Wednesday and Thursday—with the excuse

of visiting Hero but managing to involve Kitt in cookie-
baking and a ramble out Ocean Avenue to the Spouting
Rock. Tuesday evening, Midge had stayed for dinner and
conversation; Wednesday, Gus invited himself to supper with
great charm and the excuse of teaching Kitt how to make
proper hamburgers; on Thursday, Andy called and suggested
that Kitt stay for barbecued ribs when she drove Gus home.
After dinner, she gave Gus, much to his surprise, a dazzling
demonstration of how to win hands-down at Ping-Pong; once
he was in bed, she and Andy lost track of time, talking, and
she and Hero ended up staying the night.

In the middle of Friday afternoon, she was leaning on the
work counter making out a list of all the things she hadn't had
time to do that week and figuring out how much catching up
she could manage that evening, when Ez ambled in some
three hours before she expected him. After his usual exuberant reunion with Midge, he informed both women that he was
taking them out to dinner and a show in Portland. Kitt's pleas
to be allowed an evening to herself were blandly brushed
aside, and her argument that she didn't want to be a third
wheel was shot down when Midge called her older brother
and got his eager agreement to act as Kitt's escort.

Ez disappeared for the day Saturday, taking Gus and Hero
off to explore the more interesting islands in Casco Bay,
which were reached by ferry from Portland. By early Saturday evening, Kitt had had it with togetherness, and explained
to Midge and Ez in simple language that she did *not* need a
babysitter.

"In fact, you two noodles, I've been desperate to get some
time to myself for the past three days. Every stitch I own is in
the laundry. I've got letters to write. April's accounts need to
be billed. I've got all sorts of things to do if you'll just give me
some time in which to do them. Now go away for a few hours,
and let me get on with it."

"Just what we need—a quiet evening at home," Ez stated.
"We'll help you and have it all done in no time at all."

"You'll tuck your girl under your arm and take yourself
off," Kitt exclaimed wrathfully. "I know what you're doing,
and it's not necessary. I am not going to be lonely. I am not
going to brood. What I am going to do is have a little time to
myself to think sexy thoughts about O'Mara! So there!

You've all been so busy keeping me busy that I haven't even had time for pleasant memories and planning what I want to do when he gets back."

"We just didn't want you to get lonely," Ez muttered sheepishly.

"I should have realized that you'd want time to dream about the . . . ah . . . more interesting episodes," added Midge, with a reminiscent look at Ez.

"Yes, well, now that you understand, how about scooting out of here and giving me some privacy?" Kitt pleaded.

"We're gone," asserted Ez, scooping Midge up and striding out the door.

By early evening, Kitt had finished the laundry, eaten a light supper, written her letters and spread out the account books and charge slips on the desk in her study. She sat down in the desk chair and took a stack of billheads and envelopes from the bottom drawer, then wrinkled her nose and groaned at the thought of spending the next three hours closed up in the small room. A glance at her watch assured her that there was still at least an hour of light left, and exclaiming "A plague on it!" she jumped up and strode toward her bedroom to find her running shoes.

With Hero romping along beside her, she loped easily down Ocean Avenue toward the sea, her hair blowing into a tangle in the brisk offshore breeze. It was a cool evening, but the exercise was keeping her comfortably warm. Glancing occasionally from side to side, she noted that several more houses seemed to be occupied and more of the yards had been tended. Obviously, a number of summer people were taking advantage of the fine early May weather to start opening up their homes for the season. She suddenly got a noseful of the sweet fragrance of hyacinths and looked around for the source, finally spotting a border of blue and pink blossoms along the walk of the house across the road.

Enjoying the sights and scents of the spring evening, she continued on as far as the Spouting Rock, where she took a breather and watched the half-tide waves force their way through the blowhole to shoot a fan of spray some fifteen to twenty feet into the air. Just as the sky began to color with the beginnings of sunset, and before she completely cooled off, she called to the exploring Hero and started back. She was dividing her attention between the sunset and the road surface, and barely noticed the red Toyota parked on the bridge over one of the tidal inlets from the river. As she went past it, she fleetingly wondered if it could be the same one that O'Mara had seen, and then promptly forgot about it as the sky flamed with burning orange and magenta. She had no reason to look back, and therefore didn't see the driver straighten up from where he had been slouched, out of sight, behind the wheel, light a cigarette and stare broodingly after her gracefully running figure.

Kitt lingered on the deck to watch the last few minutes of the sunset and then went in to shower and don her comfortable terry caftan. Deciding that the billing could wait until morning, she settled down on the sofa with a cup of coffee to watch a Neil Simon comedy on the *Saturday Night Movie*. She was laughing when the phone rang, and there was a sense of *déjà vu* as she dumped Hero on the floor and scrambled to answer it, tripping over the hassock and grabbing up the receiver with a breathless "Hello."

"Do you always answer the phone with this panting eagerness," came the deep voice, "or is it just when you sense that I'm calling?"

"O'Mara! Where are you? You sound so close. Are you home?"

His chuckle sent waves of heat through her vitals, and she almost didn't hear him say, "No, love. I'm in Geneva, but we've lucked out on a good connection. How are you? What are you doing? I half thought you might be off somewhere with the odd couple."

"I talked myself out of it. Everybody has been so busy this week keeping me from being lonely that I haven't had a minute to myself. It's been heavenly this evening—just me and Hero and Neil Simon."

"Well, you should be safe enough with that combo. What have you been so busy with?"

Kitt recapped her week for him, sensing his delight and satisfaction at the deepening relationship between her and Gus. Finally, she asked, "How is your trip going? Have you been able to see the people you wanted to talk with?"

"Most of them, at least the important ones. I'm running about a day behind right now, but with luck I'll make it up next week. If it hadn't been so difficult to set all this up, I'd come back tomorrow. I miss you, love."

"I miss you, too. Memories are okay, but they're not as warm as you are."

"How am I supposed to take that?" he teased.

"Mmmm," she murmured noncommittally. "Besides, I feel as if we left off in the middle of things. I wanted to know . . . oh, all sorts of things. You know what I want."

"Indeed I do, love. The same thing I want. Don't worry so, my Kitt. We'll have it. Believe me. Don't you understand just how much that meant, that last night when you turned to me so instinctively, so desperately in need of physical closeness? Think about it, Kitt. Let the need build up, feed it, concentrate on it, until it fills you to the point of forcing out the panic."

"Oh, God, O'Mara, don't you think I *have* thought about it? I've been trying not to, or I won't get any sleep or be able to concentrate on work."

"Never mind sleep. You can sleep after I get home. Right now, it's more important to overcome your fears."

"All right," she sighed, "but I'll probably be a total wreck by the time you get back. Black rings around my eyes, hollow cheeks and shaking hands. Then what will you do?"

"Kiss everything better," came the husky voice. "And with that thought, I'm going to say goodnight. I'll call you in a few days. I love you, my Kitt. Hold the thought."

"Oh, yes. And I love you, O'Mara. Goodnight."

She'd lost the thread of the movie and finally turned it off and wandered along to bed, leaving a note for Ez to take Hero out. Drowsily, she replayed the conversation with O'Mara, feeling the uncoiling of desire as she remembered the warm, husky sound of his voice telling her to think about needing him. And, oh, how she did need him! She wanted to be naked with him, to look at him, to touch him, to stroke her hands over his warm, smooth skin, to feel him—NO! She couldn't think about that or she would have to remember Leon, and that was impossible. She didn't want to remember anything about Leon and what he used to do to her. It had nothing to do with O'Mara and how he touched her, loved her, would make love to her. He wouldn't be like Leon. He couldn't be, could he? But how could he not be? There was

only one way to be completely joined as one, and how could it
be any different with O'Mara?

*It would hurt! It had to! It always did! Can I possibly love
him enough to let him hurt me like that? Oh, God,
ohgodohgodohgod—*

"Kitt! What's wrong?" The lights flicked on and Ez came
swiftly across the room to drop down onto the edge of the bed
and gather a sobbing Kitt in his arms.

"Easy, easy now. Calm down and tell me what's the
matter."

Held firmly in one strong arm while his other hand stroked
back her hair and gently rubbed her shoulders, Kitt gradually
quieted to soft gulps of air as she tried to ease the ache in her
chest.

"Oh, Ez, what am I going to do? I can't . . . no matter how
much I want him . . . he can't help but . . . There's no other
way, is there?"

"You do know that you're not making a bit of sense, don't
you?" He tipped her head back against his shoulder and
examined her tear-stained face and despairing eyes. "Get
your breath back, and then tell me calmly what's happened
and who's upset you like this."

"All right," Kitt said wanly, moving to sit up by herself.
"Let me go and wash my face first."

"While you're doing that, I'll make some coffee. No, tea
would be better. Have you got some of that orange and spice
stuff?"

"Second shelf of the cabinet to the right of the sink. I'll
only be a few minutes," she said over her shoulder as she
closed the bathroom door.

Wrapped in a warm robe but still feeling chilled to the
bone, Kitt sat curled up in a corner of the sofa with her hands
clasped around a mug of hot tea and told Ez about the phone
call from O'Mara. Lounging at the other end of the sofa,
facing her, he listened without comment until she came to the
end of her recapitulation. He waited, watching her stare
broodingly into her empty mug, but she didn't say anything
else.

Finally, he asked, "Was that what upset you? Talking to
O'Mara? If you've told me all of it, I can't understand why
you were crying. I think he's making good sense about

concentrating on your need for him to overcome your fears. Does that have something to do with the state you're in?"

Quietly but insistently, he questioned her, coaxing her to talk, patiently waiting while she struggled for words and, eventually, hiding his surprised relief when she told him what had led up to her crying jag. For years, he had tried gently and subtly to bring her around to discussing with him exactly what Darcy had done to her. She had talked to him about the physical abuse—the punching, slapping, biting—which explained her fear of violence, but he had known that there must have been appalling experiences of sexual abuse to account for her terror-stricken reaction to being touched by any man other than himself. Until O'Mara came back into her life. Ez wasn't quite sure why it was different with him; perhaps because O'Mara was her first love, a strong but innocent love in the time before Darcy had brutalized her, and somehow in her subconscious she knew that O'Mara would never have hurt her. However, consciously, after her experiences with Darcy, she was convinced that physical love was a painful, unpleasant act. Ez had long wanted to discuss this part of her marriage with his twin, to try to make her understand that a sexual relationship between two people who loved each other was the ultimate pleasure, and never the ugly act forced on her by Darcy. However, Kitt had never been able to face those memories and put her thoughts and feelings about them into words.

Now, at last, O'Mara had provided the catalyst that was needed to bring down the barriers to memory and allow Kitt to talk openly about Darcy's sexual attacks, his abuse of her body and her deep-rooted fear of ever again being in a physically vulnerable position with a man.

It all spilled out, at first in a jumble of disconnected words and phrases, and then, as the pressure of initial revelation eased, she paused to pull her thoughts together and managed to give him a coherent description of just what Darcy had done and her reactions. Ez heard her out, saying very little, knowing that the very act of verbalizing all the terror and pain was part of a necessary healing process. At last, she stopped speaking and wiped away the tears that had been trickling, unfelt, down her cheeks.

Ez came to his feet and reached for her empty mug. "You

need something a bit stronger than tea. I seem to remember
seeing a bottle of brandy in the cupboard."

He disappeared into the kitchen, returning a few minutes
later with two brandy snifters. Handing one to Kitt, he
dropped back down onto his end of the sofa and swirled the
deep amber liquid around in his glass, watching her out of the
corner of his eye, waiting for her to regain her composure.

"You okay?"

"Mmmm. Sorry about that. I didn't mean to fall apart all
over you." She lifted apologetic eyes to meet his understanding gaze.

"Try not to be any more feather-witted than normal," he
said in mock-disgust. "Who better than I could you fall apart
on?"

"Thank God you're not trying to teach English," she
groaned, laughing weakly.

"There's nothing wrong with my English. A little creative
usage is what keeps a language alive. And don't think you're
going to sidetrack me into a discussion of my syntax. I want to
know if you're afraid of O'Mara."

Kitt caught her breath at the suddenness of the question.
She had started to relax, and was feeling sleepy after the
intense emotionalism of the past couple of hours. The effort
of dragging up all those ugly memories and forming them into
words had drained her, and she'd had no thought of any
further deep discussions right now.

Trying to collect her thoughts, she could only repeat,
"Afraid of O'Mara?"

"I don't mean in the normal way of things. I know you're
not. Remember, I've seen you kiss him and quite happily let
him put his arm around you." He lifted an inquiring eyebrow
as he added, "I'm not sure, of course, how much further
contact you've accepted, but it's certain sure that you haven't
been to bed with him."

Kitt's quick, upward look at him had a hint of rebellious-
ness in it. "How do you know we haven't . . . been to bed
together? Maybe—"

"Knock it off, Sis. All I've got to do is look at him when
he's watching you, and I can practically see a cloud of sexual
frustration hanging over his head. And don't bother making
any dumb remarks about his being able to get all he wants

someplace else. Of course he could. I've seen the way women look at him. If he showed the least bit of interest in any one of them, she'd be all over him like wet wallpaper. However, he's only interested in one woman, and that's you. So, he'll wait you out. Now answer my question—are you afraid of him?"

"No, not of O'Mara." She wrapped her arms around her upraised knees, bringing one hand up to her mouth and nibbling on her thumbnail. "I can . . . he can . . . it's all right between us up to a point. We've come a long way together in just those few days before he left. He makes me . . . want him . . . respond to him . . . but when it's reaching the point where his . . . arousal is unmistakable and . . . I have to think . . . no; I don't really *think* about it . . . it's more of a reaction. . . ."

"Stop a minute, Kitt, and get your thoughts together. Slowly, now. Take it one step at a time. It doesn't scare you when you're sexually aroused?"

"No. It's fine. I mean, I like it, and I don't want him to stop touching me." She was slightly flushed, but somehow not really embarrassed. Although she and Ez had never discussed their personal sexual experiences, they had in earlier years talked about sex in general. In fact, Ez had been Kitt's main source of information when she had finally developed her belated interest in men as something more than fellow athletes.

She lifted her head and looked at him, unflinchingly meeting the eyes so like her own, and she felt the tension draining out of her as she received his silent messages. It was time, now, to talk about her most pressing fear. She knew he would tell her the truth and help her to accept it even if it were as bad as she expected.

He started to speak, and she held up a staying hand. "No. Let me tell you. I know what your next question is. Yes, it's O'Mara's arousal that scares me. At least; the . . . physical evidence of it does. I'm fine now, even with his arms around me, until I feel *that* against me, and then the panic starts. Not in my mind. That's so fuzzy with wanting him that I don't think. It's some defensive trigger in my system. The minute my body feels that hard ridge pressing against it, all my muscles knot and I start fighting to move away from it. It's a threat. It's going to hurt me."

"I understand what you're saying," Ez said slowly, thinking it through. "To you, it's a weapon, an instrument of pain rather than pleasure, because you've never felt pleasure from that part of a man, thanks to that bastard Darcy. And his repeated raping of you caused so much pain that your system is . . . programmed . . . to equate an erection with agony. Damn! I wish to hell O'Mara had taken you all the way that last summer!"

"So does he. So do I. If he had . . ."

"If he had, your initial experience would have been beautiful, because he cared enough about you to make sure it was. Then, if somehow you'd still had an experience like Darcy, both your mind and your body would have had an existing pleasurable memory to offset the ugliness."

"I think you're right, Ez. I'm not afraid of O'Mara's kisses or his hands on me. He did all that before and I loved it. It hasn't been all that difficult to accept that part of lovemaking again. And I have no trouble in touching him. It's the rest of it. I love him, Ez, but I'm not sure if I can let him hurt me."

"Idiot! Why would he hurt you? He loves you practically to the point of obsession. The last thing in the world he would do would be to hurt you in any way."

"But—" There was a mixture of anguish and pleading in her expression. "How can he help but hurt me if he . . . ?"

There was a waiting silence as Ez groped for the true meaning behind her half-finished question and Kitt watched him with a faint light of hope in her eyes, willing him to have an acceptable answer for her.

Suddenly, it all fell into place, and Ez quickly schooled his expression as he finally understood the full extent of her fears. At least, he thought he did, but perhaps—

"You know why it hurt so much with Darcy, don't you?" he asked carefully, watching her face closely for every nuance of response. At her hesitantly questioning look, he continued, "It's a very basic fact, Sis, that a woman has to be ready to take a man, or he's going to hurt her. Did Darcy ever . . . arouse you . . . make love to you or touch you . . . before he—" Kitt's hair flew as she violently shook her head, her eyes reflecting remembered anguish.

"Damn him!" Ez's fist thudding onto the arm of the sofa shook the room. "It's all right, Kitt," he said quietly on an indrawn breath. "I know this is hard for you to talk about, but I can't help you to understand . . . Well, I have to know a few basics before I can explain—"

"Ez," she interrupted, husky-voiced, "I do know about . . . the need for . . . being aroused and . . . and . . . ready before . . . Well, he never did that. He never even tried. He just . . . sl-slammed into m-m-me." Her arms were wrapped tightly around her knees, and she rocked back and forth in pain, slow tears seeping from under her closed eyelids. "Oh, God, it hurt so. It hur—"

The raw, hoarse words were smothered against Ez's shoulder as he pulled her into his arms, his muscles flexing in a crushing hold as he tried, desperately, to absorb some of her pain. He leaned his head against hers, his thick chestnut hair falling forward to blend with hers, and muttered a litany of basic Anglo-Saxon under his breath. He didn't stop until he felt her hands patting his shoulders and heard her hiccupping laugh in his ear.

"Ez, good grief, you really did learn some new words from O'Mara," she choked, struggling for a light tone and almost making it. His arms loosened as she pushed back slightly to look at him, rubbing her hands across her cheeks to wipe away the last tears.

"Never mind my vocabulary." He brushed his fingers across her face and pushed her hair back, leaving his hand resting at the back of her neck. "Kitt, you *know* that O'Mara would never, never do anything remotely like that to you. He's a gentle man and he loves you. He would take great care that you would be more than ready for him before he'd even try to join with you. Don't you know that?"

"Oh, yes. At least, I know that he would try to be careful, but . . ."

"But what?" Ez watched her intently, knowing that there was something beyond the fear of rape, since it was clear that she knew O'Mara would never do that to her. He suspected what her real fear was, and willed her to put it into words. It wasn't going to help her for him to say it. She had to dig it out, face it and talk about it before she could accept his explanations and reassurances.

Still sitting in the curve of his arm, facing him with her legs curled up under her, she fixed her eyes on her hands as they

abstractedly toyed with the top buttons on his shirt while she
tried to pull together her drifting thoughts. Her mind felt
sluggish, as if it were resisting her efforts to delve into its
deepest recesses and uncover its hidden fears. She groped for
the words to explain an apprehension that, in this day and
age, should not even exist. Theoretically, she knew it was
stupid. But in her experience—and that was the problem. It
was her experience that had thrown her back into this state of
primitive, visceral, female fear of—

"He's much bigger than Leon." It was a thready whisper.

Ez waited a moment to see if she were going to add
anything. He brought his big hand down from her neck to
clasp and still her agitated fingers, watching the gilded lashes
come down to hide her eyes, while he interpreted her slightly
ambiguous statement. Nibbling on his lower lip, he rapidly
considered his options. It was obvious that this was no time
for either clinical discussions or locker-room terminology.
Plain speaking was going to sound too insensitive to her in her
overwrought state. It was a time for indirection and a very,
very careful choice of terms.

"O'Mara?" She nodded, and he said, faintly questioning,
"I take it we're not talking about height or muscular development?"

"No." It was still a whisper, but perhaps a bit stronger.
"It . . . he . . . Leon wasn't entirely . . . in proportion. I
mean, for such a big man he was . . . uh . . . not as big as
you might expect . . . or as he wanted to be, but he
said. . . ."

He saw her lashes flicker and felt the clenching of her
fingers within his clasp. Soft-voiced, he helped her out,
phrasing his questions carefully. "Are you saying that he
was . . . built on the small side where it usually counts with a
man?" She nodded. "And that seemed to bother him?"
Another nod. "And he said that it's not how much you've got
that counts but how you use it?"

Her head came up, her eyes opening wide in surprise.
"How did you know?"

The corners of his mouth twitched as he answered, "It's a
typical boast of an insecure male. As an educated guess, I'd
say that sometime in his early years, perhaps in his first
attempt at a sexual experience, a girl laughed at him or

ridiculed him, which could have made him so self-conscious that he fumbled his next attempts and gained some more negative comments. Add to that some of the crude teasing that goes on in locker rooms, and you've got all the ingredients for turning a basically insecure adolescent boy into an insecure man with a highly developed, but well hidden, sense of sexual inadequacy and a desire to 'get even' with all those girls who laughed at him."

"Why me? I never laughed at him."

"You were the prize, a woman whom all his friends admired and liked. He scored points by winning you. But then he made damn sure you would never have any desire to laugh at him. That's probably only part of the story. It would have taken a psychiatrist to dig out all the causes and effects. It's no good raking over the ashes now. You were originally making some point about O'Mara."

She dropped her eyes to study his chin, murmuring, "He's . . . bigger. Much."

"Well . . . it's been some years since I've seen him stripped. Not since the last time a gang of us went for a midnight swim at Crofts Pond. Remember it?"

"Sure. You guys always chased all the girls away so you could go skinny dipping. What about it?"

"Just that, as I recall, O'Mara was pretty much built to scale—all over—and since he was already twenty-two at the time, I don't imagine he's changed."

"No." She looked at him uncertainly. "If. . . ."

"Say it," he coaxed softly. "I can't answer you until you ask me the question."

She stiffened her back, took a deep breath, closed her eyes and let the words tumble out. "If Leon was so small and he hurt me so badly, how can O'Mara help but hurt me even more since he's much larger even if he's as careful as he can be because I must be small too or Leon wouldn't have hurt so much and it won't do any good to be sure I'm ready if—"

"Whoa, Kitt. All right, I've got the question."

"Yeah. But do you have an answer?"

"Oh, yes," he said thoughtfully. He shifted into a slightly more comfortable position, but still facing her, and took her hands in a firm clasp with both of his.

"Out of idle curiosity, Sis, if this size business has been

bothering you, why didn't you ask your doctor about it on one of those annual checkups you have?"

"It wasn't. Before, I mean. I never thought about it until . . . until O'Mara . . . I took him by surprise a couple of times. Oh, that sounds . . . what I mean is that I got carried away and . . . sort of pressed up against him when he wasn't expecting it and . . . he reacted. Just for a minute, and then he moved us apart before I panicked or anything. But for those few seconds I could . . . feel him against me . . . you know? . . . and I . . . Well, later, when I was remembering how he felt, I realized suddenly that he was much bigger than Leon, and then I . . . remembered some basic biology and things I'd heard some of the girls in the dorm back in college joking about and. . . ." Her voice trailed off and she looked at him hopefully. "So what do we do?"

"*You* stop worrying, for one thing." Ez smiled at her, shaking his head slowly. "Really, Kitt, the things that pop into your head sometimes. Listen to me carefully, you noodle. First, the question of size is easily resolved. If you were thinking with your usual efficiency, you'd have figured it out for yourself. We're twins. Right? As close to identical as male and female can be. Right? Same hair, same eyes, same facial structure, same coordination, same long bones. I'm tall for a man; you're proportionately tall for a woman. Right? Right?" He waited for her wide-eyed nod of agreement, noting the dawning of understanding deep in the smoky eyes.

"Yes. Well, like O'Mara, *all* of me is definitely in proportion. Understand? Therefore, it's logical to assume that all of you is in proportion, too. Hmmm?"

"Ohhhh."

"Indeedy."

"I never thought of that, Ez." Her mouth widened in a delighted smile. "How could I have been so dense?"

"Hah! Because you've been walking around mush-minded ever since O'Mara strolled into the shop that first day."

Kitt's smile suddenly faded. "Wait a minute. If you're right about this, how come it was so painful with Leon?"

"Just what I told you before. Size wouldn't matter if you were . . . dry . . . and your muscles were tight with fear. Which leads us to the second point I want to make. O'Mara has undoubtedly had considerable experience. He's not the celibate type."

"I know that," Kitt said hastily. "He used to take out a sandpiper now and then during those summers, and I know he's had a number of casual relationships over the years. He told me. It doesn't bother me, Ez. After all, one of us should know what we're doing."

"True. And knowing the type of man he is, I'd say he does it very well. He'll be very careful with you, and he's got enough control and experience to know how to judge your pace and match it. He won't try to hurry you. It would help both of you, I think, if you could tell him beforehand just what you've been telling me about your fears. Especially about this size thing. I doubt if he's guessed that one; I didn't. He can reassure you about that in ways that a brother can't. Do you understand?"

"I think so," she said slowly. "At least, I've got the drift of what you're talking about. Enough so I'll leave it to him to explain the rest."

She freed one of her hands to push her hair back in a characteristic gesture, and then reached for her brandy snifter. Ez waited patiently while she took a couple of slow sips, his eyes moving from the slight frown between her brows to the white teeth nibbling at her bottom lip.

Finally, she looked at him, her face relaxing into serene smoothness, her eyes clear and direct. "What you said before about my thinking in terms of an instrument of pain rather than pleasure . . . I think you're right. That's just how I've been feeling about it. I haven't been able to see it any other way because— No, it's more than that. Everything is tied in together. I've been trying to overcome that instinctive panic, but at the same time I've been building up another fear that's feeding that one, and I've managed to dump myself into an endless whirlpool. As soon as a little bit of one fear drains out of the bottom, I add another one to the top."

"Well, we're making progress," Ez said encouragingly. "Now that we've identified all the elements, what are you going to do about them?"

"Oh, psych myself out of them, I guess. You've lifted a weight by explaining away that size thing I got hung up on. That should help me reason through the rest of it, as long as I keep the emphasis on O'Mara and how we feel about each other. I do trust him, you know. We've made a lot of progress, and I was sure that everything would be okay until I started worrying that he wouldn't be able to help but hurt me. However, *now* I'm sure we can overcome whatever's left."

"One thing that will help right now is sleep," declared Ez, standing up and pulling Kitt to her feet. Flipping off lights, he pushed her ahead of him toward the hall.

"By the way," he said idly as he detoured into the kitchen to deposit glasses and mugs in the sink, "have you met your neighbors yet?"

"Which ones? The houses on both sides belong to summer residents, and I don't think any of them have been up yet."

"Oh? Hmm. There was a car parked against the front fence of that house when I came home." Ez waved a hand toward the east, indicating the old saltbox-style house on the downriver side of the shop.

"Odd," Kitt said musingly. "Wonder why they'd leave it out front? There's a driveway on the far side. I'd think they'd want it off the street."

"Maybe they think it's more protected under those trees." Ez yawned hugely as he pushed open his bedroom door. "Oh, well, maybe you'll meet them tomorrow. You okay now? Try to get some sleep, owl eyes. Once O'Mara's back, it'll all work out much easier than you think. Good night, Sis."

"Night." Kitt hesitated in the doorway and looked back at him. "Ez? Thank you."

"Any time." His mischievous grin flashed as he added, "But it would be a restful change if we could sometime have one of these analytical discussions before two in the morning."

Chapter 18

As the days of O'Mara's absence continued to pass in their erratic stop-start way, Kitt began to feel as if she were on a ferris wheel. Her mood would lighten and rise to hopeful heights as she dreamed of the life they would have together: of Gus playing big brother to a smaller version of himself and a coltish, laughing little girl; of the beautiful house on the Rock filled with love and the sound of happy children; of the private world that she and O'Mara would find in that exotic suite on the second floor. But sometimes, when she closed her eyes and thought about being with him in that big bed, her fears would start to shadow the joy, and she'd wonder if she really would be able to overcome her inhibitions and anxieties. Stopping and starting, rising and falling, the wheels of mood and time moved forward through one week and into the next.

Periodically, Kitt forced herself to blank O'Mara and her sexual hang-ups out of her mind and tend to business. Ez had left his wagon for her and taken her Camaro back for a week, so she was able to make two fruitful trips to the distributor's warehouse in Portsmouth and restock the shop. Midge's friend, Joanne, who had filled in on those afternoons of Kitt's shopping spree, had expressed interest in working on a regular basis in the afternoons until her college semester was finished, and then full time for the summer. With Midge's enthusiastic encouragement, Kitt hired the quiet, dark-haired girl, and quickly decided that Joanne was just what they had needed.

The three women worked very well together. Kitt and Midge furnished the flair and imagination necessary to design interesting, innovative displays and to select the kind of stock that would appeal to the broad range of tastes catered to by a resort-town bookshop. Joanne, much to Kitt's delight, actually enjoyed keeping records, filing and generally organizing paper work and catalogs. With a sigh of relief, Kitt happily let her take it all over, and they set up a schedule so that Joanne had time to spend upstairs in Kitt's study as well as down in the shop.

For most of that week and into the next, they were all busy rearranging the shop to accommodate the new stock, one of the major chores being to shift the paperback area around to make room for a new, extensive romance section and to expand the sections for science fiction and westerns. Aside from answering inquiries and waiting on customers, they didn't have time to pay much attention to idle browsers except to ask if they needed assistance. It was the beginning of May and the weather was good, so there was an unusual number of early tourists in town, most of whom seemed to spend part of their time in the bookshop. Neither Kitt, Midge nor Joanne took any notice of one particular young man among the several strangers who visited the shop more than once over that week and a half.

Kitt's evenings were becoming divided between the Rock and her apartment. Gus's after-school visits continued on the days that he didn't have baseball practice, and Kitt usually ended up taking him home in time to join Andy for supper. Gus had taken his father's admonitions to "look after Kitt" seriously, and he urged her to go home early so that she wouldn't be driving after dark. Although she wouldn't have minded going a bit later so that she could spend some time with Andy, she laughingly gave in to Gus's scoldings and went home early and safely to spend the evening alone. Until the Monday night almost two weeks after O'Mara had left.

It had been a strenuous weekend. Ez and Midge were in top form and had insisted on taking Kitt along to a wildly exuberant birthday party for a friend of Midge's which had lasted most of Saturday night. After a few hours of sleep, they hauled her out Sunday morning to go jogging and then to meet "the gang" for a morning-after brunch which ended up in a hilarious game of touch football. By this time, Kitt was totally relaxed with these friends of Midge's. It had been made clear that she was considered "Mike Talbot's girl" by the men, and that no one was going to get too close. If anyone did have an urge in her direction, Ez's size and narrow-eyed just-try-it smile were enough to banish the thought. Easy with these new friends, Kitt agreed Sunday evening to go along with Midge, Ez and the crowd to dinner and a disco in Portland. It was another enjoyable but late night, and she drifted through Monday half-asleep.

At four-thirty Monday afternoon, Midge called Kitt to the phone. "I think it's Gus."

"Oh, Lord, what's wrong?" cried Kitt, as she dodged around a customer and headed for the desk with long strides.

"Hello? Gus?"

"Hi, Kitt." His cheerful voice settled her fears.

"Hi. What's up?"

"I've got to stay a little late for baseball practice. Could you pick me up, Kitt? And could you call Andy and tell her we'll be late? You'll stay for supper, won't you? And bring Hero?"

"Yes to everything. What time should I pick you up and where?"

"Coach said we'd be through at five-thirty. We're at the ballfield next to my school. You know where it is?"

"Yep. See you at five-thirty, Gus. Hit 'em all out of the park."

"I am. I am. Thanks, Kitt. Oh, Kitt?"

"What?"

"If you came a little early and maybe got out of the car to watch . . . ah . . . well, the guys know you're going to be my mother and . . ."

"You'd like to let them get a look at me. Hmmm?" Kitt chuckled.

"Will you?" he asked eagerly.

"Sure. I'd like to meet your friends, Gus. See you soon."

"Great, Kitt! 'Bye."

Leaving Midge to close the shop, Kitt collected Hero and went to meet Gus. He beamed with delight and pride as he introduced her to his coach and his friends and fairly jumped with excitement when she offered to fill in at second base for the last fifteen minutes of practice, replacing a boy who had to leave early. Chuckling to herself at the doubtful looks on the other boys' faces, she dug one of Ez's baseball gloves out of the storage compartment in the back of the wagon, settled Hero safely behind the backstop fence and headed for second base.

She paused at the coach's tentative "Miss Tate?" and

turned to smile reassuringly at him. "Don't worry. I used to teach phys. ed. I've also been playing baseball since I was half the size of these guys."

Twenty minutes later, an ecstatic Gus was bouncing at her side as they headed for the wagon, calling back over his shoulder, "Didn't I tell you guys she was great?"

Laughing and ruffling his hair, Kitt prodded him into the front seat and motioned Hero after him. "Calm down, Gus. Fasten the seat belt and hold onto Hero. Come on, now. Andy's expecting us by six."

Waving to the boys running off toward their suppers and tooting goodbye to the others who were being picked up, they pulled away from the field and, with several other cars, took the next left to go around the block and back toward the ocean. Kitt was busy with handling the big wagon and talking to Gus, and she didn't notice the red Toyota which followed along three cars behind them. They lost the following cars as they turned down a side street, and when Kitt looked into the rearview mirror before making the turn onto Ocean Avenue, the road behind her was empty.

Andy had made Gus's favorite spaghetti sauce, and they feasted on spaghetti à la Gus, garlic bread and spinach salad. The highlight of their evening was a call from O'Mara just before eight. After talking with Andy and Gus, he asked for Kitt.

"You're an unexpected bonus, love. I was going to call you later; I didn't expect you to be at the Rock tonight."

"You never can tell where I'll be these days," Kitt said laughingly. "And where are you now? Last Thursday you called from Oslo, and before that it was Rotterdam, and before *that* it was Geneva."

"And now it's London. This should be the last call, love. I've got one more interview set up for either tomorrow or Wednesday, and then I'll be heading home. The next time you hear my voice in your ear, you'll feel the hot breath that goes with it."

"Hmmm. That sounds promising," murmured Kitt, glancing around to make sure Gus was out of earshot before she teased, "What else am I going to feel?"

"The phone melting in your hand if you don't stop that seductive purring." She could feel his deep chuckle vibrating right through her, and she closed her eyes at the sudden flush of heat tingling over her skin.

"Kitt?"

"Ahh . . . I'm still here. You're a toad, O'Mara, doing this to me when you're well out of reach."

"What am I doing to you, love?" She squirmed with frustration as she heard the thread of laughter in his mock innocent voice.

"You just wait till you get home, you beast."

"You have no idea how much I'm looking forward to that, my love."

"When? When will you be home?"

"I don't know exactly. This meeting is up in the air. The guy is difficult to get to, and I've got to wait for a call. It's supposed to be arranged sometime in the next two days. As soon as I'm through, I'll get the first available flight out. Don't worry, love, you'll be the first to know when I get back."

"Well, hurry it up, toad-prince. This is the longest two weeks I've ever spent."

"Too true. I've thought of some very interesting ways we can make up for it, though, and you can be sure you'll enjoy every minute. Now that should give you something to think about until I see you again."

"Indeed it will. Two more sleepless nights. Oh, damn."

"Don't be silly, Kitt. I need you rested and full of energy. Know why?" He laughed at her answering groan. "Of course you do. Now pull yourself together and say goodnight nicely before you have Gus and Andy wondering why you're blushing."

"Beastly man. But I love you. Goodnight, O'Mara," she whispered.

"Goodnight, love."

The promise in O'Mara's warm, deep voice kept flowing through her mind, and Kitt was more than a bit distracted for the rest of the evening with Gus and Andy. She found it more difficult than ever to tear herself away from the house, and stalled for an extra half-hour after Gus went to bed before finally collecting Hero and saying good night to Andy.

The dusk of evening was deepening into night and the darkening sky was filling with stars as she started the drive home. She was driving automatically, most of her attention turned inward to thoughts of O'Mara's return, and it took a minute or so for her to realize that the car was slowing down despite her steady pressure on the accelerator.

"Oh, rats! That damn gas gauge!"

Her mind now focused on the present, she quickly looked around and discovered she was on Ocean Avenue near the Spouting Rock. With its last bit of momentum, she guided the big wagon off the road onto a flattened, informal parking place, which had been worn down by people stopping to watch the blowhole.

"Well, Hero, let's admit it—it's my own fault. Ez wanted to take this heap back with him to get that gauge fixed, and I only got him to leave it for another week by promising to keep a close watch on the mileage. I *knew* I should have filled it this afternoon, but I've been half-asleep all day."

She drummed her fingers on the steering wheel for a few minutes while she considered her options: wait for a passing car and try to get a ride to a gas station, jog home, or find a house with lights on and knock on the door. Checking her watch and discovering that it was after nine, she told herself to forget about getting gas that night—all the local stations were closed. The car was off the road and should be all right until morning.

"Looks like you're going to get your run a bit early tonight, dog." She leaned across the passenger seat to push down the door locks, front and back, opened her door and got out, reaching back for her shoulder bag and then checking the locks on her side.

"Come on, Hero, let's go. Easy now, we're only jogging."

Within fifteen minutes, Kitt was in her living room calling the police to let them know that she'd left the car deliberately and would get it in the morning. She was yawning when she hung up the phone, and decided that enough was enough. Sleep was what she needed more than anything right now, even if it was still the middle of the evening. She checked that the deck door was locked, flipped off the one lamp she'd bothered to light and found her way down the hall by the glow of the streetlights shining into the big bay window in her bedroom. There was enough light so that she didn't need to turn on any lamps while she got ready for bed. She stayed awake just long enough to set the alarm for six-thirty and to feel Hero snuggle against her legs.

It was ten minutes to ten when the glare of headlights moved slowly down Elm Street from Maine Street, remained stationary for a couple of minutes at the foot of the street and then flashed across houses, fences and the front of the bookshop as a red Toyota turned onto Ocean Avenue, moved slowly past the shop and turned the corner toward Dock Square. The driver's face was a white blur in the streetlights' glow as he turned to look at the empty parking lot in front of the shop and then leaned closer to the car window to look up at the second floor, noting the absence of lights and the blackness of the bay window, indicating that the inside shutters were still open.

At quarter to eleven, and again at eleven-thirty-five, the same red Toyota made the same slow circuit down Elm Street onto Ocean Avenue, past the shop and around the corner to Dock Square. At twelve-twenty, the pattern changed. The Toyota idled at the end of Elm Street until the driver was sure that no cars were coming in either direction, and then the headlights went out and the dark car turned onto Ocean Avenue and then into the driveway of the house beside the bookshop, coasting down into the dark shadows at the back of the house before stopping. Two or three minutes passed before there was a soft click and a flash of reflected light on chrome as the driver's door opened. It was another minute before a denser shadow could be seen moving out of the car and resolving itself into a medium-tall, thin figure.

Slowly, carefully, he pushed the car door closed, worrying about loosening the tape which was holding down the automatic switch for the interior light. He peered across the backyard of the house, trying to see if there were any obstacles, and finally started moving slowly across the grass, feeling for each step. Suddenly, he stopped with a whispered "Damn" as he saw the deep shadows become defined as a thick lilac hedge between this house and the bookshop. Turning, he retraced his steps, and then, keeping to the grass verge, moved along the drive to the front of the house. He paused in the shadows at the corner, making sure no cars were coming, then moved quietly and swiftly along the fence under the trees and across the grass strip edging the bookshop parking lot, then into the deep shadow at the foot of the outside stairs. He was sweating and his heart was pounding with a fear-induced surge of adrenalin as he leaned against the side of the shop to catch his breath.

His restless eyes caught the reflection of headlights far down the road, and he quickly ducked around the stairs, crouching far back against the wall underneath them. Panic rose into his throat, choking him, as he watched the oncoming lights while his mind screamed: *It's her! It's her!* His fingers turned white as he gripped his hands together and pressed them against his mouth. She might not see him under here, but that damn dog would smell him or hear him. Not that it was very big, but it could bite, and God knew what *she'd* do. She was as tall as he was and strong, and that ape of a brother of hers had probably taught her some nasty tricks. Oh God, how did—

The car went by and it was dark and quiet again.

He wiped the sweat from his face with the sleeve of his dark sweater and rubbed his hands dry against the faded jeans that loosely fit his thin legs. Edging out from under the stairs, he held his wrist out into the dim light from the streetlights so he could check his watch. Twelve-forty-three. She was never out this late on a weeknight, so she must be staying over at O'Mara's place like she had a couple of times before. She couldn't have gotten a ride home, because the lights hadn't been on at all. She never went to bed before eleven-thirty or twelve; she always took that mutt out at about eleven—but she hadn't tonight. It had to be tonight. There might not be another chance before that bastard O'Mara got back, and tangling with him was not in the cards.

Cautiously, he put a sneakered foot on the first step and slowly shifted his weight up onto it, lifting his other foot to the next step. His hands were spread out to his sides, palms against the wall, as he inched his way up the stairs, holding his breath and praying that no cars would come up the road before he reached the deck.

Fortunately for his peace of mind, he could not see Hero's head come up and turn toward the open bedroom door, his ears standing straight up as he strained to hear again the faint whisper of an alien sound. There it was. A barely audible growl only lasted for a few seconds as the tense dog rose to his feet and soundlessly dropped to the floor. Silently, pausing every few steps to listen, Hero ghosted down the hall and across the living room, stopping in a "point" position three feet from the deck door. The long drapes were closed across the window-wall, and he could only listen and try to identify the soft, brushing sound. Then the low growl came again as the dog heard a footstep on the deck and a faint metallic tick-tick against the door.

Basenjis are incredibly strong and athletic, and can easily clear a five-foot hedge in one bound. It was no trouble for Hero to leap over the sofa on his mad dash to get Kitt. He was a dark blur going down the hall, and a hurtling projectile as he launched himself from inside the bedroom doorway in one tremendous leap that carried him ten feet across the room to land in the middle of the bed, jarring Kitt half-awake. She quickly came to full alertness as a growling Hero pushed his nose frantically against her face, licking her cheek and tugging at her hair with his teeth.

"Okay, okay, Hero. I'm up. What is it? What's the matter, boy?" Her voice was low but urgent, and she wasted no time in swinging out of bed and scrambling into a robe. Instinctively, she didn't turn on a light; she could see well enough in the light from the street as she silently followed Hero down the hall. She saw him leap over the sofa and take a few more steps toward the door before he stopped and froze in position, growling softly as he stared at the door.

Kitt hesitated at the end of the hall, watching Hero and listening intently. Then she heard it—the faint scratching of metal on metal at the door. She strained to see through the drapes, but it was too dark outside to see shadows through the heavy fabric. Whispering a breathy "Quiet, Hero," she took two slow steps into the living room and stopped to listen again. Now, she could faintly hear harsh breathing and a soft curse, as well as the scratching.

Her hands came up to press tightly over her mouth, holding back a nearly uncontrollable scream as she felt the numbing ice of terror racing through her body. She staggered with the force of the terrified shriek of *NOT AGAIN! NOT AGAIN!* that tore through her mind, momentarily deafening her. Panicked, she turned from side to side looking for a way out.

Not the stairs. They're too close to the door. He'll catch me.

Oh, no, no, no, ohgodohgodohgod. O'Mara, please, please, I need you. Helpmehelpmehelpme. Ez, where are you? EZ! O'MARA! O'MARA! DON'T LET HIM—

Hero leaped into her arms with a pleading "Rowr rowr," and butted her chin with his nose. She blinked and realized that she was down on one knee and panting for breath. The heat of anger started driving out the chill of fear, and she gritted her teeth as she determinedly forced her mind into logical thought. It seemed like hours had passed, but she knew it was only a couple of minutes. Even so, if whoever was trying to open that door knew what he was doing, he'd have been inside long ago. O'Mara would have had it open in seconds!

She put Hero down on the floor and slowly stood up. Her mind racing, she stared at the door, listening to the increasingly frenzied scratching and muttered curses.

Steady, girl. It can't possibly be HIM. So it's someone else. A sneak thief who thinks the place is empty? Doesn't matter. He's an amateur at picking locks, that's for sure. Maybe a kid? Get rid of him first, and then call the cops. How? And what if he smashes the glass? A weapon. I need a weapon. I'm not taking on anyone barehanded again if I can help.it.

Shrugging out of the restricting robe, she took three long, quiet steps to the hall closet and eased the door open. Carefully, trying not to knock anything over, she felt along the left-hand wall until her hand touched leather and then slid her fingers up to the top of Ez's golf bag and closed them around the metal shaft of a club. She eased it up and out of the bag and backed away from the closet, catching the other end of the club in her free hand to keep it from hitting the wall.

She swung around and, wrapping her right hand tightly around the taped grip of the club, moved quickly but quietly around the sofa and across the room to the switch for the outside lights. She was next to the door, so she kept her voice down to an urgent whisper as she commanded, "Hero, wake him!"

As the first notes of the earsplitting banshee howl echoed off the walls, Kitt flipped the switch, flooding the deck, stairs and parking lot with several hundred watts of light. For a brief moment, she clearly saw the black form of a thin male figure outlined against the drapes. She heard a frightened cry, and then the figure dove for the stairs. Even over Hero's howling, she could hear the thudding feet, and then a cry and a series of bumps as he evidently fell down the last few steps.

Letting out the breath she hadn't realized she was holding, she leaned the golf club against the wall next to the door and bent over to rub Hero behind the ears.

"Quiet, dog. Good boy. That was one of your best efforts to date, and it couldn't have come at a better time. Now, you keep your ears cocked while I call the cops."

As she reached for the phone, she heard an engine rev and then the sound of tires skidding on gravel, followed by the roar of an engine as a car accelerated rapidly down the road toward the ocean. Quickly, she dialed the police number and explained what had happened, adding what information she could about the direction the car was traveling although she knew that it could have turned off on any one of several side streets. With assurances that a cruiser would be there in a few minutes and a strong admonition to stay inside and not to open the door to anyone but a police officer, Kitt hung up the phone and dashed for her room to get dressed.

She had just time to yank on jeans and a sweater before a cruiser pulled into the parking lot, and she was still barefoot when she opened the door for the two officers. Nervously, with flashes of old memories distracting her, she faced them in the middle of the living room and let out an "Oh!" of relief when she recognized Eddie Bancroft, one of Midge's brothers.

"Hi, Kitt," he said, smiling easily, recognizing the signs of tension. He motioned to the other officer, continuing to speak in a casual, reassuring tone. "This is Joby Evens. Joby, I don't think you've met Kitt Tate, Ez's sister. The desk sergeant said someone tried to break in, Kitt. Scary experience. Why don't we sit down for a few minutes while you tell us what happened?"

Gradually relaxing as she talked, Kitt quickly described the events of the last fifteen minutes. The two men were laughing over her method of scaring off the intruder when another officer tapped at the door and entered.

Nodding to Kitt, he addressed Eddie and Joby. "We've checked the area. Looks like he parked down at the end of the

Stevens' drive. The gravel's all chewed up where he shot back out of there, and there's some rubber on the street. Must have taken off like a bat. Found this near the bottom of the stairs." He held out a small plastic envelope containing a thin, flat strip of metal. "Could be a lockpick. He might have dropped it. You looked at the door, yet, Eddie?"

"No. Waiting for you. Kitt says he must have been working at it for several minutes. Good chance we'll get some prints."

The three officers stepped through the half-open door and turned to examine the lock.

"Didn't know much about what he was doing," Eddie muttered. "Look at those scratches. Okay, Vince," he turned to the third officer, "do your thing. That metal doorframe looks nice and clean. Have you polished this lately, Kitt? Whose prints might be on here besides yours?"

Kitt stood just inside the door, hands tucked in her pockets. "As a matter of fact, I had to clean the glass and wipe down the edge this weekend. Midge and Ez got a bit carried away, and we ended up with marmalade all over the place. The only prints on there should be ours."

"We'll need your prints for comparison. Okay? What about Ez? Is there anything around that you're sure he touched?"

"Try his room. I haven't cleaned it since he left this morning. And you might find his prints in the bathroom, but they'd probably be mixed with mine."

For the next half-hour, the men worked at taking finger-prints and making a careful search of the ground around the stairway and the house next door. After Vince took a set of fingerprints from Kitt, she fixed coffee for everyone, and then sat down with Eddie and Joby while they asked more questions.

"You see, Kitt," Eddie explained, "it seems a bit strange for him to try the deck door. There was more chance of him being seen on those stairs or the deck than if he'd just whipped around back under the deck and gone for the back door to the shop. Besides that, if he were looking for money, you'd think he'd go for the shop and the cash register rather than for the apartment."

"Lots of businesses have alarms hooked up to their doors. Maybe he thought he could get in upstairs and then come down from inside."

"Maybe. But I've got a feeling that he was sure you were out and wouldn't be back. Why?"

"Well, I've stayed overnight at the Rock a couple of times. Otherwise, I'm usually home before nine."

"Somehow . . . I wonder . . . You haven't noticed anyone hanging around lately, have you? Or any particular car behind you when you're out?"

"Nooo, not that I can remember," Kitt said slowly. "But there was—No, that's too farfetched."

"What is it? Look, Kitt, if there's been anything unusual, tell us."

"Well, it still seems silly, but two weeks ago, on the last night we went out before he left, O'Mara mentioned something about a red Toyota that seemed to have been following him for a couple a days. We decided that it was probably a tourist who just happened to be going in the same direction. He only saw the car a few times."

"Have you seen it again since he left?"

Kitt stared at the wall, her eyes unfocused, as she thought back over the past days. "I didn't pay much attention . . . Down beyond the Yacht Club, where the road widens, there's nothing much there for a ways . . . no houses or shops . . . a few times when I've been running with Hero in the evening, there's been a red car parked along the road . . . usually near the inlet . . . but I haven't noticed anyone around it."

She looked apologetically at the two men and shrugged. "I really didn't look at it closely. It was just there. I'm not at all sure about the make."

"Okay. It's a start. Anything else?"

Kitt frowned, trying to capture a nagging memory. "There was something Ez said. Ha! Now, I remember. Last weekend —not this past one, the one before—he came in late Saturday night and mentioned that my neighbors must be here—the ones you mentioned—Stevens?—because there was a car parked next to their front fence."

Eddie and Joby exchanged glances, and Eddie said slowly, "They haven't come up yet. They're from Pennsylvania, and they don't come up until mid-June, after school's out. Think hard, Kitt. All you saw was a shadow against the drapes. About your height and thin. Have you seen a man like that hanging around?"

Before she could answer, a familiar voice spoke from the doorway. "So nice of you to invite me to the party. Can I touch this door?"

"Midge!" Kitt exclaimed. "Whatever are you doing here at this time of night?"

"I called her while you were fixing coffee," Eddie said. "Figured everyone would be happier if you weren't alone here for the rest of the night. I don't want to tangle with Ez over our not taking care of you."

He'd pushed the door open for Midge to come through, and she dumped her jacket and a bulging totebag on the sofa on her way to the kitchen. "Anybody else want more coffee? You look wrung out, Kitt. Are you all right? Do you know who it was, Eddie?"

"Thin guy, about Kitt's height, probably driving a red Toyota. Seen anyone like that hanging around lately, Miss Beady Eyes?"

Midge leaned across the breakfast bar, obviously thinking hard. "Doesn't ring any big bells. We've been really busy in the shop, and I haven't paid much attention to the browsers. There have been a lot of early tourists. Let's see, a red Toyota. Friday afternoon, when you came back from Portsmouth, I was rearranging one of the window displays, and I think a red car pulled into the other side of the lot just after you. Yes. It was red. I noticed it while we were unloading the wagon because the guy was just sitting there, smoking and staring . . . no, it was more like he was reading something he was holding down out of sight."

"Did he get out of the car?" Joby asked. "What did he look like?"

"He didn't get out. I think we were on our third trip out to the wagon when I noticed that he was gone."

"So what did he look like?" asked Eddie, a bit impatiently.

"Let me think a minute," muttered Midge, moving back into the kitchen. She came out into the living room with her coffee and sat on the edge of the sofa, closing her eyes in concentration. "I just saw his profile. Looked thin-faced, bony, kind of hollow cheeks, nothing-brown straight hair worn kind of long, gray sweatshirt."

She opened her eyes and looked anxiously at her brother. "Does that help?"

"Yeah, some. Of course, we don't know if this all ties

together, but . . . possible, possible. Do either of you remember seeing him any other time?"

Kitt shook her head. Midge shrugged and said, "Not specifically. But that doesn't mean anything. He could have been in the shop half a dozen times, or on the street. There've been a lot of visitors wandering around with all this good weather. If we weren't looking for him and he was hanging back in a crowd, we wouldn't notice him."

"Okay," said Eddie, standing up. "We can't do anything more here right now. What about Joanne, Midge? Do you think she might have noticed this guy?"

"I don't know. She's pretty observant, and she's been waiting on more customers than we have this past week. We'll ask her tomorrow when she comes in."

"What time is that?"

"Around two, I think. Kitt?"

"Tuesday? Yes, two."

"I work the four to midnight tomorrow, so talk to her and I'll stop by right after four. Meantime, you two lock up tight tonight and keep your eyes open tomorrow. If you think you see this guy, call the station right away. Understand? No funny stuff, Midge. You let us handle it."

The rest of the night was uneventful, except for Hero's perplexed visits to Ez's room as he tried to figure out why Midge was sleeping in the big bed. Kitt slept so deeply that she hardly moved until Midge woke her at nine, and she was quite unaware that the younger woman had been up since seven and had had a long talk with Ez about the events of the night.

Midge didn't enlighten her. When she'd asked Kitt about calling Ez, Kitt had decided against it on the basis that there wasn't anything he could do except worry. But once she was in bed, Midge had second thoughts about that. There was a lot he could do—especially to her, if he arrived Friday afternoon and found out that she'd kept the news of a threat to Kitt from him for four days. She decided to call him first thing in the morning.

Even though Kitt was still asleep, Midge didn't take any chances on being overheard. She called from downstairs and caught Ez just waking up. By the time Midge got halfway through her first sentence, he was wide awake and swearing, but he listened without any other interruption to her story.

"Okay, I've got it. You were right to call, moptop, although I can't do much at the moment. I'm nailed down here with finals until Thursday noon, but I can get someone to cover for me on Friday so I can get up there by mid-afternoon on Thursday. I think Eddie's on the right track. It's not a random break-and-enter. Someone's watching Kitt and wanted to go through her things. He doesn't seem to want a confrontation, so she's probably safe enough, but I don't want her left alone. Do you know when O'Mara's due back?"

"Sometime in the next two or three days. He wasn't sure just when."

"If he gets there before I do, make sure you tell him what's happened. That idiot sister of mine is just as apt to decide not to worry him, either. Call me if anything else happens, and you be careful, too. She'll probably insist on staying there at night to keep him from trying it again. Can you sleep over? Leave the outside lights on all night and keep the bedroom doors open so Hero can roam. Ask Eddie to show you how to block the sliding doors so they can't be opened. Don't forget the back door downstairs, and it might be a good idea to leave a light on in the shop. Eddie will make sure that the cruisers keep a close watch on you. Can you handle all that, honeypot?"

"Sure. Remember, Godzilla, that I've got all kinds of people I can call on for help if I need it. Kitt might be ready to take on a weirdo with a golf club, but I'd rather have half a dozen brawny cops behind me. And if they're not available, I can always stand on the deck and holler down the river. Those working boatmen are a tough bunch, and most of them know me. They'd come on the run. Don't worry. We'll be fine until you and O'Mara get here."

Ez's chuckle vibrated through the receiver. "I don't doubt it for a minute. Take care, pet. And keep a rein on Kitt. You haven't seen it yet, but she's got a hell of a temper, which she just might lose if this guy tries anything else. If she's mad enough, she's just as apt to forget that violence terrifies her and try to take him on herself."

Midge wandered back upstairs cherishing a vision of an angry Kitt brandishing a golf club and chasing a terrified young thug through Dock Square. By the time she woke Kitt at nine, Eddie and Joby had stopped on their way off-shift to take care of returning Ez's wagon, and Midge had recapped her conversation with Ez. As a result, and unknown to Kitt, by the middle of the morning the word had been passed along the river to the "native" fishermen and lobstermen, and an unobtrusive but constant watch was started on the bookshop.

In a burst of unexpected generalship, Midge rallied her forces to make sure that someone was with Kitt in the shop when she had to leave to attend classes. She also organized various muscular male relatives to accompany Kitt on her morning and evening runs with Hero, and to "ride shotgun" when she went anywhere in the car.

With a bland disregard for the truth, she overrode Kitt's protests at such coddling with the comment, "It's for my sake mostly. After all, what could a little thing like me do if this guy attacked you?"

Kitt stared at her in total disbelief as she recalled how this "little thing" handled her six-foot-three-inch, 230-pound brother. However, argument availed her nothing and, like it or not, Kitt found herself practically smothered in brawny young men whenever she set foot out the door. By Tuesday evening, she laughingly gave in and began making friends with her "babysitters," since she had a strong suspicion that they would soon be her in-laws.

Chapter 19

Eddie's hunch that someone was watching Kitt became a certainty Tuesday afternoon when they talked to Joanne. Not only had she seen a thin young man fitting Midge's description several times, both in the shop and parked in the area in a red car, but she had spoken to him. Midge wasted no time in calling Eddie.

Leaving a disgruntled Midge to mind the shop, he took Joanne and Kitt upstairs to talk to them undisturbed.

"Tell me everything from the beginning, Joanne. We can't be positive," he cautioned, "that this is the same guy who tried to break in last night, but it's too much coincidence to overlook if he really has been keeping tabs on Kitt."

Obviously distressed, Joanne looked apologetically at Kitt. "I'm really sorry, Kitt, but I never gave him two thoughts." She turned to Eddie appealingly. "You know how it is around here once the weather gets good, Eddie, and the tourists start piling in. There's always a certain number of guys wandering around looking over the 'local talent.' We don't pay much attention usually," she continued with a half-smile, "unless he's super-looking. Well, this one wasn't, and I probably wouldn't have remembered him at all if I hadn't seen him so often."

"How often?" Eddie asked.

"Last week he was in the shop three or four times. I'm not sure exactly. We were busy, but Midge and Kitt were reorganizing the stock most of the week, and I stayed behind the desk waiting on customers and generally keeping an eye on things. That's probably why I noticed him. Normally, we'd be taking turns at the desk. Anyhow, he didn't buy anything —just browsed around for a while and left."

"You said you spoke to him. When?"

"Yesterday. He—"

"Wait a minute," Eddie interrupted. "Back up to last week. Let's try to get a sequence. What about seeing him in a car? Was that yesterday or before?"

"Both. Early last week, he was sitting in a red car at the edge of the parking lot when I came to work one afternoon. The next day, I saw him in the same car parked in front of the Stevens' place when I went out on an errand for Kitt. I'd seen him in the shop a couple of times by then, and I guess I sort of stared at him, because he drove off. And then, Saturday noon—remember, Kitt, you went up to O'Mara's to have lunch with Gus?—well, I carried that big order for Mrs. Burnham out to her car just after you left, and I saw the same red car turning around in the drive across the street and then going back down the road."

"Following Kitt?"

"I don't know. She'd been gone a couple of minutes by then, but if she's the one he was watching, he might have guessed where she was going. It didn't occur to me that he was interested in Kitt." She flushed a becoming pink and said diffidently, "He looked about twenty-two or three. Without really thinking about it, I just sort of assumed he was shy and trying to get up the nerve to speak to Midge or me."

Eddie grinned at her with the familiarity of long acquaintance. "Normally, you'd be right, but I think you struck out on this one. Now, what happened yesterday?"

"He came in a little after I did, at one, and browsed around the paperback section. Kitt and Midge were working in the back, and I was busy with some customers for a while. Just as the last of them left, he came over with a couple of westerns and started talking to me while I was ringing them up."

"What did he say?"

"Oh, he asked if it was my shop, and when I said no and pointed out Kitt as the owner, he asked if she were nice to work for and how long she'd owned the place. He said something about a good-looking woman like that having lots of boyfriends, and I said that she didn't, that she was going to be married soon. He said something like 'Oh, yeah? He must be somebody special. She could take her pick.' I didn't think it was any of his business, so I didn't mention Michael Talbot or O'Mara. I just said, 'He is,' and then another customer came up and he left."

"And when did you see him in the red car?"

"That was later. I left around five to do some errands, and I was walking home when Kitt went by on her way to pick Gus up at the school. I stopped at the corner to wait for a break in traffic, and the red car with that guy driving passed me going in the same direction as Kitt, but he was several cars behind her. I still didn't pay any attention, because there are a lot of places he could have been going on that road."

Eddie leaned back and sighed. "Too many coincidences. Just too damn many. What do you think, Kitt? Any idea why someone would be watching you?"

Shaking her head, she said emphatically, "No. None at all. And the descriptions of him that the girls have given don't ring any bells."

"Could be he was hired by someone else."

"Who? And why? The one enemy I might have had has been permanently out of the picture for over five years."

"Anyone trying to get to Ez through you?"

"Ez doesn't make enemies. No, not Ez. And that leaves

O'Mara. He was in a dangerous occupation for several years. I'm not sure how those things work after someone . . . retires . . . but maybe somebody from his past is . . . what? Seeking revenge for something? Getting even? Oh, it all sounds like something out of one of his books! I can't believe this. Any of it. And that innocuous little man doesn't sound like someone who would be mixed up in O'Mara's past life. You said he must be a rank amateur at lockpicking, and he certainly sounded terrified when Hero and I routed him. He's not in O'Mara's league at all."

"Maybe. Still, it seems like the most likely possibility. About all we can do right now is keep a close watch on you, try to spot the guy and pick him up and wait for O'Mara to get back. So far, we've come up blank on the fingerprints, but we've sent them to Washington and may hear something in the next day or two. Thanks for your help, Joanne. Glad you have sharp eyes and such a good memory. I want to see Midge for a minute, and then I've got to report in. See you later, Kitt. Don't worry, we'll be keeping a close watch on you tonight."

"You can try," said Kitt, laughing, "but probably all you'll see are your own cousins and brothers, to say nothing of your mother and Angie. You should see the duty roster Midge drew up! I'm apparently going to be hip-deep in Bancrofts for the duration. Not that I don't appreciate it, but she has gotten a bit carried away."

Chuckling to himself as he ran downstairs, Eddie decided it was just as well Kitt didn't know about the rest of Midge's protective measures.

Much as Kitt appreciated everyone's concern, by Wednesday noon she was desperate for some privacy, and finally took a stand with Midge as they finished lunch.

"Listen, pixie, if I don't get some time all to myself, I'm going to go up a wall. I'm one of those people who need a certain amount of solitude. So, this afternoon, while you and Joanne mind the shop, I'm going to lie out on the deck in that lovely sunshine and work on my tan. You can post a guard at the foot of the stairs if you want, but I don't want to *see* a human being for the next two or three hours. All right?"

Midge gave her a long, considering look and saw the signs

of strain around her eyes and mouth. "Okay, Kitt, I guess we have all been hovering over you, but we really do mean well. We're concerned about you. And besides that, we've all got visions of the havoc Ez and O'Mara would wreak if anything happened to you!"

"I might have known," Kitt groaned. "Even when he isn't here, that man is taking over my life. Go away, you traitor, and let me have some peace and quiet."

"I'm going." Midge chortled. "But you might consider my tender bottom, which would be covered with unsightly blisters if Ez thought I hadn't taken proper care of you."

"I can see that the very thought has you shaking in your size-fours," drawled Kitt, a sardonic gleam in her eyes. With a saucy twitch to her hips, Midge headed for the stairs and had one foot on the top step when Kitt's voice halted her. "Wait up. What about Gus? Is someone going to be with him during practice?"

"It's all taken care of. My cousin Roger, the one who stayed at the Rock last night, will be there. He knows the coach, and he'll explain what's going on. He's also got a car, and will bring Gus here after practice."

"Roger. Big, blond, all-state tackle?"

"That's the one. Don't worry, Kitt, he's also smart and quick. He'll take good care of Gus. They got along fine last night, and Andy liked him, too. If O'Mara doesn't get back today, he'll stay at the Rock again tonight."

"Sounds like you've got everything organized, pixie. Okay, scoot now, and let me get out into that sun."

Kitt spent ten minutes rooting through boxes in the storage room before she finally unearthed an old bikini. With teeth-gritting resolution, she put it on and walked out into the bright light of afternoon, breathing a sigh of relief that only Hero and the seagulls could see what she felt to be yards of bare skin. It was just as well for her peace of mind that she didn't know how many monitoring glances from the nearby boats suddenly became fixed and heated, and how many loins stirred at the sight of her long, slim legs and lithe, near-naked body.

Kitt had tacked some lengths of canvas to the railing around two sides of the deck to cut off the light wind blowing upriver from the ocean, making a suntrap in one corner.

Now, she and Hero sprawled in boneless abandon on a padded exercise mat, and she felt the tension draining out of her in the soothing warmth of the sun.

It was one of those lovely May days with which Nature rewards the hardy souls who endure the wild, often destructive storms of winter on the Maine coast. Although the sun was bright in a clear blue sky, the soft ocean breeze kept the temperature in the sixties and low seventies. Landscaped yards and wild areas alike were bursting with the endless colors of the amazing variety of flowering trees and shrubs that grace New England. The pervading scent of lilacs drifted on the air, mingling with the tang of salt in a strangely heady blend.

It was very quiet and peaceful on the deck, and Kitt half-drowsed in the heat of the sun. She drew in deep breaths of the strong scent drifting up from the cluster of white and lavender lilac bushes in one corner of the backyard and from the lilac "fence" along the Stevens' property line. Since it was midweek, there was little traffic on the road, and only the occasional cry of a gull and the soft rushing of the river flowing out with the ebbing tide disturbed the afternoon quiet.

Indolently, she stretched and settled more comfortably on her stomach, half-opening her eyes to look at Hero. She reached over to stroke a firm hand along his side.

"Silly dog," she murmured. "You're baking. Turn over. It's a wonder you don't sunburn."

He lifted his head, muttered "Rrrarrow" and rolled over on his other side, relaxing back into bonelessness and heaving a sigh of contentment.

Totally relaxed, Kitt let her mind drift aimlessly, but within a few heartbeats found her inner vision filled with tanned skin, a sensuous mouth, bright blue eyes and soft masses of dark hair. She groaned softly as she remembered the touch of his hands and mouth on her. Her muscles tightened and she pressed her hips hard against the mat as she felt desire coursing through her at the memory of that last night—the strength of his arms around her, his fingers pressing into her buttocks as he pulled her into the warm length of his body, the muscles of his back flexing under her exploring hands, the taut urgency of his tongue in her mouth and the hot, weak sensation in her belly as she pressed it against the hard bar of his manhood.

Restlessly, she turned her head the other way and pushed her hair back from her flushed face. Sexual arousal had brought her fully awake, and now she consciously shifted her mind to the bookshop and concentrated on the pros and cons of finding another part-time person for the summer. She was still thinking about it as she drifted into a light sleep.

She didn't hear the slight sound of the door sliding slowly open and then closed, or the cat-footed pad of tennis shoes across the deck or Hero's "Whuff" of recognition. She didn't feel the large body sitting down beside her, or the pressure of a hard male hip against her thigh.

In fact she was not aware that she was no longer alone until her mind foggily registered that the large, warm hand sliding gently up and down the length of her back was *not* part of a pleasant dream. Even then, the languorous stroking felt so good that she kept her eyes closed for another few moments. Finally, she couldn't hold still any longer and, like a contented cat, flexed and stretched her back muscles with a sinuous arching movement and groaned, "Mmmmmm. O'Mara."

His deep chuckle sounded from behind her, and there was a very satisfied note in his voice as he teased, "That's encouraging, love. Now, tell me how you knew my touch even in your sleep."

She looked over her shoulder at him and wrinkled her nose, laughter in her eyes. "Probably the same way you would know my touch. At least, you'd better." She dropped her head back down on her folded arms, but kept it turned so she could watch him out of the corner of her eye as he continued slowly stroking her back. "You're looking rather good for someone who's been jetting all over the place for two weeks. No bloodshot eyes, not a trace of a beard, no dark circles. When did you get home?"

"Now. I've just driven up from Boston. You're getting a bit pink around the edges, love." He reached for the suntan cream lying beside the mat and started rubbing it into her back. "I slept for most of the flight from London and changed clothes and shaved before we landed. Idiot, I told you this was a working trip. Have you been picturing me living it up all over Europe? I'm saving that until I can take you with me."

Kitt was only half-hearing him. A large part of her mind was busy coping with the sensations ebbing and flowing through her body from the sensuous movements of his hand over her back. She was vaguely aware that he shifted slightly, and glanced up to see him pulling his knit shirt off over his head and tossing it onto a chair.

"O'Mara, what are you doing?"

There was a thread of laughter in his voice as he answered, "Getting a tan. What do you think I'm doing? Are you blushing, or is that sunburn?"

"Of course I'm not blushing. Why should I? I've seen you lots of times without a shirt." Despite her best efforts to keep her tone matter-of-fact, her voice faded at the end. *I've got to tell him about the prowler. He should call Eddie right away.* She forgot her train of thought, and also forgot to breathe, as she was caught up in the crashing impact of his total maleness. Unthinkingly, automatically, she half turned to lean on one elbow, and her other hand reached out to brush, flat-palmed, over the thick, soft mat of curls on his chest.

With darkening eyes, he watched her gaze move over his shoulders and chest, follow the narrowing mat of hair down to the waistband of his jeans, and then flash back up to his face. She stared with unconscious longing at the wide, sensuous mouth; she didn't realize that her lips had parted to let the tip of her tongue run slowly across her bottom lip and that her fingers were playing in the thick curls on his chest.

For a few moments, they both seemed almost drugged with sun, the scent of lilacs and salt tang, and rising passion. Then, slowly, O'Mara reached down to take hold of Kitt's upper arms, pulling her up to sit facing him.

He brushed his lips across her cheek, and his voice was husky, almost whispering in her ear, "Put your arms around my neck, love, and kiss me hello. I'd like to see what two weeks of thinking about us has accomplished."

"It's kept me awake nights, for one thing," she whispered as she obediently wound her arms loosely around his neck. She tilted her head back to look at him, her smoky eyes wide with desire, and he caught his breath as he realized that for the first time there was no trace of fear in her expression. She managed a shaky smile as she saw how dark his eyes had become and read the barely controlled passion in them. "It's also interfered with just about everything else in my life. I've missed you so mu—"

The word and her breath were stifled, and rational thought disintegrated, under the hot pressure of his mouth on her half-parted lips. Her arms tightened and one hand buried itself in his thick hair. She felt his long fingers cradling her head, holding her still as her mouth opened further for his exploring tongue. Heat swirled and bubbled and then drained away from deep in her body, leaving her with a hollow, aching need. She vaguely felt a tug at her nape and then another between her shoulder blades. His hand slid between their lightly touching bodies and then away, and dazedly she realized that he'd taken off her bikini bra.

Suddenly, blazingly, the last tiny, cold knot within her flamed into white heat and disappeared, and there was no trace of fear or panic, no withdrawal, no control. Only a driving need to get closer to the warm, hard, male strength of him. Even before she felt the pressure of his hands spreading across her back, she was arching against him to press her naked breasts and stomach into his soft fur.

Loving the feel of the silky curls brushing her sensitive skin, she squirmed against him, rubbing her taut nipples and swelling breasts across his chest. He growled deep in his throat, and the gentle exploration of his tongue became an urgent thrusting as his arms closed around her with a force that would have cracked the ribs of a smaller woman. Utterly lost in a scorching red haze of long-denied sexual need, they wrapped themselves around each other, fingers digging into arms, shoulders and muscles with a fierceness that would leave bruises. They swayed back and forth, jolted off-balance by the power of the unleashed passion surging between them.

It went on for endless minutes until, finally, it was all too much for Kitt and, still clinging to him, still kissing him, she began to cry silent tears. Dimly, he became aware of tasting salt, and loosened his hold on her arm to brush his hand across her cheek. Lifting his mouth away from hers, he took a deep, ragged breath, held it for a moment, and then let it out slowly. He relaxed the tight grip of his other arm and eased her slightly back from him so he could look at her.

He savored the signs of passion in her face and eyes, knowing that she was seeing the same evidence on him. With a gentle hand, he smoothed back her hair, brushed the tears away and pressed her head down onto his shoulder. Eyes closed, he rested his cheek against her sun-warmed hair and reveled in the feel of her adventuring hands as they slowly moved over his bare shoulders, down across his chest and around to his back. He cradled a firm breast in his hand, pressing his palm against the tight nipple, and sucked in a quick breath as he felt her tongue trace a warm, wet path along his collarbone.

She shivered with reaction as his deep voice, hoarse with emotion, growled in her ear, "My beautiful Kitt. All of you. I've waited so long to be able to love all of you. And I'll make it beautiful for you, my Kitt. You can believe that now, can't you?"

She stretched up against him to reach his neck with her mouth, and her breasts pressed into his fur again as he slid his cradling hand away and down the length of her body, his fingers pushing under her bikini pants to slowly stroke the smooth, taut skin of her buttocks. "Oh, yes," she promised, her voice husky with love. "It's gone—the fear and the panic. All I can feel now is . . . I want you. I want to feel . . . *you* . . . inside me . . . part of me."

Her words and the plea in her voice jolted through him, and his exploring hand reflexively gripped her buttock. "Ooo'Maraa," she groaned. "Easy. I'm going to have some very strange bruises. How would you like me to grab you?"

He froze into immobility as he felt her hand move down his back, then around and down over his ribs to his stomach, where it hesitated.

I can't. She felt the roughness of fabric under the heel of her hand, but her fingers were still resting on warm skin. *Yes, I can. I've dreamed about touching him. I've thought about it. Now. I need to know that I can be as loving and giving as he is. As he needs me to be. Move your hand, Kittredge. Prove to both of you that you really are all over the fear. Do it NOW.* She pressed her hot face into his neck and slowly, hesitantly, slid her wide-spread hand down over the tightly stretched denim, pausing as her fingers brushed against his hard, pulsing maleness.

The words were a warm, breathy moan in her ear. "Touch me, love. Please."

She moved her hand fractionally closer and hesitated again. "Help me," she whispered against the heated dampness of his neck.

She was suspended in a haze of erotic longing where seconds seemed to stretch on and on. She almost jumped when she felt his hand on hers, gently encouraging, until her fingers curved around him, tentatively examining the strangeness and then becoming bolder as she felt his heart hammering against her breasts, and his breath, uneven and hot, in her ear.

With their unique ability to link thoughts and feelings, she felt the powerful tide of joyful relief surging through him and mingling with his intense arousal as he experienced the full measure of her loss of fear and her determined overthrow of inhibition in her desire to please him. She knew he was clamping an iron restraint on his own inclinations, and giving her time to test her newly awakened seductive urges.

Almost with a will of its own, her hand moved more confidently over him in a tactile discovery of the dimensions and strength of him, and her mind blanked out in the force of molten desire that flamed through her, only infinitesimally weakened by the tiny tendrils of lingering apprehension. Although he was almost as mindless as she was, he sensed the hint of uncertainty and its cause. He also knew that it would only take another few moments of this powerful, growing sexual tension before they'd be naked and lost in each other on that mat, uncaring and unaware if Midge, Gus and half the town stood around and applauded. Which was entirely possible, and not at all what he wanted for her.

His hands closed around her arms, lifting and holding her away from him. "Kitt, we have to stop this now," he grated in a voice thick with need. "Look at me, love." He cradled her face with one hand, shaking her slightly until she blinked open dazed eyes and finally focused them on his face.

"O'Mara?" she whispered, her brightening gaze noting the sheen of moisture on his skin, the flush fading from his cheekbones, the warm glow of love subduing the hot blaze of passion in his eyes, and she knew that he was seeing the same things in her.

Suddenly, the last wisps of fog cleared from her mind, and realization crashed through her in an instantaneous replay of the preceding minutes. Her eyes and mouth snapped wide open as she stared at him in shocked, delighted incredulity.

"O'Mara! I did it!" she squealed, flinging her arms around his neck, her expression changing to triumphant joy as she scattered kisses over his laughing face, exultantly whooping, "I really did it! Oh, you are a beautiful man . . . and you're mine . . . all mine . . . I love you . . . and now we can . . . spend hours . . . weeks . . . months! . . . in that gorgeous huge bed . . . and you can teach me . . . all sorts of fantastic things . . . and between times . . . we can live in that . . . *Arabian Nights* fantasy of a bathroom . . . and . . . O'Mara?"

"What, love?" he gasped, still laughing.

"How do you make love in a hot tub?" she asked curiously.

"Very carefully," he answered with a grin. "Taking due care not to drown each other. Whatever made you think of that?"

"Er . . . something I heard."

She gazed at him with a happy smile, feeling lightheaded with the exhilarating sense of release from a long nightmare coupled with the powerful, sweeping tide of love flowing between her and this strong, passionate, yet gentle man. Gradually, they quieted, and she discovered she was angled half across his lap, held securely in the curve of one arm and resting against his upraised knees. His free hand was trailing lightly over the smooth, warm skin of her thigh, while his interested eyes traced their own tingling path down her nearly naked body. She watched his possessive examination of her firm breasts and slim, supple form. The gleaming blue eyes flicked back to meet her look of fond indulgence.

First startled and then amused, he said with mock-menace, "If you're smart, you shameless wench, you'll stop looking at me like a doting mother offering treats to her good boy." His caressing hand wandered over her bare hip and across her stomach, strong fingers gently massaging her tautening muscles, as he leaned forward to nip at her earlobe and growl, "Keep tempting me, and I may give *you* a few treats you aren't expecting."

She laughed up at him. "Tease!" she dared. "You wouldn't. Not when Midge might come up here at any minute. Or Gus or somebody else."

"Midge," he said smugly, "knows better than to let anyone up here." And his hand closed caressingly over her breast while he trailed nibbling kisses down her neck.

"Oooooh . . . no . . . wait," she panted. She grabbed his wrist, but then loosened her hold to run her fingers over the soft mat of fur on his arm. "You beast! . . . You made *me* stop . . . and now you're. . . ." Her voice died away in a low moan as his hand moved to cup her breast and his warm mouth closed over the peak, his tongue flicking teasing circles around the hard nipple.

Her back arched and she was raising her hands to his head when he stopped, lifted and turned her, and she suddenly found herself kneeling beside him, hands clutching his shoulders for balance, while he laughed up at her with wickedly gleaming eyes. He bent forward to press a quick kiss on her belly, and then rose to his feet in one lithe move, picking up his shirt and tossing it to her.

"Here, temptress," he chided, laughing, "put this on before you stand up in front of the world and all the boaters. Unless, of course," he added teasingly, "you have more treats for me."

Her eyes flashed silvery fire as she lifted her upper lip and growled at him.

He grinned appreciatively. "You must have learned that from Hero, and you do it very well, love. What are you doing? You've got it on backward. Here, let me help you. Hold still, wiggle-worm. God, you've got at least four arms. There, you're decent." He pulled her to her feet. "Come on. I've brought you a present."

Ignoring her eager questions, he tugged her after him into the living room. "It's on the sofa."

She turned and took a step forward, then stopped short, staring incredulously at the dress draped over the sofa. It can't possibly be the same one, she thought, as her mind formed a picture of a much younger Kitt turning and gliding in O'Mara's arms, enjoying his admiration of her softly swirling dress patterned in shades of blue and green. Slowly, still half-convinced it was a mirage, she moved to the sofa and picked up the dress. Holding it against herself with both hands, she swung around to look at O'Mara in delighted wonder.

"It's the same," she said dazedly. "I swear it is. Same colors, same swirly pattern, same design. Oh, you darling, how ever did you find a dress just like that one?"

"I didn't," he stated, his face mirroring her pleasure. "I spotted the material in a shop window in Zurich on the second day of the trip. I must have stood there for five minutes staring at it, trying to figure out why it looked familiar, until I finally remembered that dress you wore on our last date. The clerk figured out the yardage from my description and—What are you doing?"

With her back turned to him, Kitt was pulling off the shirt he'd just lent her. "Trying it on, silly." She dropped the dress over her head, catching the halter top as the soft folds of the skirt slithered down her legs. Nimble fingers zipped and hooked, and she spun around to face him, sending the skirt whirling and floating around her legs.

"I love it. I love you." She took a couple of dancing steps toward him and threw her arms around his neck, going up on tiptoe to kiss him, her mouth lingering on his as she felt his arms close about her.

For a few moments, he held her against him, enjoying her newfound confidence as she eagerly explored his mouth, before finally easing her back a few inches so he could look at her. Well pleased with her response to his gift, his mouth widened in a slow, satisfied smile.

"You're welcome," he murmured teasingly as his hands tightened on her hips and one eyebrow lifted in mocking inquiry. "I can't wait to see how you'll thank me for your ring."

"What ring?"

"The one I'm having made for you. No, don't ask. I'm not telling you any more. It's a surprise."

"Why do I feel as though I'm in the middle of one of your plots? Oh, all right," she said crossly over his laughter. "I won't ask—I'll let it all just happen. Now, finish telling me about my dress." She gazed at him expectantly, while her hands, seemingly of their own accord, drifted up to play in the curls on his chest.

"If you don't stop *that*, my girl, we'll be finishing this discussion in your bedroom . . . in a couple of hours. Or maybe longer." He grabbed her hands, chuckling at her rapidly changing expressions of chagrin, disappointment and, finally, a very feminine awareness.

"Oh, no. Get that seductive gleam out of your eye, my love. When I take you to bed for the first time, it's *not* going to be in the middle of the afternoon with a strong possibility of being interrupted in the next half-hour." Turning her around and giving her a light slap on the bottom, he added, "Why don't you run and change, while I fix some coffee? And be a good wench and cover up some of that distracting skin! We've got to discuss your skinny admirer, and I'd like to do it before Ed Bancroft shows up."

Startled, she turned back and gasped, "How did you know?"

"How could I not know? I came in through the shop, and Midge practically climbed up me in excitement, talking at approximately fifteen hundred words a minute, with nary a breath in between them. However, I will say that she's done a masterful job organizing protection. I think she's got half the town involved. Can't imagine why he hasn't been spotted, unless you and Hero scared him into the next state."

Which was not entirely true. He could think of a couple of reasons, the most likely being that the rather inept house-breaker had decided to lie low for a few days before getting up the courage to try again. It was highly unlikely that he'd realize how many times he'd been spotted and just how much had been pieced together about his activities.

O'Mara automatically fixed two mugs of coffee, his agile mind busy considering various possibilities. He didn't think that a howling dog and a flash of light would permanently frighten off a man who had apparently spent over two weeks on a concentrated spying project. There was no question in O'Mara's mind that the spy was an amateur; he was much too obvious to be a professional. Mouth twisting in a disparaging smile, the big ex-spy briefly considered just how easy it would be to keep a close watch on an unsuspecting Kitt without ever being noticed.

Poking around for something to nibble on, he discovered that the cookie jar was full of chocolate chip cookies, and helped himself to a handful before settling down at the breakfast bar to wait for Kitt. Munching absently on a cookie, he stared at the refrigerator while he went back to second-guessing their scrawny spy and planning his personal campaign to catch him. O'Mara was much more interested in getting his hands on the young man and doing his own questioning than in helping the police pick him up. He doubted if the watcher had gone too far away, although if he had a modicum of sense, he'd have acquired another car. The trick was going to be in lulling the police or tossing them a red herring, calling off Midge's watchdogs and making it appear to anyone watching that everyone had given up interest. Then, with Ez's help—

"Hi! What are you so deep in thought about?" Kitt dropped onto the stool next to him and reached for her coffee. "I see you've raided the cookie jar."

"Mmmmm. They're good, even better than Andy's. You make them?"

"Of course. And don't eat them all, greedy, they're for Gus." She grinned at him, reaching to break off a piece of the cookie in his hand and nibble on it.

Glancing at the clock, he said, "I understand he's going to be here shortly, and so is Ed Bancroft. Now tell me quickly, before we're interrupted, just what's been going on."

"I thought Midge told you."

"She did, but I want to hear your version. Indulge me, love." He turned the full impact of a coaxing smile on her, and she gave in—albeit with a gleam in her eye that said clearly "I know what you're doing"—and concisely reviewed the recent happenings.

He listened attentively, sipping coffee and eating cookies, occasionally offering a piece to Hero who was sitting on his foot. It only took Kitt a few minutes to run through the facts and answer his two or three questions.

"What do you think he wants? Why would anyone be watching me?" she asked anxiously at the end.

"I'm not sure. There's a couple of things that come to mind, but—" He smiled at her reassuringly. "Let me think about it. Meanwhile, you stop worrying. I'm not about to let anyone bother you. Or Gus." He caught himself up, on the verge of mentioning that Ez would be there tomorrow, deciding that the fact of Ez coming up a day early would make her think things were more serious than they actually were. Briefly, he debated telling Ez to come up Friday as usual, but concluded that things would move faster in the direction he wanted them to go with both of them working on the problem. And the sooner the better.

"O'Mara?" Kitt's voice brought him back to the present. "Have you thought of something?"

"Lots of things," he said blandly. "For instance, I didn't finish telling you about your dress. After I bought the material in Zurich, I didn't have time to do anything with it until I got to Stockholm. I was going to be there for several days, so I found a dressmaker, sketched the dress I remembered and described as many details as I could recall, and she had it ready for me the day before I left."

"Sometimes, O'Mara, you are just too much. I can't believe you remembered that dress so perfectly after all these years."

"Well, it was a rather special dress, and a *very* special night." He leaned toward her, catching and holding her gaze. "The dress is only the beginning of what I remember . . . in vivid detail . . . sight, sound and . . . touch."

Again, Kitt had the odd feeling that the world was sort of going away somewhere. Her mind seemed to up-anchor and drift on a tide of pure sensation. *He's giving me hot flashes again. How can anyone have eyes that color? Maybe they just look like sapphires because of that dark tan. He must have spent most of his trip outdoors. I'll never win an argument. All he has to do is look at me like that and,* "if he doesn't stop it, I'll start taking off my clothes again, right now."

O'Mara threw back his head and shouted with laughter. Kitt turned flaming red and clapped both hands over her mouth.

"Oh, damn," she wailed, "did I say that out loud?"

He was wiping away tears and still breaking up in spurts of laughter when they heard thudding feet on the stairs and Gus yelling, "Dad! Hey, Dad, when did you get home? Did you hear what happened to Kitt?"

He ran across the living room, Hero at his heels, and threw himself into his father's arms. Over O'Mara's shoulder, Gus winked impishly at Kitt and teased, "Hey, Kitt, aren't you glad he's back? Now you'll have someone besides me to hug and kiss you. I'll bet Dad's even better at it than I am."

O'Mara grinned at him. "You know it."

Kitt stood and stretched, then leaned over to reach out and hook a finger around Gus's belt, pulling him toward her until they were nose-to-nose. Crossing their eyes, they giggled at each other, and then Kitt said, in a comforting tone, "Don't feel bad, Gus. It's just that he's been practicing longer. Give it a few more years and you'll be every bit as good at huggin' and kissin' as he is." Her voice dropped to a loud whisper. "Maybe even better."

With a smile that could only be described as doting, O'Mara watched the easy rapport between his son and a Kitt who seemed to be getting younger and gayer with every passing hour. He listened to their laughing give-and-take as they raided the refrigerator and cookie jar. Appreciatively, he let his eyes wander over Kitt's slim but far from delicate form, admiring the snug fit of her white jeans and slate-blue knit shirt. She turned and caught him at it, and for a long, intense moment, her gaze locked with his in a heated exchange of silent messages that fairly scorched the air between them. At last, with visible effort, they broke the contact and turned their attention back to Gus, both of them secure in the knowledge that their long wait for total fulfillment of their love was almost at an end.

Chapter 20

By Thursday afternoon, Kitt was feeling more than slightly frustrated. She was also developing a strong desire to lay unfriendly hands on the scrawny cause of her immediate problems. Heaving book cartons out of her way with wild abandon, she stomped around the storeroom sorting out a huge UPS delivery and wishing vindictively that she could throw the heavy cartons right at the head of her pesky watcher.

She finally slumped down on a stack of boxes to catch her breath and rub her aching arm muscles. With a rueful grimace, she chided herself for getting so worked up in the first place. It really was rather stupid. After all, there was no question in either her mind or O'Mara's that they had overcome her fears and would be able to have a normal physical relationship—if one could call the strength and depth of their need for each other "normal." And if they had waited this long, surely another day or two wouldn't matter.

But it did. She'd wanted, expected, needed to be with him last night, and had spent half the evening in a state of heated anticipation, barely aware of all the comings and goings as O'Mara got things organized his way. Her mind was centered on being alone with him that night, all barriers gone, free to be naked and loving with him, learning how to please him, discovering at last the full measure of joy and ecstasy that he'd promised her. She'd wanted to sleep in his arms and awaken in the morning to find him beside her. Her eyes had savored the long, strong line of his back as he leaned forward talking to Eddie and Roger, and she'd thought about taking a shower with him and running soapy hands over that same back. As if he felt her eyes on him, he'd turned his head and captured her in that glinting blue gaze, a slow, sensual smile widening his mouth as he read her mind.

Damn! She kicked a carton of books in remembered frustration, and then pulled her foot up into her lap to rub her bruised toes through the soft suede of her ankle boots. For a fleeting moment, she wished it had been that aggravating man's shin she'd kicked. He knew, *knew*, what she'd been thinking about all evening and, if he was so damn clever, there must have been some way he could have worked things out so that they could have spent the night together. But, oh, no. She'd ended up with Midge again, plus Roger happily sprawled out in a sleeping bag in the living room playing guard dog, while her almost-mate took himself back to the Rock and that lovely big bed—alone! And all because of some nosy little twit.

Muttering unprintable imprecations, Kitt settled herself cross-legged on her stack of boxes and stewed. She knew she was letting her disappointment over the ending to the evening get out of proportion, but she'd built up such hopes and had assumed that O'Mara was just as eager as she was to end the waiting. Well, to be fair, he probably was. And in a way, she could understand why he had decided to wait until they'd solved their little mystery. It would be a distraction to have to keep one ear cocked for lockpickers or be worrying about the cops checking in periodically or calling with news. But still—

"Kitt! What the hell is the matter with you? Are you sick?"

Ez's bellow jerked her back to the present, literally, as she jumped and whacked her head against the wall.

"Ow! You great oaf, what are you trying to do—scare me witless? And what are you doing here, anyway? It's only Thursday," she snapped crossly, rubbing the back of her head. "I wasn't sick until you came roaring in here. Now I've got a headache. Pea-brain!"

"What am I supposed to think? Midge says you're back here unpacking books, and I find you sitting there, rocking back and forth and muttering to yourself like a demented Buddhess."

"There's no such thing as a Buddhess," growled Kitt with a decidedly unfriendly scowl.

"Don't nitpick. Why are you in such a rotten mood? You can't be that worried about this idiot housebreaker. He sounds like a total twerp. Even Midge could probably take him with one hand." He stared at her consideringly, and then said in a disgusted voice, "O'Mara! If that man doesn't do something about you soon, I'm damn well going to lock you in a cold shower!"

Kitt jumped to her feet and stood, hands on hips and chin jutting out, spitting like a cat. "If you're implying that I'm . . . oh, you . . . well, I'm not . . . and besides, he's already doing something . . . NO! I mean, he just . . . we only . . . STOP LAUGHING, YOU GREAT GORMLESS GOAT!" yelled Kitt, stamping her size-nine boot down within an inch of his toes.

"Hey, you two, if you're going to have a knock-down rip-snorter, how about going out back? You're making the customers nervous. At least, the ones who aren't laughing." An exasperated Midge stood in the doorway, head tilted back as she glared up at them.

The twins blinked, shook their heads, looked down at Midge and then grinned at each other. In unison, they bent over the small figure, each of them patting one of her shoulders and kissing a cheek.

"Now, now," Kitt crooned, "everything's just fine."

"Don't fash yourself," Ez rumbled. "We never fight."

Midge looked from one to the other and rolled her eyes up to the ceiling. "You are both," she said emphatically, "noodles."

Clasping his big hands around her waist, Ez picked her up and held her at arm's length. "While you, me wee small elf, are mizzy-mazed," he announced in an atrocious attempt at an Irish brogue.

Laughing, Kitt backed out the door. "Ah . . . if you two would like to say a proper hello or whatever, I'll help Joanne mind the shop for a while."

"You'd better clean up first. You look like you've been sweeping chimneys," Ez said absently as he lowered Midge to stand on a carton and wrapped his brawny arms around her small body. Kitt tactfully closed the door before going along to the lavatory to wash up and brush her hair to reasonable neatness.

Joining Joanne behind the desk a few minutes later, she asked quietly, "Did Ez happen to mention what he was doing here a day early?"

Joanne glanced up at the taller woman with a decidedly guilty look, and finally mumbled, "Midge called him early Tuesday morning, and he . . . I, ah, think he got somebody to cover for him so he could come up as soon as possible. Well, not knowing exactly when Mr. O'Mara would be back and . . . Well, I think he was worried about your being here alone."

Kitt quirked a sardonic eyebrow at the fidgeting girl and drawled, "Alone? Tell me five consecutive minutes that I've been alone since Monday night. If I haven't had someone at my shoulder, I've had them outside the door or at the bottom of the stairs. Drat! I told her— Oh, well, I should have known she'd call him."

"What's funny?" asked a bewildered Joanne as Kitt started to laugh.

"I could almost feel sorry for that poor little man. Can you imagine having both Ez and O'Mara after you, mad as hell and ready to commit mayhem?"

"They didn't look all that mad," Joanne tentatively offered. "I mean, when Mr. O'Mara was here earlier, he seemed very calm and cool about it. He was joking with everyone and teasing Midge and me."

"Yeah. Well, let me warn you, Joanne, with men like Ez

and O'Mara, the time to watch out is when they're really working at being cool and calm and they're smiling with their teeth clamped together. I'd give odds that Ez was one of the calls O'Mara said he had to make last night." Kitt stared contemplatively at a Beatrix Potter poster and said thoughtfully, "Now what, I wonder, have those two hatched up?"

"We haven't been hatching up anything," protested Midge, coming up to lean against the other side of the desk and looking rather moony-eyed and a bit disheveled.

Eyes gleaming with understanding amusement, Kitt explained, "Not you. Ez and O'Mara." She glanced at the ceiling, listening to the resounding footsteps of her twin. "Do you know what they're brewing up?"

"Uh-uh. Not me. Ez just told me to keep my tail tucked down. Is that significant?"

Kitt flung her hands up in a "Who knows?" gesture. "It depends on what they're planning to toss around—blasphemy, bull or bodies. Macho males and their mysterious plotting! Honestly! They don't act any older than Gus sometimes. Why make a big intrigue out of this? They could damn well tell us what's going on."

Midge and Joanne exchanged knowing looks as Kitt banged a frustrated fist down on the desk, her flushed cheeks and flashing eyes indicating a rare display of temper. Neither of the younger women was aware that most of her mini-tantrum was due to her disappointment of the previous evening.

"I'm sure they'll let us in on it sooner or later," Midge said placatingly, prudently backing out of arm's reach as Kitt cast a menacing glare in her direction.

The rather pithy comment on the tip of Kitt's tongue stayed there when the thud of large feet descending the stairs heralded Ez's appearance. His casual attire of jeans and T-shirt was set off by the copper and white of Hero, draped around his neck like a living scarf and riding comfortably on his broad shoulders.

"Where do you think you're going?" demanded an irate Kitt. "Now that I've got all that muscle power available, I mean to make use of it to heave those book cartons out of our way."

Dropping a casual arm around Midge's shoulders, Ez leaned against the desk and gave his disgruntled twin a long, considering look. Joanne unobstrusively sidled away and started clearing off the reading table, staying well out of range of any potential fireworks.

Slowly shaking his head, Ez bent toward Midge and whispered thunderously, "This is all O'Mara's fault, you know. If I ever saw a woman who needed to be—"

"It's HIM!" Joanne hissed frantically.

"Where?" "Who?" The other three crowded around her where she stood frozen by the reading table, staring out the window.

"Across the street in front of Sea Wrack's window. See him? The skinny guy with his back turned? Blue jeans and a red T-shirt? That's him."

"Are you sure?" Ez demanded. "Midge?"

"I . . . I think so. I'd have to see his face to be sure."

"I saw his face before he turned all the way around," Joanne said. "It's the same guy who was in here. Oh! Watch! He's turning again."

Ez moved a couple of steps closer to the window, his eyes glued to the thin figure idling in front of the gift shop.

"Damn! Someone's coming in," Midge cried.

"Spread out," Kitt said. "We can't all be standing here like this."

Ez spun around and started for the stairs, grabbing Midge's hand and towing her along with him. "Joanne, keep working at that table, but keep an eye on him for a few minutes. If he leaves, try to see where he goes. Kitt, take care of the customer and stay away from the window."

"Where are you two going?"

"Midge'll watch him from your room while I call O'Mara. We've got to find out what he's driving if he's dropped the red Toyota."

"Ez—" Kitt ground her teeth together as Ez and Midge raced up the stairs. For the next ten minutes, she discussed cookbooks and valiantly kept a friendly smile on her face. She left her customer trying to make up her mind between French, Italian and Chinese cuisine, and strolled over to join Joanne.

"Is he still there?" she whispered, keeping her back to the window.

"Not outside," answered Joanne in a low voice. "He went into the shop a couple of minutes ago."

"I can't stand this," Kitt hissed. "When she decides what

she wants, take care of her, will you? I'm going upstairs to find out what Ez and O'Mara are plotting now."

Kitt's long legs easily took the stairs two at a time and, when she found the living room empty, carried her swiftly down the hall to her bedroom, where she discovered an intent Midge staring out the window at the shop across the street.

"Where's Ez?" Kitt asked tautly, glancing around the room and finding only Hero sprawled on her bed.

Midge eyed her warily and carefully explained. "He went to meet O'Mara out of sight of the shop. He . . . ah . . . said he didn't want to waste time answering questions, so he dropped off the back of the deck, cut through the backyard to the river and whistled one of the boatmen over to take him up to the landing."

"I hope he grows warts in his ears!" Kitt seethed. "I hope they both do!"

"Oh, Kitt, you know they won't take you with them," Midge protested. "Ez said you'd have a frothing fit at being left out of things, but he and O'Mara can't be sure if there's just this one guy, and they aren't about to let you take any chances on getting hurt. Come on, now, and calm down. They mostly want to find out what car he's driving and maybe where he's staying. Ez said they'd be back for supper. In fact, they're bringing it with them. Lobster, I think."

"Feed the beast and soothe her ruffled feathers?" Kitt asked sweetly.

Midge choked back a gurgle of laughter, taking her gaze off the gift shop long enough to give Kitt a teasing look. "What kind of beast has feathers?"

"A flying dragon?" Kitt sighed in exasperation and then started to smile. "Oh, all right. So I'll wait until the big macho males come back, thumping their chests and twitching their tails in triumph. Yuck! I still don't see why we have to camp up here, protected like some fragile Victorian maidens." She flopped across the bed on her stomach, reaching over to scratch Hero behind the ears. "Oh, stop laughing, you pea-sized pixie."

"It's too funny," Midge gasped. "I saw O'Mara kissing you goodnight last night, and he sure wasn't acting as if you were anything like fragile. If Ez hugged me like that, I'd have half a dozen broken ribs and two collapsed lungs!"

"Er . . . ah, yes . . . well, we, ah, got a bit carried away and . . . he, um, may have a few bruises, too." Kitt struggled to maintain a blasé look, but spoiled it by blushing a deep pink under Midge's knowing gaze.

"I wouldn't be surprised. You two are something else again, you know. I can almost hear the crackle of flames when you look at each other, to say nothing of—Hey! He's leaving!" Midge edged closer to the big bay window, staying behind the thick foliage of a huge Swedish Ivy plant and peering through a gap in the leaves.

"Where's he going?" Kitt scrambled off the bed to stand behind Midge and look out over the top of the plant. "Do you see Ez or O'Mara?"

"No, but they'd stay out of sight anyway. He's heading for the square. See him? He's just in front of those two blondes."

"I see him. But where— Oh, my, how sneaky!"

"What?"

"Look. On the far side of the gas station. See that gray Mustang? That's Andy's car, and that's O'Mara slouched in the driver's seat."

"Are you sure, Kitt? It doesn't look like him."

"I'd know him even with that silly cap pulled down over his eyes. Clever. Chances are the guy wouldn't know Andy's car well enough to spot it. It doesn't exactly stand out like the Mercedes or the Renegade."

"Especially parked in with those other cars. Oh, look, there's Ez!" Midge pushed the ivy aside and leaned into the bay. "Now I see what they're doing. Ez is following him, but staying back out of sight and watching O'Mara for signals. Hey, he must be going for his car. O'Mara just beckoned Ez over."

"I see them. They're going to follow him. Damn. Surely, they've got sense enough not to try to take him in the middle of the afternoon with all the world looking on."

Midge glanced down into the parking lot as she stepped back from the window. "Looks like Joanne might have her hands full. Maybe we'd better go downstairs," she suggested tentatively. "There's not much else we can do until they get back."

Kitt stuck her lower lip out and summoned up a glower. "I could always stomp around and throw things at the walls," she threatened, and then broke up in laughter at Midge's alarmed expression. "Never mind me. It's that aggravating man who's put me in a temper; and it's up to him to get me out of it."

Not for a moment did Midge imagine that Kitt was referring to Ez.

The rest of the afternoon flew by with a steady stream of customers keeping the three women busy. Shortly before closing, Kitt heard the thudding of male feet running up the outside stairs, followed by the sound of footsteps and male laughter overhead. Impatient for news, she rushed everyone through the closing and then raced Midge for the stairs.

"Whoa, love!" O'Mara halted her headlong dash across the living room by stretching out a long arm and grabbing her wrist, giving it a strong tug that tumbled her down on top of him where he lay sprawled full-length on the sofa. He laughed up into her indignant face while his strong hands shifted her into a comfortable position against him.

"Your temper's showing, tiger lady," he teased. "Be a good Kitt-cat now and take your elbows out of my ribs."

Her glare gradually changed to a smoky blue invitation as he slowly stroked his hands down her back and across her bottom, his supple fingers lingering to knead her firm buttocks. With a throaty, "Mmmmmm," she slid her arms around his neck and brought her mouth down on his. Her hair spilled forward around their faces in a chestnut curtain as her light, teasing kiss rapidly deepened to passion when his urgent hands ground her hips against his and he shifted to bring a hard thigh up between her legs.

The intrusive sounds from the kitchen brought them back to a belated sense of time and place. Midge's outraged squeal of "Ez!" and his answering roar of laughter effectively broke the sensual spell that Kitt and O'Mara were weaving around each other, and she lifted her head to look down into his flushed face with dazed eyes.

"This was *not* one of my better ideas," he said ruefully. "We're not safe together in public—at least, not at the moment." He brought one hand up to push her head down beside his and whispered in her ear. "You were right. All that abstinence wasn't good for me. Now that I can hold you, I can't keep my hands off of you." He gently nipped her earlobe, and she could hear laughter in his voice as he added, "And you're no help, love, melting all over me every time I touch you."

She pressed her open mouth against his neck and traced moist circles with her tongue before teasing, "You don't like it?"

"Mmmmm. I love it. So much so that we are definitely going to get off this couch while you've still got your clothes on."

Reluctantly, they untangled themselves and sat up. He finger-combed her hair back into reasonable order while she tugged her cotton-knit shirt into place. His abstracted gaze followed the motions of her hands and then lingered on her breasts and the hard jut of her nipples pressing against the fabric. She groaned and leaned toward him as his hands cupped her breasts, his thumbs lightly stroking the taut nipples.

"O'Mara, please. . . ."

"Oh, hell!" he growled. His hands slid down to her waist, and he stood up, simultaneously bringing her to her feet.

"I don't care what those two are cooking up," he muttered, impatiently pushing the thick swath of hair back from his forehead. "There's safety in numbers right now. Come on, temptress, and stop that giggling. It's not funny."

"It is so, grumpy. All these weeks, and now that we finally can, we can't."

He pushed her toward the kitchen, stating positively, "Oh, yes, we can. And we will. In fact, we are."

"When?" she challenged, swinging around to walk backward, laughing at him while her eyes flashed a "Dare you!" message.

Before he could answer, his attention was diverted by the scene in the kitchen. The slow smile lighting his face spun Kitt around to find out what was so amusing. Her shoulders started to shake with silent laughter as she took in the picture of Midge perched on the edge of the high counter, her arms and legs wound around Ez while he kissed her, holding her small body close to him with obvious care.

"Wonder how many more ways he's going to find to overcome that height difference," O'Mara murmured in Kitt's ear.

"I'm more concerned about his forgetting someday and giving her a bear hug. She'd end up looking like a half-used tube of toothpaste!"

"Right now, I want to eat." O'Mara let his deep voice out in a roar. "Ez! Food! Lobsters! Salad! Dinner!"

It was enough. With a growled "I'll get you for this, O'Mara," Ez swung Midge off the counter and onto her feet, and the four of them made short work of getting supper onto the table. Despite their many questions, Kitt and Midge gleaned only the information that their skinny nuisance was now driving a blue Chevy and staying at the Day's End Motel. All questions as to how O'Mara and Ez were going to make use of that knowledge were firmly fended off. Resolutely, the men kept the conversation light, steering it into a fast and funny exchange of ideas for the most unusual wedding of the decade for Kitt and O'Mara.

Later, in the comfortable coolness of a delightful spring evening, the four of them relaxed on the deck, finishing a bottle of wine and listening to the soft sound of the river. Kitt, mindful of the size of the men in her life, had furnished the deck with sturdy redwood settees and loungers, their hard contours softened by colorful canvas-covered cushions. Ez was ensconced on a lounger holding Midge on his lap, while Kitt and O'Mara shared the long settee with their feet propped on a low table. Hero, finding his usual lap filled with Midge, had settled down on O'Mara's lap with only a mild 'Rrrorrow" of complaint.

Kitt rested her head back against the hard warmth of O'Mara's arm, which was draped across her shoulders. It was a clear night, and she stared dizzyingly up at the silver canopy of stars, wondering vaguely why she felt slightly muzzy-headed. After a few moments of uncomplicated thought, she decided it was partly the wine, partly the scent of lilac, salt and lime aftershave, but mostly the effect of O'Mara's long length pressed close to her right side. Her abdominal muscles tightened instinctively, and she shifted her hips in a restless, tingling response to his nearness.

"I know just what's bothering you. I promise I'll take care of it soon," he whispered. She could sense his smile, and her breath caught as the warm, moist tip of his tongue traced her ear.

The corners of her mouth twitching in a repressed smile, she turned her head just enough to slant him a doleful look. "Promises, promises. All I ever get is—"

The rest of her sentence was lost against his mouth. After a few moments, and long before she wanted him to, he drew away. His soft chuckle at her instinctive move to continue the kiss earned him a light punch in the solar plexus.

"Beast! You've got a stomach like a rock wall."

"Only when someone aims a punch at it," he explained. "Now, if you were to rub it gently . . ."

"You *know* what that would lead to, and you keep telling me this is not the time for further lessons. Mine, that is. You already know everything." She turned her head against his shoulder to look up at him with mock-admiration.

"Too true," he countered smugly, stroking a caressing finger across her lips and watching her face soften with desire. "I do like that look in your eyes, love. Maybe we should send those two on a long moonlight swim, hmmm?"

"Too cold. How about down to Boston for pizzas?"

"Ez would probably do it, too. On the other hand, he may well be trying to figure out how to get rid of us."

They glanced over at the couple in the lounger and, after one unbelieving look, Kitt buried her face in O'Mara's shoulder to stifle her laughter while he shook in silent glee. Ez had lowered the back of the lounger until he was lying almost flat, with his head propped up on a cushion. Tiny Midge, perched cross-legged on his chest, was leaning forward, shaking her finger and talking intently down into his laughing face. In an apparent effort to emphasize her point, she suddenly started bouncing up and down, which only made Ez, obviously unaffected by having some hundred-odd pounds thumping onto his chest, laugh harder and grab her hips to keep her from tumbling onto the floor.

"Would you two mind speaking up?" O'Mara called. "If the dialog's as exciting as the action . . ."

"Ooops!" gulped Midge, clapping both hands over her mouth and staring at them in dismay.

In a smooth, fast move, Ez was suddenly sitting up on the edge of the lounger with Midge balanced on one strong thigh. "Enough of this levity, folks. It's a little after eleven, O'Mara. What do you say?"

"What are you talking about?" asked Kitt, looking apprehensively from one to the other. "What are you going to do?"

"Yeah, what?" chimed in Midge with a touch of belligerence.

"We'll tell you inside," O'Mara said. He nudged Hero off his lap and stood up, pulling Kitt along with him. Ignoring all female questions, the two big men quickly flipped protective covers over the deck furniture, collected the wineglasses, and shooed the women ahead of them into the living room.

O'Mara slid the door shut and locked it, then reached for the drawcord and closed the drapes before turning around to meet Kitt's demanding gaze. "All right, love. Now, we'll tell you. We're going . . . hunting. I definitely want to talk to this young man before the police find him. It could well be that I won't want any public records of whatever is behind this."

"Oh, no." Kitt sank into a chair with her arms wrapped around herself, staring at him with a half-fearful, half-angry look. "You can't just— How do you know he's alone in this? There may be more of them. And what if he's got a gun or something? If he was really scared the other night, he may have gotten a weapon by now."

"Come on, Kitt," Ez growled. "One skinny guy. You were ready to take him on with a golf club."

"I didn't have any choice, dammit," she snapped, anger at their apparent foolhardiness momentarily overcoming her fear. "I was all alone here, with no time to call for help. But you two don't need to do this. If he's outside watching, all you have to do is call the cops and let them pick him up. Confronting armed thugs is their job, not yours."

"Kitt, Kitt," soothed O'Mara, dropping to one knee in front of her and taking her shoulders to give her a slight shake. "I'm sure he's not armed, and there's no evidence that anyone else is with him. We'll be just fine." He cupped her face between his hands and smiled at her reassuringly. "Will you please not worry so? I have had quite a bit of experience at this sort of thing, you know."

"But—"

"Come on, you faintheart," Ez said encouragingly. "Can you really see one skinny weasel giving the two of us any trouble?"

Kitt looked from one to the other, lines of strain starting to show in her face. With a gentle touch, O'Mara stroked his fingers over the tension marks and then leaned forward to kiss her lightly but lingeringly. "Stop fretting, love," he said softly. "I promise you we'll be all right. You and Midge have a cup of coffee, and we'll probably be back before you're finished. Okay?"

She looked at him for a long moment, then wrapped her arms around his neck and pressed her cheek tightly against his. "Okay," she murmured shakily in his ear. "But if you let anything happen to you, I'll never forgive you."

He held her close for a few moments and then stood up, pulling her to her feet. "Go make the coffee, toad-kisser." He turned her in the direction of the kitchen and started her on her way with a light slap on the bottom before heading for the stairs. "We're going out the back way downstairs, and we'll lock the door behind us. We'll come back via the deck. Don't open this door until you're sure it's us. Come on, Ez, stop fooling around and let's go."

Ez dropped Midge back onto her feet and started after O'Mara. "Stay loose, girls. You've got a whole bag of golf clubs." He winked at Midge, adding, "Take care of Kitt."

"Oh, sure," agreed Midge, looking up at her tall friend. "I can just see it now."

Kitt managed a shaky laugh. "I'll bash him with a golf club while you and Hero bite him on the legs." She listened to the receding footsteps and then drew in a deep, steadying breath. "Well, sprite, let's go make that coffee."

It was the longest twenty minutes Kitt could remember. She paced and sipped coffee and tried to listen to Midge's distracting questions about her summer plans for the shop. She had no idea what she answered. Resolutely, summoning up all her willpower, she tried to erase the insistent visions of Ez and O'Mara lying in pools of blood and surrounded by scrawny young men toting every kind of weapon from ancient pikes to modern automatics. It was ridiculous, she knew, to put herself into a panic. O'Mara knew what he was doing, and he wouldn't take foolish chances with either himself or Ez. But what if there were two or three instead of just one, and what if they had guns, and what if—

"Kitt! Snap out of it!"

She blinked and looked bewilderedly at Midge. Glancing

around, she realized that she was sitting on the edge of the sofa, clucthing her coffee mug so hard that her fingers had cramped, and that Midge was bending over her, looking distressed.

"Whew! I thought you'd gone into a trance. Now stop being so silly. You know perfectly well that either of them can handle just about anything and, together, they're enough to scare the stitches out of Frankenstein. Well, aren't they?"

"Oh, yes," Kitt murmured vaguely, her mind concentrated on her rapidly changing feelings. The metallic taste of fear was in her mouth and her hands were still unsteady, but gradually a deep welling of revulsion for her weakness was rising from within her. She had survived very real violence before. She had overcome crushing fear and fought back. True, it had left her emotionally crippled for a time, but she'd struggled long and hard with Ez's help to get herself back together. And she'd done it. Now, with O'Mara's help and love, she'd overcome the last great barrier to a complete, fulfilled life, and she'd be damned if she'd let her overactive imagination wreck everything at the first challenge!

"I am NOT a plate of spaghetti!" Kitt leaped to her feet and glared at Midge.

The younger woman grinned back at her. "Who the hell said you were? I take it you are now getting a grip on yourself. Good. Because from the sounds on the stairs, our heroes are back."

Midge ran to the door but didn't flip the lock until she heard Ez's "Open up, girls."

Chapter 21

Ez pushed the sliding door all the way open to allow room for himself and the young man held firmly at his side by the tight grip of Ez's large hand around his upper arm. Kitt took one quick, all-encompassing look at her twin as he moved into the room with his captive, and then her gaze flew to O'Mara, who was strolling lazily through the door as if he had been doing nothing more than taking an evening walk. His hair isn't even ruffled, she thought indignantly, and here I've been worrying myself into a purple funk. Which he would probably tell me is all my own fault for not listening to him. She glowered at the smug look he sent her, and briefly considered methods of taking him down a peg or two. Almost reluctantly, she shifted her attention to the very nervous man now sitting uneasily on one of the captain's chairs which Ez had placed in the middle of the room.

For a moment, no one spoke. Four pairs of unfriendly eyes examined the unprepossessing figure in the chair. About as tall as Kitt, he was pale and skinny, with thin, mousy hair straggling over his shirt collar and pale blue eyes set in an unremarkable face. Those eyes were darting rapidly around the room, lighting fleetingly on first one face and then another. It was obvious that he would have bolted for the door or stairs if Ez's big hand on his shoulder hadn't been holding him in the chair.

Kitt was beginning to relax now that O'Mara was at her side and she could feel the reassurance of his arm around her. She looked up at him questioningly.

"This," he said, flipping his free hand toward their unwilling guest, "is Stanley Portman. According to his driver's license, he's from Delaware."

"Listen, you . . . you had no right—" Stanley Portman's voice was light and pitched high with tension. He was sputtering now with fear which he was trying to turn into outrage. "What did you bring me in here for? You had no right to go yanking me out of my car. Damn you, you're a couple of thugs. I could bring charges against you for assault. Bastards! You're twice my size. You—"

"Shut up, Stanley," growled Ez, tightening his hold until the younger man groaned. "All we want to hear from you is your reason for spying on my sister, and what you were looking for when you tried to break in here Monday night."

"I . . . I don't know what you're talking about." His voice couldn't quite hold steady and, almost against his will, his eyes flicked to Kitt and then quickly away. "I don't even know your sister. I'm on vacation. Nothin' wrong with that. Just been lookin' around the place."

Kitt, watching him from the security of O'Mara's arm, could feel his fear. In a way, she could almost feel sorry for him. Ez and O'Mara in an unfriendly mood would curdle the blood of a much stronger man than this one. Mentally shaking her head, she wondered how long he thought he could hold out against the two of them. She leaned against O'Mara, listening to the staccato rap of insistent questions and the stumbling, stammering answers, and knew that it was only going to be a matter of minutes before Portman broke. He was sweating now, his hands clenching the chair arms. Ez wasn't even holding him down anymore; he was standing off to the side alternating with O'Mara in the rapid-fire interrogation.

Suddenly, Portman dropped his head in his hands and screamed, "All right! All right! I'll tell you."

They stared at him for a few silent moments. He panted in harsh gasps, as if he'd been running. Finally, he slumped back in the chair, defeated, his wary eyes skittering from one face to another. He looks like a trapped rabbit, thought Kitt, even to the twitching nose. How could I have gotten so worked over a weakling like that? Of course, even a weakling can turn on you if he's scared enough and cornered. On that thought, she turned in alarm toward O'Mara.

"Now what's boiling up in that overactive imagination of yours?" he teased in a low voice. "No, don't tell me. Just have faith, and stop worrying about everything. Don't you think I can take care of you?"

"Oh, yes, I *know* you can." Her answering grin was a bit wavery, but there was no sign of weakness in the hug she gave him as she reached to press her warm mouth to the hollow below his ear.

"First things first. I'll take care of you later," he whispered. His tender expression faded as he turned to Portman, and was replaced by a cool, controlled and quietly menacing demeanor. "All right, Portman, let's have it."

With a pathetic show of bravado, Portman attempted a sneer and glared weakly at O'Mara. "Your wife sent me!"

Three of his listeners looked startled. O'Mara merely lifted an eyebrow and stated, "*Ex*-wife, you mean. Why did she send you, Portman?"

"To watch her." He pointed at Kitt. "Laura—"

O'Mara cut him off. "Why you, in particular? How do you know Laura?"

"She's my cousin, second or third or something. Our mothers are good friends, and me and Laura always got along. So when she asked me to come up here and get evidence—"

"WHAT EVIDENCE?" O'Mara roared, startling everybody. He stepped away from Kitt and took two long strides toward Portman. The younger man cowered back from O'Mara's blackly threatening look and his menacing growl of, "What's that bitch up to, Portman? I told her she wasn't getting any more money out of me. Once was a favor, and that was IT."

"You owe her—"

"Nothing. Not one damn thing." O'Mara was towering over the cringing figure in the chair.

"B-but you w-won't even l-let her see h-her k-kid."

O'Mara leaned over the chair, braced with his hands on the arms, his blazing blue eyes practically blistering the terrified man's skin. "You listen carefully, you—Laura abandoned my son when he was less than a week old. She has never tried to see him, never asked about him, and doesn't give a damn about him. If you don't want to believe me, ask her own mother and father."

"But she said—" Portman began tentatively.

O'Mara cut him off with a seldom-heard gutter term and straightened up, pushing back his hair angrily. "I don't care a damn what she told you. She's lying. She's already tried to threaten me with a court action to get Gus. She doesn't stand a chance. Her own father is quite willing to testify as to her complete lack of interest in him for the past nine years."

"Uncle George would testify against Laura?!" Portman's voice rose to a squeal, and his shock at this revelation was evident.

"Damn right he would. Daughter or not, he has no use for her and the way she's been living. He's too upset over the effect on his wife to have any sympathy for Laura. She's really done a number on her mother, and her father isn't about to let her have a shot at messing up Gus. And believe me, neither am I. She's not going to get within a mile of him. Furthermore, she knows it. She's just out to try and cause me as much trouble as she can in the hope that I'll pay her off to shut her up."

Portman now looked totally abject and a bit sick. "Oh, God, you just might. You don't know what she's planning. She's going to make an awful stink and give your girlfriend there as much trouble as she can."

Both O'Mara and Ez moved toward the sorry figure drooping in the chair. Kitt stepped back, looking apprehensively from one man to another, asking uncertainly, "But what can she do to me?"

"Portman?" O'Mara snapped.

"L-Laura knows somebody up here, and she found out you were . . . were old friends with these Tates and y-you were spending all your t-time with her." He pointed a trembling finger at Kitt and quickly looked back at the big, threatening figures looming over him. "So she called a cousin of ours who works for the government and spun him some kind of story, and he checked them out. Mostly her. Then she asked me to come up here and watch her and make notes of how many times you visited her and how long you stayed and if she saw any other guys and—"

"And just what would that prove?" O'Mara demanded. "Kitt and I are both adults, and free to see each other whenever we please. What did Laura think she could do with that kind of information?"

"Yeah, well . . . she . . . ah . . . wanted me to get proof that you stayed overnight here or, better yet, that she stayed over at your place with you. Then Laura was going to tell you that she'd call the papers and tell them that you were carrying on with her in front of your kid."

"Unless, of course, I paid up and kept paying up? There's just one thing I don't understand about this, Portman," O'Mara drawled sarcastically. "Where's the threat? Why should she think the press would be interested beyond the gossip value of my name?"

"Don't you know?" Portman's pale eyes widened in surprise. He pointed at Kitt and cried excitedly, "Her name's not Tate. It's Darcy, and she killed her husband!"

For endless seconds, everyone but Portman stood as if turned to stone. Kitt's mind completely blanked out in shock, and she swayed on the point of unconsciousness until Ez's bellow jolted her back to alertness. And then, for a few minutes, everything moved so fast that there was no time for thought.

Ez's roar of rage would have put a bull elephant's maddened trumpeting to shame. It rattled every dish and window in the building and deafened everyone in the room. It even checked O'Mara's instantaneous reflexes for the two seconds it took Ez to leap for Portman and snatch him from the chair. By the time O'Mara moved, Portman was dangling a foot off the floor, with both of Ez's huge hands wrapped around his neck. Ez was shaking him like a big rag doll and yelling a steady stream of curses in half a dozen languages. The initial horror of Portman's accusation was forgotten by O'Mara, Kitt and Midge, who now had only one joint thought—to keep the berserk Ez from choking Portman to death in his blind rage.

Kitt and O'Mara lunged at Ez from either side, grabbing his wrists and trying to break his hold. All of them were shouting at him, but even O'Mara's deep voice couldn't be heard over Ez's continued bellows. Portman's face was rapidly darkening. O'Mara stepped back a pace and brought the edge of his hand down in two fast, hard karate chops on Ez's forearm, numbing it from elbow to fingertips. His right hand dropped away from Portman's neck, but in a blind reflex he swung from his unimpaired shoulder and knocked O'Mara halfway across the room. As soon as Ez's right hand had dropped, Kitt grabbed his left thumb with both hands, working her fingers between the rigid thumb and Portman's neck. Bracing her feet and leaning back, she used a combination of her weight and her considerable strength to loosen Ez's grip enough so that Portman could draw in gasping breaths. Simultaneously, O'Mara clamped Ez's right arm in a tight hold and fought to shift him off-balance. It was like trying to move Crest Rock. Ez's great muscles bulged and heaved as he tried to shake off Kitt and O'Mara.

Knowing the full horror of the true story, Ez had literally gone berserk at the incredible accusation from Portman, and he was in those minutes utterly blind and deaf to anything around him. Unaware of Kitt and O'Mara, his only reality was Portman and the need to destroy this threat to his twin.

In normal circumstances, O'Mara was just about an even

match for Ez. Now, however, the conditions were definitely abnormal, and it took all of O'Mara's 200 pounds and well-developed muscle power just to hold onto Ez's right arm and keep himself on his feet. He didn't want to use any of the disabling blows that he knew, since in Ez's maddened state he would have to use so much force that broken bones and/or damaged nerves would be a distinct possibility. He couldn't believe that Ez could hold out much longer—he was already holding Portman's 150-odd pounds at arm's length with one hand, with most of Kitt's 135 pounds suspended from the same arm, while O'Mara was letting his other arm take most of his 200 pounds. How long it might have taken Kitt and O'Mara to wear Ez down they would never know, because at that point Midge finally managed to include herself in the action and, in her unique style, brought Ez back to his senses.

Although it seemed like an hour, it had been less than two minutes since Ez erupted. Midge had been darting around the struggling tangle of tall bodies, trying to find a way to help but knowing she was too small and light to make any impact. When he threw O'Mara off, she tried to grab Ez's flailing arm, but backed off when O'Mara yelled, "No, Midge!" Suddenly realizing how useless she was, she stopped, took a good look at the situation and made a quick decision.

Kicking off her sandals, she dodged around O'Mara's braced feet to come up behind Ez. She jumped, grabbed a fistful of shirt for leverage, and scaled his back until she was sitting on his shoulders with both thighs clamped tightly around his head. Shifting to get her balance, she simultaneously clapped one hand over his mouth, pinched his nose shut with the other hand and started drumming her bare heels vigorously against his chest.

Not even Ez in all his rage was immune to suffocation. For a few more seconds, muffled roars echoed from behind Midge's hand, but finally he opened his left hand to let Portman drop in a heap to the floor. As soon as they felt the tension leave his body, Kitt and O'Mara let go of his arms and dropped down onto the rug, panting and rubbing aching muscles.

Once his arms were free, Ez grabbed Midge's wrists and pulled her hands away from his face. He took a couple of deep breaths, tilted his head back against her stomach so he could look up into her face, and asked in a perfectly normal voice, "What do you think you're doing, wench? You almost smothered me."

"I was saving your children's lives," she said in a tone of sweet reasonableness. "If you had strangled that son of a sick flounder, you'd have spent the next ten years in prison, and how the hell do you think we'd have managed to have kids under those circumstances? By mail?"

Ez grinned at her, said "Stupid" fondly, then lifted and flipped her and set her on her feet in front of him. His eyes went over her head to rest on Portman, still crumpled in a heap on the floor and gasping for air. Midge's alarm bells started ringing at the look on Ez's face and, planting both small fists in his diaphragm, she pushed him slowly backward, step by step, until he was sitting on the breakfast bar. Scowling determinedly, she stepped between his outstretched legs, turned around to plaster her back against his chest and stomach, pulled his arms around her and said grimly, "There now, you'll damn well stay put or you'll have to knock me over. You just let O'Mara straighten him out."

O'Mara rose lithely to his feet and reached out a hand to Kitt to pull her up. As her eyes met his, Portman's last words boomed and echoed in her mind, slamming and battering at the impregnable wall sealing off that last unbearable memory. Wrenching pain jolted through her head as, cracking and crumbling, faster and faster, the wall came down and her mind filled with the spinning horror of Leon's death.

With a wordless, anguished, guttural sob, she lunged into O'Mara's arms, burying her face in his shoulder and wrapping her arms around him in a rib-cracking stranglehold. Terror consumed her as she felt her mind sliding from sanity into an airless limbo, and she clung with desperate arms to her only remaining reality while the unspeakable nightmare memory crashed through her.

Reacting instinctively to her panic and rising hysteria, O'Mara clamped strong arms around her in a tight hold, trying to absorb the shocks as deep, hard, dry sobs jolted through her body. Frantically, she turned her face against his shoulder, seeking the security of warm, living skin, and he felt her panting breath against his throat as she finally pushed his collar aside and pressed her face against his neck. He brought up a hand to brush her hair back and rubbed his cheek against hers, murmuring loving reassurances and encouragement. All of his mental forces were concentrated in trying to break through her surging terror and make an emotional-mental connection with her. He slid his hand under her hair and kneaded the knotted muscles at her nape, while the soothing murmur of his voice continued in her ear.

Finally, after long minutes, the healing tears started, pouring down her face and his neck, soaking his shirt collar and trickling down his chest. She took deep, shuddering breaths and felt the first easing of terrifying pressure in her mind. Life, pulsing, loving, warm life was moving through her. She could *feel* his skin against her face, his hand on her neck, the warmth and strength of his body against hers, and she could *hear* the words of love and reassurance he was speaking. And then, suddenly, as if circuit switches had been flipped, her linkage with him was *there*. Love, with all its soothing, calming, supporting strength, was flowing into her, crowding out the mind-bending terror, releasing the last bonds of nightmare memory, vanquishing once and for all the lingering effects of the past.

Midge watched the two tall figures locked together so tightly that they seemed to be one. She could feel Ez, tense and distraught, half-rising and then settling back. After a few minutes, he let out a relieved sigh and relaxed, and she twisted around to look up at him.

"She's all right, now," he whispered. "O'Mara can give her something I can't, and he knows how to cope with her."

"Do you mind, Ez?"

"No." He smiled down at her in a way guaranteed to uncurl her hair. "It was inevitable that sooner or later we'd each find our own mates. It's a double bonus that we like each other's choices so much."

"Isn't it," Midge agreed faintly, looking like she'd just seen her first Christmas tree.

"Stay put, Portman!" O'Mara's sharp command brought everyone's wandering attention back to the unfinished business of the evening. Portman dropped back into his chair and huddled there miserably, obviously wondering what further disasters the evening would bring.

Kitt, still in the circle of O'Mara's arms, wiped the last tears away and looked up at him. There was sympathy and understanding in his eyes, together with an odd waiting quality in the intensity of his gaze as he said quietly, "I'm going to tell him the true story. Do you want to stay, or wait in your room until we're through?"

Her first impulse was to run for her room, and she started to draw back, feeling his arms loosening from around her. Then she stilled, hesitating as her eyes remained locked on his and she realized the significance of that waiting look. This was something she *had* to face to complete the healing process. Before all the shadows could be completely banished, she would have to recall in detail that last encounter and endeavor to put it into perspective; to accept that it was the irrational act of a madman rather than any kind of normal retaliation of an angry man; and to *know*, in the deepest recesses of her mind, that such a thing could never happen with O'Mara, no matter how aggravated he might become with her.

"I'll stay," she sighed, and saw the warm approval in his eyes before she moved back into his arms, resting her forehead on his shoulder and linking her arms around his waist.

O'Mara looked steadily at Portman over Kitt's shoulder and started talking in a flat voice, much as though he were reading a report. "I don't know or care whether Laura lied or someone misread a file, but not only did Kitt *not* kill her ex-husband, he died while *he* was trying to kill *her*. Some four months after Kitt divorced Darcy for physical cruelty, he . . ."

Kitt squeezed her eyes shut and clenched her teeth as the sound and fury of vivid memory drowned out O'Mara's voice and she lived again, in her mind, those final, fatal minutes with Leon.

She was finishing washing up her lunch dishes, listening to the laughter and talk from the Saturday afternoon crowd around the swimming pool. It was a sizable apartment complex, and there must have been close to a hundred people scattered around the big courtyard with its Olympic-size pool. She glanced out the window and decided to wait a while to go swimming. With luck, the crowd would thin out later, and she'd have more room to do laps. She turned back toward the sink to reach for a towel to dry her hands and paused at the sound of shouts and screams coming from the central hallway. Picking up the towel and wiping her hands, she started for the archway into the living room, and then froze at the shocking sound of Leon's voice yelling obscenities and ordering her to open the door. She leaned against the archway as her knees went weak with the fear chilling through her. How had he found her? This was the other end of the state!

Immobile with shock, she saw the door shake under the force of Leon's hammering, and then heard a wordless, enraged roar and a crash as his foot splintered the door beside the lock. Panicked, she unfroze and spun around, searching frantically for a way out. The kitchen was a trap. She turned and started to run for the outside-balcony door across the living room just as Leon smashed the hall door off its hinges and charged into the room.

She'd never make it. He was too close. Swerving away from him, she caught a quick glimpse of his huge figure swaying on his widespread feet, his head swinging from side to side as he searched for her. His face, twisted with rage, teeth bared in a snarl, eyes reddened and bulging with madness, was imprinted on her mind. She heard a woman screaming and knew it was herself. He saw her just as she lunged for the door and leaped after her, catching her arm and flinging her back across the room. Staggering, trying to stay on her feet, falling over a chair and rolling, rolling, seeing him coming after her, people crowding around the doorway screaming and yelling.

Her hand hit the leg of a dinette chair, and she grabbed it, lurching up on one knee to fling it at his legs. He stumbled over it, half-falling, and she came upright and picked up the other chair just as two brawny young men pushed through the doorway and grabbed Leon.

Relieved to know it was over, she set the chair down and leaned back against the wall, overcome with the release of tension. It took too many seconds for the scene in front of her to penetrate her numbed mind. Both young men were crumpled moaning on the floor and Leon was almost on her before her sluggish reflexes leaped to life. Grabbing the back of the chair with both hands, she rammed it at his chest and raced for the balcony door, the only clear exit from the trap of her apartment. She could hear him behind her, his enraged bellows deafening her, and she spun and spun again, snatching up lamps, ashtrays, end tables, another chair, anything movable, and flinging them at him in a frantic effort to slow him down. One more step. Ohgodohgod, the catch! Wet with the

*sweat of terror, her fingers slid off the catch to the sliding screen
door. Panting, sobbing, she tugged at the door. "Now, bitch!"
She flung a look over her shoulder. Pure rage charging the last
steps, hands reaching for her. She dove to the side, and his
maddened charge carried him right throught the screen, ripping it entirely out of the frame.*

*She jumped up to her feet and hesitated just an instant in the
doorway. His momentum had carried him, stumbling and
falling to one knee, all the way across the wide balcony which
ran the full length of the second floor. In seconds, he'd be on
his feet. Run! Run! She leaped through the doorway and raced
for the stairs at the end of the balcony. People, all kinds of
muscled young men by the pool, enough to stop him . . . yells
and screams behind her and more down below . . . people running across the courtyard . . . obscene roars and the
deck shaking with his thudding, racing strides . . . he was
close . . . too close . . . sirens . . . thank God! . . . run! . . .
almost there . . . no, don't look back . . . where are those
cops? . . . NOOHGODNO—*

*He cannoned into her, knocking her flat, his hands reaching
for her throat. Panic. No breath, numb, dazed from the weight
of him smashing her down, that madman's face wavering,
melting into grotesqueness through a red haze, can't move,
can't breathe, hands, huge strong hands to break my neck, kill
me, HE'S GOING TO KILL ME! NO! MOVE! ROLL! FIGHT
YOUFOOLFIGHTFIGHTnownowrunrun . . . men   grabbing . . . they've   got   him . . . no . . . runrunrun . . .
he's coming . . . they can't stop him . . . ugh, noletgoletgo
. . . kicking, punching, tearing, blood on his face, hands,
arms, don't let him get a lock around you he'll crush your ribs,
knee him knee him . . . runrun . . . oh god won't anything
stop him no not over the railing smash his nose adam's apple
somethinganything . . . get away away . . . railing . . . police
whistles . . . hang on . . . tired, so tired can't stop fighting
hurry nononoNONONON—*

". . . and the railing, already weakened from Darcy and
Kitt ramming into it, broke away, and they both fell just as
half a dozen cops ran into the courtyard. They saw the end of
it and said that it looked as if Darcy pushed Kitt away and
tried to grab the edge of the balcony but missed. Kitt did

catch an upright with one hand, but the weight and momentum of her falling body tore it lose. However, it was enough to swing her at an angle, and she landed on the canvas awning over a first-floor patio. It broke most of the force of her fall before it collapsed, and she lucked out with only a broken arm, cracked ribs and a mild concussion. Darcy fell straight down onto a concrete walkway and broke his neck. He was dead before anyone could reach him."

"Jesus," Portman breathed.

O'Mara, emotionally drained for the moment, rested his cheek against Kitt's soft hair, loosened the tight hold of his arms and started kneading the tense muscles in her back. She kept her head down on his shoulder, forcing her breathing to steady, regaining control bit by bit under the soothing movement of his hands, and finally relaxing the aching clamp of her fingers, which she'd dug into him those last few moments. Her chest hurt, and she realized that she'd been holding her breath through that last terrifying replay of the chase down the balcony and its end.

"It's over," O'Mara whispered in her ear, and she knew he meant *all* of it—the long years of fear and pain, the struggle to cope with the ugly memories, the fight to become a healthy, well-balanced, loving woman again, and the ultimate need to face that final, unbelievable memory.

She lifted her head and looked at him serenely with a quiet, accepting smile. "It's over," she agreed softly.

He held her face gently between his hands and brushed a light kiss across her lips. "And our time is about to begin," he promised.

His hands dropped to her shoulders, and he held her away from him. "Now, Ez and I are going to escort Portman to his car and see him on his way. We'll also take Hero for a short run. It would be very nice if you gals had some fresh coffee for us when we get back," he said coaxingly.

"But—"

His mouth stopped the rest of her protest. "Later," he murmured against her lips.

Kitt looked at him intently, seeing the promise in his eyes and noting that his mouth had a particularly sensual softness to its usually firm contour. After all the hours she'd spent imagining what making love with him would be like, this was all she needed to turn her insides warm and hollow with desire. Only his firm hands on her shoulders kept her from sliding her arms around him again and pressing her body against his.

He not only read the desire and need in her eyes, but he could feel the heat of it reaching out and touching him. "Later," he said again, his voice husky with promise and an answering need. He turned her around and gave her a light slap on the bottom to start her on her way to the kitchen.

"On your feet, Portman. Don't worry about him," he said as Portman flinched away from Ez. "He's not going to touch you again as long as you do just what you're told."

O'Mara opened the door and motioned Portman through ahead of him. Ez followed them, with Hero tagging at his heels.

Chapter 22

Kitt stood by the breakfast bar, staring at the closed door and listening absently to the receding voices. Her knees felt strangely weak and her body seemed to be full of warm bubbles. That husky "Later" drifted around in her mind, first loud, then soft, flowing like a tide. Listening to it, feeling it, she knew it was the goal, the climax, the new birth that she'd been reaching for with increasing eagerness. "Later," and it was a promise that parted her lips expectantly. It was as inevitable as moonrise that tonight was "Later"—it was at last the right time, and she felt only anticipation and a yearning excitement. No more fears. No more questions. No more shadows of the past. Just a rapidly increasing urgency to be with O'Mara, alone, naked, enveloped in each other. "Later," and she would know at long, long last the meaning of fulfillment, the oneness that they had denied themselves so very many years ago.

She would probably still have been standing there with slumberous eyes and a face flushed with sexual arousal if

Midge hadn't pushed her down onto a stool and forced her attention back to practical matters.

"Ye gods, Kitt," she laughed, "if O'Mara walks in and sees that look on your face, you'll never make it as far as the bedroom!"

"What?" Kitt slowly focused on Midge and then, in an instant replay, heard her last comment. The light flush deepened to fiery red, and she tried desperately to think of something innocuous to say.

"Oh, Kitt, that man had better do something about you right quick, before you start howling at the moon," Midge chortled.

"Yes, well, Ez said much the same thing this afternoon, and I rather think he's going to. Do something. O'Mara, I mean. About me. Oh, damn!" Kitt was completely flustered and suddenly felt as if she had an excess of hands and feet and didn't know quite what to do with any of them. She jumped up, exclaiming distractedly, "Drat! I forgot the coffee."

Midge pushed her back down onto the stool. "Never mind. I've already made it, and you'd better have a cup before you deteriorate into a heap of crumbs."

Between the strong coffee and Midge's bantering, Kitt managed to control her definitely overheated imagination and to regain her normal count of hands and feet. Although part of her concentration was devoted to listening for returning footsteps, and she had a tendency to see blue eyes wherever she looked, she did make an effort to pay attention to Midge's speculations about what Laura would say when Portman reported to her. She glanced at the kitchen clock every few minutes, wondering if it were slow.

"Where did they say they were going? Shouldn't they have been back by now?"

Midge adopted a look of extreme patience and spoke with exaggerated simplicity. "They are sending that creep on his way. Then, they are taking Hero for a run. Then, they will be back. Be calm. Be cool." She flung her arms wide and declaimed at the top of her voice, "HE WILL RETURN!"

When Ez and O'Mara walked in a minute later, they found both women rocking with laughter. Midge finally managed to gasp, "You guys want your coffee now?"

"No," answered Ez, taking her hand and leading her

toward the door. "The coffee was to keep you two busy." He slid back the door and paused, turning Midge around. "Say goodnight to Kitt and O'Mara now."

"Goodnight, Kitt and O'Mara," she echoed obediently, with a twinkle in her eyes and an impish smile.

Ez winked at O'Mara. "Enjoy yourselves," he murmured with a smug grin at Kitt.

She stood up, looking questioningly from the closed door to O'Mara and then, in alarm, she scanned the room. "Hero! Where is he?"

"Waiting in Ez's car," he said, smiling faintly, an intent, heated quality in his darkening eyes. "Come here, love, and stop worrying about Hero or anything else." He pulled her into his arms and kissed her lightly, his lips cool and salty from the night air. "Hero and Ez are going to sleep at the Rock tonight. Gus will be ecstatic when he wakes up in the morning. You, my love, are going to be ecstatic a good deal sooner than that."

"Oh." It was a breath against his cool lips, warming them. Her arms rested across his shoulders, and her long, supple fingers played in the soft thickness of his hair.

"Oh, indeed. Also ah and hmmmm." He was in no hurry now. He kept his mouth a breath away from hers, his lips barely brushing hers when he spoke. Slowly, he moved his hands downs her back until he could slide them under the edge of her sweater. "Midge is going to open up in the morning so we can sleep late."

"We can?" Dreamy, abstracted. Words were only half-comprehended. They were far less real than the warm hands gently memorizing the contours of her bare back. Under their light pressure, she swayed closer until her breasts just touched his chest. "If we took off some of these clothes, this would be even nicer."

"Hmmm. Why didn't I think of that?" She could sense his smile and delicately outlined his lower lip with the tip of her tongue. She felt as if clouds of tiny butterflies were swirling through her. Every square inch of tissue, every nerve ending in her body was pulsing and quivering with sweet tension. Vaguely, she heard him whisper, "Happy birthday, my lovely Kitt."

"It's tomorrow." She was muzzily aware of faint surprise;

with so much happening, she'd forgotten all about her birthday until he mentioned it.

"I know, but tomorrow arrived ten minutes ago." His voice was becoming as slow and dreamy as hers. Without conscious thought, his hands dropped to her hips, spreading over their firm curves and pressing her belly against his. "You're right," he murmured huskily. "This would be much, much better without all these clothes."

"Why don't we take them off, then?" she whispered, trailing her fingers down to start unbuttoning his shirt. He interrupted her after three buttons to pull her sweater off. "Finish what you started, love. Why do you persist in wearing these silly bras? You don't need them."

"If you're trying to tell me I'm too small, I already know that," she muttered. She pushed his shirt off his shoulders and tugged it down over his arms.

He shook free of the shirt to let it drop to the floor and brought his hands up to cover her breasts. "Sweet idiot. Where do you get these strange ideas? Your breasts are just right. They fill my hands very nicely, or hadn't you noticed?"

His tongue was burning patterns down the side of her neck. Its heat flashed through her, and she wriggled against him, fitting her hips to his hardening contours. She could feel the growing pressure of his aroused manhood against her belly, and then his spread fingers gripping her buttocks to hold her tightly against him.

"You beautiful witch," he groaned as his mouth opened wide against hers and his urgent tongue sought, found and tempted hers into an erotic, twining, sliding duel. They swayed on their feet and Kitt's knees were buckling, when O'Mara lifted his mouth, his breath coming in harsh gasps.

"I think . . . it's definitely . . . time for us to . . . go to bed. Believe me . . . you'll enjoy it much . . . better than the floor." He pressed his palms against her hipbones to move her half a dozen inches away from him. He was almost undone by the darkly luminous message in her exotic eyes, and his hands tightened on her for a long moment before they glided softly up her naked torso, briefly caressing the taut breasts, and closed over her shoulders.

"Wait right there. Don't move." Reluctantly, his hands dropped from her and, with a visible effort, he turned away to move swiftly around the room, locking the door and switching off lights. Finding his way by the dim glow of the hall light, he returned to catch her hand and lead her willingly down the hall to her moonlit bedroom.

Dazed with arousal and anticipation, Kitt paused uncertainly in the bedroom doorway. For a few seconds, her wandering attention focused on the shifting light and shadow playing over his bare skin, and she didn't hear his "What is it?" until he tapped her cheek with one long finger and repeated it a second time.

"Oh . . . ah . . . I've got to . . . I'll be back . . . just a minute." The room seemed unaccountably airless, or perhaps it was just that she kept forgetting to breathe. She hovered in the doorway, and one hand drifted up to slowly stroke the thick fur on his chest.

His teeth flashed white in the shadowed darkness of his face as he teased gently, "You were about to go in the other direction. And the sooner you go, the sooner you'll be back here." His voice dropped to a husky seductiveness. "Then we can both play as long as we want."

She was naked when she floated back into the bedroom, but couldn't remember having taken off the rest of her clothes. Somehow, she knew she'd find him naked, too. He was. The lean, beautiful, muscular body and long, sinewy legs were silhouetted against the moon-washed window where he waited for her. She never felt the soft carpet under her feet as she drifted across the room and into his arms.

It was all so natural, so inevitable. Something that had always been meant to be, that had been waiting and had now come to its proper time. There was no awkwardness, no fumbling, no hesitation. Her arms lifted to slide around his shoulders as his hands smoothed gently down her back, exerting just enough pressure to mold the full length of her naked body to his. Her parted lips were against the warm, smooth skin of his neck. She felt his breath on her ear as he whispered, "My beautiful Kitt, I love you so much and I've waited so long for you."

"O'Mara." It was an exhalation. He sensed it more than he heard it, and knew it was all she had to say. It wasn't a name; it was a one-word summation of all she knew about love and loving and all she would learn with this man. It was every term of endearment, every loving plea, and all the myriad ways of saying "I love you" refined and reduced to their ultimate essence in one three-syllable word. It was the answer to all her questions and, understanding that, she had nothing left to ask. She had gone beyond thinking or feeling in terms of hands, skin, arms and all the other elements that create separate sensations. There was only the one overwhelming sensation. "O'Mara." All of existence was, for this time, encompassed in "O'Mara."

Rising passion and building need blazed and flowed between them until they became one undeniable force. They were without words, without thought. In lazy, loving midnight reminiscences in later years, neither of them would ever recall moving across the silvered room to the bed, or even the details of their first joining. It all happened with the inevitability and naturalness of dawn. Standing together by the window, they had become one emotionally, and in moments they were lying on the wide bed completing their oneness.

This was the end of waiting. The beginning of total togetherness was *now*. No time for kisses and strokings. No need for further arousal. She was on her back, neither knowing nor caring what was supporting her, only aware of his descending body. As she felt his weight pressing on her, she opened to him, and with one strong, slow thrust of his hips, they were complete. He filled her last emptiness, and she enclosed him lovingly in her tight, heated sheath. Eyes closed, totally concentrating on each other, they could feel not only their own sensations but each other's. She didn't need his guiding hands; she *knew* how he wanted her to move as he *knew* just what she needed.

They made their journey together to the heart of a nova, bursting with its brief, brilliant blaze, and falling slowly back through space in a soft silver glow.

Neither of them moved for a long, long time, except for the instinctive relaxing of muscles. Her arms slid down until just her hands rested lightly on his hips. Her head fell back against his arm. When his taut neck muscles loosened, his head sank onto the pillow of her hair, turning slightly so that his mouth touched her neck. Slowly, their hearts and lungs regained their even rhythms. For several minutes, he could feel the tiny aftershocks of climax from deep inside her. They lay, still joined, sharing the sweet, drugged euphoria and an unexpected sense of homecoming.

"Love?" A soft whisper. She felt his breath feathering on her neck.

"Why didn't you tell me it was like that? I never imagined . . ." Her whisper trailed off as she lost the thought in remembered wonder.

"How could I describe it? You had to be here." His fingers stroked the silky skin of her shoulder, and he kissed the sensitive hollow below her ear. "I always knew we'd be special together, but I never dreamed just how special."

Her hands drifted over his back in tactile exploration of the ridges of his spine and the curving lines of muscle. "It's like being in a whole new world. Or a different dimension of the old one." Her voice was slow, soft, dreamy. "It's beautiful. You're beautiful. And I love you."

"Couldn't you call me handsome instead of beautiful?" She could feel his smile against her neck.

"Handsome is for looks. Beautiful is for heart and soul and all of it together. You're beautiful." She shifted her head so she could look at him. "My mind is only semi-functional right now, and I don't think I'm explaining things too well."

"You're doing just fine. I know exactly what you're trying to say, because I feel the same way about you." His eyes were intent on her face for several moments, reading the fulfillment, seeing signs of the growing confidence of a well-loved woman. His smile combined love and deep satisfaction, and it stopped her breath.

"Happy birthday, my Kitt," he murmured, a wicked glint in his eyes. "Did you like your first present?"

"I loved it." Her answering smile was deliciously seductive, and her eyes smoked at him. "Did you say 'first'? Are there more?"

He shifted to lean over her on his elbows, both hands cupping her face. He moved his mouth over hers in a touch as light as the brushing of moth wings. "Oh, yes, my birthday girl, there's more. In a little while. And much more later. And tonight you'll have your ring." He flicked the corners of her lips teasingly with the tip of his tongue. Tensing, preparing to lift his weight from her, he said contritely, "I must be heavy for you. Sorry, love, but I didn't want to move."

She wound her arms around his waist and shifted her legs slightly to cradle his hips more comfortably between her thighs. "No. I'm not exactly fragile, and I like you where you are."

He relaxed again on her, sliding his hands under her shoulders and burying his face in her neck, whispering, "If I stay here, my seductive witch, 'a little while' is going to be a damn short while."

"Why do you—Oh. Ohhhhh . . . oh, yes. Please. . . ."

Always, afterward, they would remember that night as the most enchanted and incredible of their special collection of magic-and-moonlight nights. A new world opened to them, and they were eager to test it, taste it, feel it, touch it. He led the way and she followed. He urged her to explore and experiment, and she stretched her wings and flew. He offered her delights, and she accepted and learned to give him pleasure. They melded passion and love and laughter and lust, and they found themselves in ecstasy.

The sky was glowing golden with incipient sunrise, and they were stretched on their sides, half-asleep, facing each other. Their long legs were still entwined, and his arms were relaxed around her. She tilted her head back against his arm to look up at him with sleepy eyes.

"O'Mara?" Her voice was husky in the aftermath of passion. The words came softly, a marvelous discovery of the impossible being possible. Her gift to him.

"O'Mara . . . it was the first time."

She caught her breath as his face was transformed with joy and wonder, and she saw the sapphire eyes glisten with tears and felt them mingle with her own as he pressed his face against hers.

Chapter 23

Kitt wriggled backward on the flat rock, and swung her feet up to sit cross-legged. The sun was bouncing off the water in eye-dazzling flashes, and she had to squint to watch the big power boat forging along well offshore on its way down the coast. Relaxed, enjoying the light breeze cooling her sun-heated skin, she wasn't thinking very strenuously about much of anything. It was the kind of afternoon when the height of ambition was to be a lazy lizard sunning on a rock.

In the distance, off to her left around the base of Crest Rock, she could hear Gus and Midge laughing and calling to each other. When she'd left them on the low-tide beach a while ago, they were discussing the merits of various tricks they wanted to teach Hero and arguing over commands and methods. Hero thoroughly enjoyed being the center of attention, and was adding his own variations to their efforts when Kitt had ambled away to explore the ledges at the base of the Rock.

The ledges and the long, narrow beach were only exposed for a few hours, before and after low tide. Although the beach was easily accessible from the road, it was not very popular, since there was no soft, dry sand for sunbathing or picnics, and the tricky tidal currents around the Rock made swimming risky. However, the hard-packed sand had become a favorite playground for Gus and Hero, giving them plenty of room to race and romp. They didn't even have to go out on the road to reach the beach, since there was a safe if rather steep path down from O'Mara's lower terrace.

Kitt untangled her legs, letting her feet dangle over the edge of the rock, and leaned back on her elbows. She tilted her head back to look up at the rugged bastion of the Rock looming above her. After a few minutes, she got up and wandered further along the ledges, stopping now and then to investigate small tidal pools. Every so often, she turned to scan the ocean, watching an occasional boat wending its way along the channel.

It was a pleasant change—one of several in this past week—to have nothing important or necessary to do. She was thoroughly enjoying a lazy Sunday on this Memorial Day weekend. It would be her last Sunday as a single woman, and that thought brought a slow, knowing smile to her face. O'Mara wasn't wasting any more time, so he had informed her just over a week ago. She stood gazing unseeingly out to sea, remembering that long, dazed lunch at the Seaside.

By the time they woke up that Friday noon, it had been too late for breakfast. Ez was having a marvelous time helping Midge with the shop, and O'Mara, with a "Keep up the good work. See you later," had swept Kitt out the door and off to lunch before she had time to say more than "'Bye." She was in a euphoric haze and couldn't seem to stop smiling. She was perfectly happy going wherever O'Mara wanted to take her, and didn't particularly care how long it took to get there. As it happened, it only took a few minutes—several miles up the coast, they pulled into the parking lot at the Seaside, an old sea captain's mansion now remodeled into a first-class restaurant. The wide veranda overlooking the ocean had been screened for fair-weather dining, and this early in the season they had no trouble securing a table by the railing. Not that it mattered. For all the attention they paid to their surroundings, they could have been sitting in a coal cellar.

When Midge asked them later which of the famous Seaside luncheon specials they had ordered, neither of them could remember. They weren't at all sure that they'd eaten anything. Ez said they'd been gone over two hours, and they'd apparently spent the time watching each other and holding hands. The only conversation Kitt could recall was O'Mara saying dreamily, "By the way, we're getting married two weeks from tomorrow." "Okay," she answered, equally dreamily. "Ez and I have arranged everything." "Okay."

Remembering it now, Kitt chuckled to herself. Ez is right, she thought, we're absolutely mizzy-mazed, the both of us. Anyone seeing us this past week would think we were a couple of love-struck teenagers. In a way, I suppose we are, but now . . . oh, it's so much more than it was then! Those telltale heated bubbles were starting to float up from her belly, and she forced her mind back to the here and now. The footing on these wet ledges could be slippery, and she didn't want to spend the first two months of marriage in a cast.

She squeezed between two big rocks and found herself at the edge of another pool, this one in a hollowed place in the ledge and deep enough for wading. She scanned the clear water for anything unpleasant before pulling off her sneakers and stepping down into calf-deep water. The usually icy seawater had been warmed by the sun just enough to be comfortable. Bending over, she scooped handfuls of water up over her long bare legs. She waded slowly across the small pool, feeling carefully for secure footing. On the far side, she found a smooth patch of ledge just above the waterline and sat down, stretching her legs out and swishing them back and forth in the pool.

She leaned back on her braced hands, enjoying the contrast of hot sun and cool water on her skin. Thanks to O'Mara, there was considerably more bare skin evident than she used to show. She thought with amusement of their shopping expedition a few days ago, when O'Mara had unexpectedly breezed into the shop and whisked her off to the Maine Mall in Portland, leaving Midge and Joanne happily rearranging all the displays.

Kitt had expected him to drop her off by Jordan Marsh and go his own way, meeting her later. He soon disabused her of that idea.

"No way," he said with a challenging grin, "am I going to let you out of my sight. You did make a reasonably good start on updating your wardrobe before I went to Europe. However, since *this* wardrobe is definitely going to be for my enjoyment, I'm going to have a hand in choosing it."

And, over her faint token protests, he did. Actually, she mused, it had been a lot of fun. He'd teased her into modeling dresses and tops which displayed an alarming amount of bare skin above the waist. Granted, he made sure her breasts were covered, but he'd only grinned wickedly and said "Good!" when she complained that she wouldn't be able to wear a bra with such low-cut backs. The flashing blue eyes and outrageously charming smile had quickly enlisted the salesgirls to his side, and they had eagerly searched racks and shelves to find what he wanted. He concentrated on summer clothes: dresses, skirts, tops, shorts and four bathing suits that she swore she wouldn't wear on a public beach. He merely quirked an eyebrow and said, "Oh, yes, you will, but only when I'm with you!" and proceeded to pick out cover-ups to go with the suits.

He'd only left her on her own once, and that was in a shoe store, with a parting admonition of "Don't forget, with me you can wear heels as high as you like." She was just writing a check for four pairs of shoes when he returned with a large box and two elegant totes, all sporting the distinctive logo of a fine lingerie shop. He laughingly ignored her questions and defeated all her attempts to peek into the bags. All he'd say was, "Later. These are just for you and me, mostly me." She blushed at the look in his eye and then kissed the smug grin off his mouth, much to the amusement of a number of people lounging around the Mall's concourse.

Kitt lifted her legs out of the water and swung around to stretch them out in the sun to dry. She glanced down at herself and smiled. The gold cotton-knit camisole top was O'Mara's choice, but the denim shorts had evolved from an old pair of her jeans. It wouldn't do to let him win them all! She still didn't know exactly what he had in those packages from Bellissima; he'd stashed them in the trunk of the Mercedes and left them there when they unloaded everything at her place. All she'd been able to get out of him was a teasing, "They aren't bras!" The man was beginning to develop a fixation about her bras. She ran one hand lightly across her breasts and laughed out loud as she remembered his scowl this morning when he caught her taking a bra out of the drawer. But she'd believed him when he growled, "If you put that on, I'll take it right off again and cut it into inch-square pieces! I keep telling you, you've got beautiful breasts, and they're firm enough so you don't need a damn bra." It had taken her half the morning and a lot of stroking before she finally got him to agree to a compromise: She could wear them in the shop, but not with him unless they were out in public and she had on something you could see through. Actually, it was no great hardship. She didn't care all that much for wearing bras either—but she wasn't going to tell him that!

Rising to her feet, she climbed the ledge around the pool to retrieve her sneakers. She glanced at her watch, only to realize that she'd left it, together with her ring, up at the house. There was no way she was going to take any chances with her ring. O'Mara had designed it with the help of a goldsmithing friend. An elegantly complex design of gold set with small diamonds and sapphires, it needed Kitt's long, graceful hand to set it off, and it had instantly become her most treasured possession. Still, she had spoken the truth when she whispered to O'Mara, "It's utterly beautiful and I'll treasure it always, but it will also always have to be my *second*-favorite birthday present." His slow, knowing smile had almost knocked her over right there in the middle of the surprise party which he and Midge had organized to celebrate the twins' thirtieth birthday.

She squinted up at the sun and then gazed speculatively at the shadows of the nearby rocks, wondering how you were supposed to tell time with any accuracy by such means. Well, using common sense and instinct, it's somewhere around mid-afternoon, she decided, and I'd better be getting back before the tide comes in. She started making her unhurried way back along the ledges, idly wondering where O'Mara and Ez had gone after lunch and when they would return. They hadn't been worried or grim, but they had definitely been uncommunicative. Surprisingly so. Unless, perhaps, it had something to do with the wedding trip.

She stopped to watch some gulls wheeling and diving around a fishing boat, her mind still puzzling over the men's secrecy. It could be the wedding trip, she mused. O'Mara is being a clam about where he's taking me. All I've been able to get out of him is that we'll be gone at least two weeks, maybe more. And *that's* only possible because Ez gets through at the university this week and can stay up here to help Midge and Joanne. The thought of her bear of a brother managing a bookshop, of all things, sent her into a fit of giggles. She had a vision of the shop crowded with customers and Ez cat-footing through them, trying to avoid knocking over standing racks or stepping on Midge.

Climbing carefully over some loose rocks, she scrambled down a steep section of ledge to reach a stretch where it leveled off. There was one more patch of loose rock to cross, and then it was uncluttered ledge around the far curve of the Rock to the beach. The few big rocks at the edge of the beach were deeply imbedded in the sand, and it was no problem to either climb over them or wade into the shallow water on the ocean side and through a wide gap onto the open beach.

She reached the next patch of rocks and started working her way across it. Part of her mind was concentrated on watching her footing, while the other part was still speculating on where O'Mara and Ez had gone. Perhaps it had something to do with Laura. She hadn't been in touch with O'Mara again, and he hadn't been able to locate her despite innumerable phone calls to her parents and anyone else who might know where she was or be in touch with her. Kitt understood that he wasn't saying much because he didn't want to worry her, but she also knew that he was uneasy about not being able to find out what Laura might be up to now and whether she had accepted Portman's report.

A rock shifted as she placed one foot on it and tested it for stability. She let her other leg take her weight and rested her hand on a larger rock for balance while she probed for the next foothold. *What was that? It sounded like—* She froze, head up, straining to hear the sound again, her eyes scanning the rocks and water to locate the source of the faintly heard noise. *There it was again. Oh, God, that's Hero and he's hurt! And that's a scream! What the hell is happening?*

Forgetting all thoughts of caution, Kitt went down over the rock pile in seconds, using both hands and feet to keep from falling, and landed running. She raced along the ledge, her long legs eating up the yards while the cacophony of snarls and yells and screams grew louder. As she rounded the far curve of the Rock, the sweep of beach came into sight, and she slowed momentarily to locate the source of trouble. It took no longer than the click of a camera shutter for the scene to register, and she was tearing down the sloping ledge in long leaping strides.

Her eyes were watching the ground ahead of her, but her mind was filled with the picture of the beach and the struggling people. In that brief look, she'd registered the presence of two unknown men, one trying to drag a fighting Gus toward the steps leading from the beach to a path to the road, while the other one was staggering around with Midge glued to his back and screaming like a banshee. Above Midge's screams, she'd heard a pained yelp from Hero and seen him just as he landed on the sand, where he'd obviously been thrown or kicked.

Kitt didn't bother to go to the end of the ledge; she jumped from four feet above the sand, took the shock of landing with bent knees and headed in a straight line for the battle a hundred yards down the beach. A large rock loomed in front of her, and she never slowed nor swerved, just took it in one long, vaulting leap and kept on going. The long athletic legs covered that hundred yards with a speed that would have turned an Olympic contender green with envy. For the first time in her life, Kitt was in a pure red rage, and the adrenalin surging through her body added incredible power to her strong, driving thigh muscles. Not even that last fight with Darcy had been a matter of total rage; there had been too much terror and desperation in the struggle for her life. Now, triggered by the threat to Gus and the brutality to Hero, Kitt was in a blind fury that more than equalled one of Ez's rare berserk eruptions.

She didn't waste any breath yelling reassurances. Her one goal was to reach the man struggling with Gus. He wasn't getting much closer to the steps. Not only was Gus kicking, punching and biting, but Hero had charged back into the battle, and with centuries-old instincts was lunging for the vulnerable spots behind the knee and ankle. Afterward, Kitt would remember seeing blood on the man's arm and rips in his trousers where Hero had already managed to get hold of him before being thrown off. With the fearless courage and highly developed protective instincts of his breed, Hero ignored his own injuries to attack, again and again, the man who was hurting one of *his* people. At the moment Kitt wasn't thinking coherently about anything except reaching Gus. She certainly had no thought or awareness of how ferocious she looked charging across the beach, her teeth bared in a snarl that matched Hero's and her eyes blazing almost as blue as O'Mara's with the force of her rage.

She was almost on them when Midge's victim spotted her. Midge was still on his back, her legs locked around his waist and her arms wrapped around his neck. She hadn't been able to bring him down, but she'd certainly slowed him up considerably. Despite being nearly deafened by Midge's howls, he heard the deep roars of "No, Kitt! Wait!" and spun around, seeking the source. In an instant's awareness, he saw two huge men plunging down a steep path from the top of the cliff and, closer, too close, a mad Amazon charging head-on

toward Jack. Forgetting she was a woman, he wrenched
Midge's ankles apart, grabbed her arms, ducked and heaved
to throw her over his head, and leaped to intercept Kitt.

She saw him coming and didn't even have to think about it.
Reflexes learned long ago shot her right arm straight out,
curled her fingers down and back, and slammed the heel of
her hand into his breastbone. It was the last thing he
expected. With his arms spread to grab her, he was wide open
and she knocked him flat and breathless. And kept on going
without even breaking her stride. Dimly, she heard male
bellows, was aware of Midge scrambling on all fours toward
the downed man, but her eyes and havoc-wreaking fury were
fixed on the man now turning toward her and violently
shoving Gus away from him. *He* wasn't expecting what he
got, either.

Again, old instincts and well-learned reflexes snapped into
operation. At the last second, her body from the waist up
turned slightly to her left, her right shoulder lifted with the
arm clamped across her ribs, she tucked her chin down
behind the shoulder, and, with her legs still driving hard as Ez
had taught her, she hit him full force with a smashing body
block that lifted him completely off his feet and dropped him
flat on his back with a resounding thud. The impact knocked
her off-balance, and her forward momentum sent her down
onto one knee and a hand. With hardly a pause, she pushed
herself up and started to leap for the feebly moving man while
a snarling Hero went by her in a copper-white blur in a direct
line for the man's throat and Gus raced up with his arm drawn
back and a sizable rock clutched in his fist. Simultaneously,
hard arms came around her from behind, lifting her off her
feet, and she heard O'Mara's "No, Hero" and "Hold it, Gus"
thundering in her ear.

Gus skidded to a stop, panting, and tossed the rock aside.
Hero swerved and slowed, turning to limp back toward Kitt.
He was favoring a hind leg but still putting weight on it, and
she didn't think he was badly hurt; his ears were up and he
was practically smiling in triumph. Gus let out a sobbing "Oh,
Hero," and dropped to the sand, gathering the dog gently
into his arms and settling him in his lap.

O'Mara let Kitt slide down to her feet and held her off at
arm's length. He examined her quickly from head to toe to

check for visible damage and, satisfied for the moment, let his gaze drift over the battlefield.

Kitt's equally quick check of O'Mara noted the signs of his desperate plunge down the cliff-path and race across the beach. He was breathing deeply; sweat ran down his face and neck and the thick pelt on his legs and arms was damp. Blood was welling slowly from several surface cuts on his bare legs—his denim cutoffs had been no protection from the rocks on that scramble down the path. Kitt was coming down rapidly from her adrenalin-powered high, and she was still somewhat bemused as she followed O'Mara's gaze and finally became totally aware of her surroundings.

Both of the unknown men were still flat on the sand, and seemed to be only partly conscious, although they were making tentative movements with their arms and legs. A choking sound drew her attention to where Ez was standing with one large foot resting warningly on the stomach of Midge's former foe. Midge apparently considered him very much a current foe, since she was trying to get back to pounding his head in the sand, an activity she had been enthusiastically pursuing when Ez had finally reached her and plucked her off her victim. He was effortlessly restraining her now with a tight one-handed grip on the back of her shorts, while he wiped the sweat from his face with his other hand. Since he was also wearing shorts, his legs, too, had a scattering of rock-cuts. The choking sound was due to his rapidly deteriorating effort to hold back laughter.

Kitt brought her eyes back to O'Mara and saw the same look of barely restrained mirth on his face. She wondered what could possibly be funny in such an appalling situation. Moment by moment, she was becoming aware of various aches and twinges in overstrained muscles, and it was coming home to her that she had put down and out two fairly sizable men. True, they weren't as big as Ez or O'Mara, but they were certainly considerably larger than she was.

Ez couldn't hold it in any longer. He stepped back, sat down on the sand and roared with laughter. That set O'Mara off, and his deep bellows joined Ez's. Kitt, Midge and Gus looked bewilderedly at each other, and then at the two nearly hysterical men.

Finally, Ez managed to gasp, "Oh, God, Kitt. For a woman

who turns to jelly . . . at the mere thought of violence . . .
you certainly mopped up . . . the beach with these two. That
was . . . without doubt . . . the best straight arm and body
block . . . I've ever seen."

For a moment, Kitt stared at her twin in disbelief as he
rocked with laughter, wiping tears away with both hands. She
looked at O'Mara, scowled, threw her head back and yelled
"MEN!" at the top of her lungs.

To the rising laughter of Gus and Midge, O'Mara pulled
Kitt into his arms, hugged her, contained his laughter long
enough for a quick kiss, and then lifted his head to watch her
growing smile. He was still chuckling and the sapphire eyes
were flashing their wicked gleam when he said, just for her
ears, "After this, there's no ques—"

"Dad, Dad," Gus's frantic voice interrupted, "who's that
woman?" He grabbed his father's arm, tugging him around
and pointing to the top of the steps leading from the beach.

O'Mara's eyes widened in disbelief at the sight of the
angry-looking brunette poised on the top step. Kitt didn't
need to hear his explosive "Laura!" to know who she was.

Everyone on the beach froze, staring at the furious woman
snarling, "You bungling idiots! How could you let one stupid
woman—" Her snarl ended in a startled squawk as an
infuriated Kitt leaped up the steps, plucked her off her feet
and started shaking her violently.

A fresh surge of anger-induced adrenalin gave Kitt the
strength to hold the smaller woman in midair with her fingers
clamped tightly under her ribs. Kitt was totally beside herself
with fury as she realized the appalling act this selfish, shallow
woman had attempted, with callous disregard of any possible
injury to Gus.

As she shook the now-screaming woman, Kitt sounded
almost like Ez as she growled. "You bitch! You miserable,
nasty, rotten-minded bitch! What were you going to do to
Gus? What kind of a slimy piece of nothing are you that you'd
turn those gorillas loose on a child? Why don't you pick on
someone your own size? I ought to—"

"Kitt! Kitt! Let go. Come on, now, drop her." "Let go,
love. You've scared her half witless."

Ez and O'Mara yelled in her ears to make themselves heard
while they tugged at Kitt's wrists and pried her fingers loose,
finally breaking her hold on the terrified Laura. The sobbing

woman dropped to the sandy path and scrabbled backward on her bottom to get well away from Kitt.

"Keep her away from me," Laura choked, turning toward O'Mara. "She's crazy! She should be locked up." The frightened but still defiant woman struggled to her feet and backed well out of Kitt's reach, rubbing her hands over her bruised ribs and working up a fine sense of injustice. "I could have her locked up, you know. Attacking me like that. You've got a hell of a nerve, Mike, letting a woman like that loose around my son. What do you—"

"You just shut up, you bitch!" yelled an incensed Kitt, squirming to get out of the hold Ez and O'Mara had on her arms. "And he's *not* your son. You never wanted him, but I do, and he's *my* son now." Twisting and pulling, Kitt tried to break loose. The two big men were hard put to hang onto her without bruising her, but they persisted since she still had the light of battle in her eyes. "Dammit! Will you two let go of me? I'll fix her so she won't come bothering any of us again."

"Kitt, Kitt, settle down," Ez crooned. "You can't go beating her up. For one thing, she's smaller than you."

"Besides that," O'Mara chimed in, "she's just not worth it. You'd get a lot more satisfaction out of seeing her marched off to jail in handcuffs, wouldn't you?" he asked with a calculating, sideways look at his seething ex-wife.

"Jail!" screeched Laura, her anger-flushed face paling to a sickly white.

"Good thinking," Kitt said in a normal tone, relaxing and finally becoming aware of Gus and Midge standing to one side and staring at her in pop-eyed amazement. "Hey, what's the matter with you two?"

Gus closed his mouth and ran to her, flinging his arms around her waist in a bearhug. "Oh, Kitt," he cried, halfway between laughter and tears. "I never saw anybody get so mad. You . . . Was that on account of me? Knocking those men out and shaking that woman?" Kitt pulled out of the men's loosened hold and wrapped her arms around Gus, hugging him tight. "Oh, Kitt, you're going to be the best mother a guy could have! Wait till I tell the guys how you charged across that beach and dumped those gorillas on their butts. They'll never believe it!"

"I hope you don't think you're going to spend the next fifty years trying to top that!" O'Mara chuckled in her ear.

Suddenly exhausted, Kitt turned to look up at him and thankfully leaned against his strength as his arm came around her shoulders and he reached out with his other hand to ruffle Gus's hair.

Laura's strident voice interrupted their moment of closeness as she demanded, "What do you mean, jail? You can't—"

"Oh, yes, we can," O'Mara snapped. "How about attempted kidnapping for starters? Then, we can add a charge of assault and—"

"Go to hell!" Laura screamed. "She's the one who did all the assaulting. And I can't kidnap my own kid!"

O'Mara fixed her with an inimical stare and in a slow, deadly voice said, "You brought those two here. You hired them or bribed them to kidnap Gus. It is kidnapping, Laura, when you take a person against his or her will or, in the case of a minor, without the consent of a legal guardian. And I am Gus's legal guardian. You have no rights where he is concerned. You gave them up. You signed documents to that effect. There is not a police officer, a lawyer or a judge who would not consider this an attempted kidnapping. Those two," he pointed at the subdued men sitting meekly at Ez's feet, "and you will go to jail if I file a complaint. In fact, I doubt if I'd even have to sign a complaint in this case. Just call the police and tell them what happened here this afternoon. As for the assault charge, Midge could bring that. They attacked her. Kitt was only defending Gus and Midge from them. Do you understand, Laura?"

White-faced, she stared at him in a mixture of fear and anger and frustration. Her eyes traveled to the tall woman standing close in the security of his arm, and then to the handsome boy who had turned in Kitt's arms to glare at her with the same inimical look that was in his father's eyes. As shallow-minded as she was, even Laura could see they were too strong for her. They were *together*, a cohesive unit, mutually supportive, mutually defensive. They defeated her.

"Take your bully boys and get out of here, Laura. Don't come back. And don't send anybody else to do your dirty work for you. Any more trouble from you, and I'll find you and turn Kitt loose on you. *I* might not be able to bring myself to belt a woman, but Kitt wouldn't mind at all plucking you

bald-headed and leaving you wishing you were safe in jail."
For just an instant, O'Mara looked as though he might change
his mind and let Kitt at her now.

"You just keep her away from me," cried Laura, backing
away. "We're going."

"Smart move," O'Mara drawled. "I assume this was all in
aid of wringing more money out of me. You can forget it. I'
told you you'd had all you're getting. I suggest you find a job.
It's safer than messing with us."

Ez nudged the two men with his foot, none too gently, and
sent them scrambling to their feet and stumbling after Laura
toward the road.

"Come on, Midge," he said, holding out his hand to her.
"Let's see them on their way." They ambled after the
departing trio, Ez calling back, "See you guys up at the
house."

Kitt let out a long sigh and leaned her head back against
O'Mara's shoulder. "I feel like I've been through a war. Oh,"
she exclaimed, straightening up and looking around, "I forgot
Hero. Where is he? Is he all right, Gus?"

"He's right behind us," said Gus, stepping out of her arms
and dropping down on the sand to pat the excited dog. "I
think he's okay, but he's still limping a little."

Kitt and O'Mara knelt down beside him to examine Hero's
hind leg and to run their hands over the rest of his body to
check for tender spots.

"Seems okay," O'Mara said. "I think that leg is just
strained. Maybe a bruise or two along his ribs, but he's not
fussing too much when I touch him."

"He's bleeding a little on his lower lip," murmured Kitt,
holding Hero's head still so she could get a better look. "Must
have jammed it against a tooth. Doesn't look too bad. It
should heal up in a day or so."

O'Mara stood up, half-lifting Kitt to her feet beside him.
He chuckled as she groaned. "Stiffening up a bit? I should
think so, love. That wasn't exactly light exercise you were
indulging in. Come on, tiger lady, what you need is a session
in the hot tub. I might even be coaxed into giving you a
massage."

She gave him a teasing, come-hither look and breathed,
"Coaxing, coaxing, coaxing."

"Witch! No, come this way. It's a bit long, but you won't have to climb that steep path."

"Hmmm. About that hot tub . . ." Kitt murmured.

"I thought you'd never ask," answered O'Mara, his smiling look promising her another new experience.

They strolled off, arms around each other, trailed by Gus and Hero.

Epilogue

The late-August night was remarkably clear, and the long, low building glowed silver-white in the brilliant moonlight. The tall lantern-lights bordering the drives, parking lots and sidewalks were dimmed by the power of Nature's night-light. Only on the shaded veranda facing the moon-bright beach was the natural light supplanted by the soft glow from the chandeliers in the ballroom. A geometrical pattern of alternating pale yellow and black rectangles stretched the length of the veranda floor. Shadows flickered across the pale yellow patches in rhythm with the music drifting from the open French doors. Periodically, the formal pattern of light and dark was broken as couples strolled slowly down the veranda, enjoying the unseasonably warm evening—it seemed more like the middle of July than the end of August—and gazing with moon-dazzled eyes at the wide white beach and rippling silver sea.

A young woman appeared at one of the French doors and stood quietly for a few moments admiring the view and letting the serenity of the evening relax some of her tension. With a deep sigh, wishing she could kick off her shoes and go for a long walk on the enticing beach, she turned back into the ballroom. Her eyes automatically scanned the room, checking for problems, making contact with an attendant here and there in the lounge and the anterooms. As activities director for the hotel, she was responsible for the planning and smooth functioning of this high point of the summer, the End-of-Season Ball. It was a long-established tradition, and was always well attended by both hotel guests and local residents. She watched the couples moving gracefully over the polished floor to the tune of a slow waltz. It was a good crowd, older, the few young people were well behaved and seemed to be enjoying the traditional ballroom dancing. There were a number of familiar faces—perennial guests, regular visitors from the surrounding area, and several who were generally well known to the public for one reason or another.

Purposely searching now, her eyes roved over the dancers until she spotted the lieutenant governor and his wife. Good. They looked happy enough. Her gaze was caught by the congresswoman who, with her husband, was occupying the best suite. She seemed to be enjoying herself, but her husband was about one drink away from tripping over his own feet, not that he was all that graceful to begin with. Not like *that* one, she thought. Now there is a man I would not mind at all directing in a few activities. Except that I doubt if his very handsome wife would put up with it for a minute. Come to that, I can't imagine him looking at anyone else. I haven't seen one of them without the other all week, and most of the time they don't even seem to know anyone else is around. Yike! Just look at that smile. Wonder what she said to him. Lordy, if a man ever smiled at me like that, I'd never let him out of my sight again.

"O'Mara. Darling beast. Oh, you wretched tease, if you don't get your sneaky fingers out of there, you're going to disgrace us both!" Kitt's attempt at indignant protest collapsed into a knowing chuckle under his blatantly sensual smile. She could feel her nipples hardening as the backs of his long fingers, tucked under the edge of her halter, stroked the outer curve of her breast.

"Mmmmm, but you're so tempting, my Kitt," he whispered in her ear, flicking his tongue around the rim and then turning his head to look into the smoky blue eyes that were promising retaliation.

"If I were not a proper married lady . . ." Her voice trailed off in a teasing threat and the wide mouth curved with delightful purpose as she shifted her hips slightly, and on the next step pressed one firm, slender thigh between his.

"Witch," he groaned, his arm tightening around her waist to hold her in place. "It's a good thing that skirt is full."

"And the lights are dim," she murmured, laughing softly. She nestled her cheek against his and moved her arm further around his neck. "You," she whispered, "are in a very sexy mood tonight."

"I'm always in a sexy mood with you," he whispered back, "or have you forgotten some of the places . . . and times . . . we've made love?" His feathering kisses along the sensitive skin in front of her ear were sending the familiar moth wings fluttering in her belly, while the vivid memory of certain of their passionate encounters heated her cheeks. His low chuckle told her plainer than words that he knew exactly what he was doing to her. She smiled to herself at the knowledge that she was doing the same thing to him.

They didn't talk during the remainder of the waltz. Totally aware of each other's arousal, they silently agreed, in their special form of communication, to keep their fire turned low for a while longer. Kitt moved her arm back to curve around his shoulder, her fingers resting lightly on the silk of his midnight-blue dinner jacket. Relaxing the tension of his tight hold, O'Mara slowly stroked his warm hand over her bare back. It was a gentling touch rather than one of arousal, and the looks they exchanged were a mixture of understanding and promise. The music swept to its climax, and they turned to walk the length of the room, arms loosely around each other, to their table in the lounge. They were completely unaware of the number of admiring and envious eyes that watched their progress.

The pretty activities director, paralleling their course toward the lounge, watched them with a longing envy, wishing she could meet a man who could bring that certain look to *her* face. She still found it hard to believe that he was Michael Talbot. Somehow, a best-selling author should be older and shorter and maybe balding, she mused, not tall, dark and possessing the wickedest blue eyes she'd ever seen. She sighed resignedly over the fact that his flashing blue glances were all directed at his wife. Pausing at the entrance to the lounge, she studied the tall, exotic-looking Mrs. O'Mara and decided that it was easy enough to see what attracted him. They are really something special, she thought, and if they had the idea that using the name O'Mara was going to make them less conspicuous, then they've obviously never seen themselves together in a mirror! I wonder if they have kids. If they do, I'll bet they're handsome.

"Another glass of wine?" At Kitt's nod, O'Mara beckoned to a waiter and ordered two glasses of white wine. He shifted his chair closer to hers and reached for her hand. "Are you enjoying your surprise, love?"

"It's marvelous, and you are still the most devious man I know!" she said, laughing and squeezing his hand. "And I fell for it. Why did I believe your agent wanted to meet me? *Does* he have a place on Cape Cod?"

"Of course not." O'Mara chuckled. "Why ever would he want a place on the Cape when he's got a perfectly lovely summer home on Long Island? But I had to have some excuse for getting you down here, alone and unencumbered by kids. Incidentally, Mal does want to meet you, and I'm taking you to New York with me next month when I go down to sign the contracts for the film sale."

"The third one in a row," she mused, "and they've taken an option on your next one before you've even started it!"

"Don't complain," he said with a teasing grin. "If you keep having babies in pairs, we're going to need the money!"

"Please," she groaned, "The twins are only four months old. I don't want to think about going through all that again for a while longer."

His gaze sharpened and he examined her face intently before catching the twinkle in her eye. Still, he didn't smile when he asked, "Are you sure you're not sorry you got pregnant so soon? We could have waited a bit." Then the slow smile came as he added, "Although I have to admit it's done very nice things for your figure."

"Tomcat." She wrinkled her nose at him. "If you're trying to tell me that I'm coming out of the top of this dress . . ."

"Not quite, but you are definitely filling it out more than you did when I gave it to you." His eyes gleamed appreciatively as they lingered on the taut material over her breasts. "At least, now, you've stopped fussing about being too small. And, no, you still don't need a bra. I thought we ended that argument over a year ago."

She laughed at him and then let her gaze drift over the lounge, pausing on the wide archway to watch the dancers swirling around the ballroom. Sighing contentedly, she brought her eyes back to the long, lean figure lounging comfortably next to her. "You really are quite sly, O'Mara." It was still her favorite term of endearment. "Not only did you sneak this dress into your bag when I wasn't looking, but you've even come up with an outfit that's almost a duplicate of that first one." She ran calculating eyes over the deep blue silk tux and the pale lemon silk shirt. "I must say, this one fits you better. Tailor-made, I bet. Hmmm? I thought so. You really have been pussy-footing around behind my back." There was a tease in her voice and her smile. "How long have you been plotting all this?"

"Since last year, just after we were married. I tried to get reservations for the end of August, but they were filled up and had been for months. This is the most popular weekend of the summer except for Fourth of July. So I called in September and made them for this year, crossing my fingers that you wouldn't be in the last months of pregnancy or just getting back on your feet from same. Of course, I had no way of knowing that you, with your clever sense of timing and extraordinary forethought, had already managed to get pregnant so as to keep all the birthdays in May."

"Ah, yes, and I did it all by myself," she mocked. "You, of course, merely sat on the sidelines and applauded."

His deep laugh attracted the attention of nearly everyone in the lounge, and many smiled at the aura of happiness and loving closeness surrounding the handsome couple.

"Little braggart. As I recall, I was a much more active participant than that. In fact, very active, and willing, and inventive . . . and—"

"Shhh. Devil! You pick the damnedest places to start these things," she moaned. The deep, seductive purr, combined with his finger stroking her palm and the heated look in his eyes, had her wriggling in her chair.

For a long minute, he held her increasingly smoky eyes captive with his, aware of her tautening breasts and rising heat. "Oh, love, I would so like to kiss you right now; but if I do, we'll probably end up on the floor, and that would really make this a ball to remember!"

It was enough to relax their tense awareness of each other, and they sipped their wine for a few moments, watching the dancers and deciding, simultaneously, to discuss other things for a while.

"I wonder if the twins miss us. Do you suppose they're old enough to realize we're not there?" Kitt asked.

"When are they going to have a chance to miss us? With Ez, Midge, Gus and Andy all deluging them with attention, we'll be lucky if they even remember who we are! Oh, and let's not forget Hero. That dog is the most efficient nursemaid since Peter Pan's Nana."

Laughing, Kitt corrected, "Not Peter Pan's. Nana belonged to Wendy, John and Michael. Did you ever see anything like Ez with those babies? He looks so funny sitting in that big leather chair with one twin in each hand, talking away to them as if they were the least bit interested in knights and castles."

"Don't knock it. He was the one who got them to quiet down that night they were colicky. Remember? I think it's that rumble that does it. Sort of stuns them to sleep. Now what's put that dreamy look on your face?"

She brought her eyes back from the dancers to meet his questioning look. "Oh, I was just thinking how lucky I am. And how happy. I've got you, and you'd be a whole life for anyone. But you brought me Gus and now the twins and, oh, it's just so much." Her voice broke on the last words, and she saw him through a blur of tears.

"You beautiful idiot," he said tenderly, leaning close to brush the tears away. "Besides, you've got it all mixed up. Don't you know you're the center of all our lives? What's between us, alone, can't even be put into words, but, added to that, you've given meaning to everything I do. I've never worked better than I have these last months—despite those many long and fascinating interludes when you've enticed me away from the typewriter."

"O'Mara, you know I never interrupt you when you're working," she protested.

"Watching you walk across a room is all the enticement I need," he said ruefully. "If you didn't spend half your days in the shop, it would probably take me at least two years to write a book. Oh, yes, it would," he stated firmly as she laughed and shook her head at him. He studied the wine remaining in his glass for a moment before returning his thoughtful gaze to her face.

"It's true, you know. We all do revolve around you. Andy was a bit worried that you might want to get involved in running the house and she wouldn't have enough to do, but she calmed right down when she found out that you'd much rather work in the shop or romp around with me than vacuum rugs. And, now, just when Gus was growing out of being dependent on her, you've produced not one but two babies for her to fuss over." Laughter gleamed in his eyes. "You may not be ready yet, but Andy can't wait for the next batch."

"Please," Kitt groaned, "will you stop talking in terms of batches? I'd just as soon extend this family one at a time."

"I'll do my best for you." His voice was a seductive tease, and he grinned as he watched the flush of color in her face.

She took a hasty swallow of wine and groped for a change of subject. "Ah . . . Gus seems to have adjusted very well to the competition. In fact, he's so proud of *his* twins that he keeps the whole town informed of their progress. Perfect strangers come into the shop and ask after Jason and Jared. By name, mind you, and they know all about their routine, diet, sleeping habits and personality quirks. Incredible."

"Not really, love, when you consider how Gus feels about you. He may adore the twins, but he thinks the sun rises and sets on you. Ever since the Battle of the Beach, you've been Wonder Woman, Cheryl Tiegs and Super-Mom all rolled into one."

"Cheryl Tiegs?! Come on, now," she exclaimed disbelievingly. "He's not old enough to—"

"He's his father's son and knows a sexpot when he sees one," O'Mara intoned pontifically. He tried to keep a straight face, but at her startled expression he broke up in laughter. "Don't worry, love. At this point, he just recognizes one; he doesn't know what to do about it yet."

"Lord, let's hope not! However, I'm keeping my eye out for a large broom. The way the girls are beginning to look at him, we're going to need one soon to sweep them off the steps."

"Oh, I wouldn't worry too much. Between Ez and myself, he's got two prime sources of experience to call on in learning how to handle women." O'Mara watched her with an expectant gleam, his lips twitching with suppressed laughter.

Kitt choked on a swallow of wine and gasped. "And you called me a braggart! Perhaps Midge and I ought to tape one of our strategy sessions, and you two would find out just how much handling you really do!"

He leaned over and kissed the indignant look off her face. "Believe me, we're well aware of just how often you two wind us around your delicate fingers. On the other hand, we've managed to surprise you a time or two."

"Mmmm. Too true," Kitt agreed with a reminiscent grin. "Ez certainly did when he greeted us back from our honeymoon with the news that he and Midge were getting married the next day, and it was damn lucky we returned on time, or he wouldn't have had a best man! I knew he was serious about Midge, but I didn't think he'd move quite that fast."

"I did," O'Mara said smugly, and then chuckled. "What surprised me was that he quit teaching to take over running the bookshop."

"Now, wait a minute!" she exploded. "You know perfectly well that Midge and I do most of the 'running,' while Ez lolls around upstairs reeling out those wickedly sexy historical novels. I can't believe how fast he does it, either. Four in less than a year, and the one that's already out is on its way to being a best seller!"

"Why not? He's damn good, and he doesn't have to do much research on that period. He already knows it backward and inside out. You, of all people, shouldn't have been surprised, love. Others may look at him and see an easygoing bear, but you've always known that he was absolutely brilliant."

He glanced at his watch and then pulled Kitt to her feet. "Come on, love, this is our waltz." At her questioning look, he just smiled and led her into the ballroom.

Wordlessly, they turned and glided around the room to the strains of a slow waltz. Kitt felt a nostalgic enchantment gradually enclosing them and dimming the reality of other people and the room around them. She was floating in a golden haze, aware only of the lean, strong body pressed to hers, warm hands holding her, and the tantalizing brush of their moving legs. He lifted his cheek from her hair, and she tilted her head slightly to look at him. It was all there in his face—love, caring, cherishing—and the power of it stopped her breath. She didn't realize that the same expression lit her face with a rare beauty. His arms tightened convulsively, and he pressed his face against hers with a wordless murmur. The gold-tipped lashes fluttered down, and she moved in a dream, confidently surrendering all control to him.

It was several minutes before she felt the breeze on her bare shoulders and the rougher floor under her feet. Opening her eyes, she caught glimpses of the moon-washed beach and realized that O'Mara was slowly waltzing her the length of the veranda. He brought them to a halt at the top of the steps and took a step back from her, letting his hands come to rest on her hips. The smile he gave her was full of devilment.

"It's a beautiful night and that's a lovely walking beach. Could I interest you in going for a moonlight stroll?"

"Weeellll," she teased, "it looks rather deserted. Will I be safe with you, sir?"

"Not for a minute. Do you really want to be?"

"No!" She laughed and pulled him down the steps and along the short path to the beach. She stopped at the edge of the sand to take off her shoes. Turning to him, she found that he had already removed his tie and undone half his shirt buttons. She watched, bemused, while he shrugged out of his jacket, took her shoes and stuffed them into the pockets, and swung the jacket over his shoulder. When he held out his hand, she slid hers into it and turned to walk across the beach with him.

They reached the hard-packed sand near the water, and she paused, tugging him to a stop a step ahead of her. Slowly, dreamily, with a remembering look on her face, she scanned the glittering water with its tempting silver path and then the bright beach stretching before them into the darkness. Her head bent as she looked down at her dress and then lifted again as her eyes traveled up his long, sinewy body to meet his waiting gaze.

"It's the same," she said wonderingly. "It's all the same."

"Almost." He waited, watching her.

She frowned. "We're older and married?"

"That, too." The devilish smile was back, and she could see silver glints in the darkening blue eyes.

"O'Mara?" It was a question, but her growing smile said that she already suspected the answer.

"We, my lovely Kitt, have some unfinished business with a sand dune."

Laughing, they began to run hand-in-hand down the long beach.

About the Author

Lee Damon is Massachusetts born and bred. She has lived in Waltham, Braintree, and Concord, and she currently makes her home in Acton. She is a descendant of an old Concord family, whose first settlers arrived in 1680.

An only child in her New England Yankee family, Lee was encouraged to become a teacher or a nurse. Instead, she studied writing, got married, acquired some secretarial skills, and promptly got a job where she wouldn't need them. She has worked as a technical editor/writer for several electronics and aerospace firms until fairly recently, when a small inheritance allowed her to start her own graphic arts company.

Having gained considerable experience in advertising and nonfiction writing, she finally turned to another longtime dream: writing fiction. In her own words, she's always been "independent, stubborn, creative, and imaginative." And now, with a nineteen-year-old son in tow, she's off and running with yet another brand-new career!

REACH OUT FOR ROMANCE
...PURSUE THE PASSION

___ **ROYAL SUITE** by Marsha Alexander
___ **MOMENTS TO SHARE** by Diana Morgan
___ **ROMAN CANDLES** by Sofi O'Bryan
___ **TRADE SECRETS** by Diana Morgan
___ **AFTERGLOW** by Jordana Daniels
___ **A TASTE OF WINE** by Vanessa Pryor
___ **ON WINGS OF SONG** by Martha Brewster
___ **A PROMISE IN THE WIND** by Perdita Shepherd
___ **WHISPERS OF DESTINY** by Jenifer Dalton
___ **SUNRISE TEMPTATION** by Lynn Le Mon
___ **WATERS OF EDEN** by Katherine Kent
___ **ARABESQUE** by Rae Butler
___ **NOTHING BUT ROSES** by Paula Moore
___ **MIDNIGHT TANGO** by Katherine Kent
___ **WITH EYES OF LOVE** by Victoria Fleming
___ **FOR LOVE ALONE** by Candice Adams
___ **MORNINGS IN HEAVEN** by Perdita Shepherd
___ **THAT CERTAIN SMILE** by Kate Belmont
___ **THE RAINBOW CHASE** by Kris Karron
___ **A WORLD OF HER OWN** by Anna James
___ **BY INVITATION ONLY** by Monica Barrie
___ **AGAIN THE MAGIC** by Lee Damon
___ **DREAMTIDE** by Katherine Kent
___ **SOMETIMES A STRANGER** by Angela Alexie